WITHDRAWN

Dr Ribero's Agency of the Supernatural:

The Case of the Hidden Daemon

Lucy Banks

Amberjack Publishing
New York | Idaho

AMBERJACK
PUBLISHING

Amberjack Publishing
1472 E. Iron Eagle Drive
Eagle, Idaho 83616
http://amberjackpublishing.com

Publisher's Cataloging-in-Publication data
Names: Banks, Lucy Ann, author.
Title: The case of the hidden daemon / Lucy Banks.
Description: Eagle, ID : Amberjack Publishing, [2018] | Series: Dr. Ribero's Agency of the Supernatural ; Book 3
Identifiers: LCCN 2018037003 (print) | LCCN 2018039011 (ebook) | ISBN 9781948705066 (ebook) | ISBN 9781948705059 (paperback : alk. paper)
Subjects: | GSAFD: Occult fiction.
Classification: LCC PR6102.A64 (ebook) | LCC PR6102.A64 C38 2018 (print) | DDC 823/.92--dc23
LC record available at https://lccn.loc.gov/2018037003

Cover Design: Emma Graves

This one's for Danny and Dyl, Zoe and Ed: the next generation of creators in the family. And for the ghost I grew up with; without whom none of this would have been possible.

Tear the Walls Down—Billy Dagger

Do what you will, it's time, it's time,
Love is the law, through filth, through grime.
We seek the pirate note, the clarion call
Repeat into nothing, do what you will.

Follow the path, lead the way,
It is the Infinite, it holds sway.
We break apart, we shatter anew
Mastering drama, I break through.

Cities spill worm, a polemicist swirl,
Cities will romp, unravel, unfurl.

Do what you will, it's time, it's time,
Night comes, and the burning flame.

Repeat into, repeat into, repeat into . . .
Chaos.

Chapter 1: The Narrow House

The alleyway was dark, silent, and eerily Gothic, in Kester's opinion.

He stumbled along the cobblestones, trying not to think about muggers lurking in the shadowy doorways. It was one of Exeter's many forgotten backstreets; quaint during daylight hours, but disquieting by night, and the decades of rain, pollution, and grime that abused the surrounding brickwork were highlighted by the weak glow of the streetlight.

Trust Miss Wellbeloved to live somewhere that looks like a setting for a Dickens novel, he thought, peering through the gloom. He checked her text message to confirm the address—*No. 12, The Mint.* She'd also added, *Come quickly, I'll explain everything.*

He certainly hoped so. Ever since he'd told his father about Anya's disappearance, not to mention her baffling message about the mysterious Thelemites, Dr Ribero and Miss Wellbeloved had been most secretive—giving away nothing, only insisting he meet them that very evening. He was exhausted, but relieved. It might be late, but at least he had a hope of getting some answers rather than spending the night wide awake, fretting.

Miss Wellbeloved's house was at the end of the alleyway; a weathered old property every bit as straight, severe, and narrow as its owner. He rapped the brass knocker, briefly breaking the quiet. A lone candle burned in the window, but otherwise, the house was entirely dark.

Kester waited, shivering.

Finally, a light went on at the window. The door opened, revealing a familiar eye, then the rest of Miss Wellbeloved's face.

"Hello, Kester," she whispered. "Fancy seeing you again so soon."

He stepped in, wiping his feet on the mat. "I know. And there was me, thinking we'd all get a restful night."

Miss Wellbeloved smiled ruefully, then shut the night out behind them.

He looked around. Her hallway was spartan yet cosy, and the wall-lamp cast an amber glow across the walls. A slender staircase led into darkness, and ahead, he spotted a farmhouse kitchen, a homely contrast to the lonely alley outside.

"Your father's getting the fire going," she said, waving him down the corridor. "Why don't you go and join him? Straight ahead, then turn left."

Kester headed along the dark floorboards until he came to a snug little room, stuffed with two oversized sofas and a stone fireplace. True to Miss Wellbeloved's word, Ribero was crouched in front of it, puffing at the kindling with alarming ferocity.

"Hi, Dad," Kester said, loitering by the door.

His father held up a finger, then blew once more on the firewood. A flame leapt up, immediately licking at the bundles of newspaper. "Aha," he said with satisfaction, prodding the pile with a poker. "Now we are in the business, yes?"

"Thanks for coming out tonight to see me," Kester said as he settled himself on the nearest sofa, watching the spreading flames.

"Though you're being rather mysterious about it all."

His father blew on the fire again, then leant backwards, massaging his neck. "That is because you mentioned the Thelemites, Kester."

"What are the Thelemites? Should I be worried? Are they going to do anything bad to Anya?"

Ribero shook his head. "Wait until Jennifer is here. Then we will tell you everything."

As though on cue, Miss Wellbeloved poked her head around the door. "Do either of you want a glass of wine?"

"Do you need to ask?" Ribero said, smoothing his moustache.

Miss Wellbeloved smiled. "It's not an Argentinian wine, I'm afraid."

"Which means it will be sub-standard. But I will accept it, nonetheless."

"How very decent of you. Kester, glass of red or white?"

"White, please," he replied and leaned back against the soft cushions, which spread deliciously around his tired back.

His father, satisfied that the fire was now alight, laid a couple of logs on top and made himself comfortable. "Have you heard anything else from this girlfriend of yours?" he asked, eyes glittering in the firelight.

Kester shook his head. "Nothing. Just one message from Anya, and that's it."

Ribero frowned. "And she never mentioned the Thelemites to you before?"

"No."

"You are sure?"

Kester smiled faintly. "I think I would remember a name like that."

An echo of footsteps down the hallway announced Miss Wellbeloved's return. She handed them their wine, then nodded apologetically at her own drink, which happened to be a mug of hot chocolate. "I simply cannot drink past ten o'clock," she said, sitting beside Kester. "It sends me straight to sleep and gives me a stinking headache the next day."

Kester smiled, noticing her hollow eyes and wan expression. "I'm sorry to land this on you, when we've all only just got home." They'd spent today driving back from Dundee, after a nightmarish week solving a particularly complex case involving a murderous fetch. He knew that the last thing they needed was another problem to deal with.

She flapped her hand at him. "Don't be silly. We're here to help."

"Why don't you start by telling us what you know, Kester?" His father leaned forward, glass pressed between his palms.

Kester shrugged, sipping his drink. "I don't really know much," he said. "I've only known Anya properly for a month or so, if that."

"Does she seem normal?" Miss Wellbeloved asked, studying his face intently.

Kester considered her question. He'd spent so long in the company of rather strange people like Miss Wellbeloved and his father that he wasn't quite sure what a normal person was like anymore.

"I *think* she's normal," he said finally. "She certainly didn't seem like she was going to disappear without prior warning, if that's what you mean."

"Did she mention any clubs or secret societies?"

Kester took a gulp of wine. It was welcome after a long, tiring day. "No, of course not. Well, only her book club. But nothing secretive."

"A book club?" Ribero fixed his gaze on Kester. "Are you sure it was a book club?"

"No, not really," Kester replied. "But why would she lie about something like that?"

"Did you ever meet anyone from her book club?"

Kester shook his head.

"Let me guess," Miss Wellbeloved said. "They meet on

Wednesday evenings?"

"How on earth did you know that?"

She nodded at Ribero, who looked grim. "Thelemites," they chanted in unison.

Kester looked at them blankly. "Please explain."

"Gosh, where to start?" Miss Wellbeloved cupped her drink, gaze roving over the fire as though seeking inspiration from the flames. "The Thelemites are an ancient secret society. There's several Thelemite lodges across the world; the Exeter branch is particularly well-established. Because of its proximity to Glastonbury, you see."

"What, Glastonbury Festival?" Kester asked, blinking.

"No, you silly boy, not because of the festival!" Ribero barked. "Do they teach you nothing at school these days?"

"Hang on, is there some link between King Arthur and Glastonbury?"

Ribero snorted, moustache bristling with unbridled irritation. "Yes, it is one of the most spiritually important places in the world, my boy! How can you not know this?"

"Remember," Miss Wellbeloved interrupted, "Kester's only been doing this job for a few months. He's got a lot to learn, Julio." She turned to Kester with a smile. "Have you heard of Glastonbury Tor?"

Kester thought about it. He was sure his housemate Daisy had mentioned it once. *Yes, come to think of it, she said she'd climbed up to the Tor with a friend,* he remembered. *She was wittering on about all the amazing "energies."*

"Is it on some kind of hill?" he asked.

Miss Wellbeloved beamed. "Yes, that's right. It used to be a spirit door, back in Druidic times. Obviously, it hasn't been operational for quite some time. These days, the only registered spirit door in the UK is inside Infinite Enterprises HQ."

"What about the doors that I open?" Kester asked.

"They are not permanent," Ribero explained. "They are different."

Miss Wellbeloved nodded. "Anyway," she continued, "back to the Thelemites. They're a secret society who believe that spirits and humans should live harmoniously together, as they used to do centuries ago."

"Hang on," Ribero said, holding up an imperious hand. "Is that how it was, Jennifer?"

"It's well documented," Miss Wellbeloved said, pursing her lips together. "For example, humans practiced shamanistic rituals to communicate with spirits."

"Yes, but to present it like it was always happy and smiley, that is not necessarily true."

She took a deep gulp of her drink. "That's not important right now. The Thelemites have been working for years to re-introduce spirits into the world. But in recent times, their methods have become . . ."

"Naughty?" Ribero suggested. The fire spat embers on the floorboards, making Kester jump.

"Renegade," Miss Wellbeloved corrected. "They are causing the government some alarm, let's put it like that."

"What do you mean?" Kester asked.

"The Thelemites are like terrorists," Ribero said, waving his glass around in his excitement. "They got involved with a lot of magick, illegal rituals to summon spirits into our world. Very naughty stuff, yes?"

"They are not like terrorists!" Miss Wellbeloved snapped. "Do try to remember that their motives are honourable, even if their methods are a bit unorthodox."

"Pah," Ribero spat, waggling his glass in her direction. "The government should have shut them all down years ago. You know that is true, Jennifer, so don't deny it."

"As if the government could!" Miss Wellbeloved replied. "You forget, the Thelemites date back thousands of years. And they're masters at appearing to behave themselves, even when they're not."

Kester frowned. "Should I be worried that they've kidnapped

Anya?" he asked, looking at them in turn. "Are they going to hurt her?"

"They're not going to hurt her," Miss Wellbeloved reassured him.

"I would not be so certain," Ribero muttered.

Kester fell silent. He could feel a headache coming on, which was hardly surprising, given the circumstances. "You're not doing much to calm my nerves here," he said eventually, mulling it all over. "Words like 'terrorist' don't exactly fill me with confidence."

Miss Wellbeloved winced. "They aren't terrorists," she reiterated, looking rather nettled. "And believe me, I should know."

"Why?"

Ribero snorted. "Because her father was one of them. And her grandfather. It's a family thing, yes?"

"Yes, it is," she snapped, crossing her arms. "But I'm not a part of the Thelemites. Not anymore, anyway."

"Why not?" Kester asked.

She rested her head against the cushions, eyes fixed on the ceiling. "I don't like their increasingly aggressive approach. But I am confident they wouldn't harm your girlfriend, especially if she's a member."

"Then why have they kidnapped her?" Kester could wrap his head around a secret organisation. He could even grasp the fact that Anya had been a part of it without telling him. But he couldn't see any logical reason why they'd steal her away.

Miss Wellbeloved shrugged. "I don't know. Perhaps she threatened to reveal their secrets?"

Kester thought about it. It seemed plausible. From what he knew of Anya, she certainly seemed feisty enough. "Would the Thelemites listen to you, if you asked them to let her go?"

Miss Wellbeloved glanced at Ribero, who stared into the fire, his expression unreadable. "I'm sure they would," she said finally. "I'll get in contact with Barty Melville tomorrow morning. He's the Master of the Exeter lodge."

"And he was a good friend of your father's," Ribero added. "I remember him. Looked like the big, fat creature who lives by the sea, you know? The blubbery one with big tusks."

"A walrus, yes," Miss Wellbeloved agreed. "Barty still has that tremendous moustache, I believe. The last time I saw him, it was virtually down to his chest."

Kester nodded. He felt marginally better now that they had a plan. "Thank goodness you know them, eh?" he said, smiling at Miss Wellbeloved. "Can't you get in touch with him now?"

She smiled. "Don't worry, Kester. Nothing bad is going to happen to her tonight. Barty will be asleep now, anyway. I very much doubt he'd bother getting out of bed to answer the phone."

"Unless he wants to shout at the person calling him," Ribero grunted. "That is what I do when someone calls me late at night."

"Quite. Anyway, Kester, try to keep calm until morning, if you can. The Thelemites have questionable methods, but they're not cruel people, and I'm sure they wouldn't harm her. Now, would anyone like some nibbles?" Miss Wellbeloved stood up, tugging her cardigan into position. "I don't know about you, but I'm exhausted. I need something to keep me awake."

"Do you want me to go home?" Kester asked. "I don't want to keep you up."

"No, that's quite alright," she replied, her expression softening. "There's something else we need to talk to you about, actually."

Oh really? Kester studied them both, trying to work out what it might be. Miss Wellbeloved winked, then trotted into the kitchen.

"What else did you want to discuss?" he asked.

His father shifted in his seat, eying Kester intently. "We were not going to have this conversation for a while," he began. "But as you are here now, it seems like a good time."

"Go on then," Kester said, perching on the edge of the sofa. "I'm all ears."

His father took a deep breath. "We know you got offered a place at the SSFE."

"How did you know?" Kester was astounded. He'd only just discovered himself that the School for Supernatural Further Education had accepted his application.

His father tapped the side of his nose. "I have my ways."

"Oh." Kester felt rather deflated. He'd been looking forward to announcing the news and seeing the look of pride on Ribero's face. *Ah well,* he thought, *I suppose it doesn't matter. They studied there themselves, it's probably no big deal to them.*

Miss Wellbeloved returned, armed with a plate of chocolate biscuits and a bag of what looked like crisps. On closer inspection, Kester saw that they were kale and parsnip crisps, which didn't sound nearly as appetising. *Trust Miss Wellbeloved to have a healthy snack,* he thought. *I bet even the biscuits are made of carob or chia seeds or something awful like that.*

"So, what did you want to talk about?" His hand hovered uncertainly over a biscuit. He was fairly sure it was chocolate, but wasn't sure he wanted to risk it.

"Taking over the business," his father said without preamble as he seized a handful of vegetable crisps.

Not this again, Kester thought, groaning inwardly. "But your health is fine," he said, gesturing at his father. "You can run the business, no problem."

Only a few weeks ago, Ribero had told Kester that he had Parkinson's disease. At times, Kester had noticed the difference: the tremble in his hands, the occasional cramps, the exhaustion after physical exertion. But on other occasions, like now, he found it difficult to believe there was anything wrong with his father at all. For a man in his late sixties, he was full of almost preternatural energy, like a jittery wind-up toy.

Ribero sighed, reaching for another handful of crisps. "At the moment I am healthy, yes," he said, flipping one into his mouth. "But not forever. Now you are studying Spirit Intervention and Business Studies, it is time for you to get hold of the ropes with me and Jennifer, yes?"

"I think you mean 'learn the ropes'," Miss Wellbeloved corrected.

"It is the same thing." Ribero studied Kester fiercely, eyes gleaming. "Soon, we will start teaching you how to manage the business. Okay?"

Kester shook his head. "I don't feel comfortable with the idea."

Ribero grunted. "It is not about comfort. It is about family honour. This is my agency. You are my son. So, you take it over."

"Well, no," Kester replied. "For starters, it wasn't your agency until Miss Wellbeloved's father gave it to you. Secondly, I'm the youngest person working in it. If you think Serena is going to take orders from me, you've got another thing coming."

Miss Wellbeloved laughed. "You're right, Serena won't be happy. But she'll come around, given time." She reached for a biscuit. "And as for it being my father's agency, you're absolutely correct. Which is why you'll be running it with me, until I retire. I have no children to pass the business down to anyway, and I'm more than happy for you to have it."

Kester swallowed. He felt overwhelmed at the prospect of taking over the agency, though he was touched at their faith in him. *I've only been a part of it for a few months,* he thought, finally daring to take a biscuit. *I'm still not totally convinced I want to be a spirit investigator, let alone the owner of a supernatural agency.*

He took a bite, then realised it most definitely wasn't choco-late. Judging by the strange, vegetable flavour, he presumed it had beetroot or something similar in it. His stomach churned. *I wonder if I could distract her, then flick it into the fire without her noticing?* However, a glance in her direction confirmed that he probably couldn't. She had eyes like an eagle.

"Luckily, I had those biscuits left over from last week," Miss Wellbeloved said as though reading his thoughts. "They've got courgette in them. You'd never guess, would you?"

He grimaced, wiping the crumbs off his shirt. "Not at all."

"So, you will take on the agency once I quit?" Ribero pressed.

He clearly wasn't going to take no for an answer.

"I presume it won't be any time in the near future, will it?"

Miss Wellbeloved and Ribero exchanged a glance. "I'm sure it won't be too soon," Miss Wellbeloved concluded. "Don't worry. We'll make sure you feel completely comfortable in the role first."

Kester rubbed his forehead. It was all too much to take in. In the space of a week, he'd run around Dorset chasing after a murderous spirit, been accepted into a supernatural school, and his girlfriend had been kidnapped by a weird cult. *Since when did this sort of thing become normal?* he wondered. *Is this how things are going to be from now on?* Not for the first time, he found himself thinking wistfully about his old life back in Cambridge, when it was just him, his mother, and nothing remotely spooky to worry about. *Those were the days.*

His phone vibrated. Kester whisked it out of his pocket and scanned the screen.

"Well? Was it Anya?" Miss Wellbeloved asked.

Kester shook his head, disappointed. "It's Mike. He wants to know if I want the tickets to the Billy Dagger gig. He offered to give me a couple for free."

"Billy Dagger, he is that musician, yes?" Ribero looked vaguely confused. "The one who wears all the silly make-up like a big girl?"

Kester chuckled. "Sort of. He's a bit of a legend, you know."

"So I have heard. I have no time for this sort of music though. It hurts my head, all those loud guitars."

Miss Wellbeloved laughed. "I used to like Billy Dagger's music, believe it or not. He's a great performer, so much energy that it's almost unnatural." She looked as though she was going to say more, before shutting her mouth and looking to the floor.

Kester grinned. He couldn't really imagine Miss Wellbeloved bopping away to a Billy Dagger tune, but then, she never ceased to surprise him. He texted Mike with an affirmative. *I may as well stay positive,* he thought, *and presume that firstly, we'll be able to rescue Anya, and secondly, she'll actually want to go on a date with me to a rock gig. Let's hope so.*

He stuck the rest of the biscuit reluctantly into his mouth, then gulped the remains of his wine. "I'm going to head home," he said, yawning. "Thanks for seeing me. I feel much better now that I know Anya's not in any danger."

"Any immediate danger," Ribero muttered ominously. "Don't trust the Thelemites too much."

"Are you sure you don't want to stay a bit longer?" Miss Wellbeloved offered, stifling a yawn of her own. "You're welcome to sleep in the spare room if you want."

He shook his head. "That's kind, but I haven't changed out of these clothes in nearly a week. I'm gagging to get into my own bed, if I'm being honest."

She nodded. "I can imagine. Let me call you a taxi."

"It's okay, I can walk."

"No, you cannot," Ribero snapped as he scooped up the poker and gave the fire a prod. "What about all the thieves and the drunk people, eh? No, they will take one look at you and have you for breakfast, lunch, and dinner. You get a taxi. I will pay."

Kester grinned. "Okay. Thanks."

Whilst he was waiting, he went through to the room next door, which Miss Wellbeloved used as a reading room. Her walls were lined with cluttered shelves, stuffed to the brim with ancient texts. With the candle flickering in the window, it looked almost medieval. He stood at the window and stared out at the dark alleyway.

I thought once we'd solved the case in Dorset, things would calm down, he thought, running his fingers over the top of the tiny flame. *But surprise, surprise, I was wrong again.* He looked up at the sliver of night sky squeezed between the narrow roofs. A few stars cast glowing circles in the black.

I wonder if Anya can see the same stars, he thought. *And whether she knows I'm thinking about her, right now.*

Pressing his head against the cool glass, he closed his eyes and hoped against hope that she did. Wherever she might be.

Chapter 2: Finding Anya

Unsurprisingly, Kester didn't sleep well. Even in the few hours that he'd managed to nod off, he'd been plagued by terrible dreams about mad Scottish spirits and faceless cults. Eventually, he gave up all hope of a restful night and sat at his desk, waiting for the feeble sun to struggle over the neighbouring rooftops.

It was a cold, grim morning, an indication of impending winter. Kester readied himself for the day ahead and waited anxiously for Miss Wellbeloved to call.

Rummaging through his kitchen cupboards, he decided to have some breakfast to take his mind off things. To his annoyance, somebody had polished off his box of Cocoa Puffs, and he knew exactly who it was. Pineapple, his top-knotted, spaced-out housemate, seemed to have no concept of personal belongings and helped himself to whatever was in the house, regardless of who had actually purchased it.

"Hello, stranger!" Daisy breezed into the kitchen, squeezing his shoulder as she passed by. She was wearing one of the most awful knitted sweaters he'd ever seen. *Are those pom-poms hanging off it?* he wondered, fighting to mask his horrified expression. *Or has it just started to unravel in the wash? It's difficult to tell.*

"Morning," he replied, pulling out some packets of pasta and praying there would be at least one small cereal box hidden behind them. "Don't suppose you've got any cereal, have you? Pineapple's eaten mine again."

"I've got some Yoga-Brite, if you'd like?"

Kester stood up, bones creaking in protest. "Um, what is it?"

"Yoga-Brite is the ultimate breakfast cereal for unlocking trapped energy. I love it, it's my new obsession. It has goji berries and spirulina and *everything*."

He grimaced. "Perhaps not." He could only imagine how rancid it would taste. "Do you have any bread?"

Daisy rolled her eyes. "I bought a fresh loaf yesterday. You know, you should try changing your lifestyle, Kester. Especially now you're losing weight."

Kester brightened, instinctively sucking his gut in, which happened to be bulging over his pyjama bottoms even as they spoke. "Can you tell?"

She gave him an appraising once-over. "Not exactly. It's just you told us you'd lost weight last week, didn't you?"

Sod it, he thought. He'd got on the scales this morning, and was thrilled to see that he'd lost seven pounds in total. *Doesn't seem much point, though, when no-one notices,* he concluded, releasing his gut again in a dejected deflation of defeat.

"Have you got work today?" he asked as he grabbed a slice of bread and chucked it into the toaster.

"No." Her face fell. "Unfortunately, I lost my job two days ago."

"Oh dear, not another one," he said, regretting asking the question already. The last thing he needed was a deep-and-meaningful with Daisy. Once she got going, her intense conversations tended to span on for several hours. "What happened this time?"

She pouted, then twiddled her pony-tail for good measure.

"My boss got cross because I was late back from lunch."

"How late?"

"Well . . ." She shuffled on the spot, picking at a stain on the cupboard door. "I didn't go back, actually. I sort of forgot. So, the honest answer is nine the next morning. I suppose I can't really blame him for being a bit cross."

"Yeah, that'll do it," Kester replied. A shrill ring from the hallway pulled his attention, and he held a finger up. "Hang on, I've got to get that. Can you pop up my toast for me before it burns?" Without waiting for an answer, he galloped out, seizing the phone. "Hello?"

"Hello, Kester, it's me." Miss Wellbeloved's clipped voice echoed through the receiver.

"Good morning," he replied, feeling happier already. There was something intrinsically reassuring about her calm, measured voice, which made him feel as though everything would be okay, regardless of the situation. "Did you speak to him?" he carried on. "Barty, or whatever his name was?"

"Barty Melville," she verified. "Yes, I did."

"And?"

There was a heavy sigh on the other end of the line. "It seems your girlfriend has been causing a bit of trouble."

Kester massaged his forehead. He could smell burning toast. A quick glance through to the kitchen indicated that Daisy had got distracted by whatever was outside the window. "Is Anya okay, though?" he asked.

"She's fine. I told you they wouldn't hurt her. But . . ."

"Yes?"

Miss Wellbeloved coughed. "The situation might be more complex than we thought. Barty said he'll see us this morning. I've checked with Julio, and it's fine for you and me to take the morning off work."

Kester looked at his watch. "What time?"

"I told him ten o'clock, so we've got to be fairly prompt."

Kester eyed the kitchen. Daisy had started to read the morning paper, oblivious to the thin wisp of smoke coiling from the toaster. He flapped a frantic hand in her direction, which she ignored.

"Well?" Miss Wellbeloved sounded impatient.

"Yes," Kester replied. "Absolutely. Ten o'clock is fine. Where do we need to go?"

"The main lodge just past Pinhoe, outside Exeter. I'll pick you up in twenty minutes or so. Okay?"

"Yes. And Miss Wellbeloved?"

"Yes?"

"Thanks for talking to him. It means a lot."

He could almost hear her smile down the receiver. "Not a problem," she replied softly. "See you in a bit."

Kester scratched his head. He wondered what Miss Wellbeloved had meant by "more complex." Whatever it was, it didn't sound promising. What had Anya done? *Oh well,* he thought, scampering to the kitchen to rescue his breakfast. *At least she's alive and well. That's the main thing.*

After munching his way through the charred remains of his toast, then diving into the shower, he waited on the wall outside, scanning the horizon for sight of Miss Wellbeloved's battered old Ford. A group of students emerged from the house next door, laughing loudly, and Kester instinctively shrank back. Although he'd loved university, he'd never felt much at home with young people, who were invariably more attractive, more confident, and infinitely cooler than he was. Which was precisely why he'd lived at home with his mother while studying, rather than living in halls.

He thought about Anya again, the only girl he'd ever met who hadn't looked at him with either revulsion or pity. She was odd, but her eccentricity was endearing rather than off-putting. *I'd thought we were getting to know each other well,* he thought, marching on the spot to warm himself up. *But this thing with the Thelemites makes me wonder if I actually knew her at all.*

A splutter of car engine startled him from his thoughts. He

looked up, just as Miss Wellbeloved's familiar Ford rattled to a stop in the road, clicking and wheezing in an alarming manner. He ran over to the passenger side and clambered in.

"Good morning," Miss Wellbeloved said, smiling. A vague drift of classical music floated from the radio like a soothing velvet ribbon.

"I'm not sure it is a good morning yet," Kester said, buckling himself in as the car pulled away. "Though thank you again for trying to sort things out. I know Anya's nothing to you, and—"

"Yes, but she's something to *you,* Kester," Miss Wellbeloved interrupted with a severe nod. "Which means we wouldn't dream of not helping her. Now, enough gratitude, let's just get this meeting over and done with." She swerved out into the main road. "I'm not looking forward to it, to be honest."

"I thought you and this Barty person were friends?"

She grimaced as they joined the long line of commuter traffic. "Barty was friends with my father, not me. Also, he and my father didn't part on the best of terms."

"Oh dear." Kester frowned. "What happened?"

Miss Wellbeloved glanced across. "Gosh, I'm not even sure I know where to start."

"Is it because the Thelemites changed? And your father wasn't comfortable with their new direction?"

She sighed. "That's the easiest explanation, yes. Put it like this, my father was always passionate about uniting the spirit and human world; he believed we could co-exist in relative harmony. However, he certainly didn't approve of the idea of inviting the spirits to live here permanently."

Kester bit his lip. "It's all a bit confusing."

"I know." Miss Wellbeloved inched the car forward, then scowled as the traffic lights went red again. "But it's something you'll need to understand, if you're going to take over the agency one day. Our industry is dominated by politics, and there's a lot of division. Some think that spirits should be locked out of our world permanently and treated as criminals when they enter. Others, like the Thelemites, believe they should come and go as they please and live here if they want to."

"And you?"

She paused, searching for the right words. "I've known some good spirits in my time, Kester. I grew up with one. A wonderful, caring spirit who lived in the oak tree in our garden. She used to play with me when I was a little girl, and leave me small presents under the branches. I believe humans and spirits can get along just fine—but I also believe that certain systems need to be in place." She switched off the radio and looked at him. "What do you think?"

"What do I think?" Kester blinked. "Honestly? I have no idea."

"You've met some spirits now, and you've worked with us for over four months. Surely you must have an opinion?"

He reviewed the question carefully. His first spirit encounter had been a hideous experience: a terrifying banshee with a face from a nightmare and a scream to match. He remembered the misplaced Japanese spirit in the woods, as small as a doll, with a tiny parasol and an expression full of pain. There had been plenty of other spirits too. A ghoul who'd had a fondness for tripping people over in a residential home in Torquay. A poltergeist who liked throwing footballs at students in the local school. And not forgetting their most recent case: the Scottish fetch who'd killed several people and had been hell-bent on murdering a few more for good measure.

"I just don't know," he said finally as he leaned back against the head-rest. "They're so different to each other. How can you apply one rule to them all?"

Miss Wellbeloved smiled in satisfaction. "Quite. I knew you'd understand. That's why we need to have a system in place; so we can allow decent spirits safe passage into this world, but keep the troublemakers at bay."

The lights went green, and they rumbled onwards up the hill, past the suburban houses, to the outskirts of the city. Kester thought about it all, feeling hopelessly torn. It seemed that there was no real solution to the problem. After all, most people in the world were terrified of the supernatural. How on earth could spirits ever live comfortably alongside them?

They drove through the village of Pinhoe and emerged into the verdant fields.

"Where is this place then?" Kester asked.

Miss Wellbeloved chuckled. "Oh, just you wait. It's quite something. You'll be amazed when you see it."

She indicated left, then turned the car down a rough, dirt track. A huddle of sheep surveyed their approach with identical impassive, chewing expressions before scattering across the field. Kester focused his attention to the end of the driveway, then gasped.

"What the hell is that?" he breathed, studying the impressive sight in front of him.

Miss Wellbeloved chuckled as she pulled the car to a halt, wheels grinding in the loose gravel. She switched off the engine, then turned to him. "What do you think?"

Kester stared in open disbelief. A huge manor house loomed over them, a behemoth of stone and black windows. However, that wasn't what astonished him. What took his breath away was the building's sheer dereliction. To one side, the roof had crumbled entirely, leaving just a shell of haphazard walls and tangled ivy.

"You can't seriously be telling me that the Thelemites meet in a place like this?" he said, opening the car door. "It's a ruin!"

She laughed and stepped out into the open. "They certainly wouldn't use the main lodge at this time of year. It would be freezing. As you can see, there's not much left of it." She gestured past the building to a narrow path leading behind it. "Come on, follow me."

He trotted after her. At the back of the house, there was a squat, prefabricated building with a spartan felt roof. It looked rather like a modern village hall, and not at all like the meeting place of an ancient cult. In fact, it couldn't have been more at odds with the main lodge if it had tried. Kester gawped.

"It's a strange place, isn't it?" he said finally.

"Not half as strange as the people who meet here," Miss Well-beloved said wryly. "Come on. Let's see if Barty's arrived yet."

She knocked on the door. Kester thought he detected movement through the frosted glass. They waited.

The door creaked open. Kester's mouth fell open.

My goodness, he thought, hastily rearranging his features into a more neutral expression. *Is that a man or a massive pile of loose flesh?*

Miss Wellbeloved caught his eye, the ghost of a smile playing at her lips. "Hello, Barty," she said softly.

"Greetings, dear young Jennifer," the man said in a rich, deep voice that reminded Kester of a Shakespearean actor. Sharp black eyes peered out from beneath a pair of astonishingly large, white eyebrows. He looked like Moses himself, Kester thought, if Moses had since put on several stone and wrinkled up like a tortoise.

Miss Wellbeloved stepped inside. "It's been a while since anyone's called me young," she replied with a laugh.

Kester watched the man shuffle to a plastic table in the centre of the room. He was as gigantic and wobbling as a hippopotamus, his size exaggerated by a shapeless garment covered in intricate stars. *He's actually dressed as a wizard,* Kester realised, stifling a snort of laughter. *I didn't even know you could buy clothes like that, except in a fancy-dress shop. Does he go out in public wearing it? Or is it for our benefit?*

Barty Melville creaked onto a seat, then invited them to do the same. His beard floated down over his neck like a misty waterfall.

"Well then," he began, eyeing each of them in turn. "We shall commence our discussion in a moment, but we must wait for Parvati first. She's informed me that she's on her way, with the young lady in question."

"Do you mean Anya?" Kester asked, leaning forward anxiously. "Is she okay?"

Barty raised an eyebrow. "Ah," he replied, with evident satisfaction. "I take it that you are Kester Lanner. Well, well, well."

Miss Wellbeloved nodded. "Gretchen's son, that's right. He's joined our agency."

Barty cleared his throat, fingers twisting at the ends of his moustache. "So I heard. I presume he has the same ability as his mother, then? To open spirit doors?"

Miss Wellbeloved's eyes narrowed. "I suspect you know the answer to that question already, Barty. I know that you have ways of getting information."

He smirked. "Touché, Jennifer." With an elaborate yawn, he eased back, confident and contemptuous as a king on a throne. Kester pitied the plastic seat beneath him, which was clearly struggling to cope with the bulk.

"So," Barty continued, "I take it the young lady is a companion of yours, young Kester?"

"She is," he replied. He wasn't warming to the gigantic gentleman in the slightest. His demeanour was knowing, and his expression unpleasantly sly, reminding Kester of a large spider sizing up two tasty flies.

"Kester wasn't aware that Anya was a member of the Thelemites," Miss Wellbeloved added. "She never mentioned it, did she, Kester?"

He shook his head.

"I'd hardly say she was a member." Barty patted his stomach reflectively. "She's only been attending meetings for a few months. Not even a year. Hopelessly out of her depth, from what I've heard."

"How did she get involved in the first place?" Kester asked.

Barty Melville smiled slowly. "My goodness, you really don't know one another very well, do you?"

"She told me she was going to a book club," Kester said defensively.

"That's what they all say."

They were interrupted by a sharp knock, followed by a creak as the door opened. A tiny woman swept into the room, brisk as a miniature cyclone, followed by Anya, who kept her head down.

Kester breathed a sigh of relief, chest loosening instinctively at the sight of her. *She looks miserable and tired,* he thought, taking in her greasy hair and hollow eyes, *but at least she's okay.*

Anya met his eyes and gave him a wan smile.

"I apologise for being late." The small woman, who was dressed in an immaculately-pressed suit, glided to the table. *She can only be about four and a half feet,* Kester thought, studying her with interest. Despite her size, there was an intimidating ferocity about her. She certainly didn't look like someone to be underestimated.

"Parvati, my dear," Barty greeted warmly. "That's quite alright. Thank you for coming at such short notice. I trust this young woman was no problem at your house?"

Parvati placed herself on the nearest chair, then turned the full force of her gaze on Kester and Miss Wellbeloved. "She was perfectly well behaved," she replied coldly. "It's a shame we cannot say the same of her conduct at our last meeting."

Anya bit her lip, glancing at Kester. He couldn't tell what she was thinking but wished he could comfort her. *She looks lost and frightened,* he thought, emotion swelling in the pit of his stomach. *How could they put her through this?*

"Anya, do you know why Jennifer and Kester are here?" Barty Melville asked. His expression suggested he was enjoying her discomfort.

Anya nodded. Then shook her head. Then nodded again. "I presume Kester's come to help me out," she said. Her voice sounded as though she'd been rubbing her throat with sandpaper. "I don't really know this other lady."

"This is Miss Wellbeloved," Kester explained. "I've mentioned her in the past. I think you've met her once."

Anya shrugged, looking confused. "I'm sorry," she whispered. "I didn't mean to get you involved in this. And I never meant to deceive you."

"Hey, it's fine," he replied, desperate to console her. "There are a few things I haven't told you either."

"Ah, young love," Barty chuckled. "Most touching. It sounds like you both have a lot to talk about. However, before we release Anya, a few issues must be discussed. Jennifer, you understand, don't you?"

Miss Wellbeloved sighed. "It depends on what she's done, Barty."

He nodded. "Very well. Firstly, allow me to introduce Parvati Chowdhury. Parvati, could you enlighten our guests here as to what happened on Wednesday night?"

Parvati pressed her palms together, creating a severe arch tipped with sharp, red nails. Her eyes bored into them, forceful as laser beams. "In the past, Anya had given us cause to doubt her loyalty," she began frostily. "We've been monitoring her carefully. Her outburst on Wednesday left us in no doubt."

"Well, you know why that was," Anya mumbled, staring out of the window. Parvati and Barty shot her a look, which she ignored.

"What exactly happened?" Miss Wellbeloved asked.

"Anya threatened to expose us all," Parvati retorted, shaking her head in horror. "Which, of course, we cannot allow to happen. In the past, this level of insubordination would have been dealt with very severely indeed."

"Thank goodness we don't live in the past then, eh?" Miss Wellbeloved tried a smile, then seemed to decide against it.

"Obviously, we cannot release her until we're satisfied that she won't reveal our secrets to the world," Barty added, drumming his fingers on the table. "It would not only threaten our ancient and most revered society, it would jeopardise your agency too, Jennifer."

Anya's head shot up. "How will it jeopardise your agency? What *is* your agency? You've never told me what you do for a job."

Kester swallowed. He'd been dreading this question for a long time. "Um, long story."

"It's not really, Kester," Miss Wellbeloved snapped. "We're a supernatural agency. However, like the Thelemites, we rely on secrecy in order to conduct our business. Do you understand?"

Anya's eyes widened. "So that's why you were always so secretive about it," she said, giving Kester a suspicious look. "Is there anything else I don't know about you? Did you know about the Thelemites already?"

Kester held his hands up in protest. "Hey, the first time I'd even heard of the Thelemites was when you texted me last night. Honestly."

Anya turned to Miss Wellbeloved. "Do you support what they're trying to do?" she asked.

Miss Wellbeloved sighed. "The spirit world is complex," she replied, looking at Barty. "For what it's worth, I believe that humans should integrate with spirits more often. But I don't think we should permit them freedom to come and go as they wish."

"Our agency actually focuses on returning them to the spirit world," Kester added.

"Only the problematic ones, of course," Miss Wellbeloved clarified, fingers twiddling nervously in her lap.

Barty snorted. "Parvati," he began. "What do you recommend we do?"

Parvati's eyes glittered dangerously. "Tell Anya that if she breathes a word to anyone about us, it'll be the last breath she takes?"

"Well, that's one way of doing it," Barty said with a chuckle, stroking his moustache. "Very well. Let's leave it there, and say no more on the matter. Anya, we're a peaceful organisation at heart, and we don't like making threats. However, what Parvati has just said shall stand. If you even say the word 'Thelemite' to anyone outside of this room, there will be consequences." His expression hardened. "Dire consequences."

"That seems fair," Miss Wellbeloved said quickly, before Anya could open her mouth. "Anya, you won't talk about the Thelemites to anyone, will you? Aside from myself and Kester, of course."

Anya glared at the opposite wall. Kester waited, biting his lip. *Why isn't she agreeing?* he thought with frustration. *Surely it doesn't even need thinking about!*

"I need an answer," Barty barked.

"Anya?" Miss Wellbeloved looked anxious.

Finally, Anya nodded. "Fine," she muttered. "But for the record, I don't agree with what you're doing."

Kester frowned. There was something *off* about Anya's voice, a deadpan tone that made her seem almost like an actor playing a part rather than a real person. *She's probably just in shock,* he rationalised, trying to catch her eye. *Either that, or she hasn't slept all night. I'm sure there's a reason for it, anyway.*

Barty smirked. "Anya, your disapproval is noted. Now, if you'd like to depart? I have other affairs to attend to."

Miss Wellbeloved rose, then gestured to Kester to do the same. "Thank you for your time, Barty. And your understanding in this matter."

Barty rose with difficulty from his chair. "Had it been anyone else but you, we would not have been so merciful. This young lady has flouted many of our ancient laws. However, out of respect for your dear father, we are happy to overlook her serious misdemeanours. For now."

"I appreciate the gesture," she replied, moving towards the door.

Barty nodded. "You know," he continued, walking slowly across the linoleum floor, "you would be most welcome to return to the Thelemites, don't you?"

Anya's mouth fell open. Kester quickly grabbed her by the arm and pulled her towards the door. "I'll explain later," he hissed, smiling nervously at Parvati as they stepped out into the open. "Let's get you out of here."

He tugged her down the path as quickly as possible, worried that the Thelemites might suddenly change their minds. Miss Wellbeloved followed, shoes clattering a staccato rhythm on the loose stones, a jarring noise against the quiet of the surrounding countryside. The only other sound was the sheep, chorusing a bleating disapproval at their presence.

"It's cold," Anya said, looking at the sky.

"The car's just over there, don't worry." Kester guided her to the car-park, still feeling rather unsettled, though he couldn't say precisely why. *Why isn't she being more animated?* he wondered. *It's not like her.* In fact, he almost felt as though he was talking to a stranger, though he couldn't work out why.

Miss Wellbeloved glanced at him, her expression unreadable. "Why don't you sit in the back, Anya?" she suggested as she opened the car door. "You look as though you haven't slept in about a week."

Anya lurched into the back, then rested her head against the seat. "I feel like my head is about to explode," she mumbled. "There's too much information to take in. And I keep thinking about Thor. I hope Wendy fed him."

"Who on earth is Thor?" Miss Wellbeloved asked, eyeing Anya in the windscreen mirror.

"It's her pet ferret," Kester explained as they pulled away. "And Wendy is her housemate." He turned and gave Anya what he hoped was his most reassuring smile. "Well, that was a bit of a close one, wasn't it? You had us all worried there."

Anya shook her head slowly. "I'm the one who's worried now."

"What do you mean?"

"I mean that you are both part of the Thelemites too! I had no idea, Kester. What else haven't you told me?"

Kester tugged at his seatbelt, the weight of her suspicion bearing down on him. "For starters," he began slowly, "we're not part of the Thelemites. Miss Wellbeloved's father used to be a member. That's all. And apparently, it was very different back then."

"It was," Miss Wellbeloved confirmed, winding down the window.

"But you're in a supernatural agency! And you never told me!" The hurt in her eyes could have rivalled a whipped puppy. Kester shifted uneasily in his seat.

"How could I have told you?" he said finally. "You would have thought I was a complete lunatic."

A hint of a smile tugged the corner of her mouth. "But the irony is I wouldn't have, would I? Because I know all about the spirit world too."

Kester wagged a finger at her. "Exactly. You didn't tell me anything about that, did you? You told me it was a book club!"

She reddened. "I would have told you if I'd have known what you do for a job!"

Miss Wellbeloved coughed as she swung the car back onto the main road. "I suspect this argument isn't going anywhere," she said. "The bottom line is, you both hid things from one another, and for good reason. But now they're out in the open."

"Yes, I suppose so," Anya agreed, then yawned. She caught sight of her reflection in the window and grimaced. "I look terrible. My hair is a mess."

"I think you look fine," Kester replied, rubbing his temples. There were plenty of other things he wanted to say to Anya, but it seemed like the wrong time, especially with Miss Wellbeloved in the car. Anya seemed absorbed with the passing landscape outside the window, her expression unreadable. He sensed that she was thinking things over and thought it best to leave her to it.

"Where was it you lived again?" Miss Wellbeloved asked as they finally approached the outskirts of the city.

Anya told her, then settled back against the window. Within ten minutes, they'd arrived outside her house—a Victorian terrace that looked almost identical to Kester's own house, only in rather better condition. *I wonder if I'll ever get invited into her home now,* he wondered, feeling depressed. *Probably not, if her expression is anything to go by. She's definitely not impressed with me.*

"I'll call you," he said as she climbed out of the car. Anya flashed a smile, which reassured him slightly.

"Okay. I'll talk to you later," she replied, tucking her hair behind her ear. "Thank you for your help, Miss Wellbeloved. I appreciate it."

"That's quite alright," Miss Wellbeloved replied, studying Anya with obvious concern. "Take care of yourself."

As they reversed down the road, Kester slumped back against his seat, feeling dejected. "I think I'm in the dog-house," he muttered as he picked at a loose thread on his trousers.

Miss Wellbeloved rolled her eyes. "She's not annoyed with you, Kester; anyone can see that. She's just overwhelmed by it all. That's why she was behaving strangely. Who wouldn't, after that experience?"

She switched on the radio. The dulcet notes of a violin concerto wafted through the car, immediately soothing his nettled spirits.

"Perhaps," he replied, unconvinced.

"Come on," Miss Wellbeloved said, nudging his elbow. "Let's head into the office. Your father will be surprised to see us back so quickly. I think he presumed Barty would be far harder to convince."

They drove into town, which was unusually quiet aside from a few shoppers wrapped up in thick coats with their heads tucked down to avoid the wintry breeze. Finally, they reached the narrow road leading to the office. Miss Wellbeloved eased her car with expert precision into an impossibly small space by the wall, then climbed out. Kester followed morosely behind, wondering whether to text Anya or not. *I don't want to look too keen,* he thought as he braced himself against the cold wind. *She already thinks I'm weird. I don't want her to think I'm pathetic too.*

They opened the door to the sight of Mike spinning Pamela around the office floor in an elaborate waltz. Kester sidestepped neatly as Pamela's sizeable bottom whisked by, barely inches past him, nearly knocking him back into the hallway. He wasn't overly shocked. Generally speaking, strange things went on in the office on a daily basis, and the sight of his two colleagues dancing around the floor wasn't nearly as odd as some of the things he'd witnessed.

"Are we disturbing something?" Miss Wellbeloved asked as she hung up her coat.

"Too right," Mike declared. He released Pamela, then bowed theatrically to her. "This genius lady has secured us a nice little job in Taunton."

Miss Wellbeloved beamed. "Really? Tell me more!"

"It's an incubus," Serena said, leaning over the top of her computer screen. "Some love-sick spirit that's been mooching around in the local swimming pool, of all places."

Kester brightened. "Hang on," he said, finger suspended excitedly in the air. "I remember reading about incubuses in my encyclopaedia!"

"It's incubi, dunderhead, not incubuses," Serena corrected, throwing him a scornful look.

"I always wondered about that," Mike said, as he slumped down on the sofa. "I mean, the plural of octopus isn't octopi, is it? It's octopuses."

"Actually," Kester interrupted, "it's a Greek-derived word, so its original plural is octopodes." He caught sight of their expressions and coughed defensively. "Sorry. Just thought I'd better set the record straight."

"Enough about plurals and singulars," Miss Wellbeloved said, flapping her hands at them all. "Does Julio know about the new job?"

Mike shook his head. "He said he wanted a nap, and that we shouldn't disturb him until lunchtime."

She looked over at his office door with concern. "That's strange. It's not his usual time for a sleep. Well, tell us more about the case, Pamela."

Pamela beamed with delight, resting herself on the edge of the nearest desk. "It should be an absolute doddle. Harmless incubus, wandering around the female changing room, moaning a bit, and generally behaving all soppy. Usual sort of incubus behaviour."

"Aren't incubuses meant to be—" Kester began.

"Incubi!"

"Aren't they meant to be a bit . . ."

Mike chortled. "A bit randy?"

Kester blushed. "Yes. I thought they were all about creeping up on people in the middle of the night and . . . well, you know."

"Getting jiggy with it?" Mike clarified with a lurid wink.

"Absolutely not," Miss Wellbeloved said sternly. "Incubi will only mate with humans if they're expressly invited to. They're not deviants, for goodness' sake."

"*Most* of them aren't deviants," Serena corrected, nails rapping on the keyboard. "But there have been isolated cases of sexual attack. Hence their reputation."

Miss Wellbeloved gave a long-suffering sigh. "For the most part," she soldiered on, deliberately turning away from Serena, "they simply fall in love. They mean well, but they can be a bit of a pain."

"It'll be an easy job," Pamela said. "They're usually easy to talk to, aren't they, Jennifer?"

"Oh yes," Miss Wellbeloved confirmed. "Providing they don't fall in love with any of us."

"I very much doubt that would happen," Serena added, casting a meaningful gaze at Pamela and Miss Wellbeloved.

"Quite," Miss Wellbeloved replied dryly. "When do we need to start?"

Pamela paced over to her desk and peered at her computer screen. "It says it's an ASAP job," she said, licking her lips. "So, I suppose if we can get started tomorrow, the government will be pleased about it."

Miss Wellbeloved rubbed her hands together. "Excellent. Exactly the sort of project we want. Quick, easy, and well-paid."

"Not tomorrow!" Mike said, slapping his forehead. "That'll be the second weekend in a row that we've worked. I need some time off."

"Get over it, Mike," Serena snarled. "It's good money, so stop whining."

"None of us want to work on a Saturday," Miss Wellbeloved agreed. "But we really must in this instance. It's too good a job to pass up." She glanced over at Ribero's closed door and stroked her chin thoughtfully. "Let's wake him up. He'll want to know."

She's worried about him, Kester thought as he watched her tap at the door. He could tell from the wrinkling of her eyes. *She's concerned that he's ill again.* To be honest, he felt rather worried himself, but he wasn't sure quite what to do about it. He didn't like the thought of his father being unwell, and more selfishly, he didn't relish the prospect of having to look after the agency if Ribero was suddenly unable to work.

"Hey," Mike said, sidling up to him. "Are you coming to the Billy Dagger gig tomorrow night?"

Kester's mouth fell open. "Oh gosh, I'd forgotten all about it. Are you still alright for me to come?"

"I said the tickets were yours if you wanted them, didn't I?" He nudged him. "Providing your girlfriend is up to it, that is."

"I haven't even asked her yet," Kester said. "But I'd love to come, even if she doesn't want to. Thank you."

"I'd like to come too," Serena piped up. A glacial tightening at the corner of her lips suggested that she might have been attempting a smile.

Mike rolled his eyes. "Alright, alright. Fine. You can come too. But only if you behave yourself, mind. And drive me back, so I can drink."

Serena opened her mouth, then shut it again. "Okay," she agreed finally. "I'll be your taxi service, if you pay for my ticket. How about that?"

Mike winked at Kester. "Fine. You twisted my arm, you conniving cow."

"And you've now got the opportunity to drink yourself silly, you alcoholic ape."

Kester laughed and settled himself at his desk, which happened to be a foldaway camping table. Thankfully, this time it didn't collapse, which it had the habit of doing at least once a day. He glanced at Ribero's office door, which had remained shut since

Miss Wellbeloved had disappeared inside. He hoped his father was alright. The office fell silent, except for Serena, who was fiercely hammering on the keyboard as though it had personally insulted her.

He gulped. *I dread to think how she's going to react when she finds out that Dad wants to make me the boss of the agency,* he thought. The mere idea of her tsunami of rage was enough to make him feel queasy.

He stretched in his chair and looked around the room with worry. *Dad might think he's found the solution, but he really hasn't. Not at all. He's just found a way to pass all the problems directly to me.*

CHAPTER 3: BILLY DAGGER

The drive to Taunton was relatively uneventful, save for Mike moaning every five minutes about having to work at the weekend and Serena telling him repeatedly to shut up. Miss Wellbeloved attempted to brief them all on the incubus case, before realising she'd left the notes at home. Finally, everyone gave up and subsided into silence. Fortunately, it wasn't a long journey.

As the van swung into the car-park, Kester peered out with interest. It wasn't at all what he'd imagined. He'd presumed that a spirit would choose some sort of crumbling Victorian building to live in. Instead, the pool was a modern, glass-fronted building, with cheery red doors and colourful posters in the foyer.

They'd been told that it would be quieter if they arrived earlier in the day. However, if the echoing whoops and splashes from the pool area were anything to go by, the entire town had turned up to have a swim.

The manager greeted them by the stairs, then apologised as he ushered them through to the staff area.

"It's not usually this lively," he explained, tugging at his tie. His twitchiness reminded Kester of a guinea pig, an impression that was reinforced by the wispy, gingery hair trailing over his ears and down his neck. "It's the weather, you see. The parents never know what to do with the kids on a day like this."

Kester glanced out the window. A strong winter sun penetrated the tinted glass. *It looks like a glorious day to me,* he thought, shrugging at the rest of the team. Pamela stifled a giggle.

"Anyway," the manager continued, "I'm Mr Gamble, or Fred, if you prefer. Please, come to my office, and I'll give you a run-through of the situation." He led them up the stairs to a room along the corridor. Apart from a window overlooking the pool area, the office was bland and featureless, with a spartan desk and a single chair for guests, which Ribero promptly sat down on. The others gathered around like a huddle of rugby players, awkwardly cramming themselves into the limited space in the corner.

"So, you have already been briefed by the government about how this works, yes?" Ribero said, rubbing his eyes. He looked tired.

"Yes, I chatted to a gentleman on the phone yesterday afternoon; I think he was called Mr Philpot." The manager sat down and started nervously tapping at the desk. "He said he'd sent the details of the case over to you."

"Yes, *someone* left those back at the office," Serena chipped in, nodding in Miss Wellbeloved's direction.

"It's not a problem," Miss Wellbeloved replied breezily. "Incubi are seldom troublesome. Why don't you tell us what's been going on?"

Suddenly, an inflatable ball bashed against the window behind the manager, spraying water over the glass and startling them all. The manager jumped, grimacing.

"Sorry about that, it happens a lot," he explained, as he adjusted his collar. "Kids think it's funny to throw things against the window. Bit of an architectural design flaw, really, having the office overlooking the pool."

"Quite. Anyway," Miss Wellbeloved continued, leaning forward, "the incubus is currently hiding in the female changing room, is that correct?"

"Yes, that's right." He looked up, wide-eyed as a child. "Can you get rid of it?"

Miss Wellbeloved bristled. "We can certainly guide *him* back to his own world," she replied, pursing her lips. "We don't like to use the expression *get rid of.*"

"How often has the incubus caused problems?" Serena asked, leaning over Ribero's shoulder. He promptly nudged her off again, leaving her momentarily off-balance.

Mr Gamble considered the question. "Not loads of times," he said finally. "I've never encountered it. A few women have run out screaming because it was moaning at them though. Don't worry," he added quickly, "we covered it up well. Told the women it was the central heating making funny noises."

"Yes, incubi can be rather loud," Pamela agreed. "Especially if the female in question is young and good-looking."

"Anything else, other than the moaning and the groaning?" Ribero asked.

The manager shook his head, then nodded. "It was floating around in the showers for a bit, Thursday afternoon. The lady who spotted it didn't like that, I can tell you. That's when I called the police, who referred me to the government."

"They probably should have just passed it to us as a regional case," Serena muttered, nudging Pamela.

"Well, it's more money for us if it's classified as a national, so keep quiet, dear," Pamela replied through gritted teeth.

"It's all very difficult to get my head around, to be honest," the manager continued. His finger delved into his ear before he wiped it on his trousers. "I didn't believe in ghosts until all this happened. It makes me feel a bit uncomfortable."

"No need to be," Miss Wellbeloved replied crisply. "Chances

of you encountering any further spirits are incredibly small these days because there aren't many left. Now, shall we get on?"

The manager nodded, then pressed his intercom. "Sharon?" he said. The line fizzled. "Sharon, will you come and escort the agency down to the changing room?"

"What agency?"

The manager sighed. "You know. The one we were talking about yesterday. Be a love, come on. I've got things to get on with." He released the button, then gave an embarrassed shrug. "Staff, eh?"

"Oh, I know," Ribero said, casting a dark look in their direction. A few moments later, the door flew open, revealing a blonde, buxom female who was squeezed into a very purple dress. Kester thought she looked like a squashed blueberry.

"Hello there, my lovelies," she greeted in a strong Somerset accent, oozing and undulating with soft, milky vowels. "Do you want to come with me, then?"

Miss Wellbeloved nodded. "Absolutely. Let's get to work, shall we?" Scooping up her handbag, she marched out of the office. The others followed suit, and they all headed back down the stairs.

"It's a crazy old thing, isn't it?" Sharon continued. She fluffed her hair absent-mindedly, a poodle-like mop of curls which surrounded her head like a cloud. "Who would have thought it, eh? That ghosts really do exist!"

"Please, keep the voice down low, eh?" Ribero scuttled next to her, eyes anxiously scanning the crowded reception area. "Remember, this is all hush-hush."

The woman made a big show of pressing a finger against her lips. "Of course, my dear. Understood. Don't worry, apart from me and Mr Gamble, no-one knows about it." She flung open the door to the female changing room, then nodded inside. "Need me to come in with you? Only I've got to get back to the desk. The queue's reached outside the door, look!"

"That's fine," Miss Wellbeloved said, observing the waiting

crowds. "May we ask that you prevent anyone from entering the changing room for a few minutes though? We need privacy to get on with our work."

Sharon looked at the crowds, rolling her eyes. "I'll do my best," she said, "but I can guarantee they'll kick off, my dear."

"Fifteen minutes should do it," Mike said with a grin.

Kester peered into the changing room. The mere thought of stepping inside a place where women took their clothes off seemed hideously indecent. *Please don't let there be any naked ladies in there,* he thought, blushing. *I think I'd have to run away if there were.* A glance at Mike's wolfish expression confirmed he was thinking the exact opposite.

"Excuse me, but there are people already getting changed in there, aren't there?" he said, looking at the others. "Surely that means that me, Mike, and Dad shouldn't go in, right?"

The others looked at him as though he was speaking in tongues. Mike poked him in the ribs. "Hey, don't pass up a great opportunity, mate," he whispered.

"It feels very wrong," Kester muttered, reluctantly following them in. "Very wrong indeed."

They stepped into the humid changing room. Kester tiptoed over the rough tiles, eyes fixed firmly to the floor. He could hear various gasps and protestations, and a blush started to creep over his cheeks. *Why didn't they ask everyone to leave before we came in?* he wondered. *It's not like we can conduct a spirit removal when there are women in their towels watching us!*

Clearly Ribero had the same thought, and he stopped, holding his hand aloft like a town-crier. "Ladies," he announced in a rich, authoritative voice. "I must ask you to hurry up with your dressing or undressing as we need to conduct a quick assessment in here."

"Of the pipework," Mike added, waving his rucksack as though that explained everything.

"The pipework?" Serena hissed. "What idiot says 'the pipework'? You mean the plumbing!"

Mike stuck his tongue out. "It doesn't matter now." He nodded towards the cluster of women who were eyeing them suspiciously, but hurrying to put their clothes on, nonetheless. "It worked, didn't it?"

Pamela meandered over to the lockers. She looked very out of place amongst the swimsuit-clad females around her. Glancing at the ceiling, her posture suddenly stiffened, alert as a bloodhound. "I can sense some residual energy over here," she called out, oblivious to the two young girls who were staring at her, mouths open, still dripping pool-water onto the floor.

Miss Wellbeloved coughed deliberately. "You mean residual leaking from the pipes, yes?"

"Oh yes, that's exactly what I meant." Pamela tapped her nose and winked. Miss Wellbeloved groaned.

"Right," Ribero said, rubbing his hands together. "That very nice lady, what was her name again?"

"Sharon," Mike prompted.

"Yes, Sharon. She is stopping any more women coming in. Jennifer, you go out to the pool and stop anyone from entering from there, okay? Then we should get the place just to ourselves, right?"

Miss Wellbeloved nodded. "Absolutely. You don't need me for this job, anyway; it should be a doddle." Without another word, she swept off her shoes and socks and headed out towards the entrance to the pool.

The others waited patiently until the remaining women had dried off, dressed, and cleared out. Finally, as the last mother ushered her children outside with a final, departing glare, they relaxed.

Mike checked his watch. "We've got about five minutes left to get this sorted out before the next lot of women come in," he said, rummaging in his bag. "Luckily, I brought the sonar detector, so I should be able to get its location pretty quickly." He pulled out a monstrous contraption, which looked suspiciously like a sardine tin with wires sticking out the top, and started to wave it around above his head.

"I'm not sure you need to bother," Pamela said, looking slightly embarrassed. "This spirit wants to be found, I think. He's leaving a clear path for us."

"Ah, don't spoil my fun," Mike said, zipping the device dangerously close to Pamela's head. "I've made a few modifications on this, I want to see how well it performs."

"We do not have the time for the silly-billy behaviour, okay?" Ribero strode over and snatched the device from Mike's hand. "You can test it out another time. Pamela, lead us to the incubus, if you please."

Mike looked mutinous. Kester patted him on the back as they followed the others. "For what it's worth, I thought it looked quite cool," he whispered.

"It's bloody genius, that's what it is," Mike muttered, shooting dark looks at Ribero's back.

They walked over to the back of the room. Kester realised where they were headed and sighed. *It would be the toilets.* He winced at the sight of the wet seats and paper all over the floor. *Why couldn't the incubus pick somewhere clean?* It smelt hideous in there; a mix of damp, chlorine, and all sorts of vaguely unpleasant bodily odours.

Pamela stiffened, then nodded, pointing to the third toilet. "He's in there," she announced, and gestured at Serena. "Go on, love. Do your thing. I'm picking up no resistance from him."

Serena pulled out a water bottle and unscrewed the lid. "Excellent," she said, jaw tightening. "Let's get this over and done with."

A low moan started to rise in the silence, like a malfunctioning boiler. Kester stared into the toilet cubicle, which looked like the filthiest of the lot, then spotted a grimy shape hovering above the cistern. He was small, wispy, and quivering like a wet cat. Kester could just about make out some sort of face, or at least a pair of beady eyes, blinking at them with unmistakable interest.

"Oh, there it is!" he said, pointing stupidly. The others ignored him. Serena started to chant under her breath, gradually extending the water-bottle towards it.

This isn't so bad, Kester thought, watching with interest. *I can handle spirits like this one. Not that he's terribly nice to look at. But at least he's not screaming, howling, or trying to kill us. That's definitely an improvement.*

"How do they know we've done our job properly?" he asked over Serena's shoulder. "The government, I mean."

"We file a report once it's in the bottle, silly. Then we drop it off to Infinite Enterprises on our next spirit-run."

"But what about spirit doors? We could just tell the government that it'd slipped back into its own realm through a spirit door, and they'd be none the wiser."

Mike chuckled. "That's very dishonest thinking, Kester."

"I wasn't planning to—"

Pamela leaned in, eager to join the conversation. "You wouldn't get away with it anyway," she said. "When you open a spirit door, it releases a surge of energy that's picked up at Infinite Enterprises, then recorded. They'd know if you made it up."

"Can we focus on the job, please?" Serena said irritably. "I want to get this done as quickly as possible."

The spirit shifted, hovering above the toilet seat. It looked remarkably like what a bad smell might look like, if it was transformed into a physical entity. Flustering and wobbling in time to Serena's rhythmic chanting, it started to edge closer.

"Aha, here we go," Ribero said with great satisfaction. "Yes, into the bottle you go, little spirit. Unless . . ." He turned to Kester, giving him a nudge. "Can you see any sign of the spirit door yet? Eh?"

Kester squinted into the cubicle, then shook his head. "Nope. Sorry."

"I wouldn't worry about it," Mike interrupted. "Look, he's going into the bottle, meek as a little rabbit. Bless him."

Serena smiled. "Just leave it to the expert," she muttered, and gave them a thumbs-up with her free hand.

The spirit started to dwindle, its tail end filtering into the open neck of the bottle. Serena nodded smugly. Then, without warning, it leapt out again and skirted over the top of the cubicle. The others stared, open-mouthed. Serena swore.

"That was your fault for disturbing me!" she shouted, pushing open the neighbouring toilet door with a metallic clang. They peered inside.

"Where has the incubus gone to, eh?" Ribero stuck his hands on his hips, scouring every corner.

"I haven't got the foggiest," Mike answered, as he shoved open every other toilet door. He looked at Pamela. "Can you pick him up at all?"

Pamela shut her eyes, then nodded. Her eyes sparkled with amusement. "Oh yes."

"Well?" Serena snapped. "Where is he, then? And don't tell me he's down the toilet. There's no way I'm going to—"

"No, love," Pamela said with a snigger. "He's up *there.*" She pointed.

Serena turned. "Where?" She scanned the line of sinks.

"No," Pamela replied patiently, shaking her head. "*There.* Above your head."

Serena craned upwards, indignantly examining the air above her. She narrowed her eyes. "Oh, I see. What the hell is it doing up there?"

Kester squinted. He could just about make out the spirit, which had shrunk to about the same size as a golf ball, flitting around above Serena's shiny bob.

Pamela covered her mouth and giggled. "Oh dear. Oh my goodness. You're not going to like this *at all.*"

"What?" Serena barked.

"Perhaps I'd better tell you outside," Pamela replied, pointing over to the door, which had started to open. "Looks like our time is up."

"Ah, this is ridiculous." Ribero glared at the stream of women pouring into the changing room. "How are we meant to work in these conditions? It is an insult!"

Mike sighed. "Don't tell me we're going to have to come back another time."

Pamela chuckled again, then leant against the nearest sink. "I don't think we'll need to come back," she said, pointing above Serena's head. "I think our little chum is coming with us."

Serena paled. "What do you mean by that?" she asked, voice glacial as a snow-drift.

"Our incubus has taken a shine to you," Pamela replied. "Bit unfortunate, that."

Serena groaned. Mike tittered, then hastily covered his mouth at the sight of her thunderous glare.

"You *are* joking?" she said, looking upwards again. "Please tell me you're joking."

Pamela shook her head. "Come on," she suggested, pointing at the other people in the changing room, who were giving them very strange looks. "Whatever we're going to do about it, we can't do it here, and we can't do it now."

Mike scurried off to retrieve Miss Wellbeloved, and the pair caught up with them in the foyer. The sharp sunlight was a striking contrast to the dinginess of the changing room, leaving them all blinking, struggling to adjust. Serena turned to them all and opened her mouth. Ribero held up a warning finger. She closed it again, following him outside to the van.

"Jennifer," he said, as he pointed back to the swimming pool. "Go and let this Mr Gamble know how we got on."

"Er, how *did* we get on, exactly?" Miss Wellbeloved looked at the empty bottle still firmly clasped in Serena's hand.

"Not great," Ribero said tightly.

"Look above Serena's head," Pamela added. Miss Wellbeloved glanced upwards, then flinched.

"Oh dear," she muttered. "That's not ideal. Still, at least we've technically moved him out of the pool, so that's a good start." She smiled weakly, then scurried back inside to update the manager.

"It's alright," Mike boomed, wrapping an arm around Serena's shoulders and waving grandly to the sky. "You always wanted a friend, didn't you, Serena?"

"Shut your face, Mike."

"Now, now; remember who's giving you a free ticket to the Billy Dagger gig tonight, young lady."

"Seriously," she replied through gritted teeth, glaring at the car-park as though it had personally insulted her. "You all need to figure out how to get rid of it and fast. There is no way I'm hanging around with an incubus."

"Ah, but he loves you," Mike said, looking up. "Don't you, mate?" The incubus let out a tiny moan, much like a mouse caught in a trap, then disappeared completely.

"Has it gone?" Serena asked with an optimistic smile.

"Nope," Pamela said cheerfully. "He's still there. He's just made himself invisible."

Serena scrabbled around above her head, swatting at the air as though trying to get rid of an annoying fly.

"Sweetheart," began Mike as he watched her with undisguised amusement. "That's not going to work. He's gone into hiding."

"I can see that!" Serena squawked, stamping her heel on the tarmac. "Oh, this is horrible!"

"It'll probably pop back again when you're trying to sleep tonight," Mike continued with a wink. "Maybe you could give it a good night cuddle." He laughed, then yelped as Serena punched him in the ribs.

"Serena, I think you should see it as a compliment, yes?" Ribero patted her on the shoulder. "It means that the spirit thinks you are a lovely lady, right?"

"He's in for a nasty shock," Mike muttered.

"Anyway," Pamela added as they bustled towards the van. "You know what to do with an incubus, don't you? I mean, this is the sort of stuff they teach you in the first year of university."

Serena nodded, yanking open the van door. "I know, I know. Ignore him, and he'll eventually go away. But I still need to get him in the bottle, otherwise we won't get paid, will we?"

Mike shimmied into the driver's seat. "That's a valid point, that is." He leaned back, giving Serena a wink. "We'd better hope old lover-ghost gets bored of you pretty quickly then, hadn't we?"

"You know the best way to make that happen," Pamela chimed, squeezing between Serena and Kester like a bean-bag compressing itself between two narrow chairs. "You need to start snogging other chaps in front of him, then he will get sad and give up hope."

"Christ, I pity the poor bloke who has to take on that task," Mike said as he started up the engine. Serena shot him another poisonous look, then glanced upwards, clearly expecting to see the spirit hovering above her head.

They waited for Miss Wellbeloved to return before they headed back to Exeter. The sun shone brightly over the passing hills, masking the winter chill that lingered on the breeze. Finally, they arrived back at the office, where they studiously got on with various tasks, biding their time until the end of the working day. Kester discovered an email from the SSFE in his inbox with dates for the forthcoming online course and a downloadable brochure, but he couldn't bear the thought of reading through it, despite knowing how irritated Ribero would be with his lack of enthusiasm.

The clock finally trudged to five. Mike leapt up like an exuberant puppet, then clapped his hands in Kester and Serena's direction. "You lucky people!" he shouted, breaking the peace of the afternoon. "In under two hours, I'll be picking you up to attend the gig of the century! Billy Dagger, eh? Amazing!"

Kester smiled wanly. He was looking forward to it, but he was also feeling distinctly jaded. He still hadn't had a chance to recover after their hectic week.

"Awesome," he said, standing up, then promptly losing

his balance and falling back into his chair as the camping desk collapsed yet again. He didn't have the energy to bother picking it up and settled for scooping his laptop from the debris instead. *When will they get me a proper desk?* he wondered without any real hope. He suspected they were just going to wait until this one broke entirely then come up with some other sort of equally cheap solution. *It'll probably be a pile of cardboard boxes next,* he thought with a wry smile. *Or they'll just get me to work on the floor.*

"Is your girlfriend coming?" Mike chucked a few contraptions into the lockable drawer in his desk, then sauntered over to the door.

Kester nodded, grabbing his jacket. "She said she was still tired from her ordeal with the Thelemites, but she'd enjoy the distraction." To be honest, he'd been delighted that she'd said yes. After her lukewarm response to him the previous day, he hadn't been sure that she'd wanted to keep seeing him. A deafening rock concert probably wasn't the best place to have a heart-to-heart about things, but at least it was a start.

"What should I wear?" Serena asked, seizing her handbag.

"Oh, I don't know. How about an evening gown?" Mike growled. "Honestly, woman, just wear what you've got on now. No-one gets dressed up for a gig."

"But I don't look great," Serena fretted as she followed him out of the door. "I need to wash my hair at least."

"Have fun!" Miss Wellbeloved and Pamela chorused after them before they emerged into the pitch blackness of the hallway outside.

"Nobody cares what you look like," Mike carried on, a disembodied voice in the dark. Kester stumbled after them, accidentally treading on Mike's foot, then teetering onto Serena, who firmly shoved him backwards. Finally, they reached the door leading down the back stairs and walked out into the car-park.

"Right," Mike concluded, pulling his coat tightly around himself. "Be ready at seven and don't you dare be late. I want to check out the support band before Dagger comes on stage."

"You mean you want to make an early start on the beer," Serena said, her eyes narrowed with disapproval.

"Well, as you're driving, I need to capitalise on the opportunity," Mike said. He smacked her on the back—so hard she nearly toppled on her heels. "You need to earn your keep, don't you, love? Especially as I'm paying for your ticket."

"Whatever." She scowled, dragged a thin scarf out of her handbag, and threw it around her neck. "See you tonight."

"Love you too, dearest!" Mike called out with a cheery wave. "Right," he said, clapping his hands. "I'm off to catch the bus. See you later, Kester."

Kester grinned as he watched Mike go. His own bus wasn't due for another fifteen minutes. *Maybe I should walk,* he thought without any real enthusiasm. *Do a bit of exercise, tone up a bit more.*

Before he could talk himself out of it, he forced his feet in the direction of home and whisked his phone out of his pocket. Anya had texted again, requesting details about the evening. He quickly replied, an instinctive smile tugging at his lips. *She doesn't sound cross at me!* he thought as he darted down the alley and out into the main high street. *In fact, she sounds quite pleased about being invited. Maybe I haven't ruined everything after all!*

The cheerful feeling continued as he walked home, and he even managed to maintain some composure when he realised that Daisy had used up all the hot water, leaving him with a shower that was about as welcoming as a bucket of ice falling on his head. Discovering that his favourite shirt had a curry sauce stain was mildly irritating, but he was determined to enjoy tonight regardless of what happened.

True to his word, Mike announced his arrival at seven o'clock, on the dot, by honking his car horn in a jaunty rhythm for a minute whilst Kester scrabbled around, trying to find his house keys. After finally locating them under a pile of empty crisp packets on the kitchen unit, he hurtled outside and climbed into the car.

At once, his ears were assaulted by a Billy Dagger song, which pounded through the sound system like a detonating bomb.

"Are you ready to rock and roll?" Mike chorused over the noise as he turned the car around in a neighbouring side road, narrowly missing two parked cars in the process.

"Um, yes? I think so!" Kester shouted, fastening his seat belt.

Mike whooped as he launched the car down the road, singing along at the top of his voice.

He's clearly in a good mood, Kester realised, watching him with fascination. In his enthusiastic state, Mike was a pure force of pent-up energy. They drove on to Anya's house, where she joined Kester in the back, before heading into the centre of town to collect Serena, who was predictably late.

"What the hell is this racket?" she screeched, settling into the front seat.

Mike flicked off the CD player, then glared. "Get out of the car."

Serena rolled her eyes. "I see. It was Billy Dagger, was it? It's difficult to tell when your eardrums are being ripped apart."

"Thank you for inviting me," Anya added, seizing the opportunity to be heard now the music was off. "It is so nice of you, and just what I needed after such a horrible week."

Mike turned around briefly, giving her a grin. "That's alright, darling," he said as he joined the busy main road leading out of the city. "My pleasure. May I say that you're looking very lovely this evening?" He turned to Serena and glowered. "Wish I could say the same for you."

"The feeling is entirely mutual," Serena retorted, rummaging in her micro-sized handbag for her lipstick.

Mike switched back on the music, at a more moderate level this time. Shifting awkwardly in his seat, Kester tried to move clear of the sticky sweet wrappers and crisp packets, only to find a stale bit of sandwich underneath his bottom.

"So, how are you?" he asked Anya, looking over at her. She

looked better than she had the day before, though he noticed she was wearing more make-up than usual, which was surprising. She hadn't really struck him as the sort to worry about her appearance much. *I don't want to look like a slob by comparison,* he fretted and instinctively sucked in his stomach.

"I'm okay," she replied with a shrug. "I thought you wouldn't want to have anything to do with me after what happened, so I was surprised you asked me to come along tonight."

He laughed. "I thought exactly the same. I presumed you'd be furious that I hadn't told you what I do for a job."

"Hey, none of us tell *anyone* what we do for a job," Serena said warningly, applying her lipstick in the mirror at intervals to stop Mike from deliberately jogging her.

"I know. I understand," Anya replied. "Anyway, I did the same, didn't I? I never told you about the Thelemites because I thought you'd think I was weird."

"In all honesty, they do seem a little odd," Kester said. "What was with Barty Melville? He looked like a whale in a dress."

"Lots of the older ones wear clothes like that, it's a traditional outfit," Anya said. She glanced out the window. "But I suppose I must be careful what I say, right?"

"Damned right you do," Mike said. "Remember, it's not just humans that belong to that society, it's spirits too. Which means they can listen to you whenever they want, and you wouldn't have a clue about it."

Anya gave him a strange look. "I know," she replied finally, toying with her skirt. "I wish I'd never joined. I just got so wrapped up in finding out the truth of it all that I didn't think about what I was getting myself into."

"Well, best not talk about it anymore, eh?" Mike added. "How about we talk about Billy Dagger instead?"

"Lord, you're obsessed," Serena drawled as she rested back against the seat. "Are we going to have to endure you rabbiting on about him the entire journey?"

"Have you listened to his latest album?" Mike carried on, ignoring her.

"Not yet. It only came out last week, didn't it?" Kester replied. *Not that I have enough money to buy it anyway,* he added silently. He was still waiting for last month's pay-cheque—he didn't have the heart to chase his father over it.

"Four days ago, to be exact," Mike continued. "It's amazing. Really weird though, lots of strange lyrics. There's obviously a subtext going on, but I have no idea what it is." He patted the compartment in the driver door before finding the CD in question. "Here," he said, flinging it into Serena's lap. "Put this on, would you?"

Serena sighed but did as he asked anyway. At once, deep, melodious music flooded the car, complete with an eerie, thumping bass-line. *Mike's right,* Kester thought, listening to the lyrics. *This is pretty odd. Nothing like his usual stuff.*

"What's this one called?" he asked as he reached over to take the CD case from Serena.

"'Tear the Walls Down,'" Mike replied automatically, his foot heavy on the accelerator as he joined the motorway. "It's awesome, isn't it?"

"What the hell is the song about?" Anya asked.

"It's probably all the drugs he's taken over the years," Serena chimed. "They've clearly addled his brain."

"Hey, don't insult his mighty brain, thank you very much," Mike barked. "Especially given the miniscule size of your own."

"You're a fine one to talk."

"At least I haven't got an incubus hovering around over my head."

Serena looked up immediately, then punched him on the arm. "Shut up, Mike. I haven't seen the incubus since this morning anyway, so I think he might have gone away."

"If he's gone back to the swimming pool, we're in trouble," Kester said, thoughtfully scratching his ear.

"Nah, we'll just send Serena over to flirt with him, she'll get him out of there again."

"Mike, you are so annoying," Serena growled, smoothing down her fringe.

They drove on through the darkness at breakneck speed. Mike mastered a route through the chaotic streets of Bristol, taking great delight in burning other cars off at the traffic lights and nearly crashing at least twice. After circling a few busy, residential streets, they finally managed to find a place to park and headed over to the venue.

"God, it's absolutely heaving," Serena commented, surveying the crowds of people spilling over all three floors and leaning over the bannisters of the cavernous reception area.

"What did you expect?" Mike retorted as he fiddled around in his back pocket for his wallet. "What I'm more concerned about is that bloody huge queue at the bar." He nudged Serena and gave her a wink. "Go on, love, work your magic. You'll get served before me because you're prettier."

She rolled her eyes. "Fine, fine. I'll get you a nice soft drink, shall I?"

"Beer, please," he replied with a warning wag of his finger. "Don't even think of making it non-alcoholic. You know the deal."

"What's that?" Serena replied, pretending not to hear over the hubbub of the crowd. "Make it non-alcoholic? Are you sure?"

"Don't even joke about it, madam."

"Hey? What was that? Lemonade?"

He flapped a hand at her as she disappeared, slipping between people with the ease of a snake through grass.

"She'd better hurry up," Mike snarled as he tapped his watch. "The support band's on in a few minutes." He hopped from foot to foot, anxiously eyeing the doors that led to the main hall.

"Where are we, then?" Kester asked, peering over Mike's shoulder at the tickets. "Are we near the front or right at the back?"

Mike waved the pieces of paper in the air triumphantly. "It's a standing-only gig, which means we can dive right down to the front."

Anya laced her arm through Kester's own, the warmth of her skin pressing against him. "My dad always loved Billy Dagger; it will be awesome to see him perform live."

"Your dad, eh?" Mike repeated with an embarrassed rub of his forehead. "Now I feel old. I forget you two whippersnappers are younger than me."

Eventually, Serena returned, weaving through the crowds and struggling with four drinks. Mike let out a sigh of satisfaction to see that, despite her threats, she had bought him a beer. Without preamble, he necked down about half the pint without pausing for breath. Kester took his, then slipped some money into Mike's pocket.

"Let me get the drinks," he said with a nod. "You gave us these tickets, it's the least I can do."

An ear-splitting buzz rang through the bar area, announcing the imminent start of the gig. The hundreds of people ceased speaking in unison, turning towards the doors like a pack of meer-kats.

"Aye, aye," Mike said with a grin. "Time to get a move on. I want to be so close to the stage that I can see the grey hairs up Dagger's nose."

"Whatever turns you on, weirdo," Serena replied before pushing past him and striding towards the door.

They milled into the general throng, squeezing through the double-doors and down the stairs, until they reached the stage, which was bathed in darkness save for a projector display announcing the name of the support act.

"Who the hell are the Grot-Monkeys?" Serena asked, apple juice cupped pertly in her hands.

"Ah, some psychedelic rock outfit," Mike replied knowledge-ably. "They're from Finland, aren't they, Anya?"

Anya raised an eyebrow. "Why are you asking me? I'm from

Denmark."

"Finland, Denmark, same place."

She chuckled. "They really aren't, you know."

The support band all looked identical to Kester: long hair draped over their faces and grubby T-shirts hanging off their skinny frames. They were passably good, or at least good enough for the crowd to start bobbing and singing along to the lyrics. Whilst they were playing, Kester took a moment or two to glance across at Anya.

Her face was illuminated by the stage lights, flickering green, red, and blue in turn; her eyes were a glittering black. *She looks like a beautiful rainbow turned into a human,* he thought, amazed by his unexpected burst of emotion. He wondered whether he'd have the opportunity, or the courage, to kiss her at the end of the evening. *Probably not,* he thought, looking across at Mike, who had his eyes closed and was holding his empty glass in the air in some sort of salute to the music. *Mike will probably say something awful like "get in there, mate," which will instantly make me feel like a colossal prat.*

The support act finished. Then, after an impossibly long wait, strobe lights started to pulse over the stage. Mike whooped in excitement, spilling his third pint over the back of a man in front, who didn't seem overly bothered.

"Aw man, I've been waiting for this for ages!" he chorused, then wrapped an arm around Serena, who looked alarmed and revolted in equal measures.

So have I, thought Kester, looking at his watch. *Billy Dagger certainly likes to keep his crowds waiting. We won't be back home until about two in the morning at this rate.*

A low hum like a swarm of bees gathering momentum filled the auditorium. Seconds later, a solitary guitar chord crashed into action followed by a deafening techno-beat. Mike howled, embraced the man next to him, and nearly knocked Serena over in the process.

"Is he always like that?" Anya shouted in Kester's ear.

He glanced over at Mike, then nodded. "Yeah." *Where's Billy Dagger, then?* he wondered as he scanned the stage. His backing musicians had assembled, only partially visible through the smoke and pulsing lights, but he couldn't see the singer anywhere. Then the rousing wail of enthusiastic calling and pointing alerted him to the fact that Dagger was emerging from what looked like a rip in the curtain at the back of the stage, floating down on a set of ropes.

"Amazing entrance!" Mike gibbered, flailing his arms with worshipful abandon. "Like a fallen angel or something. Beautiful. *Just beautiful.*"

"Oh, for goodness' sake, Mike, it's not God himself descending from heaven, you know." Serena crossed her arms, but her expression revealed she was more impressed than she was letting on.

"It is," Mike corrected. "Seriously, Dagger is like a god to me. Come on, look at him. No-one that cool can be human."

A cacophony of noise silenced them all as the first song, one of Dagger's classics from the 1970s, kicked in. The crowd went wild, thumping and stamping as one until the floor beneath their feet vibrated. In spite of natural introversion, Kester felt an irresistible urge to join in. He attempted a few experimental bounces before catching sight of Anya's puzzled expression and stopping.

After a few more old songs, Billy Dagger launched into a song from his latest album. Kester immediately recognised it from the car on the way up.

"What was this one again?" he shouted.

"'Tear the Walls Down'!" Mike bellowed back, leaping around like a maniac. "Man, it sounds even better live than on the album!"

Kester could see what Mike was getting at. The singer, even though he was in his sixties, was slight, sprightly, and full of attitude, with a fetching sneer, spiked hair, and a tight leather T-shirt. His voice was also impressive, almost unearthly when he hit the high notes, like a bird caught in a trap.

"He's such an incredible performer," Anya said, gazing entranced at the stage.

"Yeah, really sexy too," Serena added, nodding. Mike and Kester looked at one another incredulously.

"He's old enough to be your dad, if not your granddad!" Kester shouted.

"Yes, but he's got a certain something, hasn't he?" Serena added, eyes following every hip-thrust and wiggle with great attention.

The song ended with a deafening crescendo and the crowd erupted in approval. Billy Dagger sauntered to the front of the stage, then pointed, finger signalling masterfully into the darkness.

"Good evening, all you people of Birmingham," he drawled. His voice snagged like velvet dragged over spikes—smooth, yet disjointed.

"It's Bristol, mate!" someone called from the back.

"Same thing, same thing," the singer crooned with a wink. "Wherever you're from, people, you must remember *to do what you will*. You dig?"

"Oh yes, we dig!" Mike roared along with thousands of other eager fans behind him. Without waiting for the noise to die down, Dagger crashed into his next song, another familiar hit that sent the audience into a renewed state of frenzy.

"It's crazy, isn't it?" Anya screamed into Kester's ear.

"Crazy and very impressive," Kester replied. Admittedly, he'd never been to a gig before, unless you counted the choral performances that his old neighbour, Mrs Winterbottom, held in the town hall back in Cambridge. Nothing could have prepared him for the noise and the excitement. The air vibrated with energy powered by an unseen current that rippled from person to person.

Dagger paused, then extended a fist to the sky. "It's time to tear the walls *apart*," he whispered cryptically into his microphone, then he slumped to the floor.

The crowd gasped as one.

Kester looked around, confused. All the surrounding faces mirrored his own—open-mouthed amazement at the scene in front of them. The singer's motionless body remained in the centre of the stage, like a puppet whose strings had suddenly been snipped.

"Is this part of the act?" he asked, scratching his head.

Mike frowned. "I'm not sure." The crowd started to murmur. Even the backing musicians on stage were looking at one another in bafflement.

Suddenly, two stage-hands bolted on and knelt beside Dagger. The audience watched, muttering and whispering, as the men checked the singer's pulse.

"Oh my god," Anya breathed, eyes wide. "What's going on?"

"I have literally no idea," Mike replied, staring at the stage. "But this is very, *very* not good." He looked like a little boy who'd had his ice-cream taken away from him, bottom lip hanging in horror and disappointment.

"Do you think he's dead?" A spiky-haired woman in front of them turned around, putting the question to them all.

"No. Not possible," Mike replied, hands knotted in an anxious ball over his stomach. "There's no way . . ." His sentence drifted into silence as one of the stage-hands shook his head before gesturing urgently off-stage. A few seconds later, the curtains were drawn. The room erupted into a chorus of outraged gasps and mutterings.

"I don't believe it!" Mike continued, as he grasped Kester by the arm. "What the hell just happened?"

Kester gazed up at the heavy, velvet curtains. "I have no idea. Maybe they'll tell us what's going on in a moment?"

They lingered by the front of the stage as the crowd grew steadily more restless. Suddenly, the screeching whistle of the Tannoy cut across the noise. Instantly, the room hushed.

"Now we should get some answers about—" Serena began. Mike shushed her urgently.

The voice over the loudspeaker crackled, then coughed. "It's with much regret," it began, "that we announce that tonight's show has been cut short, due to unforeseen circumstances. Please be assured that we are currently attending to the health and wellbeing of Mr Dagger, and we will be in touch in due course regarding the possible rescheduling of the performance. At present, we'd like to ask you to leave quietly by the entrance doors."

"I want my money back!" a voice bellowed from the back. He was quickly silenced by a sea of disapproving tuts.

Mike shook his head, his shoulders slumping. "I don't believe it," he whispered as he followed the slow-moving herd of people towards the exit. He looked back at the stage hopefully, as though expecting the curtains to miraculously open again. "The one time I manage to get Billy Dagger tickets, and he collapses. What are the odds?"

"I'm sure there'll be other times," Serena said, patting his arm.

"Not if he's gone," Anya countered, as she swiftly linked arms with Kester.

"What do you mean, gone?"

"Dead, of course. You know."

"He's not dead!" Mike sniffed. "No way."

"Shall I get you another beer?" Serena asked with uncharacteristic kindness, ignoring the fact that she was being jostled from all sides by chaotic throngs of people.

Mike shook his head. "No. Not even alcohol will make me feel better. Let's go home."

The drive back was sombre. Mike refused to even put the radio on, claiming it would be depressing to hear any kind of music after the disastrous evening. Instead, he slumped in the passenger seat, glaring out of the window whilst Serena drove down the silent motorway. Finally, they arrived back in Exeter, stopping at Anya's house first.

"Well," Anya said finally as she scrabbled out of the backseat. "Thank you again for giving us tickets, Mike. I know the gig was cut short, but Billy Dagger really was very good."

Mike grunted and rolled his head against the window, eyes cast mournfully to the sky.

Kester nudged Serena on the shoulder. "You might as well drop me off here too," he offered. "I only live ten minutes away. It'll save you turning the car around."

Serena looked over at Anya and nodded knowingly. "Fair enough," she replied. "See you Monday."

"Bye. And thanks again, Mike!"

Mike muttered something in response, which was partially drowned out by Serena revving the engine. The car zipped off into the darkness before disappearing out of sight at the bottom of the road, leaving them in silence.

Kester shifted uneasily on the spot. "So," he began, but he couldn't think of anything else to say. "Er. Yes. So . . ."

Anya raised an eyebrow and laughed. "So, what, Kester?" She looked ethereally beautiful with her eyes glowing in the moonlight.

Kester took a deep breath, then chuckled. "Oh, nothing." *I'm such a pathetic coward,* he thought, blushing furiously, glad that the darkness was hiding his red cheeks. *Any other man would just lean over and kiss her, not stand around dithering like an idiot.* He gestured lamely down the road. "I guess I'll just—"

To his shock, she leaned over and kissed him squarely on the lips. His eyes widened and finally closed. *Oh my god, she's kissing me!* he thought in shock, then remembered himself and focused on kissing her back. *What if I'm doing it all wrong?* he fretted. *What if my breath smells?*

Her lips were soft, pressing against his with delicious intensity. Gradually, he relaxed into the moment, losing himself to the warmth of her body. He placed a hand on her hip, panicked that he was being too forward, then swiftly removed it.

After a while, Anya retreated. He was relieved to see that she was smiling. "I think if I waited for you to kiss me, I would be waiting a long time," she said with a wink.

Kester massaged the back of his neck. He felt hideously embarrassed and, at the same time, rather pleased with himself. "I liked it," he replied, then he felt like an idiot all over again.

"So did I."

"Oh, really?"

She giggled. "Kester, you are very funny. That is why I like you."

He beamed. "Thank you. I like you too."

She leant over, touching his arm. "I have to go to sleep now," she said, looking up at the darkened windows behind her. "But I wanted to say thank you."

"What, for the tickets tonight?" he said. "That's Mike you need to thank; it was his suggestion."

Anya shook her head. "Not just that. For rescuing me from the Thelemites. For looking out for me."

He scuffled his shoe on the pavement. "Any time."

"Good night, then."

"Yes, good night." Kester watched as she walked to her front door, remaining rooted in position even after the front door had closed quietly behind her.

She kissed me! he thought and brushed his mouth tentatively with his finger. It might have been his imagination, but he could feel the residual heat where her lips had been. *My goodness, someone actually gave me a proper kiss! She didn't even look disgusted once it was over!*

With renewed energy, Kester spun around on his heel and bounced off down the road, suddenly feeling that life had got very much better indeed.

Open Your Eyes—Billy Dagger

Hold out your hand, little boy.
Touch the great unknown, little boy.
I confess, I spit Maria,
I spurn your church,
I prefer them, elites of truth.

Step through the door, little boy.
Open your eyes, little boy.
I, male hematite,
Will be your guide.
Lend me your heart, your youth.

Don't let them shut the door.
Don't let them lie no more.
Join them, elites of truth.
Drive deceivers to the floor.
Open your eyes.

CHAPTER 4: THE HAG O' THE DRIBBLE

The mood was predictably sombre in the wake of Billy Dagger's death, made worse by the fact that it was a Monday morning. Mike's depression radiated through the office like smog, with every sigh from his desk indicating a fresh wave of misery.

To make matters worse, Serena's mood was even more sour than usual, thanks to the incubus making a surprise return on Saturday night. According to her furious report, he had woken her at two in the morning by leaping out from behind her bed and affectionately rubbing her ear. The same had happened the night after, which explained her hollow eyes and irritated expression.

"Dearie me, it's like someone died in here," Pamela exclaimed after two hours of working in relative silence. "Shall we have a sing-song to cheer ourselves up?"

Mike shook his head solemnly. "It'd be sacrilegious. Can't you tell I'm in mourning?"

"Yeah, I don't think anyone's in the mood," Serena added. "How about we just get on with our work instead?"

Kester looked up from his book—*Spirit Intervention for Beginners*. Miss Wellbeloved had lent it to him for his forthcoming studies at the SSFE, and his head was aching from trying to understand it. "Pamela, Mike's very upset," he reminded her, observing Mike's dejected expression, partially obscured behind a sea of crackling wires and metal oddments.

"I am," Mike replied, cradling his head in his hands. "I cannot believe Billy Dagger is dead. And we saw him die. It's awful."

"Presumably, if you sell the tickets, they'll be worth a fortune though," Serena said without looking up from her computer screen. "I checked on eBay; people are going mad for Billy Dagger memorabilia already."

Mike glared at her indignantly. "Don't be so *crass,*" he hissed. "A legend has died, and you're telling me to cash in on his death?"

"Someone else is already selling their ticket on eBay, and it's currently over £120," she replied, giving Kester a grin.

"Really?" Mike scratched his chin thoughtfully. "That's pretty good, isn't it?" He caught her eye and added, "Not that I'd consider it, of course. It'd just be *wrong.*"

"This ticket has still got six days left on the auction. It'll probably sell for far more than that."

Mike grunted but looked more cheerful regardless.

Miss Wellbeloved emerged from the stockroom, pen tucked behind her ear, still peering at her notepad. "Right, that's the spirit counting done," she announced. "Kester, how are you getting on with *Spirit Intervention for Beginners*? Nearly finished it yet?"

Kester massaged his brow and winced. "It's a bit difficult to understand. If this is a book for beginners, I dread to think what the advanced copy's like."

She laughed. "Well, it's on your reading list and you've got to write that essay before you start the course, so I'd get cracking if I were you."

Kester groaned. He'd read the email yesterday detailing his pre-course assignment. *Undertake research into the process of inter-*

vening meaningfully with spirits, it had stated, *and write up your findings in a five-thousand-word essay with key points outlined in a PowerPoint presentation to share with your fellow students online.* Any other topic, he would have been fine writing about. But spirit intervention? It wasn't exactly something he could research in the library. Thankfully, the email had also included a few Swww websites for him to refer to, which he desperately hoped would prove useful.

The morning trudged past uneventfully, only interrupted by his father sweeping into the office just after Kester had polished off his sandwiches. Easing off his jacket with a grandiose shrug of the shoulders, Ribero hurled it at the hook on the back of the door—missing, as usual. Miss Wellbeloved scooped it from the floor with a long-suffering sigh.

"Everything alright, Julio?" she asked, smoothing her hair back into position.

He nodded, then pointed to his office. "I need a smoke, yes? Give me ten minutes." Without further explanation, he strode towards the door, flung it open, and disappeared into his inner sanctum.

Kester glanced at Miss Wellbeloved, who bit her lip.

"Is he okay?"

She chewed her lip nervously. "Let's hope so."

After half an hour had passed, Kester crept towards Ribero's office door. He knocked tentatively. The low rumble in response was presumably an admission to enter, so he did.

The usual cloud of smoke greeted him as he went in. His father sat in the midst of it all, as regal in his armchair as a king holding court over his subjects. Kester noticed straight away that the hand holding the cigarette was shaking—and badly.

"Hello Dad," he began and sat down on the swivel chair opposite his father.

Ribero attempted a smile, then swallowed. "How can I help you, Kester?"

Kester shuffled in his seat, examining the ruby-red geometric rug, the cluttered desk, the nicotine-stained ceiling. He remembered vividly the first time he'd entered the office—the day he'd found out that Ribero was his father. It had only been a few months, and it surprised Kester just how much he'd grown to care about him.

"I wanted to check you were okay," he said gently.

Ribero sat in a strangely rigid, upright position, as though an iron rod had been forced up his spine. Kester wondered if it was an attempt to control the tremors currently running through his body.

Finally, Ribero nodded. "I have been better," he admitted, glancing down at his hands. "Today is not so much a good day, I don't think. It is the Parkinson."

"Parkinson's," Kester corrected. "Dad, if you weren't feeling well, why did you come in? No-one would have minded if you'd stayed at home." *Because you don't do much work these days anyway,* he added silently, then immediately felt guilty for thinking it.

His father frowned. "Staying at home would not be good," he stated, before stubbing his cigarette out in the ashtray. A wisp of smoke plumed out in its wake, like a tiny spectre floating to the ceiling. "If you give into it, then it is worse, right?" He grimaced, rubbing the small of his back. "I just wish it didn't make me feel so stiff. And it is making me slow. Like an old man. I don't like it at all."

"Well, you are an old man," Kester said with a grin, then wished he hadn't.

Ribero stabbed a finger in his direction. "Just you wait 'til you are old. It is no matter to laugh about, let me tell you."

"No, I'm sorry." Kester shifted uneasily in his seat, quailing under the force of his father's glare. "Well, if there's anything I can help with at all . . ."

Ribero sighed. "Get us some new business, perhaps? That is what we need. Though I do have some good news. I had an email from that government man, you know, the one with the silly name?"

"Curtis Philpot?" Kester guessed. He'd met the man at Larry

Higgins's offices only a few weeks ago, though it felt like far longer.

Ribero slapped his thigh. "Yes, Philpot. That is his name. Thank you, Kester. I forget these things sometimes."

"What did the email say?"

"Ah, good things!" Ribero brightened. "He said we handled the Scottish fetch case very well. He commended you on your spirit-door opening skills. Without you, we couldn't have done it, could we?"

Kester blushed. "It was good teamwork, not just me."

Ribero waved a hand in his direction. "Ah, you are modest, like a little mouse. You need to find your roaring lion, Kester. Get your confidence, right?"

Kester thought back to Saturday night, when Anya had kissed him. *That certainly helped with my confidence,* he thought as he bit back a smile. "I'm getting there," he said. "I'm starting to study for the BA in Spirit Intervention and Business Studies, you know."

His father brightened. "That is good news. Then you will be ready to take over the agency in no time, right?"

Kester flinched. "Well, I don't know about that." He glanced at the door. "Did you want me to bring you a coffee or something?"

"You are a good boy." His father smiled. "That would be nice. A cream cake would be good too."

"Oh, but that means I'll have to go to the shop and—" He caught sight of Ribero's expression and sighed. "Okay. I'll go and get a cream cake. Anything else?"

"Get one for yourself too, if you like. Ask Jennifer to take the money out of the petty cash, right?"

Kester patted his stomach. "Can't. I'm on a diet. I've lost quite a bit of weight, you know."

His father scrutinised his stomach, then nodded. "Yes, I can see it. Your gut is a little bit smaller. Now go and buy me cake."

Kester grinned as he closed the door quietly behind him. The others were silent, studiously tapping at their keyboards.

He held up a hand. "I've got to go to the bakery. Does anyone else want a—"

Serena suddenly shrieked and started flapping wildly at the air above her head. "No! Not again, seriously!"

Kester folded his arms crossly. "I was only going to ask if you wanted a cake, as I was buying one for Dad. There's no need to—"

"Not the cake, stupid!" Serena glowered at the ceiling, then grimaced. "I don't believe it. It's *back again.*"

"What's the problem, love?" Pamela asked, craning her neck over the computer screen.

"Yeah, you mad witch, what are you waffling on about?" Mike added as he leaned back, settling himself for a show.

"It's the sodding incubus, isn't it!" Serena barked. "It just started stroking my hair." She glowered at Mike, as though he was personally responsible.

"*He's* not an *it*, Serena," Miss Wellbeloved interjected. "Show some respect." She squinted at the air above Serena's head. "I can't see anything. Are you sure it wasn't just a fly or something, buzzing around you?"

Mike guffawed. "You're not getting worked up over a tiny incubus, are you?"

Serena levelled her gaze at him, delivering a look that would have made a lesser man wilt on the spot. "You try being woken up in the middle of the night by something nibbling at your ear," she snapped, nails rapping dangerously at the desk.

"Oh, the poor bastard," Mike continued. He was clearly taking great delight in Serena's discomfort. "Being in love with such a cold-hearted wench. It must be torture."

Serena shook her head. "I need help getting rid of *him.* Every time I reach for the water bottle, he wiggles away and hides himself."

"Get Luke down to help you!" Pamela beamed at the prospect. They'd all got to know Luke as Lara before finding out he was transitioning from female to male, and during the short time they'd worked together, they'd all become very fond of him and his ceaseless optimism. Unfortunately, the same couldn't be said for his boss, Larry Higgins, who they all agreed was an arrogant moron. Dimitri Strang, the grim-faced psychic for Higgins's agency, wasn't much better in Kester's opinion, though Serena had seemed rather taken with him.

"What, you think just because Luke has fancy equipment, he'll have any better luck sorting the spirit out?" Serena retorted.

"You need to lure the incubus out with your natural charms," Mike replied as he winked in Kester's direction. "Wear something pretty. Invite him to dinner. Then work your magic."

"I'm not inviting him to dinner, and don't be such a childish idiot." Serena glared at him with open dislike. "You love this, don't you? This is one just big joke to you."

"Yep," Mike confirmed cheerily. He swivelled back to his desk and scooped up his latest contraption, fiddling with the screws at the bottom. "I can't deny it, Serena. I think it's hilarious."

Kester cleared his throat. "None of you have answered my question," he continued as he grabbed his satchel. "Do any of you want a cream cake, or is it just my father?"

Pamela beamed. "If you're buying, then I'm eating, Kester. Make mine a chocolate éclair, please, love."

"Just a carrot cake for me," Miss Wellbeloved added.

"I want the biggest, chocolatiest cake in the shop, please," Mike declared, with a contemplative pat on the stomach. "And no holding back. I'm starving."

Kester rolled his eyes, feeling distinctly jealous. He was hungry too, but he didn't dare cheat on his diet, not when he was doing so well. "Okay, fine," he said, swinging his bag over his shoulder and trying not to look too begrudging. "I'll be back in a few—"

"Ah! Kester!" The call, though muffled by his father's office door, was unmistakably urgent.

He quickly raced back. "Dad? Was that you?" *It sounded like he was shouting,* he thought as he tugged at the handle. "Dad?"

"Ah! Come quickly!"

Kester glanced across at Miss Wellbeloved, who looked as

concerned as he was. Without waiting for permission to enter, he threw open the door.

"Dad?" At first, he thought Ribero was being sick. He was bent over double, head suspended between his legs, moaning in pain. "Dad, what's wrong?"

"It is the cramp, yes? Cramp in my legs!"

Kester bent down and touched Ribero's calf. "What, just here? A cramp?"

"That is what I said, idiot boy!"

Kester frowned. "Is this a symptom of Parkinson's disease too?"

"Ah, just massage my legs, please! Quickly, it is agony!"

Kester rubbed his father's legs. He could feel the tension of the muscles, spasming underneath his father's immaculately pressed slacks. "Is that any better?" he asked eventually as he eased the pressure of his massaging.

His father nodded. Breathing heavily, he straightened, eyebrows knotted with pain. "Perhaps I should not be here today," he muttered as he shook out one leg, then the other. "My pills are at home. I need my pills."

"Then let's get you home," Kester said firmly. "We can manage here, it's a quiet day anyway. You need to rest."

"I need my pills," his father repeated, hands tremoring in his lap. He suddenly looked very old and very vulnerable. Kester wanted to hug him, to tell him that everything would be alright, but he wasn't sure it would be appropriate.

"Do you need someone to go and get the pills?" he asked finally, not sure how else he could help.

Ribero shook his head mournfully. "There is no point. It will pass before you get back. Go on, you go. I will be fine."

"Are you sure?"

"Yes." His father paused and pressed his hands down urgently, pinning them against his thighs to stop them shaking.

Kester left his father's office, then he quickly relayed the situation to Miss Wellbeloved, who immediately called for a taxi to take

Ribero home. Ten minutes later, Ribero left the office, so dejected he could scarcely take his eyes off the floor. Kester guided him down the stairs, then returned to the office, feeling utterly depressed. It was horrible to see his father like that—not just because he was in pain, but because he was obviously embarrassed by it.

"We need to have a private word," Miss Wellbeloved muttered as she glanced surreptitiously at the others. She nodded to Ribero's vacant office.

"What about my chocolate cake?" Mike asked. "I'm hungry!"

"Not now, Mike. If you want a cake so badly, get off your bottom and get it yourself," Miss Wellbeloved barked. Without another word, she ushered Kester into the office and closed the door.

Kester sat in the swivel chair, waiting for her to speak.

"Kester," she began, then paused. Her hands wound restlessly around one another, pressing into her thin lap.

"You're going to say that we need to prepare to manage the agency without Dad, aren't you?" he guessed.

She looked at him and nodded. "His condition seems to have become rather worse recently. He can't keep coming into work like this. He needs to be at home."

Kester sighed. He studied the rug whilst waiting for his brain to come up with an appropriate answer. "What do you propose we do, then?" he asked finally.

"Without your father, we should all manage just fine when it's a small job. But if we get another national job, we must accept that we'll need help."

"We managed okay with the Scottish fetch last week," Kester reminded her. "Dad didn't join us for that job until the very last minute."

"But we had Larry Higgins and his crew to assist us," Miss Wellbeloved replied. "You might think Larry is a prat, but you can't deny that Dimitri and Lara were useful."

"Luke," Kester corrected automatically.

"Yes, of course. I'll remember in the end," Miss Wellbeloved said with a smile.

Kester leaned forward, studying her intently. *She's got a plan up her sleeve,* he realised, *and she's just been waiting for the right time to talk to me about it.*

Miss Wellbeloved flinched under his scrutiny. "What are you thinking, Kester?"

"I'm figuring out what you're trying to suggest." Kester continued, "Are you saying we should hire more staff? I hardly think we're in a position to do that, are we?"

She laughed. "No. We're certainly not. I had something else in mind, actually."

Kester raised an eyebrow. He knew that expression very well. It meant that his instincts were right, and that Miss Wellbeloved had come up with a plan. "Go on?" he encouraged.

"If we get a national case," she began, choosing her words carefully, "then I suggest we merge with another agency to ensure we can cope with the volume of work involved. That'll mean we're in a much stronger position to pitch for jobs."

"You're talking about merging with Larry Higgins, aren't you?" Kester sighed. The logic of the argument was good, but the thought of working with Larry again wasn't pleasant at all. Throughout the Scottish fetch case, he'd been negative, argumentative, and, perhaps most annoyingly of all, highly pompous.

Miss Wellbeloved shrugged. "Would it be so bad, working with them? Luke and Dimitri were great to work with. We made a good team."

"Yeah, they were fine," Kester agreed, "but Larry was a total nightmare." He shuddered. "Plus, Dad hates him with a vengeance. He's not going to be delighted at the suggestion that we buddy up with Larry's agency, is he?"

Her eyes twinkled. "Well," she began, "Julio keeps saying you need to take more control of the agency. And I'm second-in-command anyway. So, between the two of us, I think we'll convince him."

You sound far more confident than I feel, Kester thought. However, he couldn't deny that the idea made sense. They'd be far more likely to win contracts with more people on board. "Surely Larry Higgins wouldn't be that keen to work with us again, would he?" he said.

Miss Wellbeloved smiled. "Actually, I talked to Larry about it a while ago. I think he'd be happy to join forces, if it meant securing more national contracts. The more nationals we win, the less that go to Infinite Enterprises, eh?"

"Sounds like you've got this all mapped out," Kester said wryly.

"I have given it some thought, yes," Miss Wellbeloved admitted. She looked at her watch. "Gosh, it's nearly two o'clock. We need to be at Beer Quarry Caves by three. Are you joining us?"

"Do I have to?" Kester asked.

Miss Wellbeloved rolled her eyes. "No, you don't," she said, "but if you do, you'll be getting invaluable experience. Which will help no end with your studies."

"It's only a preliminary visit, isn't it?" Kester frowned. He'd overheard Serena and Pamela discussing the new case this morning, and he hadn't liked the sound of it at all. The words "hag" and "dribble" had been used, which hadn't exactly filled him with enthusiasm.

"Yes, and that's all the more reason for you to come," Miss Wellbeloved concluded. "It's just a brief chat with the staff, and a quick look around the caves."

"It's that 'quick look around the caves' part that's bothering me," Kester replied. "Caves are dark and scary. In fact, it's fair to say that I really, *really* hate caves."

Miss Wellbeloved stood up and extended a hand to the door. "Come on. I insist you come with us. It's another easy case, and you need to get used to these things if you're going to take over the agency one day."

Kester groaned, but followed her out nonetheless.

After gathering up the necessary equipment, the team headed out of the office, ignoring the wintry chill outside. They bundled into the van, which was even harder to get started than usual. Mike informed them all, with more than a hint of resentment, that it was because of the long journey they'd had to make up to Scotland and back.

"If you put pressure on the van, she doesn't like it," he grumbled as the engine finally spluttered into life.

"Mike, it's a car, not a person," Serena sneered, then she nearly fell into Pamela's lap as Mike accelerated, then jerked the van around the corner.

"It's definitely got colder, hasn't it?" Kester pulled his coat more tightly around himself. They'd only been in the van a few minutes, but already the combined heat of their breath was misting up the freezing windows.

"It is November, mate," Mike replied, deftly swinging the van into an available space in the busy traffic. "What do you expect?"

"I heard there was snow up on Dartmoor," Pamela said as she rubbed her hands together. "Perhaps it'll snow down here too."

"As long as there's no snow on the way to Beer Quarry Caves, I don't mind," Miss Wellbeloved said. She fiddled with the controls, then sighed. "We really must get the heating fixed in this van, Mike."

"Why are you telling me?" he asked, concentrating on the road. "Ribero's the one who holds the company purse-strings. Get him to book it in for a service."

"Perhaps you could fix it, as you're such a whizz with machinery?" Serena asked, sarcasm dripping from every word.

"Fat chance," Mike retorted. "I can only work with machines that were built after the Industrial Revolution. This relic is beyond even my capabilities."

"So," Kester interrupted, leaning forward, "is this some sort of hag we're going to investigate then?"

"Spot on," Miss Wellbeloved confirmed. "It's a hag o' the

dribble. We don't get many of them down these parts, but they're certainly not unheard of."

"Hang on a moment." Kester had a whole range of unpleasant images in his head now and wasn't sure which one to settle on. *Is this some sort of witchy thing that dribbles everywhere?* he wondered with a grimace. *She'd better not dribble on me. I only washed this shirt last night.*

"You want to know what a hag o' the dribble is?" Serena guessed with a dramatic roll of the eyes.

"Go on then, spoil me," Kester retorted. "What is it?"

"A hag o' the dribble is a fairly minor spirit, but a nuisance nonetheless," she began.

"Not a nuisance, just *different,*" Miss Wellbeloved corrected.

"Yes, yes. Whatever." Serena's lips tightened. "Anyway, it likes to collect stones and throw them down on unsuspecting people. Which is where the name comes from. The spirit sends down a dribble of stones. Do you see?"

Kester wrinkled his nose. "I thought you said this was a minor spirit? Lobbing rocks at people's heads doesn't sound minor to me. That sounds horrible!"

Miss Wellbeloved chuckled. "Fortunately," she said, wiping the condensation from her window to see better, "everyone who visits Beer Quarry Caves has to wear a hard-hat anyway, so they're well protected."

"Well that's alright then," Kester said sarcastically. He couldn't think of many things worse than being in a dark cave and getting pelted with rocks by a mad spirit. He sighed as they reached the outskirts of the city and joined the busy main road, which was filled with commuting cars.

Forty minutes later, they pulled into the cave's car-park. It was quiet, and the surrounding trees loomed over them, creating an unsettling, oppressive atmosphere. Kester got out and stretched, then spotted the dirt track leading up a steep incline. *Oh good, we're walking,* he realised with a sinking heart. *Yet again, we've got to trudge for miles in the cold. Hooray.*

"Is everyone ready?" Miss Wellbeloved asked with a bright smile.

Mike slammed the van door and saluted. "Ready and at your service, ma'am."

She gestured upwards. "Come on, then, let's go. I hope you all wore sensible shoes today, it's apparently quite slippery down in the caves."

"Oh great, now you tell me," Serena groaned. Kester glanced down at her shiny red stilettos and laughed. *You'd think, by now, she'd have realised that high-heeled shoes aren't great for this line of work,* he thought, marching ahead with the others.

At the top, a little old man with a face like a badger came scuttling over to greet them, waving vigorously at them all.

"Aha," he declared as he panted to a halt. "You must be Dr Ribero's Agency." A yellow hard-hat perched on his head like a scoop of ice-cream on a particularly small cone.

"Mr Smelter, I presume?" Miss Wellbeloved extended a hand, and the tiny man beamed.

"Absolutely correct, madam. And I must say, I am delighted you were able to come at such short notice. This isn't the first incident we've had at the caves. There have been many over the years. In fact, I believe your father once came out to deal with a particularly tricky ghoul, many years ago."

"Goodness me, it must have been a very long time ago if my father was still in charge of the agency," Miss Wellbeloved said dryly. She gestured to a large basket by the side of the cabin, which was full to the brim of battered hard-hats. "I presume we each need to wear one of those?"

"Quite so," Mr Smelter twinkled, giving his own helmet a tap. "We don't want your precious heads to get hurt by low-hanging rock, do we?"

"Or by spirits throwing pebbles at us," Kester muttered as he grabbed a hat.

"Whilst we're walking down to the caves," Miss Wellbeloved began, "I wonder if I could ask you a few questions?"

"Yes, of course," the old man agreed. He led them back out to the dirt track, then pointed downwards, where the gravel path disappeared into the gloom of the trees. A soaring mass of rock flanked the path at the bottom, steely grey and rather forbidding. Kester sniffed. The air had a distinctly moist, mossy smell to it, which he always associated with caves. *It's the smell of wetness, trapped underground,* he thought as they began to trek downhill. *All those creepy subterranean rivers that people explore, only to be never seen again.* He shuddered.

"When did the spirit start making itself known?" Miss Wellbeloved began, slowing her pace to ensure Mr Smelter could keep up.

"Only a few days ago," he replied cheerfully. "It started throwing small stones at our visitors' heads and producing an awful moaning noise. Very loud, it was."

Mike dropped back to join them. "What did the visitors think?"

Mr Smelter chuckled. "They were all terrified. Thankfully, when it first started, I was the one leading the tour, so I told them it was just another visitor pretending to be a ghost. Then I got them out of there pretty sharpish."

"That was quick thinking," Miss Wellbeloved said, nodding with approval.

The old man shrugged. "As I said, I've seen this sort of thing before. I know how important it is to keep it hush-hush."

"Well, it definitely sounds like a hag o' the dribble," Miss Wellbeloved concluded. "It's exhibiting classic behaviour."

"The last one we had was the same," Mr Smelter said. "About fifteen or so years back. Could it be the same one? That one went away on its own in the end."

"Entirely possible," Miss Wellbeloved said as she pondered his comment. "They occasionally return to the same place, unless you give them a good enough reason not to."

"For example, if you keep packing them off to the spirit world until they get bored and give up," Mike added, jauntily skipping over a loose pile of stones.

Miss Wellbeloved gave him a look. "Not that we normally have to do that, as most spirits are highly amenable," she tutted.

They rounded the corner. Kester looked up and gasped. The sight was formidable, to say the least. A sheer rock-face hung above them, lichen-coated and dank in the dim light. Tucked at the bottom of the rock was a pair of roughly-cut entrances barred with thick metal gates. *It looks like the entrance to an ancient prison,* Kester thought as his stomach did an involuntary lurch. It wasn't a promising start.

"Looks like a nice, welcoming spot," Pamela said with a giggle.

"It's got atmosphere, hasn't it?" the old man agreed, giving her a wink.

Kester gulped. He personally didn't find it amusing at all. *Yet again, another location that looks as though it's straight out of a horror film,* he thought, feeling his chest tighten. "Is there light in the caves?" he squeaked.

Mr Smelter laughed. "A bit, yes. Plus, we've got this." He rapped the headlight on his hat, then inserted a key into the lock, yanking the gate open with a loud screech. To Kester's horror, the noise echoed forlornly through the unseen caves beyond.

"How exciting!" Pamela exclaimed, oblivious to the sombre surroundings. She skipped through, her footsteps replicated against the vast, damp walls. Kester winced, then scurried after her. *Better that than being the last one to come in,* he thought as he took one final look at the outside world. *It's always the people bringing up the rear that get picked off first.*

They followed Mr Smelter down a dark, dripping passageway to the first of the caverns, a huge space only interrupted by squat pillars carved out of the rock. "Is this a man-made cave?" Kester asked as he looked around in bafflement.

"Yes, it was an old quarry, like the name suggests," Mr Smelter confirmed. His voice boomed unnaturally in the darkness. "Romans used to quarry down here. Some of the country's finest cathedrals are made from Beer stone, I'll have you know."

"Impressive," Kester whispered, surveying the surrounding walls. In the silence, he could imagine ancient quarrymen, chiselling relentlessly against the rock. *I wonder if the Romans had to put up with spirits too?* he thought. He imagined a burly Roman centurion running screaming from a spirit and grinned.

"Do you want to take us to the spot where you first heard the hag o' the dribble?" Miss Wellbeloved asked as she pulled her cardigan tightly around herself. "Then we can proceed with the preliminary investigations."

Mr Smelter nodded, headlight casting long shadows over the uneven floor. "Yep. I'll lead you there now. Can I stay and watch?"

"We won't be doing much today, to be honest," Miss Wellbeloved replied as she followed him into the next chamber. "Mike will take a few readings, and Pamela will assess the environment, but I doubt the spirit will show itself. They're notoriously secretive when we're around."

"Because they know that we're about to get rid of them," Serena added. She cursed as one of her stilettos splashed into a puddle.

"Whoops, mind your step, Serena," Mike said, deliberately nudging her out of the way. "Don't want your heels getting stuck in any holes."

Kester couldn't make out Serena's hissed response, but he was certain it contained a swear word or two.

Winding a path through the blackness, they finally reached the largest cavern of all—more an underground warehouse than a cave. Mr Smelter pulled to a stop, then pointed ahead. "This is the spot," he declared as he patted the nearest stone pillar. "We call this place the Saxon area. Can you see? The walls have been carved differently. It's much squarer than the Roman zone."

"Fascinating," Kester said, enrapt. He let his gaze travel over the flat planes of the rock face, wondering about the people who'd quarried here hundreds of years ago.

"Look at him, he's in his element," Mike said and poked Kester in the ribs. "You're such an academic, aren't you?"

"More like a nerd," Serena laughed.

The wall-lights flickered briefly. Mr Smelter frowned, and they fell silent.

"I take it that doesn't usually happen," Miss Wellbeloved said eventually. She surveyed the cave coolly, then gave the others a nod.

"No, it doesn't," the old man replied slowly. He adjusted his headlight to full brightness just as the main lights went out. Kester squealed.

"What happened?" he said, focusing on the disembodied faces of his team-mates, lit only by the meek light radiating from Mr Smelter's hat.

Mike tittered. "What do you think happened? The lights went out, didn't they!"

"But I don't like it," Kester protested. He was aware that his voice had taken on a whining quality, not dissimilar to one best suited to a small child, but he couldn't stop himself. *Why do spirits always do things like this?* he wondered as he peered anxiously into the pitch black. *Honestly, it would help a lot more with spirit and human relations if they'd leave the lights on every so often.*

He heard a slap in the darkness and leapt in fright before realising it was Pamela clapping her hands.

"This is excellent," she exclaimed. The light shone down on her face and made her look unnervingly like a Halloween pumpkin. "I can pick the hag o' the dribble up strongly! She's very close."

"Oh no," Kester said automatically. Every hair on his body prickled in fright.

"That's fantastic news!" Miss Wellbeloved said enthusiastically. "If we can capture the spirit today, that's even better." She rubbed her hands together, eyes twinkling in the beam of light.

"That'd suit us too." Mr Smelter seemed completely unfazed by the events, which made Kester feel even sillier by comparison.

A low moan interrupted them, and Kester groaned. *I knew it,* he thought as he swung his head around, fighting the urge to run blindly in the general direction of the exit. *I knew it would all kick off if I joined them. It always does. These spirits save their tormenting just for me.*

"What's the hag going to do?" he whispered, anxiously peering around.

"Don't worry, mate," Mike replied, in a reassuringly calm voice. "There's no reason to be worried."

"That's easy for you to say, but it's—"

"—I've picked something up," Pamela interrupted suddenly. She grasped at the nearest person, which happened to be Kester. Kester shrieked in response, leapt backwards, and collided into Serena, who swore at him loudly.

"Goodness me, what's going on?" Miss Wellbeloved said crossly, voice raised to make herself heard over the crescendoing moan of the spirit. "Can you all please compose yourselves whilst I try to converse with the spirit?"

"Blame this idiot here," Serena snarled with a deft poke in Kester's side.

"I really don't like this at all," Kester muttered, then yelped as a pebble struck him on the nose. At once, a shower of tiny stones pelted them all, mostly bouncing harmlessly off their hard-hats and onto the floor.

In the weak light, Kester could see Miss Wellbeloved frowning. "It seems that the spirit is frustrated," she said and pulled herself straighter. "Hag o' the dribble, tell me more. What is the problem? Are you lost in here?"

The moaning noise whirled around their heads, bringing with it a fresh fountain of pebbles. Kester clutched onto Mike, not caring what the others might think of him. *Mike's the biggest, toughest person here,* he thought, *and that's all that matters right now.*

"Good news, everyone," Miss Wellbeloved said quietly, holding up a hand to deflect the next succession of tiny stones. "The hag o' the dribble wants to return to the spirit world. She has had enough of being here, but she can't find her way back. She's trying to tell me something about a disturbance, some significant spirit activity that's making her upset, but I don't understand what she means."

"That's interesting." Pamela's voice floated through the dark, sounding almost ghostly. "Can you try to find out more? We need to know if there are any serious issues going on."

"Not that we'd be able to do much about it," Serena added.

Miss Wellbeloved whispered a few more sentences under her breath, then announced, "She mentioned a daemon, then wouldn't say anything more. Goodness knows what that's meant to mean."

"Well, let's not worry about that now," Pamela said. "Let's get this hag back where she belongs, eh?"

Miss Wellbeloved glanced at Kester, who was now practically under Mike's armpit. "Kester, is there any chance you can summon a spirit door?"

"None whatsoever," he squeaked. He burrowed against Mike's chest as a fresh barrage of gravel hit his hard-hat.

Serena tutted loudly. "Kester, for goodness' sake, can you stop cowering like a giant baby and at least have a go? It would make life a whole lot easier."

"Yeah, I wouldn't have to take the spirit all the way to London to drop it off at Infinite Enterprises, would I?" Mike added, gently prising Kester away.

"Yes, but I'm scared!" Kester protested. The others looked at him with expressions of pity, embarrassment, and mild disbelief. "Remember I've only been doing this for a few months," he added weakly.

"You'll excuse our colleague," Serena snapped. "He only stopped wetting the bed recently."

Kester opened his mouth to retort, then promptly snapped it shut as a load of loose gravel hurtled through the air, landing directly on his tongue. *Why in my bloody mouth?* he thought incredulously as he spat on the floor. "Give me a moment," he wheezed.

Miss Wellbeloved sighed, tapping her foot on the floor.

Finally recovered, Kester squinted into the darkness. *It's no use,* he concluded with a gulp. *I can't even think straight in situations like this, much less concentrate on seeing a spirit door.* He hated the pressure of it all, the expectation of the others weighing down on him. For the briefest moment, he thought he saw a glimmer in the air, but it disappeared in an instant. *Not that it was probably ever really there at all,* he thought glumly. *I might as well admit it, I can't conjure up this spirit door anymore.*

"I can't see anything, sorry," he muttered, promptly feeling like a failure.

Serena snorted. "Mike, get me the spirit storage unit," she said, clicking her fingers in his direction.

"You mean the water—"

"Yes, that's exactly what I mean." Even though he couldn't see it in the dark, Kester could well imagine her cross expression.

Mike paused. "What makes you think I've got it?"

"Because I saw you put the bottle in your bag! Didn't you?"

"No. I put in a chocolate bar for later, but not a water bottle."

Serena snorted. "Are you serious? How are we meant to trap this spirit, then?"

"I thought this was just a preliminary visit! Anyway, since when has it been my responsibility? You're the one who—"

Pamela cleared her throat. "Luckily for you two, I've got my thermos flask in my handbag."

"Everything alright?" Mr Smelter asked, sounding confused.

Miss Wellbeloved took the opportunity to deliver Mike and Serena one of her iciest glares, grey eyes glowing in the light. "Yes, absolutely fine. Don't worry, we'll have this sorted in a jiffy."

Kester detected a rummaging noise in the darkness, then a low hiss; which he presumed was the sound of whatever liquid had been in Pamela's thermos hitting the floor.

"At least someone came prepared, eh?" Pamela said with a chuckle and passed it to Serena, who promptly held it aloft and started to chant.

"Funny way to do it," Mr Smelter commented, as casually as if he'd been discussing the weather. "Still, who needs fancy equipment when something basic will do the job, eh?"

"Yes, that's what we've always thought," Miss Wellbeloved replied. Mike let out a laugh, then quickly disguised it as a cough.

Only a minute or so later, the moaning ceased. The wall lights flickered back on, bathing the chilly cave in a welcoming glow. Kester massaged his brow. Now the lights were on, he felt even sillier than before. *Okay,* he conceded, aware that the others were looking at him with a vague blend of irritation and pity, *perhaps that wasn't as frightening as I thought it was going to be.*

"If only all spirits were as easy to deal with as that one, eh?" Mike said. He hoisted his bag over his shoulder and gestured to the exit. "Shall we? I believe our work here is done."

"That was marvellous!" Mr Smelter clapped his hands together, looking suitably impressed. "I can't believe you dealt with it so quickly. Many thanks. I'll be sure to give you all free passes to the cave. You're welcome here whenever you like."

"I'm sure Kester will be pleased," Mike said with a nod in his direction. "He can swot up on the history of quarrying then. You were getting into it earlier, weren't you, mate?"

"I found it very interesting indeed," Kester retorted primly, refusing to be baited.

"Come on, everyone." Miss Wellbeloved started to follow Mr Smelter back through the network of caverns. "Time to head back."

It was a relief to emerge out into the open. The scent of cool, damp foliage hit them immediately—a welcome change from the still, suffocating air of the caves. After bidding Mr Smelter farewell and returning their hard-hats, they trooped down the hill to the van. Kester wasn't sure if it was the shock of emerging out into the open or the worsening weather, but he felt sure the air was even colder than before; there was a crisp tang on the breeze that suggested snow wouldn't be out of the question.

Mike threw open the van door and bowed to the ladies. "Job

well done, I think."

"I should say so," said Pamela. "I wouldn't mind a few more jobs like that, eh?"

Miss Wellbeloved climbed back into the van. "Yes," she said uncertainly. "Though I'm still concerned about what the hag o' the dribble said about the spirit disturbance."

"It's probably nothing," Mike replied, sticking the key into the ignition. "You know what some spirits are like, they babble about any old nonsense."

"Possibly." Miss Wellbeloved rummaged in her handbag and pulled out her phone. "It was vibrating while we were in the caves," she said, peering at the screen. "I wonder who was calling me?"

"Perhaps it was Dad?" Kester suggested over the rheumatic roar of the van's engine.

Miss Wellbeloved pressed the screen, then frowned. "That's strange," she said. "It's a London number."

"Infinite Enterprises?" Mike suggested as he drove the van back onto the country road.

She shook her head. "No, it's not them. Whoever it was has left a message. Be quiet for a minute whilst I listen to it."

They sat, waiting patiently as Miss Wellbeloved pressed the phone to her ear. Her frown deepened. Kester glanced at the others. *I wonder who it is?* he thought. Whoever it might be, Miss Wellbeloved certainly didn't look happy to hear from them. Finally, she put the phone down and turned around, biting her lip.

"Well?" Pamela leaned over, nearly crushing Serena in the process. "Who was it, love?"

"Curtis Philpot," Miss Wellbeloved replied with a curt nod. "An emergency, apparently. I need to call him back as soon as we get back into the office."

"What sort of bloody emergency?" Mike spluttered, driving against the hedgerow as a car attempted to squeeze past them on the narrow road. "Don't say it's something to do with the Scottish fetch. I'm done in with that case."

"No, it was nothing to do with that," Miss Wellbeloved said. She looked out of the window with a concerned expression. "I'm worried it's more serious than that, actually."

"Like what?" Kester asked with a sense of foreboding. He didn't like the look on her face. It suggested something awful was going on—something so bad that she couldn't even bring herself to tell them about it.

Miss Wellbeloved shook her head. "Let me get more information from Curtis Philpot," she said decisively. "Then we'll take it from there."

Kester leant back, frustrated. *No sooner do we solve one problem than another one crops up,* he thought, feeling rather put out. And by the look on Miss Wellbeloved's face, this problem wasn't going to be as easily solved as the hag o' the dribble.

CHAPTER 5: THE DAEMON AND THE DOOR

Upon returning to the office, Miss Wellbeloved immediately vanished into the quiet refuge of Ribero's office to return Curtis Philpot's call. The others waited fretfully, glancing at each other with growing confusion as the minutes ticked on.

She's been nearly an hour, Kester thought, eyeing the clock for the tenth time, fingers drumming against the desk. *What's going on?*

They attempted to get on with work, though they were unable to stop their gazes from continually flicking to Ribero's door, expecting Miss Wellbeloved to emerge at any moment. To distract himself, Kester tried to read a few more paragraphs of *Spirit Intervention for Beginners,* but the words seemed to slide off the page without even coming close to making sense in his brain. The thermos flask containing the hag o' the dribble sat on Serena's desk, momentarily forgotten.

Finally, Kester closed the book with a sigh. It was no use. The words might as well have been written in Hebrew as far as he was concerned. "I wonder what they're talking about?" he asked finally, to no-one in particular.

A flurry of sparks erupted from the pile of knotted wires on Mike's desk. Mike swore under his breath. "I don't know, mate," he said tersely as he pulled his chisel out from the mess. "I'm not a psychic, am I? Ask Pamela."

Pamela looked up from her computer. "What was that?"

"I told Kester to ask you what Miss Wellbeloved was talking about, as you're the resident psychic."

"Ah yes, very funny." Pamela reclined in her chair, which creaked loudly in protest. "If only it worked like that, eh? Serena, are you going to pop the hag into storage? If you would be so kind as to move it into a water bottle, that'd be appreciated. I'd like my thermos flask back."

"Can't I just do it tomorrow?" Serena whined. "I'll have to release it then get it back into another bottle, which is such a hassle."

"I'm sure the hag o' the dribble loved being trapped with the remains of your tea, Pamela," Mike added. He yanked another wire free, then cursed as a blue flame blazed from the end.

"It was potato and leek soup, actually."

"Oh, even better. Imagine being cooped up with the smell of leek and potato for hours on end. Poor thing."

Finally, Ribero's office door swung open. Miss Wellbeloved came out, wearing an expression of pure exhaustion. She leaned against the door-frame and shook her head in bewilderment.

"You were a long time," Pamela said, rising from her seat. "What on earth was all that about?"

Miss Wellbeloved pressed her hand to her forehead. "Good-ness," she said faintly. "I don't even know where to begin. Would someone please make me a cup of tea?"

"Why not make it something stronger?" Mike suggested. He pointed at the clock. "It's already nearly five o'clock. Let's head to the pub and chat there."

"Well, if you're all happy to do so?" Miss Wellbeloved looked at them all. Everyone nodded, desperate to find out what Curtis

Philpot had said.

It's obviously something major, Kester thought as he flung his coat on. *I haven't seen her looking this harassed in ages. And that's saying something.*

They ventured out into the cold. The city streets were unusually empty, apart from a few homeless people congregated in miserable huddles outside an empty shop. Kester scooped out a few coins and dropped them into a particularly dejected-looking man's hat. The man grinned and offered Kester a salute in response.

Miss Wellbeloved patted him on the shoulder. "You're a kind boy, Kester."

He smiled. "I've seen you do the same thing many times."

"Well," she said as she leant in closer. "If you can't be kind to those around you, who can you be kind to, eh?"

He thought about it, then nodded. "And of course, you mean being kind to spirits too."

"I do. And regardless of what the others might say, I won't change my view on the matter. Spirits may be very different to us, but they have feelings too—of that, I can assure you."

Kester thought back to all the spirits he'd encountered so far. They had all been so bewilderingly diverse that he found it hard to form an opinion on the matter. However, he did agree with Miss Wellbeloved that every creature should be given respect, regardless of where they were from or how sinister he might find them.

The pub was pleasingly deserted as they went in, not to mention deliciously warm. Bill the barman was in his usual position behind the beer taps, reading a newspaper. Apart from the sound of the pages turning, it was completely peaceful.

"Shut that door after you, if you would be so kind," he said with an affable wink. "It's bitterly cold out there."

"There's going to be snow on Dartmoor, apparently," Pamela said, looking longingly over the wine list.

"How are things, Bill?" Mike surveyed the draft ales, then pointed at the one closest to him.

"Picking up for the festive season, my good man," Bill replied. With expert precision, he pulled a pint, removing the head with a flick of his pocket knife. "And yourself?"

"Busy and bonkers," Mike said.

Bill stroked his beard thoughtfully. "It'll calm down after Christmas. It always does. What can I get the rest of you?"

The others placed their orders. Mike leant over the bar and nodded deliberately. "We're actually here to discuss business, you know."

Bill gave him a knowing look. "Ah yes, and that means you'd like to be left to chat in privacy, right?"

"That would be ever so much appreciated," Miss Wellbeloved said, sipping at her drink.

"Anything for you," the barman said. "Though I'd still love to know what you lot all do for a living. It's all very mysterious."

"We're double-agents for the government," Kester said.

Bill studied them all, then laughed. "Forgive me for saying this, but you're not exactly James Bond, are you?"

"Oh, I don't know, love," Pamela chimed as she picked up her glass of wine. "I was quite a looker in my time, I think I could have given Ursula Undress a run for her money."

Mike spluttered, spraying ale over the bar. "Undress? *Undress?* You're thinking of the wrong sort of film, love!"

"What? What did I say wrong?"

"It's Andress, you mad woman. I don't want to think of you undressing, thank you very much."

Pamela erupted into giggles, which soon set everyone else off, including Kester. He hadn't realised how tension-laden the atmosphere had been until now, and was grateful for the light relief.

Finally, Bill wiped his eyes. "On that note, I'll leave you all to it. I'll be out in the kitchen if you need me."

Still chuckling, they picked up their drinks and sat at the table in the corner, which was conveniently close to a snug radiator. Kester found himself squashed against the wall by Pamela's considerable thigh, then compressed even more tightly as Mike squeezed in too.

"Right then," Serena announced. She tapped a perfectly manicured nail against her glass. "Let's get to business. What the hell is going on?"

Miss Wellbeloved cleared her throat. "Major problems, unfortunately. Gosh, I'm not even sure where to start."

"How about at the beginning?" Mike suggested, slurping at his pint.

She nodded. "Very well. The government have received a letter of a rather unpleasant nature."

"Surely that's nothing unusual," Pamela said with a laugh. She leaned back against the wall, squashing Kester even more in the process. "They're not exactly a popular lot, are they?"

Miss Wellbeloved shook her head. "This letter was serious. It was a threat, to be precise. A dangerous threat that could shake our society to its very foundations."

"What sort of threat?" Serena asked with a suspicious look. "And who was it from?"

Miss Wellbeloved took a deep breath. She clasped her glass tightly in both hands, pausing before replying, "It was from the Thelemites."

"Are you serious?" Kester studied her expression, then laughed. "Come on. Really? We only went to see them a couple of days ago, and they looked pretty harmless to me." He thought back to his encounter with Barty Melville, who he'd thought looked like a manatee in a dress. *Hardly a major cause for concern.* Parvati Chowdhury, the tiny woman with the fierce glare, had been more intimidating, but hadn't exactly looked like a serious governmental threat.

"The Thelemites are a large organisation," Miss Wellbeloved said. "Barty Melville is just one of many."

Mike placed a hand on the table. "Hang on a minute," he said slowly. "This doesn't add up. Since when have the Thelemites ever gone around making threats? That's not their style, is it? I mean, they like to stir things up and cause trouble, but they're not terrorists, for goodness' sake."

Miss Wellbeloved shook her head. "I'm not sure anymore," she replied. "If what Curtis Philpot told me is true, they've changed a lot."

"What was the threat?" Serena asked, looking worried.

Miss Wellbeloved paused. "To create a *permanent door*," she whispered eventually, then clasped a hand across her mouth.

Mike laughed. "That's ridiculous. It's not possible, for starters."

"Infinite Enterprises managed it," Miss Wellbeloved reminded him.

"Yeah, but only through cutting-edge technology and millions of pounds," Mike replied, slopping his pint without noticing. "The Thelemites haven't got the resources or the skills to achieve that."

Kester coughed. "Hang on a minute," he said, feeling more confused by the moment. "Can you rewind a bit? What door do you mean? And why is that a threat? I don't quite follow."

"A spirit door, of course!" Serena snapped. She fixed him with a stony glare. "Christ, do we have to explain every last detail to you? When are you going to catch up, eh?"

Kester chose to ignore her. "But aren't there spirit doors around anyway? I mean, how do the spirits arrive here? I'd presumed there were spirit doors all over the place."

Pamela snorted and wrapped an arm over his shoulder. "Goodness me, no. Not anymore, anyway."

"So how do the spirits get into our world?" Kester asked. He was now completely baffled. *Probably this is something I should have verified a long time ago,* he thought, seeing the incredulity on the others' faces.

Mike took a deep breath, placing his pint firmly down on the table. "You see," he began, as though explaining a simple concept to a dim-witted child, "spirits can come in and out of our world whenever they like, using their own energy force. But not many choose to, because it's difficult to do so."

"That's right," Miss Wellbeloved added. "It's generally only the spirits that *really* like humans that make the effort."

"Like Serena's incubus," Mike added.

"Stop calling it my incubus!" Serena screeched. "You're just doing it to wind me up."

"So, you see," Miss Wellbeloved continued, ignoring Serena's outburst, "normally, it's not too much of a problem. Spirits turn up occasionally, but at present, they're relatively under control."

"Yes," added Pamela, "they enter our world, we hear about it, then we capture them. Job done."

". . . and then you take them to Infinite Enterprises, who returns them to their own world, using their official spirit door," Kester concluded. He knew that much, given that he'd done a few of the London spirit-runs with Mike and had seen how it all worked. Not that he'd ever been inside the Infinite Enterprise building, a vast, glass behemoth in the centre of the capital, but he'd watched Mike deliver the spirits in their water bottles to official-looking men and women in suits, which was enough to emphasise how important the company was.

"However," Miss Wellbeloved continued, "if you create a permanent spirit door, there's nothing to stop spirits entering our world in a blink of an eye, without any effort at all. Unless you police it carefully, like Infinite Enterprises does with theirs."

"So, it's a bit like a border control?" Kester said, trying to get it straight. "If you open a spirit door without monitoring it properly, there's no controls at the borders, so spirits can come and go as they please?"

Miss Wellbeloved nodded. "I don't love the analogy, but I suppose so, yes."

"Which means," Mike added, "that if the Thelemites manage to create a new door, we've got a *huge* problem. We'd be overrun with spirits, and there'd be nothing we could do about it."

Kester shuddered. He imagined a world where the streets

were filled with howling banshees, unpredictable poltergeists, and sinister ghouls. It didn't even bear thinking about.

"But you don't think they can create another door?" he asked, looking at Mike.

"Nah," Mike said, voice muffled as he downed the remnants of his pint. "Take it from me, the technology needed to create a spirit door, let alone keep it open, is formidable. You'd need millions just to make it, not to mention millions to keep it in operation."

"Remember the Sun-Doors, Mike," Miss Wellbeloved warned.

Mike scoffed and slammed his glass on the table. "Come on, Miss W. When was the last Sun-Door built, eh?"

"Sun-Doors are ancient gateways that used to be used as spirit doors thousands of years ago," Pamela whispered helpfully in Kester's ear. "There's a few still remaining, though no longer in operation. In Bolivia, Egypt, places like that. People believe that spirit-door openers created them, using the sun's power to keep them open."

"What if they've discovered the ancient secrets of harnessing the power of the sun to create a spirit door?" Miss Wellbeloved said. "If ancient civilisations managed it, what's to stop the Thelemites from doing the same?"

"No, I don't buy that at all," Serena said. "Experts have proven it's just a myth; there's no way of achieving it in real life. You know that. Plus, you'd need a spirit-door opener to get things started, which I very much doubt the Thelemites have, not to mention—"

Mike held up a hand, interrupting Serena mid-flow. "Hang on a minute, my friends."

They looked at him questioningly. He held up his empty pint glass as though presenting a trophy, then pointed to the bar. "I need a refill," he declared. "And because this is a serious meeting, I'll even offer to buy a round."

"Blimey, what's happened?" Serena snorted as she presented him with her glass. "Mike's buying a round? Mike's actually reaching into his pocket, wiping the cobwebs off his wallet, and purchasing other people some drinks for once?"

Mike gave her a wink. "A simple thank you would suffice."

The others waited while Mike summoned Bill from the kitchen. Whilst the drinks were being poured, Kester mulled over what he'd learned so far. To be honest, he didn't understand what the fuss was about. *After all,* he reasoned, *if the Thelemites don't have the ability or funds to create a spirit door, that means it's just an empty threat, doesn't it?*

Finally, Mike returned, wielding a tray laden with alcohol. "I come bearing gifts."

Bill gave them a cheery wave and disappeared back into the kitchen.

"I hope you don't mind me asking," Kester began, reaching for his pint and wishing that Mike had just ordered him a soft drink instead, "but why is this a big deal? It doesn't sound like the Thelemites pose any serious threat, do they?"

"Hear, hear," Mike agreed, wiping the foam off his upper lip. "Sounds like the government have got in a flap over nothing."

Miss Wellbeloved shook her head. "I haven't even told you the half of it yet."

"Oh lord." Pamela leaned heavily on the table. "Go on, then. Break it to us."

"The Thelemites also informed the government that a very old, very powerful daemon has now joined their ranks."

"Whoa there," Kester said, pushing his glasses up his nose. "What did you say? A daemon? Like a devil?" He didn't like the sound of that at all.

"No, not like a devil," Miss Wellbeloved snapped. "Goodness me, why do people always think that? The original meaning of the word 'daemon' means 'genius' or simply 'spirit'. It's not necessarily malevolent at all."

"But when they are malevolent, they're bloody terrifying," Mike said, pint momentarily forgotten.

"That's interesting," Pamela muttered. "Remember what the

hag o' the dribble said? About a daemon and picking up spirit disturbances?"

Miss Wellbeloved nodded grimly.

"What's this one like, then?" Kester said, already suspecting that he didn't want to know the answer.

"This particular daemon has a long history of living among humans. Much like Dr Barqa-Abu, the djinn who will be teaching you at the SSFE. For centuries, this daemon has behaved himself impeccably, inhabiting human bodies and living among us—"

"Excuse me?" Kester squealed. "Inhabiting human bodies? Like a daemonic possession?"

"Not at all," Miss Wellbeloved replied tightly. "Some humans happily allow daemons to inhabit their bodies, especially when the daemon makes them wealthy, beautiful, and successful."

"They do possess people against their will sometimes, to be fair," Pamela noted, then quickly added, "but only on rare occasions," after catching Miss Wellbeloved's eye.

"Daemons are remarkably charismatic, clever creatures," Miss Wellbeloved continued. "And they absolutely love living with humans. That's why there are still a few of them around. Believe it or not, one used to work for the government many years ago."

"He ran for Prime Minister, actually," Pamela said. She laughed. "Can you imagine? A daemon Prime Minister? That would have been interesting."

"That particular daemon was, and still is, a highly respectable creature," Miss Wellbeloved reminded her. "Last I heard, he was living on a Caribbean island and raising lots of money for good causes across the world."

Kester felt vaguely more optimistic. "So, is the daemon that's joined the Thelemites a nice spirit then?"

"Well," Miss Wellbeloved paused, chewing the side of her nail. "This daemon is certainly a character. For several decades, he's adopted the human form of an international rock star, actually." She nodded with great deliberation in Mike's direction. "I believe you're especially familiar with him, Mike."

Mike's pint glass faltered mid-air, just inches from his lips. His eyes widened. "If you tell me it's Billy Dagger, I might actually drop dead of a heart-attack."

"Yes, it's Billy Dagger," Miss Wellbeloved confirmed. Mike let out a noise not unlike a squawking parrot. Kester gasped. *Surely not,* he thought. The timing was uncanny given they'd seen him perform only a few days earlier.

"Why didn't you say something before?" Kester asked. He felt a little rattled. The performer he'd seen leaping around on stage had been almost eerily talented, but he'd had no idea he'd been watching a spirit in action. He recollected Billy Dagger's ethereal voice, his boundless energy, and formidable stage presence, and nodded. It did make sense, in a strange kind of way.

"I didn't know myself that Billy Dagger was a daemon." Miss Wellbeloved shook her head. "Daemon identities are closely guarded, for their own protection. The government only releases details in extreme cases such as this. Normally, even the supernatural agencies would have no idea."

"Why not?"

She sighed. "Because unfortunately, even supernatural agencies can't be trusted to behave themselves with spirits. Concealing daemon identities is part of the spirit-protection programme. But of course, if daemons wish to reside in our world full-time, they need to apply for a permit, just like any other spirit."

"That means they must declare their whereabouts or get deported back to the spirit world," Pamela whispered.

"Gosh." Kester leaned back against the wall and mulled it over. It was difficult to take in. He wasn't sure if he was missing something, but he still couldn't see what the real problem was. Judging by the expressions on Mike and Serena's faces, they clearly felt the same.

Miss Wellbeloved coughed, guessing their thoughts. "You're wondering why the government are taking the threat so seriously, aren't you?"

"Just a bit," Serena confirmed.

"Well," Miss Wellbeloved said and gestured for them to move closer. "That's not the end of it, I'm afraid. Someone broke into Infinite Enterprises two evenings ago."

"What?" Mike slapped the table and all the glasses teetered alarmingly. "Not possible. No way."

"Not possible for a human," Miss Wellbeloved corrected. "But not entirely impossible for a spirit, as you know. If they were incredibly powerful, like a daemon."

"But why would anyone want to break in?" Serena said, looking aghast. "I mean, it's not as though they can steal the spirit door, is it? The equipment they use to open it must weigh the same as a herd of elephants!"

Miss Wellbeloved shrugged. "That's just it. No-one knows why Infinite Enterprises was broken into. Nothing was taken, but it was clear someone unauthorised had been in the premises. In particular, down in the archives department. Certain files had been rifled through."

Pamela shuddered. "Now, *that's* more worrying. What on earth were they looking for? Information on how to open a spirit door, perhaps?"

"I suppose the next question is," Mike said with a nervous twiddle of his thumbs, "what's our role in all of this?"

"We've been called upon to assist with the case," Miss Wellbeloved said. "So has Larry Higgins and, of course, Infinite Enterprises. Various other supernatural agencies have also been informed and called upon to investigate further. Quite simply, when someone threatens the security of the entire country, it becomes a problem for us all."

Mike ran a hand through his hair and glanced over to the door. A group of young men entered a second later, still in their office suits, breaking the quiet with laughter and stomping feet. Bill emerged a moment later, clutching a tea-towel in one hand

and a glass in the other. He greeted the men warmly, then nodded meaningfully to them.

"I think quiet-time might be officially over," Mike muttered and looked at his watch.

"What's the conclusion then?" Pamela downed the last of her wine quickly, eyes still fixed on the noisy young men.

"We've all been called to the Infinite Enterprises offices for an emergency meeting," Miss Wellbeloved said. She looked awkward.

Mike groaned. "I can guess what you're about to say," he said as he examined her expression. "You're going to tell me we've got to go tomorrow, aren't you? Is it tomorrow? Please don't say it's tomorrow."

"Nine o'clock sharp," Miss Wellbeloved confirmed.

Mike groaned. "Are you serious?"

"I've got to book our train tickets tonight," she added. "We'll need to meet at six o'clock at the train station."

"You're joking," Kester said.

"Regrettably not," Miss Wellbeloved replied. She looked over her shoulder at the men, who were now raucously tucking into pints and numerous bags of crisps. "I suggest we all go home and get as much rest as possible. It's going to be a busy day tomorrow."

They gathered their belongings, preparing themselves to go out into the cold once again. Kester had a sudden thought, and pulled Miss Wellbeloved to one side.

"Will Dad be going tomorrow?" he asked.

Miss Wellbeloved shrugged. "Ideally, yes," she replied. "Philpot expects to see him there. But if he can't manage—"

"—we'll just have to manage on his behalf," Kester concluded as he straightened his jacket. They pulled the door open, waving at Bill on their way out.

"Yes, that's correct." Miss Wellbeloved looked anxious. "I'm sure we'll cope."

It was a clear, dark winter evening, and the moon glowed overhead, white as ice, narrowly framed by the buildings surrounding them. *Why does the moon always look like it's screaming?* Kester wondered and shivered. He'd never been able to understand why other people saw a smiling face in the moon's surface when all he could see were begging eyes and a mouth stretched wide in horror.

Miss Wellbeloved patted his arm, startling him out of his thoughts. "See you all tomorrow," she said as she nimbly crossed the road. "Sleep well."

Serena snorted. "Unlikely. I have no doubt that the sodding incubus is going to pop out at some point in the night."

"Just enjoy it," Mike said. "You love the attention, really."

Serena shot him a poisonous glare, then stalked up the road. "I'll see you tomorrow morning," she shouted over her shoulder without waiting for a response. Her words were swiftly lost on the freezing breeze.

"I brought the car in today," Mike said. "Do either of you two want a lift?"

Pamela nodded. Kester considered it, then shook his head. "It's okay," he said. "I need to call Anya anyway, and it's easier doing it outside the house, where Pineapple and Daisy aren't listening in on my conversation."

"Suit yourself, sir." With a flourish, Mike linked arms with Pamela, hoisting her along the pavement. "Come on, my lady. Let's get you home."

"You're an old charmer, you are," she giggled.

Kester watched them depart, then headed up the hill, pulling his phone out of his pocket and trying to ignore the chill numbness already settling into his fingertips. *If it doesn't snow soon, I'll eat my hat,* he thought, shivering. To his surprise, Anya answered almost immediately.

"Gosh, that was quick." Kester crossed the road, deliberately avoiding eye-contact with the gang of football-shirt-wearing men loitering outside a nearby pub.

"I am glad you called. I'm worried, Kester."

"Really?" He dug his free hand into his pocket. It didn't provide much warmth, but at least it was out of the wind. "What about? Is everything alright?"

"I think someone is watching me."

He frowned. "Why? What makes you think that?"

"My bedroom light. It keeps flickering. And it is cold in here." Her voice was so low that Kester struggled to hear her.

"Could it just be that your lightbulb is going?" he suggested. "Also, it is bloody freezing cold at the moment."

"No," she said with a sniff. "This is different. Every time I look down at my book, the light flickers. When I look up, it goes back to normal. And my room, it is so cold, I can see my breath. But my radiator is on. To be honest, I am a bit scared."

Kester paused. *Is she being paranoid?* he wondered. Certainly, if he'd just been kidnapped by a supernatural organisation, he'd be fairly paranoid too. However, flickering lights and unnaturally cold temperatures did sound distinctly like spirit activity.

"Do you want me to come over?" he asked.

Anya paused. "No," she said. "It's okay. Miss Wellbeloved, she said that they wouldn't hurt me, didn't she? Mind you, I don't feel comfortable being on my own."

Kester swallowed hard. "I'm sure you are safe," he said, choosing his words carefully. "But it never hurts to be cautious, does it? Would you like to come and stay at mine for the night?"

His question was met with silence followed by a giggle. Kester felt confused, then suddenly realised what he'd said. He blushed, heartily relieved it was too dark for any passers-by to see him.

"That's very forward of you, Kester."

"Gosh, I really didn't mean it like that," he bumbled. "I mean, you can sleep in my room, and I'll sleep on the sofa. Of course."

Anya laughed. "I know you didn't mean it like that," she replied. "You are too much of a gentleman. Thank you for the offer, but I think I will stay here for now. I might come over if it gets worse, though. My housemate is here, so I will be fine."

He nodded. "I'm sure you will be. But keep your phone with

you, just in case." *After all*, he reasoned, *there's no reason why the Thelemites would come after Anya. If it is them, they're probably just using one of their spirit members to check she's behaving herself.*

"What have you been doing tonight?" she asked, changing the subject.

"Ah, just down the pub. You know." He briefly entertained the thought of telling her what he'd found out about the Thelemites but decided against it. It was classified government information, after all.

"Was that with your workmates? What were you talking about?"

"Nothing much," Kester lied, crossing his fingers instinctively in his pocket. "Just having a relaxing drink after work, nothing else."

"Oh." She sounded disappointed.

"Anyway," Kester continued, darting nimbly around a group of young women walking along the pavement. "If you need someone, just call me, okay?" he continued. "I'm happy to come over, if it makes you feel safer."

"Thank you, Kester." She sounded genuinely grateful. "I am glad I met you."

His blush deepened. "Really?"

"Yes." She chuckled. "You make me feel protected. That is a nice feeling."

He beamed, forgetting all about the cold for a moment. "Wow. I don't think I've ever been told that before."

"Well, now you have. I'd better go, I haven't had my dinner yet. Thanks for listening, Kester."

"It's a pleasure," he replied, meaning it. "Have a good evening. And don't worry about the light flickering. It's probably nothing."

"I know," she replied. "Good night, Kester."

He hung up and stuffed his phone back in his pocket, feeling extraordinarily pleased with himself. *She said I make her feel protected,* he thought and felt his breath catch, just a little. *No-one ever says things like that about me. Maybe I'm not as useless as I thought.*

A glance at his watch told him that it was nearly seven o'clock.

The thought of wrapping himself up in his duvet, blocking out the cold, and thinking about Anya was very tempting indeed. Except he knew that he needed to think about tomorrow's emergency meeting instead, not to mention the news that Miss Wellbeloved had just relayed to them.

Billy Dagger, eh? he thought, once again feeling incredulous. *How is it even possible that the singer I saw die on stage only this week was actually a daemon in disguise? Not to mention, tangled up with the Thelemites, who I didn't even know existed until a few days ago.*

It all felt rather surreal, which was probably why he was struggling to take the information in.

If only I could just have a break, he thought as he staggered up the road. The night air bit into his skin, making his eyes water. *Just a few days off to recover, rather than this relentless onslaught. That would help.*

However, he was certain there would be no days off soon—if Miss Wellbeloved's worried expression had been anything to go by, things were only going to get more chaotic.

CHAPTER 6: INFINITE ENTERPRISES

Getting out of bed at five in the morning was one of the worst things Kester had endured in recent months, which was saying a lot. Frost laced his window panes, which would have been pretty had it not emphasised how freezing cold it was. *This is ridiculous,* he thought as he gazed out into the darkness. The trees in the neighbour's courtyard were swaying violently, suggesting a stiff breeze to accompany the coldness. *Why am I doing this?* He toyed with the idea of calling in sick, then imagined his father's look of disapproval and thought better of it.

After a lukewarm shower and a hasty rummage for some fresh clothes, Kester stomped out the front door, resisting the urge to slam it behind him. *And now I've got to run to the station because I've left it too late to call a taxi,* he realised, checking his watch. *Could this day have got off to a worse start?*

Half an hour later, he staggered into the station, chest burning, eyes watering. He spotted the others immediately, huddled by the ticket office, wearing identical expressions of irritation. Kester wheezed, bent over double, then clutched his knees.

"Seriously," he panted, "don't even think about having a go at me. I ran all the way."

"We can tell," Serena said. She surveyed him from head to toe. "You're covered in sweat."

Kester straightened, coughed, then noticed his father, who was wearing his usual fedora. "What are you doing here?" he asked, blinking rapidly.

Ribero scoffed. "It is my agency, yes? Why would I not be here, silly boy?"

Without warning, Miss Wellbeloved nudged Kester towards the gates. "No time for that now." She flicked a ticket in his direction. "If we miss this train, then we'll be late for the meeting, which won't do at all."

Just as she finished her sentence, the train pulled to a halt at the platform, the screech of brakes echoing around the cavernous space. Cursing, Miss Wellbeloved broke into a trot, haring towards the stairs with surprising spindly elegance. The others followed, and Kester reluctantly brought up the rear, wondering just how much more sprinting he could possibly cope with in one morning. His clothes were drenched in sweat, and he dreaded to think how awful he'd look when he finally reached Infinite Enterprise's smart London office.

Boarding the train just as the guard blew his whistle, they collapsed in the nearest seats with a collective sigh of relief.

"I never want to do that again," Kester muttered. He pressed his head against the window, fighting to gain control of his racing heart.

Mike moved his rucksack under his feet, then leaned over. "Think of it as a free gym session," he said with a wink. "You'll get a rippling six-pack in no time."

A rustle from across the aisle distracted them both. Ribero was rummaging in his briefcase, depositing a succession of objects on the seat next to him. Finally, he pulled out a napkin followed by a croissant and a tiny jar of jam. A further search produced a tiny silver knife.

"That's a decadent breakfast, Dad," Kester commented, eyeing the croissant yearningly. He'd completely forgotten to bring anything for himself.

Ribero shrugged. "Ah, if you are going to eat, you eat properly, right? None of this junk food."

"I agree." Miss Wellbeloved gave an approving nod.

"I thought you'd be staying at home today," Kester continued, watching his father's hands, which looked far less trembly than the previous day.

Ribero raised an eyebrow. "Trying to get rid of me, eh?"

"No, of course not." Kester grinned, settling himself more comfortably into his seat. "I'm glad you're here. Just surprised, that's all."

"I heard you all did great yesterday at the wine quarry caves, yes?"

"It's Beer Quarry," Miss Wellbeloved tutted. "Honestly, I think you do it on purpose sometimes. You've lived here for decades, there's no way you didn't know its proper name."

"Ah, but wine is nicer, right?" Ribero patted the corner of his mouth, then applied another smear of jam to the remains of his croissant. "Beer is such a nasty *British* drink. Ugh."

"I'll let the good people of Beer know that you think they should change their town's name then," Miss Wellbeloved retorted. "Now, shall we start talking about today?" She cast an eye around the empty carriage before adding quietly, "there's a lot we need to discuss before we go to the meeting."

Pamela yawned. "Really? Can't we just catch up on our sleep instead? I'm ever so tired. Hemingway kept barking in the night, he was driving me mad."

Kester grinned. He'd spent a few nights at Pamela's house when he'd first met Dr Ribero and his agency, and he remembered her shaggy dog very well, not to mention all the hairs he deposited liberally over every surface he passed.

"No, you cannot go to sleep," Miss Wellbeloved said severely. She reached into her handbag and pulled out her notepad. "I received a brief from Curtis Philpot yesterday evening, and I need to pass the notes on to all of you."

Serena stretched out on the chair. "Oh, go on then," she muttered. "If we must. I'm still not convinced it's as serious as the government thinks, though. It sounds like an empty threat to me."

"Someone broke into Infinite Enterprises, one of the most secure buildings in the UK," Miss Wellbeloved barked. "Don't tell me that's not serious."

"Alright, alright," Serena sighed. "Keep your hair on."

"Someone not get a very good night's sleep?" Mike asked with a gleeful glint in his eye. "Old lover-boy incubus keeping you up again?"

Serena's lips pressed so tightly together they practically disappeared. "It's not funny, Mike. Nothing about this situation is funny. Show some sympathy."

"Well, the incubus certainly has stamina, doesn't he? Keeping you up all night long, what a legend, eh?"

"Can somebody make him shut up?" Serena scowled. "It's far too early in the morning to deal with his stupidity."

Pamela shook her head. "I very much doubt it, love."

"*Anyway*," Miss Wellbeloved interrupted, peering at them disapprovingly over the top of her glasses. "Listen to these notes, please."

They all shifted in their seats and waited patiently. Outside, the first hint of dawn glowed weakly over the distant fields, casting a feeble glow over the surrounding empty seats. Kester rubbed his eyes and stifled a yawn.

"Right," Miss Wellbeloved continued. "Firstly, I need to let you know something important." She glanced at Ribero. "Larry Higgins will be there."

"Ah, the Higgins," Ribero spat, arms crossed. "Hopefully, he may have an accident on the way in, eh? Maybe something nice and terminal."

"I'll pretend I didn't hear that. Luke and Dimitri will be there too."

"Who else?" Pamela asked as she rifled through her bag. Finally, she pulled out something wrapped in foil, which turned out to be a pile of huge cheese sandwiches. Kester's stomach rumbled in response.

"Curtis Philpot will be present, of course," Miss Wellbeloved said. "Lord Bernard Nutcombe will be joining by conference call too, so you all need to be on your best behaviour."

"That's the Minister of the Supernatural, isn't it?" Kester said. He'd heard the man mentioned before, usually with a term of abuse added at the start or end of his name.

"Yep, good old bog-brush Nutcombe," Mike confirmed with a dramatic roll of the eyes. "Can't stand the man. On the few occasions I've had the misfortune to talk to him, I've thought he was a complete and utter—"

"—and two Infinite Enterprises officials have also been assigned the case," Miss Wellbeloved interrupted. "Mr Ian Kingdom-Green and Mr Cardigan Cummings, to be precise. I've never met them, but I've heard they're the best of the best."

Kester raised an eyebrow. "Cardigan? Is that a name?"

"Absolutely," Miss Wellbeloved confirmed. "I believe the gentleman in question has West Indian roots."

"I've heard them mentioned before." Mike tapped his leg thoughtfully. "Where have I heard their names?"

"Ghost-Con," Serena replied. "They won the prize for 'Best Investigative work,' remember?"

"And the year before, I believe," Miss Wellbeloved added. "So, we're in excellent company."

"And there's even more opportunity for us to look crap by comparison," Mike said gloomily. He folded his arms. "It's going to be a bloody disaster."

"Now, now, less negativity, please," Miss Wellbeloved said,

returning to her notes. "There are some other items on the proposed agenda. Firstly, the briefing will contain some highly sensitive information, especially regarding the daemon Hrschni." She caught sight of Kester's blank stare and quickly clarified, "the late Billy Dagger."

"Yes, this is private stuff that normally even people like me don't get to know, okay?" Ribero said with a severe waggle of the finger. "Very top-secret stuff. You tell others, and—" He sliced his fingers across his neck, complete with enthusiastic sound-effect. "*No more you.* Get it?"

"Oh, come on," Mike scoffed. "This isn't the dark ages. They're not going to murder us because—"

Ribero repeated the neck-slicing action, then nodded meaningfully. "Don't underestimate how far people will go to protect secrets, Mike."

Mike rolled his eyes but remained silent.

"Anyway." Miss Wellbeloved coughed significantly, flicking back through her notes. "This is going to be a collaborative effort, and as a result, we may have to go to London quite a bit. There may be other travel requirements too, but don't worry, Curtis Philpot has said he'll pay travel expenses in full prior to booking."

"Anything else?" Serena asked, examining her nails.

"Yes. There are various files that Infinite Enterprises will be sharing with us today. Particularly on Hrschni—"

"Can we just call him Billy Dagger?" Mike asked with a plaintive look. "I'm not ready to think of him as a daemon just yet."

"If that suits you better, that's absolutely fine."

"How come Infinite Enterprises have the files on Billy Dagger then?" Kester was curious to find out more about how it all worked. Even though he'd been with the agency for a few months, there was still a lot that baffled him.

Ribero cleared his throat. "They hold all the archives, you see? Every file on every spirit—you'll find it there."

"Not to mention every file about us," Mike said darkly. "And plenty of information you probably wish they didn't know about you."

"Really? So there's a file on me?" Kester swallowed. He didn't much like the thought of that.

"Of course there is, boy!" Ribero nodded imperiously, then gestured at Pamela. "I see you have a spare cheese sandwich there. May I?"

"You've just had a croissant!" Pamela placed a protective hand across her remaining sandwich. "And I'm ever so hungry."

"But I am ever so much your boss, right? So I need the food more than you. Your cheddar cheese is smelling very nice."

Pamela tutted and handed over the sandwich. "Doesn't seem very fair."

"Life isn't fair," Ribero declared, biting into the bread with a grin. "This is very good. Thank you."

"Hang on," Kester said as he shuffled around in his seat. "This file about me, the one at Infinite Enterprises. What sort of information does it contain, exactly?"

"Oh, just the juicy stuff." Mike gave him a leery grin. "All the stuff you want to keep private, basically."

Miss Wellbeloved reached across and patted Kester on the arm. "Don't panic, Kester. It's nothing too private. Just details about your role in the agency, your specialist skills, the cases you've worked on so far. That kind of thing."

Serena sniggered. "You look a bit worried, Kester. What have you been getting up to that you don't want people to know about?"

Kester chose to ignore her and stared out of the window instead. The train ploughed on through field after field, past provincial towns and tiny villages. The sun finally rose, casting a mildewy light through the clouds and making everything seem far bleaker than before. *It's the one thing I dislike most about this time of year,* Kester thought, sighing. *Everything is always bleached of colour.*

Finally, the rolling fields gave way to a more urban landscape. Patchwork seas of rooftops gradually merged with concrete tower-blocks and glassy skyscrapers. More people boarded the train until they were surrounded by a swarm of suits and briefcases. The bustle and noise was infectious, and Kester found himself feeling perkier despite his tiredness. Apart from driving in occasionally with Mike on the spirit runs, he hadn't been to London for years. Even though he'd lived in Cambridge with his mother, he'd never felt much of an urge to visit the capital. They'd been far more comfortable staying at home in familiar, safe surroundings.

The train slowed, clacking along the rails towards the station. Mike and Serena, who had managed to both fall asleep leaning against one another, both woke simultaneously, then sprang apart like two dogs sprayed with water. Kester bit back a chuckle as he watched Serena hastily wipe a line of dribble from her lips.

"That was quick." Mike stretched out, taking up most of the space around him.

"It did not feel quick to me," Ribero grumbled, glowering at the woman standing next to him who kept bumping her handbag against his shoulder. "It felt like a very long, unpleasant journey."

"Well, we're here now," Miss Wellbeloved said as she popped her book into her bag. "We just need to catch the underground train to Holborn, then it's a short walk from there."

Finally, the train ground to a halt, the doors sliding open with a metallic whine to let them out. Kester fought to remain upright as the throng of commuters shuffled on either side, carrying him along in a tidal wave of motion. He looked over his shoulder and saw the others looking similarly disgruntled.

"Hang on, Kester, I've got your tube ticket," Miss Wellbeloved called out, as she brandished the tickets in the air, like a flamenco dancer waving a fan. "You can't get to the underground without it."

Kester wrestled a path back to the others and tried to ignore the swearing and nudging from the city workers as he did so. He felt uncomfortably out of place, and the continual pressure of bodies around him made him hot and bothered.

They passed through the ticket gate as a group, then headed to the underground station, which was no less crowded. In fact, if anything, it was worse: stuffy, stale, dingy, and crammed to the brim with commuters and tourists. After waiting for ages for a train with enough room on it to squeeze all of them on, they finally departed and whizzed through the black subterranean tunnels.

"Are we late?" Ribero asked as he watched Miss Wellbeloved check her watch for the tenth time in five minutes.

She shook her head. "Not quite yet. Come on, this is our stop."

After another flap with the tickets, they finally emerged outside again and stood on the street corner, taking in the cityscape in front of them. Cars and double-decker buses zipped up and down the road in front of them, and tall, neo-classical buildings formed a solid wall of impassive grandeur and severity.

"Which way do we bloody well go?" Mike shouted as he peered up and down the street.

"Fortunately, I looked it up last night," Miss Wellbeloved retorted. Taking Ribero's arm and nodding at the others, she pointed to their right. "Come on, it's only a short walk this way."

They scurried down the busy pavements. Kester still found it difficult to adjust to the seething masses of people, not to mention the noise and the musty smell of car-fumes. He found himself suddenly missing the peace of Exeter with its surrounding greenery and sleepy ambiance. *I think it's safe to say I could never survive in a city like this,* he thought as he fought to keep up with the others.

"There it is," Miss Wellbeloved announced. She paused and pointed ahead. "See?"

Kester looked up. Then up a little bit more. The vast, glass-fronted offices of Infinite Enterprises towered above them, dwarfing the surrounding buildings. He gawped. On the occasions that he'd driven into London with Mike on a spirit run, they'd always dropped the spirits round the back. The front was far more intimidating, which was saying something.

"Gosh, it's a bit . . . *fancy,* isn't it?"

Miss Wellbeloved nodded. "They are the largest supernatural agency in the country, hence the ostentatious building," she said.

"Shall we? We're running the risk of being late."

They marched up to the entrance, which was obscured by frosted glass. A huge metal sign, complete with gold frame, announced the company's name.

"How come they choose to be so conspicuous when they're a supernatural agency?" Kester asked as Ribero pressed the intercom button.

"Sometimes, the best place to hide is in full view of everyone else," Miss Wellbeloved said. "People just presume Infinite Enterprises is a standard London business."

"And," Mike added, "if anyone does check online, they have a false business website. The government's created fake business details for them on all the other major sites too."

Ribero pressed his ear to the intercom, frowning. "Hello? It is Dr Ribero and his agency." He paused, then shrugged. "I think that did the trick, yes?"

They waited. A quiet buzz followed, then the glass door slid open, releasing a welcome burst of central heating. Miss Wellbeloved raised an eyebrow at the others, then stepped into the building.

"Whoa," Kester exclaimed as the door slid shut behind them. He hadn't meant to express himself quite so loudly, but the interior had taken him by surprise. If the outside had been grand, the inside was even more imposing. Polished onyx floors ran the entire length of the endless reception area, and soaring metal pillars supported the high ceilings above. At the end of the room, a receptionist peered at them disapprovingly over his computer screen.

"Hello there," Miss Wellbeloved said as she smoothed her hair. "We're Dr Ribero's agency, here for the nine o'clock meet—"

"I know who you are," the receptionist interrupted, tapping at the keyboard that Kester noticed was made of glass and metal. "Could you please form a queue and take turns to press your finger on the glass pad? Then I'll present you with your passes."

Kester craned his neck over the top of his father's shoulder.

There was a black glass pad embedded in the desk, which Miss Well-beloved dutifully pressed her finger against. A red flash emerged briefly from underneath.

"Next, please."

"What is it?" Kester whispered to Pamela.

"Fingerprint scanner," she replied. "It's so only verified people can access the rooms within the building."

"Gosh, it's like a police station, isn't it?" he joked as he stepped forward to the glass pad.

"I assure you," the receptionist drawled, looking at him as though he were a particularly unpleasant form of cockroach, "what the police use is far inferior to our system."

"How?" Mike challenged as he leant over the desk. "What makes it so good, apart from the fact that you've used some posh, black glass?"

"It is 150 times more sensitive than standard police fingerprint equipment," the receptionist snapped. "Which means if your finger so much as tickles any surface, we'll know it's you, simply by scanning the area, in a millisecond."

Mike squidged his finger against the glass. "I think I've left a dirty mark," he said deliberately and gave the receptionist a wink. "You'll have to clean that now."

Miss Wellbeloved gave him a warning look. "How long will it take for our passes to be created?" she asked with an anxious glance at her watch.

The receptionist ducked down, then brought out a box of passes with a flourish. "Already prepared. Please clip them to your tops and have them clearly visible at all times." He watched them all fumble with their passes, then pointed to the line of lifts to their right. "You need to go to the 14th floor and turn left. The meeting is in the Flamel suite."

"Thank you very much," Ribero declared, patting his pass. "We'll head up straight away, right?"

"Make sure you use the fingerprint control as you pass through the door on the 14th floor," the receptionist continued with a hint of a smirk. "You'll then have thirty seconds to pass through."

"Why only thirty seconds?" Serena asked.

"Security." The receptionist gave a particularly nasty smile. "After that time, a series of lasers are emitted along the wall."

"And what do they do?" Pamela asked.

"They're not strong enough to kill you, but they'll singe your flesh enough to make you pass out, I should imagine."

"Oh lovely, some barbequed Mike, just what I fancy," Serena snipped as she strode towards the lifts.

"It'd go quite nicely with that sarcastic sauce of yours," Pamela quipped. The lift doors slid closed with a hiss, surrounding them in a perfect cube of gold-tinted mirrors.

Kester couldn't actually tell that they were moving until a minute bump announced their arrival. They stepped out into a seemingly endless corridor with a stern-looking walnut door to their left.

"Passes at the ready, everyone," Miss Wellbeloved said. She eyed the walls with suspicion, presumably to try to figure out where exactly the lasers were fired from. One by one, they pushed a finger against the reader, before passing hurriedly through into the next section of corridor. An enormous set of double-doors, complete with bronze plaque, announced their arrival at the Flamel suite.

"Here goes nothing," Mike muttered with a nervous titter.

Ribero waved a hand, then rapped at the door. "It *is* nothing," he said firmly. "Don't be intimidated by shiny signs and big doors, Mike."

A tinny voice shouted at them to enter. Ribero opened the door with a flourish. Kester peered over his shoulder, feeling both terrified and exhilarated in equal measures.

"I should have known you'd be late." Larry Higgins, who happened to be closest to the door, twisted round to look at them all with an expression of complete contempt. "Are you lot ever on time?"

Miss Wellbeloved tutted. "It's only a few minutes past nine o'clock," she said before smiling at the other people in the room. "Though we are sorry if we've held things up at all."

Curtis Philpot, who looked even spindlier than when they'd seen him last, shook his head. "It's not a problem," he declared, gesturing at the empty seats around the vast, glass table. "Commuting across London can be rotten at times."

Kester sat at the nearest seat, then he looked around the room with interest. Luke and Dimitri, who were sat seated either side of Larry, each gave him a wave, though Luke's was considerably friendlier.

"Why, fancy seeing you all here so soon!" Luke drawled, giving him a wink. He'd dressed in a sharp three-piece suit, though the cowboy neck-tie was still in place.

"I know, can you believe it?" Kester chuckled. He looked round at the remaining two people at the table: a towering man with a mane of flowing brown hair and the roundest eyes he'd ever seen, and a shaven-headed black man, who had roughly the same size and build as a barge. They made an intimidating pair.

"Now that we're all here, I'll get the formalities over," Curtis Philpot began, twisting at his tie. He gestured to the two unfamiliar men. "Allow me to introduce Cardigan Cummings and Ian King-dom-Green, who are unequivocally the finest spirit investigators at Infinite Enterprises."

The two men nodded and surveyed the others with interest. Kester couldn't take his eyes off the pair of them—one theatrical and grandiose, the other impassive and unreadable. He was looking forward to hearing them speak.

Philpot quickly introduced the others, then flicked on the projector screen and dimmed the lights. "Right, let's get down to it then," he began with a nervous twitch of his eyebrow. "We need to act quickly on this, and of course, it goes without saying that everything we discuss in this meeting is strictly confidential."

The others nodded. Kester bit his lip, hoping he wouldn't say anything stupid by mistake.

Philpot clicked his mouse, and the screen at once filled with a 3D image of a building, which Kester guessed was Infinite Enterprises.

"Firstly," Philpot started, pointing at the screen, "let's begin with where the building was broken into." He tapped again, and the screen zoomed in, rotating to focus on the subterranean levels. "For those of you who don't know, these are where the archives are kept. It's a vast underground warehouse of files, both on computer and on paper. We're talking files that go back centuries."

He tapped again, checking to see they were all following. The screen zoomed in once more, to a corner of the underground room. "This is where we discovered evidence of a break-in. In fact, it didn't look like the intruder had made any effort to conceal the fact they were there. Papers were scattered on the floor, and one of the computers showed evidence of a hacking attempt."

"Did they succeed in hacking into the computer?" Miss Wellbeloved asked.

Philpot shook his head. "They did not. However, most of the files are replicated in hard copy anyway. We merely use the computers as back-up and ease of access for Infinite Enterprise's staff."

"So, what did they take?" Higgins asked, brows furrowed with ape-like concentration.

"Nothing." Philpot shrugged. "We can only presume that the intruder found what they were looking for and memorised or photographed the details."

"And what were they looking for?" Dimitri asked. He leant forward, arms folded, as severe as a court judge.

Philpot shrugged. "We have no idea. The spirit in question must have rifled through the files with phenomenal speed."

"Anything picked up on CCTV?" Mike asked.

"No. But then, spirits are adept at invisibility, so in this case, CCTV is unlikely to help us."

"Have you tried slowing down the footage to see if you can detect movement?" Serena suggested. Dimitri looked across at her and smiled wolfishly. She blushed.

"Of course we have, madam." All eyes turned to the new speaker; the Infinite Enterprises investigator with the flowing hair, not to mention his impressively bushy beard. *Ian Kingdom-Green, I presume,* Kester thought, noting the man's mildly theatrical tone. *He looks like he'd be more comfortable in a Shakespeare play than working for a supernatural agency.*

Ian Kingdom-Green continued, acknowledging their attention with a nod of the head. "My colleague and I have scrutinised the CCTV footage in great detail, not to mention the files themselves and the point of entry."

Beside him, Cardigan Cummings nodded. "That is correct. We found very little to go on, I'm afraid."

Kester bit back a smile. *For such a muscular man, this Cardigan Cummings has a surprisingly gentle voice,* he thought. It made him feel far less intimidated by his rippling biceps, which looked as though they would burst out of his tight suit at any moment.

"What did you find?" Miss Wellbeloved nudged her glasses up her nose, eyes flitting from face to face.

Ian Kingdom-Green swept his hair over his shoulder. "My dear lady," he continued, "all we could surmise was that this was an *exceptionally* powerful spirit. No other creature could have broken through our defence systems."

"Any ideas who?" Ribero asked, eyeing him with undisguised wariness.

Philpot raised a hand. "We're reluctant to speculate without due evidence," he said. "However, given the recent events with the Thelemites, we wonder whether the intruder might have been Hrschni."

"You mean Billy Dagger," Mike corrected.

"Billy Dagger is merely the body Hrschni has been inhabiting for the last few decades," Philpot said sniffily. "Prior to that, he has inhabited some of the finest humans our world has ever known, such as—"

"Suffice to say, the daemon Hrschni cannot be thought of as mere mortal," Ian Kingdom-Green interrupted with a sweep of his arm, which nearly collided with Philpot's laptop. "He is of the genus daemon-demonichai, one of the most ancient known creatures of the spirit realm."

"Up until recently," Philpot continued, hand hovering protectively over his computer, "Hrschni was the model spirit resident. Always completed his permit applications on time, always attended registration, and submitted to regular checks. Then he pulled a rather dramatic stunt at a concert and went off the radar."

"Though the Thelemites have taken great pleasure in telling us that he's joined their forces on a permanent basis," Cardigan Cummings offered with a tight smile.

"We were at that gig," Kester piped up. "It was pretty dramatic, you're right."

Philpot studied him with interest. "That's useful," he said with a twitch of his nose. "Having eye-witnesses may yet come in handy. Who knows?"

"Yeah, he was my hero," Mike said glumly. "I can't believe he was a bloody daemon all along."

"Yes, Hrschni was *born* for the stage," Ian Kingdom-Green declared, eyes rolled heavenward. He clutched his chest, as though imploring his heart to calm its beating. "Such a performer. However, now we must accept, though it pains us to do so, that Hrschni's intentions are not as honourable as we once believed."

Cardigan Cummings nodded. "Put more simply, this daemon has turned, and he and the Thelemites are threatening not just Infinite Enterprises but everything this world holds dear."

Kester gulped. The two investigators from Infinite Enterprises were impressive, both in stature and in what they were saying. He felt particularly small and silly by comparison.

Philpot cleared his throat. "Shall we continue?" The others

nodded, and he clicked his laptop. At once, a photocopy of a letter appeared on the screen. Kester started to read, then realised what he was looking at.

"So this is the letter they sent you," Ribero declared, twiddling his moustache thoughtfully. "I now see why you are so alarmed."

Philpot nodded. "Quite. As you can see, this threatens not only Infinite Enterprises, but the world as a whole. It's deeply concerning."

Kester quickly scanned to the bottom.

> *Dear controllers of the spirit realm,*
>
> *Your time is nearing completion, and your reign in the sun almost ended. The door will be opened. The two worlds will come together again. Your season of control is about to cease.*
>
> *Them, elites and sceptics alike, will fall. Do what you will, for you cannot avoid the inevitable. Love is the law. The door will open again. Repeat into nothing. The door will be opened.*
>
> *We are coming. Be prepared.*
>
> *The Thelemites*

He shivered. The words had a hypnotic, incantatory quality, which somehow made them far more sinister.

"What does it all mean?" he asked as he looked at the others.

Philpot straightened his jacket. "It's typical daemon word-play, of course. They do love riddles and puzzles, it's like an obsession for them."

"And there are direct references to the Thelema cult," Larry Higgins added. "'Love is the law.' 'Do what you will,' all that nonsense."

Kester was confused. *I knew I should have looked up the Thelemites before coming to the meeting,* he thought. None of the others looked at all baffled, and he didn't want to reveal his stupidity by asking.

"The door mentioned in the letter is obviously a reference to the spirit realm," Miss Wellbeloved added, chewing her fingernail.

"We suspect that their target is actually the spirit door here at Infinite Enterprises," Philpot said. "Hence the warning to 'be prepared' at the end."

"But no-one can access the spirit door apart from official personnel, can they?" Serena asked as she tucked her hair anxiously behind one ear. "Your security measures are second-to-none."

"Or so you always tell everyone," Mike muttered ominously.

"Their security measures *are* second-to-none," Philpot asserted as he rapped at the table to emphasise the point. "However, Hrschni is possibly one of the most powerful daemons the world has ever seen. Which means—"

"Which means you're not quite sure *what* he's capable of," Higgins barked, leaning back in his chair with a look of disapproval. "Because you always presumed he'd behave himself."

Philpot glanced across at Cardigan Cummings and Ian Kingdom-Green, who both shrugged. "Yes, I suppose that's the truth of it," he conceded. "But in fairness, in the millennia that Hrschni has lived in our world, he's only ever demonstrated exemplary behaviour. We've got records dating back centuries that mark him as a respectable, decent daemon, with only love for humans."

"This is all most worrying," Miss Wellbeloved said. She massaged her temples and exhaled deeply.

"There's something bugging me about that letter," Mike interrupted. "I don't know what it is, but there's something not quite right about it."

"*Nothing* is right about it!" Higgins spat, giving Mike the most withering look he could muster. "It's meant to be deliberately puzzling, isn't it? That's what daemons are like!"

"What do you think is not right?" Dimitri asked as he carefully plucked a piece of fluff from his shirt sleeve.

Mike frowned. "I don't have a clue," he admitted eventually.

Higgins grunted, folding his hands against his chest. "Valuable input, as ever."

A series of beeps interrupted them. Philpot pressed a finger to his lips, silencing them all, then pressed his keyboard.

"Hello there, sir!" he said and gave the others a serious nod.

"Is everyone assembled?" The voice on the other end of the call sounded rather nasal, as though speaking with both nostrils stuffed with tissue.

"Yes, sir; everyone is present." Philpot pressed another button, and at once, a video image appeared on the projection screen. Kester studied the face with interest. *This must be the famous Lord Bernard Nutcombe,* he realised. For a Minister of the Supernatural, he didn't look particularly impressive. And Kester could now see why the others kept saying his hair was like a toilet-brush. Black bristles protruded not only from his head, but also from his chin, upper lip, and—from what Kester could tell—even his nose. In fact, he looked more like a polished chimney sweep than a politician.

"Ah yes." The minister eyed them all, then nodded. "A few new faces, I see. Shall we proceed? I have exactly nine minutes until my car arrives to take me to the House of Commons."

"I've given them the basic debriefing already, sir," Philpot said as he gestured to his laptop.

Nutcombe looked distinctly unimpressed, looming down on them like an enormous, floating deity. "As I'm sure you can imagine," he began, "this needs to be dealt with swiftly and effectively. We've also enlisted the help of a couple of other agencies in the country, notably Whilshin & Sons, who are gathering intelligence for us."

Philpot nodded. "The main Thelemite lodge is in London, so naturally, we've arranged for surveillance of the premises. However, Exeter is also a principal Thelemite lodge, which means that Dr Ribero and his team are ideally positioned to investigate there."

"The other principal lodges are at Cambridge, Oxford, and Whitby in North Yorkshire," Nutcombe continued, attempting to smooth his hair without any discernible success. The bristly strands simply bounced back the moment his fingers left their surface. "We may have to investigate activity in those locations too."

"We're looking for undercover information, which means investigative work." Philpot nodded upwards at Nutcombe's disembodied head on the screen. "This isn't an exercise in charging in like a bull in a china-shop. This needs to be subtle, swift, and effective."

Nutcombe cleared his throat. "We may need someone to infiltrate the Thelemites, though of course, this is dangerous."

"Allow me," Ian Kingdom-Green declared, hands clutched in excitement. "I am a master of many roles and can adopt any personality you choose. I'd infiltrate their meetings in the blink of an eye."

Nutcombe covered his mouth, suppressing what might have been a cough or sarcastic snigger. "Thank you, Mr Kingdom-Green. However, the suggestion is impractical. The Thelemites are already familiar with you, regardless of how magnificent your theatrical performance might be."

"Could I do it?" Luke asked, eyes shining. "I'd be happy to give it a shot, and I guess they wouldn't know my face."

Nutcombe peered down the length of his considerable nose. "And who might you be? The latest whipper-snapper to join our ranks?"

Luke looked at the others and winked. "You can call me Luke, sir."

Nutcombe squinted at the screen. "Very well, whatever your name is. We now know that the Thelemites have had access to our files, thanks to the break-in. Which means they may well be familiar with you too. That's the problem, we have no idea how much they know about us."

"Perhaps your girlfriend could do the honours," Serena said, pointing at Kester.

Kester glared. "She absolutely could not," he snapped. "She's already been kidnapped by them; I'm not having her put in any more danger."

Nutcombe leaned forward, suddenly looking more interested. "What's this?"

"Kester's girlfriend was a member of the Thelemites until very recently," Serena said, ignoring Kester's furious stare. "She might be able to help."

"Well now, that *is* interesting," Nutcombe said as he stroked his chin. He turned and fixed his gaze on Kester. "Is this correct?"

Kester reddened. "Well, yes, but—"

"We'll have to interview her, see what we can learn about the organisation's current practices," Nutcombe said, eyes boring into Kester's own.

"No, you absolutely cannot do that," he blurted. The others stared, mouths open in collective horror. Across the table, Ribero flapped his hands urgently, which Kester ignored.

Nutcombe raised an eyebrow. "Why not? Presumably, the young lady has invaluable information—information that may assist with this vitally-important investigation."

Miss Wellbeloved raised a hand. "If I might interrupt," she said with an imperceptible nod in Kester's direction, "the young lady in question was actually held captive by the Thelemites, if only for a short period of time."

"And they threatened her!" Kester spluttered. "They said if she spoke a word about what she'd learned from them, they'd hurt her."

"They didn't actually say that in so many words," Miss Wellbeloved said carefully, glancing in Kester's direction. "But they certainly made it very clear that she would suffer in some way if she spoke out about them."

"Well," Nutcombe said, leaning forward. "I can guarantee our best men would protect her. This is too important a lead to simply let go, I'm afraid. Now," he continued and nodded down at Philpot. "If you'd like to distribute the dossiers and make arrangements for the initial investigations? I'll leave it in your capable hands, Curtis."

"Absolutely," Philpot flustered. He reached into his satchel and withdrew an enormous pile of folders. They sat in front of him, a formidable wall of text to be waded through.

Nutcombe nodded with satisfaction. "Excellent. I see you're well prepared, as ever. Ladies and gentlemen, it's been a pleasure meeting you all. I trust you'll resolve this matter with utmost speed and professionalism."

Higgins sidled a glance in Ribero's direction and sneered. Ribero narrowed his eyes.

The screen went blank. Philpot closed the laptop, then distributed the folders to the team leaders. "Our first task," he began, "is to work out their motivation. What's caused the Thelemites to behave like this, after all this time? Why now?"

"They've been getting more radical for some time," Miss Wellbeloved added with a worried look.

Philpot nodded significantly. "Yes. You'd know all about that. I know about your family's connections to the organisation."

Ian Kingdom-Green and Cardigan Cummings looked at one another, then over at Miss Wellbeloved, who blushed.

"Second task," Philpot continued, bustling his laptop back into his bag as he spoke, "is to work out what they plan to do. And how they plan to do it. We'll be using the Infinite Enterprises intranet to stay in touch from now on, as it's far more secure than standard emailing. All other cases are low priority until this one is solved. Understood?"

They all nodded. Through the tinted glass, Kester saw the winter sun duck behind a cloud, like a child hiding. He felt a sudden sense of foreboding. *This isn't going to be an easy case,* he thought, taking in Miss Wellbeloved's look of barely-concealed panic. He glanced over to Serena and frowned. *And thanks to her, I've got to worry about Anya's safety too.*

He sighed. It was going to be a long, difficult few weeks. He could tell.

Chapter 7: Nosing Through Phones

The days that followed the meeting in London were hectic, to say the least. The phone rang frequently, and Miss Wellbeloved patiently fielded suggestions, requests, and urgent demands from Infinite Enterprises, even at the most inconvenient times. Meanwhile, the weather grew colder, and the high street windows began to fill with tinsel, fairy-lights, and all the other trappings of the festive season. It was only six weeks until Christmas, but none of them felt able to get into the spirit of things, not even Pamela, who was usually the first to seize the chance for a celebration.

Infinite Enterprises had sent through the login for their intranet, which allowed them unrestricted access to the vast underground archives. No-one seemed particularly excited about this apart from Kester, who spent the best part of three hours rifling through old files.

It was fascinating to browse the records of daemons on the system. They were all, without exception, residing in the bodies of famous or wealthy humans; and all were known for their kindness, generosity, and decency. Kester gasped as he perused their statistics. All the daemons had "age unknown" written in their files, but their estimated dates of arrival in the human realm were formidable. Hrschni's first human possession was recorded in 1055 in Winchester, though the file suggested he'd been around many centuries before that. It made Kester dizzy to think about it. *He's been here thousands of years,* he realised, thinking back to the energetic performance he'd seen from Hrschni while he was masquerading as Billy Dagger. *Who would have guessed?*

He'd also read through his own file, though he had respectfully resisted the urge to nose through the rest of his team's. In contrast to Hrschni, the information on him was short and concise, stating his age, education, previous address, and specialist skills. He almost laughed out loud when he noted they'd listed him as a "spirit-door opener." *If only they knew how unreliable I am at doing it,* he thought, remembering how he'd only managed it recently after being chased by a large, angry bull.

A hand slammed a piece of paper onto Kester's makeshift desk, startling him. He looked up from his laptop to see Ribero peering down at him, eyes twinkling mischievously.

"Stop reading about yourself, you vain boy, and do some real work."

Kester hastily shut down his file. "It was research," he protested.

Ribero jabbed at the paper. "This is your work now. Ian Kingdom-Kong has just phoned—"

"Kingdom-Green," Kester corrected automatically.

"Whatever. The big, hairy, ape goon. He wants us to work on deciphering the letter, okay?"

Kester sighed and glanced down at the print-out. "It's the letter that the Thelemites sent Infinite Enterprises."

Ribero launched into a round of applause, sarcastic expression firmly in place. "Bravo, genius child!" he shouted. "Now, get on with it. See what you can work out; you are good with puzzles like this. Pamela and Mike are going to help you."

Mike looked up from his desk. "Why me?"

"Because you are doing the silly thing with wires and metal again, not doing any proper work. Now is the time to use your brain."

Mike muttered darkly and threw his screwdriver down. "I'm not sure what help I'll be."

Ribero scoffed. "Nor me. But at least you will be earning your money rather than playing with tin cans, yes?"

Pamela pushed her chair over the carpet, then plunked herself down beside Kester. "I do like doing things like this," she said with a beatific grin. "It's like doing a good crossword in the morning, isn't it? Gets the juices flowing."

"Enough about the juices," Ribero barked before stalking back towards his office. "But Serena, that reminds me. A coffee, please."

Serena scowled, rapping her fingernails on the desk. "Get Pamela to do it, it's her job."

"It certainly isn't, young lady!" Pamela pointed at the kitchen. "Go on, off your bum."

"Yeah, get off your bum," Kester echoed darkly. He still hadn't forgiven her for mentioning Anya in the meeting the other day. Not that Serena seemed at all bothered. *She doesn't even seem to notice when I'm angry at her,* he thought as he watched her storm to the store cupboard to boil the kettle. *It's like water off a very skinny, mean duck's back.*

Mike dragged his chair across the floor, landing next to Kester's desk like a falling boulder. "Come on then," he said gloomily. "Let's get this over and done with."

"At least it a short letter," Pamela said.

Kester moved his laptop to one side and spread the paper neatly across the desk.

"'Dear controllers of the spirit realm,'" he read aloud. "'Your time is nearing completion, and your reign in the sun almost ended. The door will be opened. The two worlds will come together again. Your season of control is about to cease.'"

"Weird stuff, isn't it?" Pamela breathed. "Very esoteric."

Kester cleared his throat and continued. "'Them, elites and sceptics alike, will fall. Do what you will, for you cannot avoid the inevitable. Love is the law. The door will open again. Repeat into nothing. The door will be opened.'"

"And let's not forget that last, dramatic line," Mike added with a fierce nod at the paper.

"'We are coming,'" Kester concluded. He looked at them both, then added, "'Be prepared.'"

"Signed, 'The Thelemites,'" Pamela finished. She rolled back in her chair and folded her hands across her knitted cardigan. "What do you make of all that, eh?"

Mike yawned. "Well," he began, looking yearningly back at his desk. "The Thelemite phrases are pretty clear, aren't they?"

"What are the Thelemite phrases?" Kester asked.

"You were told to read up on the Thelemites, Kester," Miss Wellbeloved reprimanded from her desk without looking up from her computer screen. "If you had done so, you would have known this important information already."

Pamela gave him a wink. "It's all pretty straightforward," she explained, and pointed at two sections of the letter. "*Do what you will* is a famous tenet of Thelema. So is *love is the law.*"

Kester scratched his head. "Yep, that still doesn't make any sense to me."

"Oh lordy, lordy," Serena groaned from across the room. "Kester, do you need literally *everything* explained to you? It's like working with a toddler."

"You're the one who has the tantrums," Kester muttered as he delivered her the most piercing glare he could muster. "Not to mention the one who uses horrible playground tactics when we're in important meetings."

"Oh, don't start wittering on about your girlfriend again," Serena drawled, clearly hitting her stride. "I only said that she'd been caught up with the Thelemites, which is true . . ."

"Let's just focus on this letter for now, shall we?" Pamela interrupted. "Okay, Kester. Crash course in Thelema. Are you ready?"

"Probably not," Kester said, still glowering across the room. Serena smiled smugly and resumed tapping on her keyboard.

"Everyone thinks Aleister Crowley invented Thelema in the 1900s," Pamela began. "Have you heard of Aleister Crowley?"

Kester pondered. "Wasn't he a devil-worshipper or something?"

He heard the sound of Miss Wellbeloved slapping her forehead in horror, and he didn't dare look in her direction.

Pamela chuckled. "No, not really. Aleister Crowley was a bit of a show-off, and he brought Thelema to public attention. But he didn't invent it. Actually, the Thelemites have been around for centuries. No-one knows how long. They were a secret society, and they believed in *true will.*"

"True will?" Kester frowned. "What do you mean?"

"Not just following desires and whims," Pamela carried on, rapping an emphatic fist on the table. "They believed that everyone had a calling or goal in life. That was the *true will.* So 'do what you will' refers to that. Refusing to stray from the path of your true destiny, if that makes sense."

"Sort of," Kester replied. He already felt a little confused. "So, what does 'love is the law' mean?"

"That's what they're governed by," Mike said. "They believe that love of all creatures, human and spirit, should guide us in our actions."

Kester pondered. "That sounds quite nice," he concluded with a glance across at Miss Wellbeloved, whose expression remained inscrutable.

"Yes, but they believe that love should govern our approach to the spirit world," Pamela clarified. "They've never liked the idea of controlling spirit access, and, in the past, many Thelemites have voiced disapproval about the government deporting spirits."

"I should also like to add," Miss Wellbeloved interrupted wryly, "that many *were not* disapproving—many understood the need for spirit migration control. Remember, my own father and grandfather were both members of the Thelemites."

"Yeah, and your dad chose to leave because he felt they were getting a bit too heavy," Mike reminded her.

Miss Wellbeloved tutted and returned to her computer screen.

"What do you think it means about the 'reign in the sun'?" Kester asked, re-reading the letter. "Is that something meaningful too?"

"Probably something to do with Nuit," Serena chimed in.

Mike sighed. "Look smart-arse, if you're so keen to show off your knowledge, why don't you just come over here and join in?"

"Well, if you're struggling already, of course I'd be happy to help," she replied and started to drag her chair across the room. Mike slumped against on the desk, causing the legs to buckle. Fortunately, Kester just managed to catch it before the entire thing collapsed to the floor again.

Serena peered over the letter, then she placed it back on the table with a deliberate nod. "As I was saying," she continued, "Nuit is the Ancient Egyptian goddess of the sky; particularly the night, as she's often depicted as being covered in stars. She's very important to the Thelemites."

"How do you know all this?" Mike asked suspiciously.

"Because I listened to the teachers at the SSFE, rather than wasting my education seeing how many private parts I could doodle on the textbooks," she replied with a sneer.

"So, you think that this is their way of saying 'night is coming,' then?" Pamela suggested, scratching her head with a pencil and dislodging most of her bun in the process.

Serena shrugged. "Could be. It's definitely a seriously-worded warning, I'd say."

"Or it could be about sun-worship," Miss Wellbeloved added. "Remember, the sun used to play an integral role in opening permanent spirit-doors, if the old myths are to be believed."

"Which they're probably not," Serena replied.

"What other unpleasant warnings are in there, then?" Mike scooped up the letter, peering anxiously at the words.

"The bit about the door opening is fairly obvious," Serena continued. "It's a threat to open a spirit door and let all the spirits roam free."

"Yes, but it doesn't give any clues about *how* they're planning to open it, does it?" Pamela pointed out.

"It's got to be the door at Infinite Enterprises," Serena said. "After all, why else would they break in there? Why else would they send this letter?"

"It does make sense," Kester said dubiously. "But isn't it a bit *obvious?*"

"What do you mean?" Serena snapped.

"Well, it's a bit unsubtle, isn't it? It's almost like that's what they *want* everyone to think."

Serena laughed. "I think you're reading too much into it."

"What about this bit, then?" Pamela said as she circled a section of the letter. "'Them, elites and sceptics alike'? That's a weird phrase, if ever I heard one."

"Yes, it is a bit," Serena admitted with a frown.

Kester pondered. "Is it referring to elite people who run the spirit agencies, perhaps?"

Pamela rested her head in her hands. "That doesn't sound right." She picked up the letter and frowned. "Why those words? They seem clunky, given the style of the rest of the letter. 'Them, elites and sceptics alike.' It's very inelegant, isn't it?"

Mike suddenly clicked his fingers, drawing all eyes to him. "Say that again," he commanded.

Pamela looked baffled. "Which bit? About it being inelegant?"

"No, no." Mike perused the letter quickly, then stabbed the paper hard. "*That bit.* 'Them, elites and sceptics.' That's it!" He looked up at the others, eyes shining. "I *knew* it sounded wrong!"

"What are you wittering on about?" Serena asked with a look of irritation and amusement.

"'Them, elites of truth'!" Mike shouted. He prodded Kester hard on the arm. "Come on, mate, you know it! 'Them, elites of truth'!"

Kester withdrew his arm to prevent another barrage of jabs. "I have no idea what you're talking about," he answered. "What's that supposed to mean?"

Mike grunted with frustration, then clicked his fingers in the direction of Kester's laptop. "Here, pass me that. I'll show you."

"Oh lord, what's he up to now?" Serena muttered.

Mike opened the internet browser and clicked through to YouTube. "You'll see," he said with a wink.

As usual, the internet was painfully slow to load. Kester watched with interest as Mike typed in "Billy Dagger," followed by "Open Your Eyes."

"I know that song," he said. "That's one of his biggest hits, isn't it?"

Mike rolled his eyes. "Of course it is." The video appeared on the screen, and he grinned with satisfaction. "Right, you lot. Listen to this."

He clicked on the play button. Instantly, the room was filled with pounding rock guitars and manic drumming, which made Miss Wellbeloved wince and bury herself even further into her seat.

"What are we listening for?" Serena asked, her sarcasm giving way to curiosity.

Billy Dagger started to sing, and Mike held a finger to his lips, nodding at the screen.

> *Hold out your hand, little boy.*
> *Touch the great unknown, little boy.*
> *I confess, I spit Maria,*
> *I spurn your church,*
> *I prefer them, elites of truth.*

"Oh!" Pamela squealed, nearly falling off her seat in excitement.

"I heard it!"

Mike pressed pause and nodded with satisfaction. "Bit of a coincidence, eh?" He beamed at the others. "I *knew* there was something about that letter that was bugging me."

Kester smiled. "Nice one, Mike. So we've got a connection to Billy Dagger. 'Them, elites.'"

"I'm still not sure what the relevance is, though," Pamela said. "Hey, Jennifer, did you hear that?"

Miss Wellbeloved grimaced. "I couldn't not hear it," she said. "It's rather loud, isn't it?" She caught the expressions on the others' faces and laughed. "I know, you're referring to the lyrics. That's an interesting connection. Are there any others in the letter?"

The rest of the team hastily looked down and scanned the words. Kester and Mike spotted it at the same time.

"'Repeat into nothing,'" they both whispered, looking at each other with wide eyes.

Pamela grinned. "Another Billy Dagger lyric?"

"It was in his last song, wasn't it?" Kester said, feeling rather breathless.

Mike nodded. "It certainly was. It's even in the last line, isn't it? Where he sings 'repeat into, repeat into, repeat into,' before finishing with the word 'chaos'?"

Serena stuck her fingers in her ears. "Please don't sing again, Mike. You sound like someone being throttled."

"But this proves it, doesn't it?" Pamela said, flapping her hands with excitement, like an oversized duck attempting to take off. "This letter is obviously trying to tell us that Billy Dagger is heavily involved or that he wrote it himself."

"You mean Hrschni," Miss Wellbeloved corrected. "Let's not forget, he's not a rock-star anymore."

Kester rubbed his chin thoughtfully. "What are they *really* trying to tell us, though? That's the big question."

"What do you mean?" Mike replied. "It's their coded, pompous way of announcing that they've got Billy Dagger working with them, that's all." He glanced at Miss Wellbeloved. "Sorry, Hrschni. I'll remember eventually, I promise."

Kester frowned. *Is it?* he thought. He personally disagreed, especially as the Thelemites had already told the world that Hrschni had joined their ranks. Why would they bother to announce it again, especially in such a cryptic way? He strongly suspected that they were missing something.

"I'm not convinced," he said eventually. "But maybe you're right. Maybe I'm reading too much into it."

Mike nodded. "Yeah. You have a habit of doing that, mate."

Miss Wellbeloved shrugged. "He also has a habit of being correct, though, doesn't he?"

"What about the meaning of the words themselves?" Kester asked. "'Repeat into nothing.' Why put that in the letter? It must mean something, doesn't it? What are they planning to repeat?"

"It's just the lyrics to the song," Mike insisted. "I don't think there's anything more to it." He gestured to the phone. "Shall we give the others a call, let them know what we've found out?"

"I'll do it later," Miss Wellbeloved said, smothering a yawn behind her hand. "I've got to provide them with an update today, anyway." She clicked her fingers in Kester's direction. "That reminds me. Curtis Philpot was asking about Anya again, and when she'd be happy to attend a formal interview." She caught sight of Kester's expression and flinched. "I know you don't want to, but Infinite Enterprises can't let go of inside information like this."

Kester folded his arms. "I'm not going to ask her. It's not right."

Mike let out a low whistle. "Your funeral, mate. Don't fancy being in your shoes when that gets back to Bernard Nutcombe."

"Yeah, he'll get really angry," Serena added, looking anxious.

"I really don't care," Kester said. "It's not right, so I'm not asking her." He looked up and noticed his father leaning against his office door, watching with interest.

"I thought you would say that," Ribero said. He puckered his lips around his cigarette holder and inhaled deeply. "You are a boy with integrity, and I respect this, yes?"

Kester beamed. "Thank you! I'm glad someone understands. There's no way I'm going to—"

"—which is why I called the young lady and asked her myself," Ribero concluded with a wolfish grin.

"What?" Kester slammed his hand on the desk, which completely buckled, trapping four pairs of knees between its plastic sides. The others bellowed with pain, then glared at Kester, who completely ignored them.

"What do you mean, you called her?" Kester pushed his chair back, letting the desk flop to the floor with a crash. "You don't even have her number!"

"I found it on your phone yesterday," Ribero replied with a wink. "You left it on your desk when you went to buy a sandwich."

"You nosed through my phone?" Kester could feel his face getting redder.

Ribero waved his cigarette dismissively in the air. "Ah, I didn't read your messages," he said. "So, any naughty business between you and your woman is still a secret."

Serena visibly shuddered.

"You had absolutely no right to snoop through my—"

"What did she say?" Miss Wellbeloved interrupted.

Ribero scratched his ear. "Well," he began slowly, eyes raised to the ceiling, "to begin with, she was not so happy. But then, when I explained, she accepted that it was the right thing to do. She is quite a strange girl, yes? Odd to talk to."

Kester stood up. Normally, he was a placid person. It took *a lot* to make him angry. However, the thought of his father trawling gleefully through his phone whilst he was out, not to mention phoning Anya and forcing her to do this risky interview, was more than he could bear. Blinking with rage, he stormed across the room and jabbed a finger directly into Ribero's chest.

"How dare you?" he shouted, pushing his glasses up his nose. "That was totally unacceptable, and you've placed Anya in real danger."

Ribero frowned. "I don't think that is the case at all. Infinite Enterprises have said they will take all measures to keep her safe . . ."

Kester shook his head. "You know as well as I do that we're dealing with a very old, very powerful daemon here. If Hrschni can break into Infinite Enterprises, he can sure as hell break into Anya's house. Christ, even a blind person could break in; it wouldn't be difficult. There's only a rusty, old lock on the door."

"Okay, okay," Ribero said placatingly as he placed a hand on Kester's shoulder. "I understand why you are cross. But you see how important it is to the case? She can give us valuable information!"

"It wasn't your place to ask her!"

"And it is not your place to stand in the way of our work!"

"I'd rather stop your work than have my girlfriend murdered!"

Miss Wellbeloved clapped her hands. "Please! Calm down, both of you!"

Kester glared at them all, stormed to the door, and grabbed his jacket. "I'm leaving," he snapped. "It's nearly home-time anyway, but if you want to dock it from my pay, feel free."

Ribero paced after him. "Look, Kester, do not go off sulking. It is not the right way to—"

Sulking? Kester thought, feeling even angrier than before. *Sulking?!* He scurried to his collapsed desk and scooped his laptop and phone from the floor. "Just in case you were thinking of looking through my private things again," he growled, stuffing them into his satchel. The others stared in horror as he yanked open the door and stalked out.

It was only when he was out in the car-park, shivering with cold and indignation, that he started to feel slightly ridiculous. *Perhaps that wasn't the best way to deal with it,* he thought, glancing back up at the darkened windows of the office. It was most unlike him to explode like that, but then, his father *had* done something completely unacceptable. Finally, he pulled out his phone, hoping a chat with Anya might settle him.

Thankfully, she answered after a few rings.

"Hello?"

Kester sighed, nimbly skipping around an icy puddle and down the narrow alleyway. "I'm so sorry, Anya. My dad just told me what he'd done. You must be furious with me."

A soft chuckle tickled his ear. "No, I'm not angry with you, Kester. Your father told me that you had nothing to do with it. He was very nice about you."

Kester felt vaguely mollified. He pulled his collar up around his neck and strode on to the high street, making sure to give the street performers a wide berth. The nearest man, dressed as a Christmas elf, threw a set of rings into the air, juggling until they became a blur. The audience cheered, moving aside to let Kester through.

"What else did my dad say?" he continued once the noise of the crowd had subsided.

"He explained why it is so important." She paused. "I understand, Kester."

"Well, I bloody don't!" he spluttered. "I'm fuming about it, actually. Dad had no right to ask you to do it, especially as it puts you in danger."

"He said that I'd be well protected."

Kester sighed. From the neighbouring shop window, a glitzy snowman whirled in giddy circles. "Well," he concluded, "we need to find out what level of protection you'll be offered before you say a word to anyone. I won't have you put in peril."

Anya giggled. "Your father recommended that I go and stay at your house for a while."

The sly old dog, Kester thought, exasperated yet rather grateful at the same time. "You're more than welcome to do so," he replied in what he hoped was his least suggestive voice. "I'll sleep on the sofa, of course."

"Well, shall I do that then? Shall I come and stay with you?"

Kester beamed, stifling his smile with a cough. "Yes, why not? It'll be nice having you around."

"Thank you. Tonight, then?"

He spluttered. "Er, yes. Crikey." *It's okay, you can handle this,* he told himself firmly, nearly walking into a bench as he did so. "I've not got any food in, though," he continued. "Pineapple raided the fridge again last night and stole pretty much everything I'd bought from the supermarket."

"We'll sort something out," Anya replied. "Can I bring Thor?"

Oh no, not the rat-ferret that likes humping my leg, Kester thought, remembering the serpentine little creature, not to mention the unsavoury hip thrusts it had performed against his ankle when they'd last met. He bit back a sigh and replied, "Yes, of course." He'd have to get in the habit of tucking his trousers firmly into his socks. *Maybe I can get away with spraying it with pepper spray when Anya isn't looking?* he wondered.

After hanging up, he felt a little brighter. *Who knows?* he thought, neatly skipping across the road. *Perhaps Dad wasn't wrong to call Anya after all. It certainly wasn't a bad move telling her she could stay at mine.*

He glanced at the passing shop window and caught sight of his paunch, the thick glasses on his nose, and his hair wafting in the breeze like a tentative sandstorm. It wasn't a great look. His heart sank a little, as it so often did when confronted with his own reflection.

As long as I don't make a prat of myself, he concluded, deliberately looking away. *That's not too much to ask, is it?*

Chapter 8: Anya's Visit

Kester lit a candle. He positioned it on the mantelpiece, moved it an inch to the left, then stepped back to survey the effect.

His heart sank. The candle-light bounced off the rusty metal of the wall-mounted heater, and looked embarrassingly small, with only a plastic cat ornament that Daisy had picked up in Japan to keep it company. *Utterly pathetic,* he thought. *Could I look as though I'm trying any harder?*

A low whistle diverted his attention. Pineapple leant against the doorframe, wearing a tight lemon-coloured vest, jeans with a crotch to the kneecaps, and a grin of idiotic proportions.

"You impressing the lady tonight?" A lavish wink accompanied the smirk. "Hoping to get some tender loving, right?"

Kester reddened. "Absolutely not," he scowled, then pinched the candle out. A stream of smoke plumed upwards to join the already-stained ceiling. "I was just trying to make the place feel a bit warmer, that's all."

Pineapple perched on the edge of the sofa and delivered a

knowing nod. "Man, I feel you. If you don't want her to be an ice-maiden, you've got to get her heated, that's right."

"Er, yes," Kester replied uncertainly. He didn't have a clue what Pineapple was talking about most of the time. "Are you going out this evening?" he added hopefully. The last thing he needed, when trying to have a nice conversation with Anya, was an imbecilic idiot with a top-knot joining them.

Pineapple ignored him. "So, she's going to be staying for a while, that right, Kes?"

Kester bristled. He hated it when people abbreviated his name. "Yes," he confirmed. "She's having a few problems with . . . with a few things. So she needs to come somewhere safe."

"Yeah, safe and *warm.*" Pineapple wrapped his arms around himself and mimed some sort of elaborate hug, which looked pretty indecent from where Kester was standing. "And to answer your question, me and Daisy are hitting the club scene, meeting with people, feeling the vibes." He spun round, finger suspended in the air like a hoverfly. "Hey, you and the lady should come with us, yeah? Get spiritually connected, man."

Kester moved the candle over to the coffee table, frowned, then put it back on the mantlepiece. "That's okay. We're alright for spiritual connection at the moment, thanks."

A familiar shock of mousey hair, tamed into two backcombed bunches, appeared round the door, followed by Daisy's beaming face. Kester was disturbed to see that she was wearing a lurid Lurex dress, which was printed with bunnies and other furry creatures. He shuddered involuntarily.

"Let's head to the pub," she suggested, linking arms with Pineapple. "Leave the two love-birds to it, eh?"

The doorbell rang. Daisy bustled Pineapple out of the room, moving aside to let Kester past. "Good luck," she whispered, slapping him on the bottom.

Fighting to rid himself of the memory of what Daisy had just done to him, Kester pulled open the door.

"Hello!" Anya shivered like a whippet on the front door step. She was weighted down with a backpack that was roughly the same size as her, plus a duvet coiled around herself. Thor slithered around her ankles, tethered by a studded lead, and fixed a beady gaze on Kester's leg.

"How did you carry all this stuff?" he asked as he reached across to relieve her of her load, carefully avoiding the ferret.

She flexed her arms. "Ah, I have the strength of a superhero, haven't you noticed?"

"That'll explain it." He pointed at her duvet. "You know you can just use mine, don't you?"

She laughed. "I presumed you would be using your duvet when you slept on the sofa?"

Kester reddened. *Oh gosh, did I just insinuate that she'd be tucked up under one duvet with me?* he thought. To add to his embarrassment, Pineapple and Daisy each gave him an enthusiastic thumbs-up before grabbing their coats.

"You have a nice evening, you wonderful, colourful people," Pineapple drawled. He looked at Anya's duvet and smirked. "Seems like you got it all prepared, sweet and nice, innit?"

Anya raised an eyebrow. "If you say so."

"And you've got a little friend too!" Daisy gushed, pouring herself beside Thor and promptly making insufferable cooing noises at him. "What an adorable otter he is!"

Anya opened her mouth to correct her, then caught sight of Kester's expression and promptly closed it again.

"You off, then?" Kester said to his housemates with a pointed glance at the door.

Pineapple wiggled his hips in a manner that made him look as though he urgently needed the toilet. "We're off, for sure. As long as you are *on*. You feel me? As in, let's get it *on?*"

Unable to conceal a groan, Kester yanked open the door and drove Pineapple and Daisy out into the cold. "And on that note," he announced, "it's probably time for you to be on your way." Before they could protest, he shut the door firmly in their surprised faces.

"Have a nice night!" Anya called, then giggled. Thor squeaked and leapt up the stairs, his lead trailing a slither of red behind him.

Kester ushered her through to the lounge, forcing himself not to dwell on what the ferret might do upstairs. The chill was palpable, even with the heating cranked to maximum. Though the boiler had finally been fixed, the radiators only ever felt lukewarm at best. He balanced himself awkwardly on the armrest of the sofa, then promptly got up again.

"Would you like a drink?"

She nodded. "Yes, please. Something strong. It's been a long day. The library was *so* quiet."

He trotted to the kitchen. Thankfully, Pineapple hadn't yet had a chance to steal his bottle of wine. Hastily, he poured out two glasses, then fretted about the generous sizes. *I don't want her to think I'm trying to get her drunk,* he thought, wondering whether it was physically possible to feel more anxious about the evening than he already did.

"Here you go," he said as he eased himself onto the sofa, which squealed underneath his weight. "Other than quiet, how was work?"

She sighed and took a hearty gulp of her wine. "Ah, you know. A few old women asking for books that don't exist. Boys wanting books but not knowing what they're called or who wrote them. That sort of thing."

Kester grinned. "Sounds taxing."

She leaned across and punched him lightly on the arm. "Yes, I know. Not nearly as serious as your job. How's it all going, anyway?"

He rolled his eyes. "Stressfully. We're having big problems with the Thelemites; they broke into Infinite Enterprises."

"Your dad mentioned it, I think. Who are Infinite Enterprises?" Anya asked.

"Oh, just some bigwigs in London. They get all the cushy jobs because they're the richest."

She grimaced. "Like any other business, then. Have you found out who broke in?"

"Sort of." Kester sipped nervously at his wine. He wasn't quite sure how much he should be telling her, and he suspected the others wouldn't approve of him sharing information. "We've got suspicions that a daemon's behind it all."

"A daemon, eh?" Anya exhaled deeply. "I heard about them from the Thelemites. What else do you know about the daemon?"

He shifted in his seat. "I probably shouldn't say too much."

"I understand." She patted his leg, a gentle move that made his skin tingle. "Though you can trust me, you know. After all, they want to interrogate me about my time with the Thelemites, don't they?"

He blushed. "I'm really sorry about my dad calling you out of the blue like that. He had no right to hassle you over the interview."

"Ah, it's fine," she said, rearranging herself delicately against the lumpy cushion. "I don't think I will be in too much danger. The Thelemites aren't going to murder me in my bed."

"But you said the other night that you felt like something was watching you?" Kester reminded her.

She grinned. "Perhaps I just said that because I wanted to be comforted by you."

Kester felt his cheeks burn even brighter. "That's a very sweet thing to say," he mumbled, sipping his wine.

"You are a very sweet person, Kester." She leaned in, eyes half-closed. He was confused, before realising she was waiting for him to kiss her. His heart leapt a little, and he moved in to meet her, closing his own eyes in readiness.

The door-bell rang, a tinny bell snapping them out of the moment. Kester cursed. "I bet that's bloody Pineapple," he said with an apologetic smile. "He'll probably have decided to return for his bongos or something irritating like that."

Anya giggled. "It's okay, honestly. You go and answer it."

He stomped out into the hallway. *That bloody bastard Pineapple,* he thought as he jiggled the key into the lock. *Just as I'm about to get a kiss, he decides to come back home again. Absolutely typical.*

A freezing gust of night air whooshed into the house as he pulled open the door. Kester flinched, looked up, then gasped. It was Serena, teetering on the doorstop and clasping some sort of box in her hands.

"What are you doing here?"

"Hello," she mumbled and shoved the box against his chest. He looked down. To his surprise, it was a box of chocolates. "I got these for you. To say sorry. Alright?"

Kester's jaw dropped open. He was aware that he probably looked like a freshly-caught trout struggling for breath, but he couldn't quite manage to close it again. "For me?" he said, looking at the box and wondering whether it contained a bomb.

"For goodness' sake, yes!" Serena frowned, tapping her finger-nails on the doorframe. "I wanted to apologise for landing your girlfriend in it the other day. It wasn't fair of me, and I know you're cross."

Kester shook his head in disbelief, not quite sure what to say. "Well," he ventured, stroking the cover of the chocolate box thoughtfully. "I suppose it's okay."

Serena smiled tightly, then looked over her shoulder. "Also," she continued, dropping her voice to a whisper, "I want to talk to you about something I'm worried about."

"Really?" Kester was confused. He'd never seen Serena looking so nervous, not to mention non-hostile. "What's the matter?"

She paused, then took a deep breath. "I'm not even sure where to start. Basically, I've got some suspicions about—"

"—Hello Serena!" Anya sidled up beside Kester, who jumped. He hadn't heard her coming, even though the hallway floorboards usually creaked under even the slightest weight.

Serena's face fell. "Oh. Hi, Anya. I didn't realise you were here." She twisted a strand of hair around her finger.

Anya smiled. "There's no reason why you would, I suppose." She glanced at the box in Kester's hands. "Oh, chocolates, that's nice! What's the occasion?"

"Nothing in particular, I was just apologising for . . . something." Serena looked about as comfortable as someone who'd sat on a cactus. "Well, I can see I've caught you at a bad moment. I'll just leave you two to it, shall I?"

"Hang on," Kester said, catching her by the arm. "What were you going to say? Something about having suspicions?"

Serena shook her head. "It doesn't matter. We can talk about it another time. It's just work-related stuff."

Anya suddenly squealed and pointed to the air above Serena's perfectly-smoothed bob. "What's that?"

A mournful yowl echoed through the chill night air. Serena scowled.

"I don't believe it!" she exclaimed as she flapped her hands above her head. "That sodding incubus!"

Kester stared in fascination. A little, brown wisp of smoke bounced crazily in the moonlight, dodging left and right to avoid Serena's frantic fingers. "Oh dear," he concluded. "You're still having problems with him, then?"

"What is that thing?" Anya asked, fascinated. A glimmer of a smile tugged at her lips.

"An incubus," Serena said in a manner that suggested she'd like to do unspeakably painful things to the spirit in question. "I tried to extinguish it on a recent job, but it latched onto me instead. Now it's waking me up every bloody night."

The incubus grew in size until its black, gleaming eyes could be easily seen in the milky light. He moaned again and hung what might have been his head down towards his shoulders.

"He doesn't look very happy," Anya commented. "Poor little thing."

"Poor little thing, my arse," Serena snapped. "You have it if you think it's so cute."

"Can't you just extinguish him when he next appears?" Kester asked as he watched the spirit weave disconsolately in the air.

"No, I told you! He disappears every time I try," she growled, glowering above her head. "It's driving me absolutely crazy." She swiped again at her head, made contact, and the spirit disappeared with a small pop, like a vacuum cleaner sucking on fabric.

"Why don't you come in?" Kester offered. He suddenly felt a bit sorry for her. *After all,* he realised as he looked down at the chocolates, *she's come all this way just to apologise, which is uncharacteristically nice of her.*

She shook her head. "No, I'll leave you to it." She turned to leave, then clicked her fingers. "Oh, before I forget, have you spoken to Miss Wellbeloved?"

"No, why?"

"Check your phone, I bet she's tried calling you," Serena continued. "There's been a lead on the case." She glanced meaningfully at Anya. "It's probably best if we don't discuss it now."

Kester nodded. "Righty-ho, I'll check for messages in a moment." He waved the chocolates with vague embarrassment. "Erm, thank you for these. That's very kind of you."

Serena frowned. "That's alright. We'll talk tomorrow, okay?"

"It was nice seeing you again," Anya said brightly. "I hope you don't mind if I have some of the chocolates too."

"Of course not." Serena pulled her leather coat around herself, eyes cast down to the ground. "Have a pleasant evening."

Kester watched her stalk down the lamp-lit street until she was just a shadow in the distance, then shut the door. "Well," he said with a bemused glance at Anya. "That was unexpected."

Anya's mouth tightened. She looked up at him, scrutinising his face. "What do you think she wanted?"

"To give me these chocolates, I think."

"No." Anya shook her head, then headed back towards the lounge. "I don't think that's what she wanted at all."

Kester frowned. She had a strange, guarded expression on her face that he hadn't seen before.

"I'm sure it's nothing to worry about," he said, passing her the glass of wine. "Did you want to watch some television or something? I need to quickly check to see if Miss Wellbeloved has left a message for me."

She nodded and reached for the remote control.

"I love that you think that might actually work," Kester said as he reached over for the main switch on the television. "But it doesn't, I'm afraid. Much like most other things in this house."

"Why have it, then?" she said, looking down at the device with bemusement.

"Pineapple thinks a broken remote control makes a nice ornament," he explained. "Despite Daisy saying that defunct technological gadgets give off bad karma."

She giggled. "Your housemates are weird."

"You'll find out just how weird after living with them for a few days," Kester replied. "Also, you might want to never leave food in the fridge."

"Why, is the fridge broken too?"

He shook his head. "No, it's not that. Pineapple apparently has a condition called food-kleptomania. Once you put anything in there, it's gone within a few hours."

She threw back her head and laughed, giving Kester the full benefit of her pearly-white teeth. "I know a way you can stop him."

"Go on."

"Dip two sticks of celery in chocolate, then put them in a Twix wrapper. That should put him off."

Kester chuckled as he flicked through the TV channels. "That's evil. Good idea."

He left her watching a programme about DIY home renovations and went out to the hallway. Sure enough, he had a missed call on his phone. Quickly, he pressed his voicemail button.

"Hello, Kester, it's me," the message began. He grinned. *Just as Serena said,* he thought. *Miss Wellbeloved. I wonder what this mysterious lead is, then?*

"I wanted to speak to you quite urgently," Miss Wellbeloved's voice continued. "There's been a sighting of Hrschni in the Thelemites' Whitby branch. Curtis Philpot has proposed that each team send a representative up there to do some observations, and I thought you'd be perfect, as you've got such a knack of spotting things that the rest of us miss. Can you give me a call back, please?"

Kester hung up and sighed. *Not again,* he thought. *I just want to spend some time at home without having to dart off here, there, and everywhere.* He poked his head round the lounge door and saw Anya had already finished her wine. In spite of the cold, she looked quite cosy nestled into the corner of the sofa. He longed to forget about work, at least for a little while, and snuggle up next to her, though, by the sounds of things, that wasn't going to be possible.

"Do you want another drink?" he offered, pointing to her glass.

She nodded. "Yes, please. What did the message say?"

He quickly filled her in, then headed out to the kitchen.

"Where this time?" Anya asked as Kester returned with the bottle of wine.

"Bloody Whitby. I'm not even sure exactly where that is."

"It's a seaside town in the north-west," she replied. "It's famous. Bram Stoker thought up the story for *Dracula* there."

Kester laughed. "How do you know that sort of stuff?"

She sipped demurely at her wine. "What can I say? I'm a sucker for vampires."

"Gosh, do I need to guard my neck when I'm around you?"

"Only at night-time."

He grinned. It felt good to have her around, just hanging out together like a normal couple. Her blonde hair draped over the sofa cushions like a blanket, shining in the lamp-light, and it made his breath catch with sudden desire. *She really is beautiful,* he thought. *What does she see in someone like me?* He glanced ruefully at his phone, then sighed.

"I'd better return Miss Wellbeloved's call," he explained. "Back in a minute."

He went through to the kitchen and stepped out into the

utility area, which was currently overflowing with Pineapple's dirty laundry.

The phone rang, then finally connected.

"Aha, Kester, there you are! And why did it take you so long to call us back, eh?"

Kester's mouth fell open. He hadn't expected his father to answer. "What are you doing at Miss Wellbeloved's house?" he asked.

"That is none of your business, nosy. Did you listen to Jennifer's message?"

Kester could hear Miss Wellbeloved's voice in the background, complete with soft music that sounded like an opera recording. *Are they having some sort of romantic evening together?* he wondered. His stomach turned at the thought.

"Yes, I listened to it," he muttered, then added mutinously, "Why do I have to go?"

"Jennifer said why you have to go. It will be good for you." Ribero cleared his throat, then laughed. "Also, there is a very special person helping with the case, and I think you should meet them."

"Who's that?"

Ribero tittered. "I am not going to tell you. It is a very big surprise."

Kester's heart sank. "I don't like surprises," he said. "Can't you just tell me?"

"No. So you need to get ready to go to Whitby, okay?"

"Why, when do you propose I go?" Kester barked, feeling angrier by the second. He glanced back to the lounge, where he could still hear the muted chatter of the television programme.

"You will leave tomorrow. It is an urgent case, right?"

Oh, you have got to be kidding me, Kester thought. "What if I refuse?" he said aloud, in a voice that was rather squeakier and more indignant than he'd intended.

"Then I call you a silly pillock."

"Well, that's good to know."

There was a rustling down the line, some muffled whispers, then suddenly Miss Wellbeloved's lighter breathing drifted into his ear.

"I'm sorry, Kester," she said without preamble. "I know you probably just want to relax for a bit. But I really do think this investigation is right up your street."

"But I've got Anya staying with me!" he protested, aware that he was starting to whine but unable to stop himself. "I was looking forward to spending some time with her!"

Miss Wellbeloved sighed. "I can understand that must be frustrating. For what it's worth, I don't imagine you'll need to be up there for long. Cardigan Cummings and Ian Kingdom-Green are going to do the longer-term stake-out. Luke's going too, if that helps?"

He shrugged. "A bit, I suppose. I guess I haven't got a choice in the matter, have I?"

"We'd really appreciate it if you went."

Kester sighed, leaning against the wall. "Okay, *fine*. What time do I need to leave?"

"The train's at half-past seven in the morning," Miss Wellbeloved replied. "There are two changes, and you arrive in the afternoon." She paused. "I'm sorry."

Kester bit back a sharp retort. He knew it wasn't her fault. "Fine," he replied through gritted teeth. "What about accommodation?"

"There weren't many available rooms at short notice, so you'll be sharing a twin room with Luke. It's a hotel apparently, right on the seafront. I'll text over the details in a moment."

His shoulders slumped. Even the prospect of a five-star establishment wasn't likely to brighten his mood. "What about Anya?" he asked. "If she's doing this interview with Infinite Enterprises, I want to know that she's being kept safe, like Philpot promised."

"Absolutely," Miss Wellbeloved replied smoothly. "I'll make it a top priority to ensure that happens."

"Alright, then." He couldn't think of much else to say. "I'd better go. I've left Anya alone in the lounge. By the way, why is Dad at your house?"

There was a substantial silence. Miss Wellbeloved coughed. "We were just keeping each other company," she said stiffly. "You know how it is, when you get old."

"Not really," Kester admitted. Whatever it was that they were up to, he probably didn't want to know.

After saying goodbye, he headed back to the lounge and slumped back onto the sofa like a disgruntled sack of potatoes.

"Oh dear," Anya said, spotting his dejected expression. "Let me guess. They want you to go tomorrow?"

He grabbed his glass of wine and promptly drank most of it. "Apparently so. Unbelievable, isn't it?"

The television programme came to an end, complete with a horribly jovial theme tune, which only seemed to mock his bad mood.

She sighed, then drained her glass too. "Does that mean I'll be here with just your housemates, then?" she asked finally.

"And Thor too," Kester said with a smile.

Her mouth twitched. "He'll be good protection if the Thelemites come to get me, I'm sure."

"I thought you said you weren't so worried about them now?" He reached over and switched off the television. At once, the room fell into soft, companionable silence.

She looked over to the window, studying the faded curtains. "I'm not worried," she said quietly.

But there's something going on, isn't there? he thought as his gaze traced a path over her face. *It's just you're not telling me, for some reason.* He wished he could read her better, but he'd never been that good at interpreting women. Or anyone, for that matter. It was as though an invisible veil had been raised somewhere inside her, masking everything from view. *Why didn't Mum teach me more about the opposite sex?* he thought with a rueful smile. *It would have been bloody helpful right now.*

Suddenly, a movement by the fireplace caught his eye. Before he had chance to register what it was, Daisy's ceramic cat from Japan teetered and fell, smashing into pieces on the tiled hearth.

Instinctively, he leapt to his feet, nearly dropping his glass in the process. "What the hell caused that?" he said with a wild glance in Anya's direction.

Anya shook her head slowly and evaluated the smashed pile of cheaply-painted china on the floor. "I don't know," she said finally, placing her hands on her hips. "Was it off-balance or something?"

His mind raced back to when he'd been fiddling about with the candle. *Did I move the cat?* he wondered, surveying the mess. *I don't remember touching it, but I suppose it could be possible. But why did it only fall over now with no-one near it?* He shivered in spite of himself. Something didn't feel quite right. In fact, if he was being honest with himself, things hadn't been feeling right for some time, and it was starting to worry him.

Anya patted him on the back, sensing his discomfort. "It's just one of those things," she said emphatically. "Nothing to be worried about, I am sure."

He shook his head. "I'm not convinced."

"What are you not convinced about?" She smiled. "Things like this happen all the time, you know."

"But we were just talking about the Thelemites and—"

To his surprise, his words were lost under the sudden, smooth pressure of her lips. His eyes widened then shut as he gave into the sensation of her mouth on his—insistent and forceful. A hand circled around his waist, and instinctively, he circled his own around her, feeling the line of her lower back smoothing out in a glorious plane above her jeans. *I don't know whether to feel elated,* he thought, *or terrified at the fact that she's now got her hands firmly on my love-handles.*

Moments drew into timelessness, then finally, she pulled away. His lips felt tender and bruised.

"You worry too much," she said with a wink and tugged him gently on the hand. "Come on."

"Come on where?" he squeaked as she dragged him out of the room.

She glanced over her shoulder, eyes glittering in the light. "We need to look for Thor upstairs."

Is that a euphemism? he wondered, then remembered Thor was her ferret. She winked at him, and he felt even more baffled. Dutifully, he followed her up the stairs like a lapdog trotting after its master, thinking, *I'm not sure if that is the most exciting thing that's ever happened to me or the most terrifying.*

"Are you okay?" she asked and gave him the full benefit of her gleaming smile. Thor appeared at the top of the stairs, wrapping himself around the top bannister like a fur scarf.

He nodded and pressed his lips together with anticipation. *Ah well,* he concluded as they turned towards his bedroom. *There's one way of finding out, I suppose.*

CHAPTER 9: WHITBY

Kester paced the seafront, struggling to get his bearings. Despite having spent most of the day relaxing on the train, he felt drained and irritable, unable to adapt to the new surroundings—especially as he hadn't had much sleep the night before.

Not that I'm complaining, he thought with a grin. It all seemed rather unreal, given that he'd presumed he'd remain a virgin until he managed to find someone who was blind, deranged, or extremely unfussy. He still couldn't quite believe that someone as beautiful as Anya liked him enough to give him a kiss, let alone spend the night with him.

Still, now probably wasn't the time to dwell on it, considering how cold it was, not to mention how much his stomach was rumbling. Tempting though it was to re-live every moment of last night, he knew he needed to get on with the task at hand.

So, this is Whitby. He took a moment to survey the surrounding landscape. Grey waters slapped against the stone harbour, and the ruined abbey perched precariously on a distant hill, its windows framing the sinking sun. *It's very different to Exeter,* he concluded. Colder, too. But it was certainly pretty, despite the steely-grey sky. Quaint, stone buildings jostled for space along the promenade, and little boats, sails flapping in the wind, bobbed beside him as he strolled onward. A man, made more of beard than anything else, sat sucking on a pipe and watching Kester with great interest before he disappeared down an alleyway between two shops. Aside from that, the street was deserted.

I suppose of all the places they could have sent me, this isn't too bad, he conceded. The place had a serenity and sense of timelessness that appealed to his traditional sensibilities. A flock of gulls suddenly streamed to the sharp cliffs on the other side of the estuary, wailing in the wind. Snapped back to reality, he rummaged in his backpack for the hotel details, then squinted once again at the address.

"Seafront Hotel, Langbourne Road." He looked for a sign, then realised he was already in the right place.

A muffled shout broke the silence. Kester turned to see Luke waving merrily, his tasselled, suede jacket rather out of place against the elegant, Victorian backdrop.

"Well, howdy-do!" Luke called, finally catching up with him. He patted Kester on the back, grinning with pleasure. "Nice to see you again. I take it you're looking for the hotel?"

Kester smiled. It was a relief to see somebody he knew. "Hi, Luke," he said, stepping around a discarded box of fish and chips. "Have you been here long? Or are you as lost as I am?"

"Nah, I'm *never* lost," Luke replied, hoisting his bag on his shoulder. "See that building right there? With the pillars and fancy windows?"

"Surely they haven't paid for us to stay there, have they?" Kester studied the hotel with amazement. It was far posher than the horrible bed and breakfast they'd had to stay in when they'd been investigating in Dorset.

Luke shrugged. "When it's a top national case, I guess they flash the cash a little."

Kester looked up with awe. Up close, the hotel was even more impressive, and he was pleased to see that it had a restaurant. *A hefty pile of food,* he thought wistfully. *That'd do me.*

The automatic doors swished open, and they walked into the polished, elegant reception. *Anya would love this,* he thought, spying his reflection in the tinted mirrors behind the desk. *One day, I'll take her somewhere posh.*

Luke caught him smiling and gave him a curious look. "My, my," he said as he flung his bag on the floor at the reception desk. "Someone looks like the cat who got the cream then raided the dairy after. What's put a grin on your face, Kester?"

The receptionist swiftly emerged from the back room and took their details. Kester blushed, grateful for the diversion. "I can't imagine what you're referring to," he mumbled.

"Yeah, right." Luke grabbed the keys and gave him a wink. "You'll tell me later, after a few beers, I'll bet. Agreed, partner?"

They climbed up the sweeping staircase to their room, a calm oasis of white with two pleasingly comfortable-looking beds. Luke promptly lobbed his bag onto the bed nearest the window. "Shotgun," he shouted, then added as an afterthought, "you don't mind if I bag the great view, do you?"

"No, not at all." Kester peered out the window, which had a tiny, iron balcony overlooking the harbour. He personally preferred to be close to the toilet in the night, anyway. "Shall we unpack now, while we're waiting for the others?"

"Nah, I reckon they'll be here already." Luke grabbed a complimentary bottle of water and promptly ripped the lid off. "You know what Infinite Enterprises are like. Always one step ahead of the rest of us."

Kester looked longingly at the free pack of biscuits by the kettle, then down at his stomach. *Don't even think about it,* he told himself firmly. "Should we give them a call, then?" he suggested.

"I don't think you need to bother," Luke replied. "I saw a person with flowing hair sitting with their back to us in the bar earlier. I'll bet that's our man, Kingdom-Green. Let's see if we can find them there."

"Good idea." Kester stifled a yawn with the back of his hand. "I need a drink to wake me up. A cup of tea would do the job nicely."

They made their way to the bar, which, as Luke had predicted, contained both Ian Kingdom-Green and Cardigan Cummings, dignified as two lords, settled in matching, velvet armchairs. Both nodded politely as they approached.

"We wondered when you'd get here," Cardigan said, extending his hand to both of them. "A pleasure to meet you once more."

"A pleasure and a joy," Ian added, and gestured expressively to the bar. "What's your tipple, good friends? I've been reliably informed that this trip is all-expenses-paid. Order whatever you will, though save the champagne for when we solve the case, eh?"

Kester smiled. "I think I'll just have a nice cuppa for now," he replied.

"Upon my word, you shall not," Ian said severely. "Make it alcoholic, for what we are about to discuss requires a flexible, open mind. Have a wine. It invigorates the senses."

I'm not sure it'll invigorate mine, Kester thought, but he nodded nonetheless. A few minutes later, he and Luke were presented with a goblet of Merlot each, which certainly looked appealing. Even better, the waiter placed a large bowl of peanuts beside them, which Kester's fingers hastily sneaked towards without him realising it.

Ian watched them seriously, chin resting lightly on his index fingers. "Ah," he breathed in satisfaction, once they'd each taken a large gulp. "And now, let the medicine do its job. A good vintage, I presume?"

"Tastes alright to me," Luke drawled and promptly downed the rest.

"How was your journey up?" Cardigan asked as he clicked his fingers at the waiter, then pointed at Luke's empty glass.

"Very good, thanks," Kester squeaked, feeling like a child talking to two seasoned academics. "And yours?"

"Likewise." Cardigan raised a glass in their direction. "Though I will confess to missing my children when I'm away."

Kester smiled. "How old are they?"

"My daughter is ten, my two sons are both five. They're twins, and every bit as much of a handful as you might imagine."

"Do you have children?" Luke asked Ian, accepting his second wine with a wink at the waiter.

Ian shook his head, his mane flowing over his shoulders. "Sadly, no. I am merely wedded to my work. Like a nun to Christ, you see."

Kester fought the urge to chuckle as a sudden image of the spirit investigator dressed up in a wimple and black gown came to mind. *It would probably suit him,* he thought. *He's dramatic enough to carry off most outfits, I reckon.*

"Ah, I know that feeling, Ian," Luke agreed as he scooped up a handful of nuts. "Work can take over everything sometimes."

"May I ask," Ian said, as he rested his wine glass delicately down on the table, "why you call yourself Luke? If it's not an imposition, of course."

"Nah, that's okay," Luke replied, grinning. "I'd better get used to people asking, I guess." He quickly outlined the facts, and the two men nodded sagely.

"A remarkably brave decision to make," Ian commented and raised his glass to Luke. "I commend you for it. 'To thine own self be true,' as Shakespeare himself did once write."

Luke doffed an imaginary hat in Ian's direction. "True that, partner."

"So," Cardigan interrupted as he lowered his glass. "We should address the matter at hand. I take it you haven't been fully debriefed yet?"

"All I've heard is that there was a sighting of Hrschni here in Whitby, and we've got to check it out," Kester replied as he settled himself more comfortably into the sofa. The amber lights and mellow jazz music filtering out of the neighbouring speakers were making him sleepy, and there was a strong temptation to simply allow Cardigan's words to wash over him while he zoned out in a trance and replayed last night in his mind.

Cardigan rapped at the table, snapping all eyes back to him. "Not quite a sighting," he said. Reaching into his jacket pocket, he pulled out a pair of half-moon glasses and slipped them on. Ian Kingdom-Green removed a notepad from his leather briefcase and placed it obligingly in front of his colleague.

"I take it these are the notes?" Luke asked, peering over Cardigan's arm.

"Absolutely." He peered at them seriously over his glasses. "According to our surveillance team, Hrschni's presence was detected two days ago, outside the Whitby Thelemite lodge. At first, they weren't certain, but then they picked up something again yesterday."

"How did they pick it up?" Kester asked. The others stared at him incredulously.

"Basic thermal or sonar detection, I presume?" Luke explained carefully, looking slightly embarrassed for Kester. "You covered that in your standard training, right?"

Kester reddened and reached for his wine glass, inwardly cursing his lack of knowledge. There was simply too much to learn in such a short space of time; he'd been thrown in at the deep end since day one.

"There's nothing basic about Infinite Enterprise's equipment," Ian corrected briskly. "Our surveillance gear relies on sophisticated kino-thermal transmissions, so sensitive that they could pick up a—"

"That's probably not important at present," Cardigan interrupted. "The fact is, we're fairly certain he's here. If it's not him, it's another powerful daemon."

"And as far as we know, there are no other significant daemons that we cannot account for," Ian added with an elegant flourish of the wrist, like a magician about to present an impressive trick.

"That's not entirely true," Cardigan said hesitantly. "There are a few other daemons that have managed to slip the net over the years, but as they haven't been any trouble so far, we haven't worried about them too much."

Ian Kingdom-Green shrugged. "Ultimately, my dear friends," he concluded, "if a daemon disappears to the far ends of the earth, there's very little we can do to locate him or her, unless someone reports strange daemonic activity. However," he continued with a significant look, "we knew where to start our search with Hrschni, and true to our expectations, he's gravitated towards one of the Thelemite lodges."

Kester stifled a burp. "If you don't mind me saying," he ventured as he finished the rest of his drink, "it all seems a bit *convenient,* doesn't it? I mean, this Hrschni is obviously clever, so why would he go somewhere where he knows we're watching out for him?"

"Unless he wants to be found, you mean?" Cardigan replied, shifting back in his seat and folding his arms over his sizeable chest.

"I guess that's what I mean, yes," Kester replied. He quickly outlined what they'd discovered the other day about Hrschni's songs and the lines repeated in the letter sent to Infinite Enterprises. "It all sounds a bit too deliberate," he concluded and waited for the others to mull it over.

"It's possible," Cardigan said eventually. "But then, the letter may not be significant at all. We know how much daemons like word-play and puzzles." The music changed, sending sombre piano notes trickling through the bar area like drops of rain. He nodded thoughtfully. "Ultimately, we have no way of knowing Hrschni's intentions at the moment. Nor the Thelemites', for that matter. Until now, we've had no major problems with either. This is unfamiliar territory for us all."

"But you'll get to the bottom of it," Luke chimed as he delivered each of them his most dazzling Texan smile. "I mean, that's what you guys do, isn't it? Ghost-Con award-winners and all that."

"We'll *all* get to the bottom of it," Ian declared grandly, reaching across the table and patting their shoulders. "We all of us have remarkable skills to offer. With talent such as this, how can we fail?"

Cardigan rubbed his chin. "Very easily, if we get complacent," he concluded. "We're dealing with an ancient, powerful creature here. Don't underestimate him."

"What's the plan then?" Kester glanced at his watch and saw it was already getting late. His stomach was rumbling furiously, and he longed to return to the soft confines of his hotel bed and order as much food as possible on room service.

"Observation, my dear fellow!" Ian exclaimed. "Our surveillance team are in position even as we speak, monitoring the lodge. We'll be using our combined abilities to see what else we can glean from the situation."

"You don't reckon it's a good idea to just knock on the door and ask 'em what they're up to?" Luke suggested, eyes twinkling.

"Probably best not to," Cardigan glanced back down at his notepad. "The energy surges reported by our crew were substantial. Which suggests that Hrschni is firing on all cylinders, so to speak."

Luke chuckled. "You mean, if I go knocking, I might get knocked flying into the next town by this daemon?"

Cardigan shrugged, taking his comment seriously. "It's a possibility. Everything we thought we once knew about Hrschni no longer applies. He's now classified as an unknown, illegal entity, and possibly extremely dangerous. As a result—"

"—proceed with absolute caution," Ian finished. "However, we do have some assistance from a real expert in the field. She'll be joining us tomorrow to help with the case."

Kester raised an eyebrow. "Who's that, then?" He remembered what his father had said the night before about him meeting someone special in Whitby.

Ian nudged the side of his nose in a highly-knowing fashion. "You'll see. It's a real honour to be working with her, actually. She's a true inspiration to us all, and one of the finest creatures to walk this earth." He clicked a pair of long fingers in the direction of the waiter and ordered a whisky. "Anyone else for another?" he offered.

Kester shook his head, then fought off a yawn. "I might head upstairs, swot up on the case," he said. Actually, he wanted to call Anya and see how she was doing back at home, but he hardly thought it was the time to mention that now.

"Don't you want to know who is joining us tomorrow?" Ian declared, as he waved his wine glass in the air. "Are you not curious to know who this great and majestic individual is?"

Cardigan pulled his arm down gently. "I believe our friends want to retire to their room," he said, then nodded at the pair of them. "They'll meet our special guest tomorrow." He winked at Ian and smiled. "We'll probably be here for the evening, if you'd like to join us later, after you've had a chance to rest and recover."

Luke yawned. "I don't know, I'm pretty beat. I'll take you up on the offer tomorrow, though, when we've busted our way through this case."

"That sounds very agreeable," Cardigan replied as they stood up to leave. "Enjoy a good night's sleep, both of you."

They headed to the stairs. Kester slid a contemplative hand along the gold-plated bannister rail and thought of Anya, back at his home, with only the dreadful Pineapple and Daisy for company. *Poor her,* he thought. He sincerely hoped that Thor was, at this present moment, busily humping Pineapple's leg.

In the room, Luke collapsed onto the bed and kicked off his leather boots. "Man, I need a nap," he declared, staring up at the ceiling. "Larry's been working us real hard recently, and I'm just about done in by it all. Plus, the hormone meds I'm taking are making me feel all over the place."

Kester sat against the padded bedhead and nodded. "How long have you got to take them?"

Luke rolled onto his side, pressing his head up against his hand. "Ages. Still," he said, brightening, "I got some good news a couple of days ago. My first operation's been booked in."

"That must feel exciting."

"Yeah," Luke said as he stifled a yawn. "And scary. It's just one of many."

"Is Larry okay with you taking time off?"

Luke grinned. "Do you know, for an old fuddy-duddy, he's been pretty cool about it all." He winked. "He ain't as bad as y'all think he is. I think he understands, though he still calls me Lara every so often."

Kester plumped the soft pillows and eased them behind his back. "I suppose it takes a bit of getting used to, doesn't it? Did you feel strange when people started calling you Luke?"

Luke chuckled. "I guess a little. But it was nice. Nice that people just accepted it." His expression darkened. "Not that everyone's been so great, of course."

Kester examined his room-mate's face. He remembered Luke mentioning his family before, back in Texas. "I take it you're talking about your brother?" he asked tentatively, not wanting to darken Luke's mood any further.

"Yeah, and the rest." Luke tugged off his socks and balled them in his hands before lobbing them across the room. "But that's life, I suppose. You wanna watch some TV and order room service? I don't know about you, but a burger and fries would be perfect for me right now."

Kester smiled. "Yeah, in a minute. I've got to call someone first."

Luke beamed. "I take it this is the same *someone* who kept you up last night? The one you've been grinning about all evening?"

"I can't imagine what you're talking about," Kester spluttered as his cheeks reddened. Then he grinned. "Well, I can imagine. And you *might* be right. But a gentleman never tells."

Luke whooped and slammed his hands on the duvet. "Good for you! Did you want me to leave the room so you can talk to her?"

Kester felt his face turn an even deeper shade of crimson. "No, that's okay. We won't be talking about anything . . . you know. Anything private." He blushed even more, until he felt as though his arteries might combust with the pressure. "I'll . . . er . . . just phone her in the bathroom. Okay?"

"Yeah, you do that," Luke drawled. "Have fun."

Easing the bathroom door shut, Kester closed his eyes, then started to laugh. It felt good to be teased about having a girlfriend, especially as it had never happened before. Splashing his face with some cold water, he rested on the edge of the bath and pulled his phone out of his pocket. Anya answered almost straight away.

"Hello," Kester said in what he hoped was an alluring voice. On reflection, it sounded a bit idiotic, and he wished he hadn't.

"Hey, you." Anya's voice sounded tired. Kester felt his spirits drop, just a little bit.

"Is everything okay? Are my housemates driving you mad yet?"

Anya chuckled. "Not quite yet. Daisy keeps calling Thor an otter, though. I don't know why."

"You could tell her Thor was a velociraptor and she'd probably believe you, you know."

"Now that's an idea." Anya paused. It sounded as though she was drinking something. "How was your journey to Whitby?"

Kester sighed. "It was fine. Long, but fine. The hotel's nice. I'm sharing a room with Luke. He keeps teasing me about you."

"Why, what have you told him?"

"Nothing at all," Kester replied as he undid his shirt collar, relaxing against the wall. "That's between you and me, isn't it?"

"If you're talking about last night," Anya said, "then yes, it certainly is." There was a silence, before she added, "I had fun, you know."

Kester gulped. He suddenly wished, more ardently than ever, that he was home with her rather than here, stuck in a featureless, white, hotel bathroom, hundreds of miles away. "So did I," he croaked, then coughed. "I really did. I hope it was . . . you know. Alright."

She laughed again. "It was better than alright, Kester. It was lovely."

He felt his heart melt, turning into a useless puddle of soppiness in his chest. *She said it was lovely!* he thought to himself and swallowed hard. *Who would have thought it, eh?*

"I thought so too," he wheezed. Catching sight of himself in the mirror, he inexplicably gave himself a wink.

"So," she continued with a hint of self-consciousness, "how's the case going? Did you get anywhere today?"

Kester sighed. "No. We had a chat with Ian Kingdom-Green and Cardigan Cummings; you remember the two agents I told you about?"

"The massive guy and the man with the silly hair?"

"Something like that." Kester opened the bathroom door an inch. Luke was busy scanning the menu, which looked like it had a photo of a very large, very tempting burger on the back cover. He patted his stomach reflectively.

"What did they say about it all?"

Kester laughed. "You're very interested in this case, aren't you?"

"Only because you are always so secretive about it," she replied with a hint of defensiveness. "And remember, I know what the Thelemites are like. I'm involved in this too, you know."

He swallowed hard. "Yes, I know. I don't mean to be secretive." *But it is a necessary part of the job,* he added silently. *Still, I suppose it's okay to share things with Anya. After all, she knows a lot about it already.*

"What are your plans for tomorrow?" she pressed. He could hear the soft tap of her fingernails against the receiver, which was strangely alluring.

"We're doing a stake-out, I think," he replied. "And there's some special guest joining us. I dread to think who."

She laughed. "It sounds like a game-show or something."

"Knowing the others, it's probably just some big-wig who's won loads of awards at Ghost-Con," Kester said with a chuckle. "Infinite Enterprises like to show off all their accolades and prizes."

"Ghost-Con?"

"It's just a weird awards ceremony for supernatural agencies," he explained, hoping she didn't press him for more details. The truth was, he wasn't quite sure what the point of Ghost-Con was himself, he but didn't want to look like an idiot for not knowing. "What are you doing tomorrow?" he asked, deftly changing the subject.

"Ah, I am getting my hair done. I thought it would look nice with more blonde and honey highlights. I look so drab at the moment. What do you think?"

He raised an eyebrow. *I hadn't had her pegged as a girl who worried too much about her appearance,* he thought, then grinned. *Maybe she's doing it to impress me.*

With this pleasant thought in mind, Kester glanced out again at Luke, who caught his eye and waved the menu cheerily. "Look, I'd better go," he said reluctantly. "I haven't eaten yet, and my tummy is rumbling so loudly, it sounds like a jet plane taking off."

She laughed. "That's never a good thing. You go and eat, then. Don't worry about me and Thor, we're fine here. Unless you think I should go back home now? I mean, it seems silly, me still being here when you aren't."

"No, stay." He paused, wanting to say more, something meaningful and romantic, but the words refused to come out properly. "Could you do me a favour?" he said instead.

"What's that?"

"As a laugh, could you pop Thor into Pineapple's bed later on?"

Anya chuckled. "You know, Thor would probably enjoy that. He was checking out Pineapple's leg earlier on, actually."

"There you go," Kester replied. "Thor and Pineapple's shin-bone. It's a marriage made in heaven. Or alternatively, stick a fake horn on his head and tell Daisy that he's the world's smallest unicorn."

"It's a plan," she agreed, then fell silent, apart from the steady, soft sound of her breath. "Well, I'll let you have your dinner."

"Good night," he said, then added awkwardly, "I wish I was there with you."

"Me too," she replied. To his delight, she sounded sincere. He hung up reluctantly, then returned to the bedroom, just in time to see Luke turn on the television.

"Hey, look what's on!" he exclaimed with an enthusiastic gesture at the screen. "*Terrington Grange!* Man, I love your English period dramas, they're just amazing."

Kester put his phone back in his pocket and raised an eyebrow. "If you say so. Don't they have these sorts of programmes in America, then?"

"Nah," Luke said, gaze fixed on the screen. "Not like this, they don't. This is *quality.*"

"So," Kester said as he slumped back on his bed and prepared to settle himself in for the evening. "Who is the special person joining us tomorrow, Luke? Do you know?"

He grinned and tapped the side of his nose. "I might do. But I reckon you'll enjoy the surprise."

Kester groaned. He hated surprises. Even his mother letting off party poppers on his eighth birthday had given him an instantaneous panic attack. "Can't you just tell me?" he begged as he perused the menu.

Luke shook his head. "Nah," he replied. "That'll just spoil the fun."

Oh great, Kester thought as he picked up the hotel phone to order. *Yet another thing to look forward to. Still, the faster we solve this case, the better. And I guess if this secret person helps us achieve that more quickly, it's only a good thing.*

Chapter 10: The Stake Out

"Now, this is what I refer to as magnificent English weather," Ian Kingdom-Green declared the following morning, without a hint of irony whatsoever. Kester followed the sweep of his hand as he gestured out to the promenade, which was already dusted with a thin carpet of snow. *I'd be so much happier if I was back in bed,* he thought and shivered, wishing he'd remembered to bring his proper winter coat. The sky was dun-white and clearly laden with more snow to deposit on them later in the day.

Luke beamed out at the sea and ran his finger along the top of the nearest bench, removing a line of frost as he did so. "This is incredible," he exclaimed with an expression not dissimilar to a child opening its stocking at Christmas. "I ain't never seen snow. It's like a picture postcard or something."

Cardigan Cummings stamped his feet reflectively on the pavement and tugged his scarf more tightly around his neck. "It's a little brisk for my liking," he commented, then pointed down the street. "But enough about the weather. Shall we head on?"

Kester looked wistfully at the hotel entrance, thinking back to the steaming full English breakfast that he'd enjoyed just half an hour ago. Already, he missed the warmth of the hotel restaurant, not to mention the cosy comfort of his duvet. "Don't we need to wait for this other person to arrive? The special visitor?" he asked, peering around for signs of anyone else about to join them. The seafront was deserted apart from a couple of elderly women who were walking gingerly along the road, clutching onto one another for dear life.

Cardigan smiled and cast a glance at Ian. "Do you think we should tell him yet?" he said.

Ian looked at Kester and shook his head. "His father asked us not to, remember?"

"Hang on a minute," Kester said with instant panic and suspicion. "What do you mean? What has Dad been up to now?"

Cardigan let out a booming laugh, which startled the nearby pigeons, who were contently pecking around by the bottom of the bench. "Oh Kester, I am sorry about all of this. I normally hate trickery, but I think Dr Ribero wanted to inject a bit of fun into the proceedings."

"You mean he wanted to poke fun at me," Kester replied darkly. He knew what his father was like.

Ian patted his shoulder comfortingly. "Let's go and meet them, shall we? Put you out of your misery." He led the way, a gallant knight venturing into the unknown. Kester skulked onwards, thinking all sorts of uncharitable thoughts about Ribero.

"The Thelemite lodge isn't too far," Cardigan said in a low voice as they rounded the corner and started to climb the hill. "It's just a bit further inland, past the museum."

"What's the plan for today, then?" Luke asked. The first flakes of fresh snow started to drift aimlessly in the air around their heads like dancing, white fireflies.

"The stake-out van is already in position," Ian said. "We'll meet with the team first, find out what's what, then proceed from there."

Kester looked at him cynically. "Are you sure Hrschni isn't aware that we're watching him? A stake-out van seems a little obvious, doesn't it?"

Cardigan gave him a deliberate nod as a young couple walked past, then continued once they were safely out of earshot. "Perhaps the daemon knows, perhaps not. Ultimately, things like this are always a bit cat-and-mouse."

Finally, they reached the top of the hill and continued past a large park, until they reached the museum: a squat, brick building flanked with pillars. Ian pointed down the road.

"You see that building with the white façade?" he asked and gave the others a nudge. Kester and Luke nodded obediently. "Well, that's the spot."

"It says it's the British Legion," Kester said uncertainly, squinting through his glasses.

Ian nodded knowingly. "Subterfuge, my friend. Remember, they're a secret society. Nothing at all to do with the British Legion though, of course," he added hastily.

Kester's gaze travelled to the other side of the road. A van was parked beside the row of houses, complete with the name and details of a construction company along the side. *I presume that's our surveillance vehicle,* he thought as he studied it intently. *Somehow, I don't think Hrschni is going to be fooled by it.*

"The van moves at regular intervals," Cardigan explained, catching his expression. "Hopefully that way, we can avoid detection." Without any further preamble, he marched up to the back of the van and rapped smartly on the door.

A few seconds later, it flew open. A harassed face, wrapped in a brightly-coloured hijab, peered out. She waved them in impatiently, then slammed the door closed behind them.

"You let the cold in," she muttered, moving over to a computer screen in the corner, which was currently showing a thermal map of their surroundings.

"Rather unavoidable, in order to actually get into the van,"

Ian commented, then baulked at the woman's steely glare. "Any further updates?"

"Yes," the woman barked, rapping away at the keyboard. A moment later, the screen flicked off. "What took you so long, guys? We've been waiting for ages."

Kester looked around the cramped space of the van. *Is that meant to be the royal 'we'?* he wondered. Unless someone was currently hiding in the foot well of the driver's seat, there definitely wasn't anyone else in here. The van had a very strange smell too, a tinge of sulphur, as though someone had been lighting matches close by.

"Lili, allow me to introduce Luke and Kester," Cardigan began, nodding at them both. "Kester, Luke; this is Lili Asadi, who leads our surveillance team." He looked around. "Where's Tinker?"

She coughed, wiping her nose across her sleeve. "Tinker's currently situated on the roof of a hotel across the road, taking photos of the building with an amplifying-heat lens. Hopefully we'll be able to determine the shape of this daemon a bit better then. At present, there's no way of confirming whether it's him or not."

"Tinker does fantastic surveillance and undercover work," Ian explained. "Though you probably won't ever meet him. He's notoriously shy."

"I don't suppose you brought me a cup of coffee, did you?" Lili asked as she placed her hands on her narrow hips. "I've been here since five o'clock, I could do with a bit of caffeine. Dr Barqa-Abu is probably feeling a bit worse for wear too."

Kester jumped so vigorously that he nearly tripped over the wires at his feet. "I'm sorry," he spluttered. "Did I just hear you right? Did you say Dr Barqa-Abu?"

Lili looked amused. "That's correct."

Cardigan winked. "That's the special guest helping us with the case, Kester."

Right on cue, the air beside Kester began to quiver, turning almost pearlescent, as though lit by an underwater light. Before he had a chance to react, or even *think* about the situation, the recognisable face of the genie appeared above him, looming down with an expression of mild irritation.

"It is a very cold day," she hissed without any other form of greeting. Bobbing and wheeling in the cramped space around them, it felt rather uncomfortably like being trapped in a tiny cage with a large, unpredictable animal.

"Good morning, Dr Barqa-Abu," Cardigan greeted, then bowed deeply. "As ever, it is a great honour to see you. I take it you weren't too inconvenienced, taking the time off work?"

The genie glimmered into faintness before sharpening once more, her black, fathomless eyes studying each of them in turn. "The SSFE understands the importance of the case," she murmured, then stopped abruptly above Kester. "Ah. I see that Gretchen and Ribero's offspring is with us. Finally, we meet in the flesh, Kester Lanner."

Kester shivered. He didn't think he'd ever heard the "s" in his name extended quite as excessively in his life. However, with the genie in such close proximity to him, he now realised where the smell of burning matches was coming from. "Er, hello," he stuttered and edged back instinctively, intimidated by the swirling form towering above him. "Nice to see you again."

The genie made a noise that could have either been a snort or a laugh, then rolled towards the other end of the van, where she promptly vanished. Kester looked around with worry, horribly suspicious that she was going to leap out again when he least expected it. To his relief, she reappeared only a few moments later and rested on the top of one of the units near the ceiling, like a large, watchful bird of prey.

Lili coughed deliberately and tapped the nearest computer screen. "Right," she continued, "here are the most recent developments. They're quite significant, so I hope you're paying attention."

"Of course, my dearest lady," Ian declared grandly. He leaned against her shoulder, caught sight of her indignant expression, and promptly leapt off again.

"We noted plenty of activity during the night," she began, shooting a final disapproving look at Ian, who shrank back with embarrassment. Clicking at the computer, she brought up some thermal footage, which they all studied intently. After about five minutes, Lili pressed pause, and tapped at the image. "Here," she said decisively. "This is what I want you to look at."

Cardigan peered intently at the screen. "There are two images. Clearly, the one on the right is human, given the level of heat produced. And the other could well be daemonic, judging by its intensity."

Kester squinted. The blurred figure on the right looked much like any other thermal image he'd seen on news reports in the past, a vibrant woman-shaped silhouette of red, yellow, and lurid green. However, the figure to the left was very different indeed. For starters, it shifted in form constantly. Secondly, it glowed unnaturally bright, and was filled with burning yellow and orange alone.

"Any idea who the human is?" Ian asked.

Lili shook her head. "It's a female, and she's slender. Quite short too. That's all we can tell at this point."

Dr Barqa-Abu swooped down to join them. Kester felt hot air rush past his face, much like a blast of a furnace. "Watch what happens next," she muttered and positioned herself in the available space beside Luke, who seemed completely unfazed.

Lili pressed play, and the footage continued. They watched, captivated, as the figures moved closer together. Suddenly, there was an explosion of colour, which filled the screen. Kester looked on in amazement as the colour shrank in on itself until it had disappeared completely—absorbed into the human form.

"Where's the daemon gone?" he exclaimed, nearly knocking his glasses off in his excitement. "Only the woman's there now!"

Cardigan let out a low whistle and patted Lili on the back. "This is interesting," he muttered. "Very interesting indeed." He looked around at the others. "So, Hrschni has chosen to inhabit another human. That could complicate things a little."

"Particularly if we don't know who the female in question is," Ian added with a worried glance at his colleague.

"Who are the females that attend this particular Thelemite lodge?" Cardigan asked.

Lili nodded at Dr Barqa-Abu, who slid elegantly in front of them.

"We've examined the profile of every known Thelemite female that belongs to the Whitby branch," the genie hissed, her pointy features drifting in and out of visibility. "There are four in total. None match the physiology of the female in question."

"Are you sure?" Ian asked.

The genie glowered, circling around him like a stalking mist. "Of course we are sure," she retorted. "The other women are all too tall, not to mention mostly too large in build. The female who is carrying Hrschni is not from the Whitby lodge."

"We've also reviewed the CCTV footage from the camera on the street," Lili added. "The woman was in a coat with a big hood, it was impossible to make out her features."

"So how are you going to get a good look at her?" Luke asked.

"That's why Tinker's using the amplifying-heat lens," Lili explained. "We're hoping he'll catch a better image with it."

Ian rubbed his beard thoughtfully. "This rather changes things, doesn't it?" He looked over at Dr Barqa-Abu, who had almost faded to invisibility once more. "What do you propose?"

The genie whirled into sharper focus, bringing with her an even more pungent smell of burning sulphur. "I suggest that I slip into the building to see what I can discover," she murmured smoothly and wheeled to a halt in front of Ian.

"Is that wise?" he replied with a glance at the others. "What if you're detected?"

The genie pulled herself up to full height. "Humans would not be able to detect me, if I wished it so," she said haughtily. "The only threat is Hrschni himself, so we would need to be sure he is not in the near vicinity."

Lili rapped the computer smartly. "I can keep tabs on that, no problem."

"And I guess the rest of us could position ourselves in the surrounding area, to watch out for any short women heading this way," Luke suggested, as he scratched his head. "How short are we talking here?"

"Very short," Lili replied curtly. "And small-framed. I'd say 5 feet or less."

Kester patted his stomach reflectively, taking comfort from the remnants of his breakfast, still filling him up pleasantly. "This all still seems a bit odd, though," he said slowly, thinking about the events so far. "I mean, why now? Why did he wait all this time before entering the body of another human?"

"What are you driving at?" Lili asked as she studied him curiously.

"It feels a bit like he's playing a game," Kester concluded with a nervous shrug. "I can't help feeling like we're all being led on a merry dance."

"So you keep saying," Cardigan said. "The only problem is, what can we do? We have to work with what we've got."

Dr Barqa-Abu floated closer to Kester, examining him with open interest. He flinched under the heat of her gaze, not to mention the eye-watering scent of her person. "You interest me," she concluded finally and shifted backwards. "You are observant, but you have not yet learned to use the right perspective."

"What do you mean?" he asked. Her comment was confusing, to say the least.

Her empty, black eyes shifted into sharp focus. "You will see," she said cryptically. "Time will show you the way, I can promise you that. However," she continued, whirling above their heads, "now we need to act on our plan. I will go into the Thelemite lodge now and see what I can find. The rest of you must ensure my safety while I am in there. I am old and powerful, but I do not underestimate

Hrschni's ability to cause harm to me, should he so wish."

"We'll safeguard you as best as possible," Ian announced with a dramatic beating of his chest. "You have my word, my good Jiniri."

"See that it is so," she hissed before vaporising into nothing. Kester looked around in bewilderment, then spotted the bright yellow shape, moving on the thermal imaging screen.

"Gosh, she moves fast, doesn't she?" He followed her as she floated across the road and entered the building.

"Of course she does, she's one of the djinn," Lili said firmly. Stalking across to a box in the corner, she rummaged around before pulling out four tiny devices, which she threw at the others. "Walkie-talkies," she explained, seeing Kester's look of confusion. "Get out there, get watching. I'm going to contact Tinker, then move the van to a safer position."

She threw open the door and ushered them back out into the cold. In their absence, the snow had picked up pace, and was already an inch thick on the pavement. Luke stamped his feet. "Jeez, you guys really know how to do winter here, don't you?"

"We have it down to a fine art," Ian confirmed, then nodded down the street. "Luke, you and Kester stand watch near the park. You'll have a good view of any passers-by there. I'll take this end of the road. Cardigan, are you okay to go around the back?"

Cardigan nodded. "Of course. Any sign of a small woman, you must raise the alarm. Got it?"

The others nodded, then parted company. Kester couldn't help feeling rather excited by it all, despite the fact that his nose was already turning to ice and his fingers were agonisingly numb. They crossed the road, and dutifully positioned themselves by the park entrance, watching as thick snowflakes landed silently all around them.

"Ain't no-one going to be out in this weather," Luke announced cheerfully as he wrapped his jacket more tightly around himself. "Even the world's most dedicated Thelemites wouldn't bother coming out on a morning like this, would they?"

"What about the world's most dangerous daemon?" Kester asked, with a wry smile. "I doubt a bit of cold would bother him."

Luke nodded sagely. "Ah, but remember: when they enter a human body, they're constrained by human limitations. That means he'd feel the cold, alright."

Kester scratched his chin. "Why do they inhabit humans, then?" he asked. "I mean, what's in it for them?"

Luke laughed. "Man, you really are green, aren't you?" Seeing Kester's expression, his expression quickly softened. "Not that there's anything wrong with that."

"That's why I've enrolled on a course at the SSFE," Kester replied stiffly. "I'm aware I'm still new to all of this."

"I know," Luke said placatingly. "Let me explain. A daemon, like any other kind of spirit, loves to be around humans. We don't really understand why. They just do. It's our energy, you see. They almost feed off it."

Kester shuddered. "I'm not sure I'm comfortable with that idea."

Luke waved a dismissive hand. "It's nothing to worry about. All spirits have their weird little ways. Many are attached to specific places. Some attach themselves to certain types of people. Daemons fall into the latter category."

"What sort of people do they like, then?" Kester asked.

"Ambitious folk," Luke replied. "Daemons thrive on attention, and as a result, they search for people with similar dreams to their own. They offer those people the world, in exchange for . . ."

"For temporary residence?" Kester suggested.

"Yeah, that's pretty much what it is," Luke concluded. "Most times, it's a real harmonious relationship. Both the daemon and the human benefit from it."

Kester coughed, sending a plume of icy mist into the air. "Would they ever enter a human without permission?"

Luke looked shocked at the mere idea. "No way," he said adamantly. "It goes against their daemon code. They're very respectful of humans."

"Well, Hrschni seems to be breaking the code already, doesn't he?"

Luke pondered the statement, eyes fixed on the clouds overhead. "I know he's already acted strangely," he said after he spat onto the snow below. "But I still can't imagine any daemon entering a human without being allowed to. It's just not their nature, period."

"Why's he suddenly acting so aggressively towards humans, then?" Kester pressed. He knew that Luke didn't have the answers, but it felt good to get the questions out in the open and try to figure out what was going on.

"I guess he wants the world to embrace spirits again," Luke replied simply. "Like they used to in the old days, before people like you and I started to control their movements."

"Before science took the place of spirituality?"

Luke grinned. "Yeah, something like that."

Kester said nothing. *I still think we're missing the bigger picture,* he thought to himself as he shifted a pile of snow underneath his feet. *The break-in at Infinite Enterprises, the secret lyrics in Billy Dagger's songs, the sudden disappearance . . . none of it is adding up. And it's driving me mad.*

They waited, eyes sweeping restlessly up and down the street. Apart from the occasional passing car, the area was deserted—almost eerily so. A lone jackdaw poked around at the dustbin beside them, the only disturbance in the otherwise deathly silence.

Suddenly, their walkie-talkies crackled quietly in their palms. They raised the devices to their ears. To Kester's surprise, Cardigan's voice came through, clear as cut glass.

"Have either of you seen anything yet?" he asked, then added, "Over."

Luke glanced at Kester. "Nope, nothing yet," he replied. "It's quiet as a tomb down here. Over."

"I've just heard from Lili that Dr Barqa-Abu is on the upper floor," Cardigan continued. "She's been in one particular room for a while now, we wonder if she's discovered something. Over."

Kester wrapped his arms across his chest and shivered. *I swear it's getting colder,* he thought as he gazed longingly back in the direction of the hotel. *I'd give anything to be snuggling up in bed watching a film right now.* A figure in the distance suddenly caught his attention, walking slowly up the hill towards them. He nudged Luke and pointed.

"Hang on a minute," Luke said quickly, pulling Kester back so they were concealed behind the wall of the park. "We've got someone coming towards us, up the hill. He's a big guy though, not a small woman. Over."

Kester watched the figure as he waddled closer, deliberate and ponderous as a bison. There was something about the way he was moving that seemed familiar, though he couldn't think why. They waited patiently as the man lumbered to the top of the hill, then started to pace in their direction.

"He's coming this way. Over," Luke whispered, squinting at the man in question.

Suddenly, Kester gasped. He fumbled for his walkie-talkie, nearly dropping it in the snow as he did so. "Cardigan?" he muttered quickly as he squinted at the approaching figure. "Cardigan, are you there?"

There was a silence. Luke nudged him. "You're meant to say 'over'," he whispered helpfully.

"Oh yes. Over!"

"What is it? Over."

"I think I know the man! I mean, I'm not definitely sure yet, but I'm fairly confident I do. Over."

Luke studied the man intently. "He doesn't look familiar to me. You sure?"

Kester rubbed at his glasses, then nodded firmly. "I definitely do." Directing his voice into the walkie-talkie, he added, "Cardigan, the man coming towards us is Barty Melville. I'm sure of it. I'd recognise his awful taste in clothes anywhere. Over."

Cardigan whistled down the other end of the walkie-talkie. "As in Bartholomew Melville, who's quite high up in the Thelemites? Over?"

"Yes, that's exactly who I mean. I met him recently. Over."

"Lili, are you listening to this? Do we need to get Dr Barqa-Abu out of there, over?" Cardigan asked tersely.

There was a crackle, then Lili's clipped, cockney tones filled their ears. "Not if he's unaccompanied by any daemons. He wouldn't be able to detect Dr Barqa-Abu in a million years, don't you worry. Over."

They fell silent as Barty Melville wobbled closer. His expansive figure was covered by a voluminous black velvet coat, which fell about him like an oversized magician's cloak. *He looks shifty,* Kester thought as he shrank further back behind the wall, making sure he was out of sight. *I knew there was something about him I didn't trust.*

Barty coughed as he passed, a deep, baritone boom that disturbed the impeccable silence of the morning, echoing around the neighbouring beech trees. A few moments later, he'd proceeded up the street, pacing a slow, inexorable path towards the lodge. Kester exhaled and looked at Luke in bewilderment.

Luke shrugged. "The plot thickens," he concluded, rubbing an anxious hand over his buzz-cut hair. "Why do you reckon he's here?"

"I don't know," Kester replied as he pocketed his walkie-talkie. "But I bet you anything he's involved in all of this."

"Not good," Luke said solemnly and kicked at a nearby pile of snow-coated leaves.

"Not good at all," Kester agreed.

They continued to keep watch with renewed enthusiasm, confident that at least one other Thelemite member would join Barty at the lodge. However, the road remained resolutely clear, while the snow started to fall even more heavily.

Finally, Luke raised the walkie-talkie to his lips. "The weather's getting pretty bad, guys," he said morosely. "Has Dr Barqa-Abu finished up yet? Over."

The line crackled. "I think she's on her way out now," Lili replied dryly. "She's certainly on the move, if the thermal imaging is anything to go by. Over."

Without waiting for further comment, Kester and Luke moved back in the direction of the van. The snow had soaked through Kester's coat, trousers, and socks, leaving him bitterly cold all over.

"Your teeth sound like a rattlesnake's tail," Luke said with a laugh as they crossed the road, wading through the settling snow. "I don't think they could chatter any more if they tried, could they?"

"I'm bloody freezing," he replied grumpily, then swore as a piece of snow fell from the tree above, falling directly down his jacket collar. "If I get hypothermia, I won't be happy."

"Hey, you think you've got it bad; I'm used to Texan weather," Luke reminded him as they approached the van, which was now parked further down the road. "This is like the Antarctic to me."

They knocked quietly on the van door, which immediately flew open. Lili peered out, then pulled them in, frantic as a flapping parakeet. "Come on, come on," she muttered. "Don't take all day about it." She pointed at their feet as they stood unhappily in the middle of the van. "You're dripping water all over the place."

"You try standing out in the snow for half an hour," Kester grumbled as he brushed his coat down. He looked around. "Is Dr Barqa-Abu back yet, then?"

As soon as he spoke, the air beside the computer shimmered, solidifying into the shifting mist of the genie.

"*She* is indeed back," Dr Barqa-Abu replied dryly, then weaved through the air towards him. "And *she* has discovered very interesting things. But we will wait until the others return."

Kester grimaced. He hoped they'd hurry up. He was in desperate need of a steaming bath and a nice, warm, comforting drink.

A few minutes later, Cardigan and Ian returned, both looking as wet and irate as Kester felt. They stomped into the van, which felt immediately cramped with Cardigan's large body and Ian's bouffant mane taking up a considerable amount of the available space.

"So," Cardigan said as he shrugged off his jacket. "Bartholomew Melville, eh? That's an interesting development."

"Did anyone else join him?" Luke asked.

Cardigan shook his head. "No. He was alone." He turned to Dr Barqa-Abu. "What did he get up to when he was inside?"

The genie flitted back towards the ceiling, her eyes darting from face to face. "Something very alarming indeed," she hissed. "But allow me to start from the beginning."

They all waited expectantly. The genie shimmered an ice-blue for a moment before fading to a scarcely visible haze.

"I found nothing of interest on the ground floor," she started, settling back into a misty, shifting cloud by the computer. "Apart from a large hall, a small office which I believe may be used by the British Legion, and some toilets. However, upstairs was rather more intriguing, to say the least."

"What did you find up there?" Lili asked, wide-eyed as a child.

Dr Barqa-Abu exhaled, a long, vibrating noise that sounded like ball-bearings dragging over the floor. "The door to the upper floor was locked," she continued. "But of course, that was no problem for me. In addition, every other door on the floor was also locked. In some cases, double-locked. Clearly, they take security very seriously. They also had sensors and alarms fitted in every room."

Ian whistled. "That's rather interesting. What are they protecting so passionately, I wonder?"

Dr Barqa-Abu's face came into sharp focus. For a moment, Kester thought he detected a dry smile playing on her lips that faded as soon as it began. "Quite," she replied, then continued her ceaseless circling of the narrow space. "Anyway, there was one room in particular that was very interesting indeed."

The others waited, hardly daring to breathe.

"There was a complex strategy drawn up on one of the walls," she continued. "Regrettably, sections were written in some form of code. However, it was clear to see what their goal was."

"To open a permanent spirit door?" Cardigan prompted. "We know that much already."

The genie shook her head, clearly nettled by the interruption. "Not just that," she snapped. "To keep it *continually* open and in their control."

Cardigan looked at Lili, then they both chuckled.

"That's not possible," Lili stated. "It costs Infinite Enterprises an arm and a leg to open it once a week, let alone all the time. We're talking *millions*."

Kester frowned. "Are there any other ways to create a permanent opening?" he asked.

"Only to create a sun-door, as they used to in the days of old," Ian declared, casting his gaze dramatically upwards as though searching for signs of ancient civilisations on the metal ceiling.

"That's never been scientifically proven," Lili added practically.

"And even if ancient people did manage it, we have no idea how," Cardigan concluded.

Kester scratched his head thoughtfully. "If Hrschni is so old," he said slowly, "might he have an idea of how it was done?"

Dr Barqa-Abu solidified briefly, her razor-sharp features coming into sharp focus. "It is possible," she said, moving closer. "I am as old as he, and I do not know how it is done, but daemons have ways of finding things out."

"Let's presume that sun-doors can be built," Kester said, massaging his temples. "What would be the main advantage?"

"To allow mass movement," Dr Barqa-Abu replied. "When a single spirit enters this world, it can take time, not to mention effort. A sun-gate enables faster travel between the realms. Much like the spirit doors that you create, Kester."

I'm not sure mine have ever been big enough to let many spirits through at once, he thought, remembering the thin, shimmering openings he'd created in the past. *Still, perhaps that's because my skills aren't terribly good.*

"So," he said finally, "it's like the difference between walking down a narrow country road or speeding down a motorway?"

The genie sighed. "If one is going to put it crudely, then yes, I suppose so."

"Probably more like comparing a sci-fi teleporter with an old Penny Farthing bicycle," Lili added helpfully. "Quite simply, spirits much prefer taking the easy route to our world, via a proper door."

"Did you find out anything else?" Ian asked as he rested against the nearest desk.

Dr Barqa-Abu nodded. "Names. I believe these were some of the key figures in the operation. But there is bad news, I'm afraid."

"What's that?" Cardigan asked, with a worried look at the others.

"They're not all human."

They groaned collectively.

"Please don't say there are any other daemons involved," Lili said, sitting next to Ian. "That would be terrible."

"A few names I did not recognise," the genie replied. "But one name was certainly familiar. *Fylgja*."

Cardigan flinched. "Tell me you're joking."

Ian stood up, electrified into action. "Fylgja went off the radar years ago."

"Over seventy years ago, to be precise," Dr Barqa-Abu clarified. "I remember it well. The first daemon in years to fail to report for registration. And of course, no-one has heard from her since."

"Christ, if she's joined the Thelemites, we're in serious trouble," Ian whispered.

"Excuse me," Kester said, once again feeling like the only child in school who didn't know the answer to a very easy question. "Who on earth is this Filljar person?"

"Fylgja," Dr Barqa-Abu corrected, pin-prick eyes burrowing into his own. "Surely you have heard of her? It was a famous incident. It shook the supernatural world to its core."

"Nope," Kester replied. "It doesn't even sound vaguely familiar." He cowered under the weight of her obvious disapproval.

"Fylgja is a relatively powerful daemon," the genie explained, flitting irritably from side to side. "Her most famous human inhabitation was inside a certain British queen, though most of the time, she chose to connect with people from the northern lands."

"The northern lands? You mean Scotland?"

"No, I mean northern Europe," Dr Barqa-Abu corrected irritably. "Even daemons favour certain parts of the world, from time to time."

"Why is it so bad if she's joined the Thelemites, then?" Kester asked.

"One daemon is bad enough. Two is virtually unmanageable," Cardigan replied.

"There's more news, I'm afraid," Dr Barqa-Abu continued. She glided closer to Kester, solidifying into a form that was clearer than he'd ever seen her before. He fought against the urge to cower as he studied her skeletal face and hollow, haunted expression.

"What is it?" he squeaked, already knowing that it was something to do with him.

"It's Barty Melville," she said as she inched even closer. "And more specifically, what he was doing in the Thelemite lodge."

"What *was* he doing?" Kester asked, even though he didn't really want to know. The proximity of the genie, not to mention the overwhelming smell of burning coming from her, was making him feel nauseous.

"Among other things, he was reading through some files," she said quietly, and for a moment, her features softened. In fact, she looked almost as though she felt sorry for him. "And those files were about your father and his agency."

"What?" Kester's head shot up. "What do you mean?"

"I mean," the genie concluded, a spectral hand touching him briefly on the shoulder, ice-blue as a glacier, "If the Thelemites possess files about your father's agency, it may be a target."

"Which means," Cardigan concluded heavily, "that your team are in danger. Serious danger."

CHAPTER 11: WORD GAMES

The train finally pulled into Exeter station at just after midnight. Kester emerged onto the cold, lamp-lit street, grateful that at least it wasn't snowing here, and readied himself for the long walk home.

He'd tried calling both his father and Miss Wellbeloved countless times on the way down, but nobody had answered. Even stranger still, no-one at the office was picking up either.

He trudged through town, exhausted and anxious. Even the sparkling Christmas lights overhead did nothing to improve his mood. *What if this Fylgja daemon has already got to them?* he thought as he paced up the high street. *After all, we have no idea where she is. She could be in Exeter already. She could have already done something to them, for all I know.*

The mere thought made his fists clench inside his pockets. *I'd make them pay if they tried any funny business,* he thought fiercely, puffing with exertion as he started to climb the hill that led to home. *If anyone's hurt Dad or Miss Wellbeloved or any of them, even Serena, I won't rest until I've found them. Even if it is a centuries-old daemon.* The dampness of his coat pressed against his already-cold back, but he hardly noticed.

Finally, he arrived outside his front door, unlocked it, and stepped inside with relief. The hallway light was on, but this wasn't unusual, given that his housemates frequently forgot to turn the lights off, not to mention the oven and other dangerous appliances.

God, it's even colder in here than it is outside, he thought as he dumped his bag down next to the stairs.

"Hello?" A tentative voice trailed from somewhere in the house.

Kester nearly tripped over with shock. He hadn't expected anyone to be up so late. Peering into the lounge, he was amazed to see Anya, sitting primly on the sofa, Thor comfortably coiled on her lap. Apart from the streetlight casting a glow over her shoulders, she was sitting in complete darkness. Her eyes shone with an almost eerie light.

"I didn't realise you'd stay up," he said breathlessly, then he instinctively clambered over and kissed her on the lips. "But I'm very glad you did."

She kissed him back—a slow, thoughtful motion that set his heart racing—then retreated. "Of course I waited up," she said, gaze flitting across his face. "I just wondered why you had to return in such a hurry. Your text messages didn't explain much. Has something bad happened? Tell me everything, I'm worried."

He switched on the lamp, which bathed the room in its usual watery light, instantly making everything feel far more normal. "Don't worry, it's nothing to be worried about," he explained, settling himself on the sofa. "I just have to be careful what I say, don't I?" He leant back, then touched a strand of her hair. "I like the new colour. Very pretty. It shows off your eyes."

Anya grinned and patted him on the leg. "You are charming, Kester. So, what happened?"

He sighed and retrieved his phone, hoping that his father or Miss Wellbeloved would have miraculously replied to his messages. However, the screen remained frustratingly empty. "Can I get a drink first?" he said as he patted Thor tentatively on the rump. "The walk home really took it out of me."

She bit her lip, then stood up. "Let me," she said. "What do you want?"

"A big, fat glass of wine, if there is any."

He waited patiently, resting his head against the welcome softness of the sofa. *I'm utterly exhausted,* though he knew that was no guarantee of a good sleep. If anything, he suspected he'd be wide awake until he was sure the others were safe.

Anya returned with a glass in each hand. She perched beside him, then nodded. "Go on, then," she pressed. Her eyes almost seemed to burn in the amber lamplight, and he felt his insides turn to liquid once again. *God, she looks prettier every time I see her,* he thought as he sipped at his wine. *It's almost like someone's switched on a lightbulb behind her face, which makes her gleam from within.*

"Barty Melville turned up," he explained finally, rubbing his eyes. Quickly, he filled her in on the rest of the details.

Her eyes widened. "That's very interesting. Do you think that your dad is in danger?"

Kester nodded and traced a contemplative finger around the rim of his glass. "The fact that he's not answering his phone isn't helping," he replied. "I'm terrified something's happened to him."

She nuzzled in next to him, stroking his tummy. "Why do you think Barty is interested in your father's agency? What could your dad possibly offer to the Thelemites? Have you got any theories?"

"That's a good question." He studied the opposite wall, eyes tracing the various stains and marks on the wallpaper. It was such an appallingly grotty house, and the filth always seemed more noticeable after he'd been away for any length of time. "I wondered at first if Barty was more interested in Miss Wellbeloved, given that her family used to be so heavily involved with the Thelemites."

Anya shrugged. "Maybe. Or maybe your dad has something that they need?"

He exhaled heavily. "Who knows? All I'm concerned with right now is ensuring that everyone's safe."

"And did you find anything else out while you were up there?"

"You're very interested in all of this, aren't you?" He raised an eyebrow.

She blushed. "Only because I know it interests you. I care about you, Kester. This is your career, so I want to know more about it. That's all."

Kester smiled and sipped at his wine. "That's sweet of you. But why don't you tell me how your day went instead?"

"Ugh. The last thing I want to do is talk about the library." She leaned over and kissed him on the cheek. "Why don't you come to bed?"

"I'm not sure I'd be up to much, to be honest."

"I mean to sleep, you funny thing! Though if you're offering . . ."

Kester glanced down at his phone again. "I might just try Dad one more time. Just in case."

She shrugged, downed the rest of her glass, then stood up, Thor snuffling restlessly at her heels. "I'll see you upstairs then."

"Yes, I'll be up in a moment." He watched her as she sashayed out of the room. Her pyjama bottoms hugged at her tiny hips in a most inviting manner, and he looked away, worried that his open leering might be considered indecent.

Think about something completely non-arousing, like concrete bollards or paper-clips, he ordered himself firmly, then raised the phone to his ear.

It rang and rang, until finally it went through to answerphone. Sighing, he slammed it on the coffee-table, then stared anxiously into space. *Where the hell are you, Dad?* he thought, aware of the bite of anxiety, nestled deep within his stomach. *And why do I feel like something is about to go very horribly wrong?*

The phone suddenly vibrated into action, startling him out of his reverie. Without pausing, he seized it up.

"Dad, where the hell have you been?" he snapped. "I've been absolutely worried sick!"

"Kester, it's me."

He took a deep breath, then laughed. "Hello, Miss Wellbeloved. Sorry about that. Where on earth have you and Dad been all day? I've been desperately trying to get hold of you."

There was a nervous clucking down the other end of the phone. Kester waited patiently, the tension in his chest already unravelling like a loosening knot. Everything was alright. He could sleep comfortably now, without enduring any more panicking—for now, anyway.

"We're at the hospital," Miss Wellbeloved said eventually. "I left my phone in the car, so I didn't know you'd called."

Kester sat upright. "What happened? Is Dad alright?"

"He's okay, don't worry. They had to keep him in because of the risk of concussion. Other than a sprained ankle, he's fine."

"What happened?"

"He was going to make some breakfast for us, then he tripped down the stairs. You know how steep the stairs are in my house, Kester."

"Hang on," he interrupted, nearly spitting out his mouthful of wine. "Are you suggesting that Dad stayed the night at your house?"

Silence hung down the receiver, weighty and strange as a sumo wrestler in a tutu.

"I can't see why you'd choose to focus on that particular detail, given that I've just told you about your father—"

"—Are you and Dad romantically involved, then?"

Miss Wellbeloved tutted. "May we move to another topic, please?"

Kester grimaced. *The wily old goat,* he thought, not sure whether to feel disgusted, perturbed, or supportive. *Even after jilting her at the altar and having an affair with my mother, he managed to weasel his way back into her bed. It's certainly impressive for a pensioner.*

"Are you still there?" Miss Wellbeloved sounded wary.

"Yes." Kester sighed and stretched his aching back. "How is he, then?"

"Your dad's fine. He was a bit shaken up, but otherwise okay." Miss Wellbeloved sighed. "It's been a stressful day, though. How did you get on in Whitby?"

Quickly, he outlined his experiences, ending with Barty Melville's interest in Dr Ribero's files.

Miss Wellbeloved cleared her throat. "That's curious, isn't it?"

"Curious?" Kester exclaimed. "I'd say it's more than that. I'd call it downright ominous. What if he's trying to find out information to hurt Dad with? Or you, for that matter?"

"I can't imagine Barty doing that," Miss Wellbeloved said briskly. "Remember, Kester; I've known him since I was a young girl. He knew my father. And my grandfather, for that matter. Regardless of what he might think about my family parting ways with the Thelemites, I doubt he'd ever hurt me."

"What about Dad, then?"

She paused. "I don't think so. It's just not Barty's style. He's petty. Arrogant. Rather ruthless at times, perhaps. But he's not a violent man."

Or perhaps you don't want to acknowledge that he's changed, along with the precious Thelemites, Kester thought unkindly. He made no reply.

"Look," Miss Wellbeloved said eventually. "Infinite Enterprises already know about this, so we'll be well protected. Your father, your girlfriend—everyone. Don't panic, Kester, it'll all be okay."

He rubbed his eyes, tiredness descending on him like a bag of wet sand. "If you say so," he mumbled. "I'm going to go to bed now, otherwise I'll never be up for work."

"Of course," she replied. "Serena and Pamela are out of the office tomorrow morning, by the way; Curtis Philpot wanted them to visit the Exeter Thelemite lodge to see if they could detect anything."

"Ah well, I'm sure I can manage one day without Serena goading me about something or other," he replied. "Good night, Miss Wellbeloved."

"Sleep well, Kester."

He flicked off the lamp. *It's all too much to think about,* he brooded in the darkness before standing up. *And the thought of Dad and Miss Wellbeloved cosying up to each other, on top of everything else, is the icing on the cake.*

The stairs creaked as he crept upwards. Pushing his bedroom door open as gently as possible, he smiled to see Anya tucked underneath his duvet, already asleep. The gentle rise and fall of her body reminded him of the waves of an ocean, tugging and pulling.

Snuggling in beside her, he draped an arm over her body, feeling the warmth of her skin. He couldn't believe how lucky he was. Growing up with his mother, he'd always presumed he'd be single for his entire life. The thought of a woman actually liking him was something he'd regarded as ridiculous. Yet here she was, sleeping right next to him.

Good night, he thought, studying her face in the moonlight. *I rather think I'm falling in love with you, Anya.*

With that delicious yet frightening thought, Kester fell asleep.

The alarm cut through his head like an electric drill. He peered at the time, then groaned. *How can it already be eight o'clock?* he thought. *It feels like I only climbed into bed a few minutes ago.* Anya groaned, rolled awkwardly against him, then buried her head under the duvet.

"Don't you have work this morning?" Kester mumbled, trying to silence his alarm clock by smacking it with his fist. So far, the alarm clock was winning the battle by a considerable margin.

Anya grumbled in response and burrowed deeper down into the bed. Kester wished he could too. His eyes felt grainy from insufficient sleep, and the prospect of spending a day at the office, fretting about the case, wasn't an appealing one.

"I'll see you later," he whispered and attempted to locate her head underneath the warm sheets. In the end, he settled for stroking her hair before sloping off to the shower.

After an irritable march through town, Kester opened the door of the office to see Miss Wellbeloved and Mike, already at their desks. To his surprise, his father was there too, resting languidly on a set of crutches. He saw Kester and gave a slow, deliberate wink.

"It is the boy!" he exclaimed as though Kester had been absent for weeks, not a couple of days.

"You alright, mate?" Mike asked, poking a pair of tweezers into what looked like a discarded take-away carton. Triumphantly, he hoisted out a mass of wires, which sparked furiously as he waved them about in the air. "You're looking a bit peaky."

"I feel a bit peaky," Kester confirmed, slumping down in front of his camping desk, which promptly buckled under his elbows. "I only got in at midnight last night. I'm suffering from severe sleep deprivation."

"Did you enjoy the nice hotel in Whitby?" Ribero asked, crutches clacking on the floor as he hopped over.

"I was only in it for one night." Kester looked down at his father's foot, which was neatly swathed in white bandages. "I thought you'd still be in the hospital."

Ribero laughed. "No, Jennifer got me out, like a prison break, yes?"

Miss Wellbeloved gave a long-suffering sigh. "Your father begged me to come and get him, so I did."

The less I know about what my dad is begging you to do, the better, Kester thought. He was still struggling to digest the idea of their romantic involvement; judging by the wary expression on Miss Wellbeloved's face, she'd guessed what he was thinking. His father, however, seemed blissfully unaware.

"So, we have got some more developments in the case, I have heard?" Ribero sat down heavily in the nearest chair. "Jennifer tells me that Dr Barqa-Abu found out many useful things."

"Yes, about Dr Barqa-Abu," Kester began, frowning. "You might have bloody warned me she was going to be there."

His father grinned. "Ah, but it was more fun as a surprise, don't you think?"

"No, not in the slightest."

"So, now we know that we've got another daemon to contend with," Miss Wellbeloved said. "Philpot was on the phone about it just before you arrived. This makes things a lot more complicated."

"And no-one has any idea where Fylgja might be," Mike commented, delicately trying to tie a knot in a wire. Another huge spark erupted, though he didn't seem overly bothered. "That wily old daemon, eh?"

Miss Wellbeloved adjusted her bun, smoothing down the loose hairs that had managed to spring free. "It is mysterious. What has Fylgja been up to all this time? Everyone assumed she'd just returned to the spirit realm."

"Is she as dangerous as Hrschni?" Kester flipped his laptop open, ready to start researching.

"No daemons are necessarily dangerous," Miss Wellbeloved replied tightly. "Remember, we still don't fully understand Hrschni's intentions, so let's not draw any conclusions. His motives may be honourable."

"Do you think Infinite Enterprises will mind if I log onto their system and look at Fylgja's files?"

Ribero smacked the table. "That is a good idea, boy. Use that big brain of yours to find something out." He leant closer, one arm hooked over the top of his crutch. "Remember, if we solve this case, then we make Higgins look like the big, fat idiot, right?"

"That's not our main objective!" Miss Wellbeloved reminded him sternly. She turned to Kester. "I'm sure they won't mind at all. See what you can find out."

Kester swiftly logged into Infinite Enterprise's Swww address. His father patted him on the shoulder, then rose awkwardly to a standing position.

"I leave you to it," he announced and hobbled towards his office. Kester nodded, hardly noticing him leave.

He located Fylgja's files quickly enough, though the sheer volume of notes was daunting. He skimmed the content as swiftly as possible, trying to locate anything relevant to their case. The latest document detailed her mysterious disappearance.

Interesting, he thought, eyes scanning to the bottom. *She vanished at the end of the second world war, after inhabiting the body of a well-known Danish code-breaker.* He tapped his fingers thoughtfully on the keyboard. *Presumably, it was easier for her to slip away, given that everyone was preoccupied with something else at the time.*

He flicked through the other pages. Prior to her disappearance, she'd inhabited several different humans and was described as an exemplary spirit, always attending registration and submitting her permit papers on time. The only negative comments Infinite Enterprises had included were about her vanity and a love of inhabiting the bodies of attractive, powerful women.

Both she and Hrschni behaved themselves impeccably for hundreds, maybe thousands of years, he mused, glancing around the room at the others. *Why have they suddenly been galvanised into action now? What's changed?*

He didn't buy into the theory that the timing was coincidental. So far, everything the Thelemites had done felt choreographed; prepared to perfection, carefully designed to lead them down a certain path. It was not a comfortable thought.

After he'd scanned the rest of Fylgja's files, he rested his head on his hands, wishing he didn't feel quite so useless. As usual, trying to advance in the case felt like wading through treacle, always a few steps behind where he needed to be. *The information's there,* he thought with a sigh. *It's just a matter of knowing where to look for it.*

He wondered what Anya was doing and whether she'd had to go to work today or not. *I might pop over to the library later and surprise her,* he thought with a smile.

"That's a very lovely simper on your face, Kester."

Kester's glanced up to see Mike grinning at him from across

the room.

"I wasn't simpering, thanks very much."

"Call it a lovesick smile, then."

"Please don't."

Mike chuckled and returned to his work. For a few brief moments, silence reigned. Kester waited patiently, arms folded. He knew Mike far too well to believe that his teasing had finished yet.

"So, you got anywhere with her yet then, mate?"

"Mike, *really!*" Miss Wellbeloved's head snapped up in exasperation like a vexed meerkat. "Is it really necessary to ask those sorts of questions?"

"Not necessary, but funny, nonetheless," Mike waved his screwdriver cheerfully. "Kester doesn't mind, do you, Kester?"

"I bloody do," Kester corrected crossly.

He clicked on Hrschni's files, in the vain hope that he might spot something that he'd missed before. However, nothing obvious leapt from the pages, just a detailed record of all the humans he'd inhabited, dating back centuries. After twenty minutes, Kester logged out of the system, and sighed heavily. The words were beginning to blur into a mass of meaningless text, and he knew it was futile to carry on, or at least not until he'd had a cup of tea to wake himself up.

"Find out anything interesting?" Miss Wellbeloved asked, looking up as he made his way to the stockroom.

"Nothing at all," he replied grimly. "The files just go on about how well-behaved the daemons were. There's nothing to hint that they'd go over to the dark side. Apart from the fact that Fylgja likes looking pretty. But that doesn't really make her a criminal."

"I do wish you'd all stop making comments like that. There's no 'dark side' involved here," Miss Wellbeloved objected above the whistle of the kettle. "And they're not criminals."

"They've gone on the run, despite knowing they legally have to register and apply for permits. And they've threatened the government. Doesn't that count as criminal activity?" Kester asked.

Mike chuckled, then cursed as the contraption on his desk produced another loud bang.

"It depends on how you look at it," Miss Wellbeloved replied with a sniff. "Did you find anything else out?"

"All I can tell is that vain Fylgja liked to hang around in Scandinavia a lot, and that Hrschni had a thing for writers and musicians," he called back as he set about adding plenty of sugar to his steaming mug of tea. "And that Fylgja seemed to have lots of experience inhabiting the bodies of double-agents and code-breakers. Presumably that's a daemon thing."

Miss Wellbeloved brightened as Kester placed a mug of black tea on her desk. "Thank you, that's just what I needed." She sipped with contemplation and stared at the ceiling. "It's unsurprising that Hrschni is drawn to wordsmiths and wordplay, and Fylgja to puzzles. Daemons often enjoy riddles, anagrams, and enigmas."

"I can relate to that," Kester replied as he eased himself back into his chair. He rubbed at his stomach and wondered if he could detect a vague hint of muscle hidden underneath the generous layer of puppy fat. He'd been attempting to do a few exercises each day, but he wasn't convinced it was having any effect yet.

"I suppose that's why he included the lyrics in the letter he sent to Infinite Enterprises," Miss Wellbeloved mused, nails rapping rhythmically against the side of the mug. "A clever word game, designed to test us all. Just the sort of thing daemons love to do."

Kester stared at his computer screen, trying to force his brain into action. *It's all a ball of knotted string,* he thought with frustration. *And once I find the end, I can start unravelling it.*

Suddenly, he sat bolt upright, spilling tea over his lap as he did so. Miss Wellbeloved looked over quizzically, then shrugged at Mike.

"Anagrams and riddles," Kester murmured and ran a hand urgently through his hair, completely oblivious to the scalding wet patch currently spreading over his legs. "I wonder. *Word-play.*"

"What are you wittering on about?" Mike asked, watching him

with obvious amusement. "Is this one of your Sherlock Holmes moments, Kester?"

Kester frowned. "It's probably nothing. Just a thought. What's a good site for finding lyrics to songs?"

"I dunno, just Google it."

Kester quickly started typing, wishing the internet connection wasn't so painfully slow. Finally, the computer whirred into action. *This might be nothing,* he thought, peering at the screen, *but then again, it might not.*

"'Tear the Walls Down,' that was his last song, wasn't it?" Kester called out as he scanned the list in front of him.

"Yeah," Mike replied, leaning forward. "Though I've heard a rumour that there's a new one being released soon; one that's been hidden in the archives—"

"Never mind that now," Kester interrupted. He clicked through to the song and started reading through the lyrics.

> *Do what you will, it's time, it's time,*
> *Love is the law, through filth, through grime.*
> *We seek the pirate note, the clarion call*
> *Repeat into nothing, do what you will.*
>
> *Follow the path, lead the way,*
> *It is the Infinite, it holds sway.*
> *We break apart, we shatter anew*
> *Mastering drama, I break through.*
>
> *Cities spill worm, a polemicist swirl,*
> *Cities will romp, unravel, unfurl.*
>
> *Do what you will, it's time, it's time,*
> *Night comes, and the burning flame.*
> *Repeat into, repeat into, repeat into . . .*
> *Chaos.*

Kester removed his glasses, polished them earnestly on his top, then studied the lyrics again. *Well,* he thought with a wry grin, *trying to understand this load of gibberish should be fun.*

He peered closer, then jumped as he felt a hand on his shoulder.

"Need a bit of help?" Miss Wellbeloved asked quietly. Without waiting for a reply, she pulled up a chair and sat down beside him. "I used to be quite good at cryptic crosswords, so perhaps I can spot some hidden meaning in this song."

Kester delicately wiped down his crotch. The spilled tea was cooling, gluing his trousers to his thighs in a rather unpleasant manner. "Yes, please," he replied, "I need all the help I can get."

The room fell silent as they pored over the lyrics again.

"Obviously 'Do what you will' and 'Love is the law' relate directly to the Thelemites," Miss Wellbeloved said finally.

Kester sighed. "We knew that much already. Hrschni already used those phrases in the letter he sent to Infinite Enterprises. And 'Repeat into nothing', don't forget that."

They carried on looking.

"Some of these lyrics are very odd, aren't they?" Miss Wellbeloved concluded, easing her shoulders with an audible crack.

"Have they got any occult meaning?" Kester asked. "What about this line? 'Cities spill worm, a polemicist swirl.' What the heck does that mean?"

"I don't even know what the word 'polemicist' means," Mike shouted from across the room.

Kester quickly looked it up on the internet. "Here you go," he said. "It means 'someone who argues in opposition to others.'"

"Like the Thelemites arguing in opposition to us?" Miss Wellbeloved suggested as she drained the last of her tea.

Kester frowned. "I'm not convinced. There's something we're missing here, I'm certain of it." He squinted with frustration, then suddenly grabbed a pen.

Miss Wellbeloved watched him with fascination as he jotted down some letters in a circle, and started rearranging them.

"What are you doing?" she asked, eyes following his every movement. "Do you think there's some sort of anagram here?"

"I suddenly noticed," Kester said as he jotted down the letters feverishly, "that 'cities spill worm' and 'polemicist swirl' use exactly the same number of letters. Even more interesting, they *are* the exact same letters. Just in a different order."

Miss Wellbeloved gasped, then laughed out loud. "Well, I never. Hrschni's been at his word games again."

A deafening bang reverberated around the office. The others looked up to see Dr Ribero, standing in the doorway to his office, finger extended in Kester's direction.

"Something exciting is happening here, yes?" he announced, then hobbled awkwardly over to the desk. "I sense it in the air. Like electricity. What is going on?"

"Kester's uncovered some hidden secrets in one of Billy Dagger's songs," Mike said. He placed his screwdriver on the table and came over to join them.

"Solved it yet?" Miss Wellbeloved asked.

Kester blinked furiously, massaging his temples. "Not yet," he admitted. "It's hard working with this number of letters."

"You're definitely on the right track," Miss Wellbeloved said excitedly. "I notice that the next line, 'cities will romp,' uses almost the same letters again, except it's missing an 's'. Three times in a row." She grabbed a pen off her own desk and started to scribble down notes.

Suddenly, Kester threw down his pen. He looked up at his father, hair flopping over his eyes, and laughed. "I think I've got it," he said breathlessly. "And it's so obvious, I'm amazed I didn't see it straight away."

"What is it?" the others chorused in unison. Kester said nothing, only flipped his piece of paper, allowing them to see what was written on it.

"'*Spirits will come*'," Ribero read aloud. He looked at the others with wonder. "And this anagram is used three times in the song?"

"Three times in a row!" Kester exclaimed. "How bold is that?" He jabbed his pen at the lyrics. "He's cheated a little with the 'cities will romp' line, as it just says 'spirit will come', but otherwise, it's a perfect anagram, repeated as a trio. Clever."

"'Spirits will come'," Miss Wellbeloved repeated and took a deep breath. "I think that's a fairly clear warning, isn't it?"

Kester leaned back and surveyed the screen with a mixture of frustration and wonder. *How clever is this daemon to leave clues like this?* he thought. *I wonder what he's like in person?* He'd seen Hrschni as Billy Dagger, and even from the crowd, he could feel his energy and creativity. *I'd imagine he's very impressive,* he concluded as he nibbled the top of his biro. *Not to mention highly intimidating.* He felt suddenly like a small rodent attempting to stalk a tiger. *I'm out of my depth here,* he realised. *But what choice do I have but to continue?*

"I presume there are other clues in there too, maybe?" Ribero muttered as he pressed over Kester's shoulder.

Kester selected a few more of the lines at random and started playing around with the letters. "Probably," he agreed, squinting through his glasses. "Why don't we all have a go at deciphering it?"

For quarter of an hour, silence reigned in the office as they all pored over the lyrics. Finally, Miss Wellbeloved squeaked with excitement, waving her notepad high in the air. "Got another one!" she announced triumphantly. "The first verse. It contains the lyric 'pirate note'. I've been playing around with it, and it's an anagram of 'tear it open'."

Mike clapped her on the back. "Nice one, Miss W. Makes sense, doesn't it? As they're trying to tear open a door into the spirit world."

Kester nodded enthusiastically. "Funny you should mention that one. I was working on 'repeat into' and I think it's an anagram of the exact same thing. Let me double-check." He scoured the letters, and sure enough, they fitted perfectly.

"The question is," Mike said as he puffed out his cheeks, "who are the lyrics designed to send a message to? Other spirits? Is

Hrschni trying to create an army here?"

"Or is he just toying with us all?" Ribero suggested, eyes shining. "Leaving clues just for the fun of it, maybe?"

The office door suddenly flew open, disturbing the hush. Serena and Pamela stomped in, huddled in their coats, still shivering from the cold.

"What are you all looking so pleased about?" Serena asked as she unwound her long scarf and draped it neatly over her chair. "Something's happened, I can tell. What's going on?"

Miss Wellbeloved laughed. "Funny you should say that." Quickly, she filled the other two in on what they'd discovered.

Pamela clapped her hands enthusiastically. "Well, that's a turn up for the books," she said, sliding into her chair. "Clever you. Who knows what other clues are hidden in those Billy Dagger songs, eh?"

Kester looked at the others. "Gosh, yes. I wonder if all his lyrics are hiding something?"

"I wouldn't fancy going through all of them," Mike added. "He's got a back catalogue of about twenty albums."

Serena peered over their notes, then laughed. "Oh dear, have you all been working out these anagrams on paper? What a waste of time! Why didn't you just use an anagram solver online?"

Kester frowned. "Are there such things?"

"Yes, they're handy if you do a lot of crosswords."

Miss Wellbeloved coughed. "You mean, if you cheat a lot at crosswords."

Serena crossed her arms defensively. "Only when I get stuck near the end, thank you very much. Anyway—" Without waiting for permission, she leant over Kester's shoulder and started typing away at the keyboard. "Here you go. Loads of anagram solvers. Just enter the words you want to check, and it'll bring up all the options."

Kester sighed. "That is pretty useful, actually. Thanks, Serena."

"Where would you all be without me, eh?"

The others returned to their desks, leaving Kester to get on with it. With grim determination, he ploughed through the rest of the lyrics, typing them into the website and trawling through the possible anagram options.

This does speed things up a bit, he admitted as he skimmed through the list of words. *But it's still hard work. Perhaps there's nothing else to find, maybe I'm just wasting yet more time here.*

Suddenly, he remembered Serena's visit the other night, when she'd come over to give him the chocolates. He looked up. She was flicking through a pile of notes, patent-leather shoe tapping impatiently under the desk.

"Serena?" he called out, keen to take a break from his work.

"Yes?"

"Thanks for those chocolates the other night," he said. "They were very nice, and it was kind of you."

Mike's head snapped up as though he'd been electrocuted. "What were you doing, giving him chocolates?" he asked, eyes narrowing. "You never bring me chocolates."

Serena shifted in her seat. "It's absolutely none of your business, Mike. I merely went over to Kester's house to—"

"You went over to his house?"

"Yes. So?"

Kester coughed loudly, breaking the awkward silence. "She was apologising for something," he explained quickly, alarmed by Mike's expression. "Which reminds me, what was it you wanted to talk about, Serena? That night, you mentioned something about having suspicions about something?"

Serena looked uncomfortable. "Yeah. Now probably isn't the time, Kester."

Mike bristled. "Was it about me?"

"For heaven's sake, Mike; why would it be? Not everything revolves around you, you know!"

Kester sighed. *I might as well leave them to their bickering,* he thought. *They've forgotten I'm here again.* Sure enough, they continued to snipe at each other, completely oblivious to the rest of the office. Kester returned to the anagrams.

He typed in "mastering drama" from the second verse; not expecting to discover anything, even though it was a rather odd expression. The website whirred into action before producing a long list, mostly of complete gibberish. However, one entry, near the bottom, made his eyes widen.

Kester spun his chair around to face Miss Wellbeloved.

"What do you call the leader of the Thelemites?" he asked urgently as he shoved his glasses further up his nose.

"The Grand Master," Miss Wellbeloved replied. "Why?"

"What does the Grand Master do?" Kester pressed, leaning forward. "What's their role in the organisation?"

The others were listening now, alert to the excitement in Kester's voice.

Miss Wellbeloved carefully put down her pen and moved closer to him. "The Grand Master is nominated in a secret ceremony," she explained, "and only the initiated few know who he or she is. They have complete power over the Thelemites. Now, are you going to tell us why you want to know?"

Kester smiled slowly, then moved his monitor around to show her. She squinted at the bright screen, scanning the list of phrases. Helpfully, he pointed at the anagram that he'd noticed.

Miss Wellbeloved drew back as though she'd suddenly noticed a dangerous snake on his desk. Her hand flew instinctively to her mouth.

"And that's an anagram of the lyric 'mastering drama', is it?" she said breathlessly, looking around at the others.

Kester nodded.

"In which case," Miss Wellbeloved concluded, "this is even more dangerous a situation than we could have imagined. We need to let your father know."

"Know what?" Pamela, Mike, and Serena called in unison.

The office door slammed open again, and Ribero's head poked out like an inquisitive tortoise. "Yes, know what? I heard my name mentioned."

"Kester, you tell them," Miss Wellbeloved ordered.

Kester gulped. "There's a worrying anagram in this Billy Dagger song. It says 'I am Grand Master'."

Mike whistled. Even Serena looked frightened.

"I take it that's a very bad thing?" Kester said finally, interrupting the silence.

Ribero rubbed his moustache. His complexion had taken on a vaguely ashen colour. "Yes," he replied simply as he clutched the door frame for support. "Yes, it is a very bad thing, indeed."

"Why?"

"Because it means a daemon is in charge of one of the most powerful organisations in the world. And there's no telling just how much more powerful it'll be if it is led by him."

CHAPTER 12: SUSPICIONS

"That sounds absolutely preposterous," Larry Higgins barked, leaning over the meeting room table. The rest of his team, and indeed everyone in attendance, looked mildly irritated—hardly surprising, given that most of them had been stuck on a train for hours to get there.

Kester stifled a yawn. After their discovery about Hrschni, they'd immediately contacted Curtis Philpot, who'd called an emergency meeting at Infinite Enterprises headquarters in London. One long train journey later, here they were, all yawning, grumpy, and longing to get back home again.

Curtis Philpot dabbed his nostrils delicately with a handkerchief, then he looked at Larry down the length of his sizeable nose. "I fail to see which part you regard as preposterous, Larry," he replied, in a dangerously smooth voice.

Larry gestured wildly at Dimitri and Luke, who shrank back into their seats with embarrassment. "I mean *all of it*," he explained, casting a look of pure venom in Kester's direction. "You can't read anything into song lyrics, surely!"

"Why on earth not?" Philpot's eyes narrowed. "It's clear that Hrschni deliberately hid those clues in his song."

Larry clucked with exasperation. "But why would he reveal his identity as Grand Master? That makes absolutely no sense. The whole thing is quite ridiculous."

Ribero smirked, stroking his moustache as though petting a much-loved cat. "Well, perhaps you can tell Lord Bernard Nutcombe about how silly you think it is, yes?"

"Well suggested, Julio. I could pass your opinion on to the Minister for the Supernatural, Larry," Philpot rubbed his hands together with Machiavellian satisfaction. Although the room was heated, the cold of the day somehow seemed to permeate the windows, easing into the room and chilling them to the core. Larry slumped back into his seat and delivered them all a glare of magnificent proportions.

Ian Kingdom-Green coughed, interrupting the silence. "I believe," he said quietly, "that the question we need to ask is—why? Why did Hrschni use his song to tell us he is Grand Master? Why inform us of his intentions?"

"I asked that exact same question yesterday," Mike said, glaring out of the window at the busy street below.

"And it is a pertinent one, my friend," Ian stated, patting Mike's arm, which made him wriggle crossly on his chair. "Is Hrschni using his songs to communicate with other spirits, perhaps?"

Dimitri held up his hand, stern as a judge. "Would other spirits be able to decipher these lyrics? Not many are as intellectual as daemons. It does not seem plausible."

"Maybe he's just targeting other daemons," Cardigan suggested. "Reaching out to gain support from his own kind?"

Kester shook his head. "It seems like an odd way to go about it. I mean, couldn't he just visit the other daemons in person and gather their support that way instead?"

They all pondered hard, leaving the room in cold, abrasive

silence.

"Alright then," Luke piped up as he pressed a finger on the meeting room table. "If this Hrschni ain't reaching out to other daemons, who is he trying to impress with these lyrics?"

"Is he trying to send a message to us, perhaps?" Kester suggested.

Larry bashed a fist on the table. "By joining the Thelemites, breaking into Infinite Enterprises and engaging in illegal activities, Hrschni has established himself as our enemy. Why would he then try to assist us by leaving clues in his songs, eh? What a bloody ridiculous suggestion."

"Positive as ever, Larry," Miss Wellbeloved chastised. "Kester may well be right. Perhaps Hrschni is toying with us."

"Oh, sod off, I don't believe that for one second," Larry scoffed. "I think we're all just going around and around in circles, when we need to take decisive action."

"And what would you do, Larry?" Philpot said, fingers drumming on the desk. "We'd welcome all suggestions. Please. You have my undivided attention."

Larry's mouth opened, then closed again like a large, disgruntled fish. "Well, I'd have to think about it for a while," he said slowly, "but I'm sure that—"

"—Well, once you've thought of something, feel free to let us know," Philpot concluded. Several people around the table attempted to conceal a smirk. Larry looked about to erupt, but wisely chose to remain silent.

"So," Philpot continued. "Let's examine the facts, shall we? I've put together a quick visual presentation, to ensure we're all on the same page." Without waiting for a response, he clicked a button on his laptop, firing the screen behind him into action.

"Here's what we know so far," he began. "There are at least two daemons involved. Hrschni is now believed to be Grand Master of the Thelemites, which is unprecedented. Never in their history have the Thelemites had a non-human leader."

"What do we know about Fylgja?" Luke asked, squinting at the screen. "Has she got any previous history with Hrschni?"

"That's a good question," Philpot said with an approving nod. "Let me move on to the next screen; we've got a more comprehensive profile on both." He clicked his mouse again. "Fylgja. We've got a long list of known previous inhabitations on file. This daemon has a strong preference for inhabiting females, and in particular, aims for clever, cunning women. Attractive as well, usually."

"Told you she's vain," Kester whispered to Miss Wellbeloved. "This daemon obviously likes to look good."

"As far as we know," Philpot continued, "there has only been one recorded occasion where Hrschni and Fylgja's path might have crossed, and that was during the second world war. Both were fighting in support of the Allies. Fylgja had inhabited the body of a famous code-breaker and was doing invaluable work. At the same time, Hrschni was in the body of a renowned fighter pilot. It's entirely possible they would have met at some point, though we can't say for sure."

"Fylgja went missing directly after the war, didn't she?" Kester asked.

Philpot nodded. "Someone's been doing their homework. Well done."

"Seems like a big coincidence," Serena said.

"Didn't take the brains of Britain to work that one out," Mike growled. Serena rewarded him with one of her most poisonous glares.

"So, that's when Hrschni might have convinced her to join the Thelemites?" Miss Wellbeloved speculated.

Philpot shrugged. "Who knows? We'll probably never know for sure. But it's possible."

"Why did Hrschi continue inhabiting humans, then?" Larry barked. "Why didn't he disappear at the same time as Fylgja?"

"Perhaps it was in his best interests to act innocently," Philpot replied. "Again, we don't know." He returned to his presentation. "We now know that Hrschni is inhabiting another human, thanks to Lili Asadi's excellent observational work in Whitby."

"That's right, he's inhabiting a woman," Luke piped up. Philpot nodded.

"But why?" Kester asked.

"I suspect it's to avoid detection." Dimitri scowled out of the window, his frustration palpable.

"How does that work, then?"

Dimitri took a deep breath. "When a daemon enters a human, their spirit energy is muffled. That means we cannot detect them nearly as easily. It is basic stuff, you see? Have you not yet learnt this?"

Kester reddened. "Not yet, no," he replied stiffly, trying to ignore Larry's gleeful expression.

Philpot rapped on the table. "Gentlemen, please. Let's continue. I believe that we need to get in touch with all known daemons on record, check that we're not facing some sort of daemon army here."

"I hardly think they'd behave like that," Miss Wellbeloved said, nervously tugging at a stray strand of hair. "We know that daemons are a highly respected species of spirit."

"And yet, two of them are now mysteriously involved with an organisation that's trying to destroy the world as we know it," Larry retorted, folding his hands over the top of his belly. "Come on, Jennifer. It's time you dropped this naïve attitude towards spirits. Or are your loyalties torn, perhaps?"

"What on earth do you mean by that?" Miss Wellbeloved bristled.

"I mean, your whole family was deeply involved with the Thelemite organisation. I only hope your previous involvement isn't affecting your better judgement."

Miss Wellbeloved blushed. Ribero hastily stroked her arm as though calming a skittish horse.

Philpot coughed politely. "No offence, Jennifer, but that was something I was rather concerned about too. I think you need to appreciate that the Thelemites have changed, and not for the better."

"My loyalties are not divided," Miss Wellbeloved muttered through gritted teeth. "I'm merely protesting about the language you use when talking about spirits. They're our equals, not our inferiors."

When it comes to intelligence, Hrschni is clearly superior to any of us, Kester thought with a slight smile. He respected Miss Wellbeloved's dedication to the spirit cause, but suspected she was fighting a losing battle. From what he could tell, most people simply weren't that keen on spirits, and wanted to keep them as under control as humanly possible.

Philpot sighed, rubbing his forehead. "Infinite Enterprises will be getting in touch with all registered daemons," he continued, nodding deliberately in Miss Wellbeloved's direction. "Larry, I'd like your team to work with our observations crew. Start talking to other agencies across the country, check that no other spirits have joined Hrschni. We need to know what we're up against here."

"Agreed," Larry said with a sanctimonious smile in Luke and Dimitri's direction.

Philpot turned to Kester. "You made such a good start with this song lyric; I think you should start exploring the rest of his music. It would be interesting to find out just how long he's been leaving us clues."

"Do you want all of us to work on that?" Serena asked with an impatient click of the tongue. "Not being funny, but it's a bit of a one-person job. Two, at most."

"I'd like someone to get in contact with Whilshin & Sons. Their company was the last one to keep tabs on Fylgja's whereabouts. They may have more information in their files. We need to know *everything* about her, if we're going to track her down."

"Got it," Serena said with obvious satisfaction. *At least I won't have her breathing down my neck while I'm browsing through Billy Dagger's back catalogue,* Kester thought with relief. Working with Serena was usually stressful, to say the least.

"The rest of you, keep a close eye on the Exeter Thelemite lodge," Philpot concluded. "We know Barty Melville's heavily involved, and we need to learn more about what he's up to. Has everyone got it? I'll send out a more detailed brief later on."

There was a murmur of agreement. Kester sighed. He'd thought the last case with the fetch was complex enough, but this business with Hrschni made it seem a doddle by comparison.

Philpot nodded, stood up, and stuffed his laptop into his briefcase. "On that note, I'm off to report to Lord Nutcombe," he announced. "He wants an urgent update of the situation. Do your best, everyone. This case is getting more worrying by the day."

"The worst thing is, we don't know what the heck they're planning to do," Luke said, stretching with a yawn. "It'd help if we could just figure out what their game-plan was."

An abrupt screech drew all eyes to the left of the room. Serena was flapping around wildly in the air, and for a moment, Kester wondered if a wasp had managed to get into the room. Then he noticed the familiar little, brown, smudgy blob above her head, which was flitting through the air like smoke in a breeze.

"Is that incubus still bothering you?" He watched with fascination as the tiny creature whirled to and fro, skilfully avoiding Serena's manic swipes.

"What does it bloody look like?" Serena squealed again as the spirit nestled on top of her head. Kester squinted. *It looks a bit like he's stroking her hair,* he thought, feeling a bubble of laughter rise in his throat.

Serena caught his expression and glared. "This isn't even slightly funny," she barked as she slammed a hand down on her scalp. The spirit disappeared with a quiet *pop,* and Serena winced at the force of her own palm.

Mike sniggered. "You poor old thing. Still, at least someone loves you."

Philpot shook his head with a mixture of disapproval and disbelief. "Surely you can manage to deal with a little spirit like that, can't you?"

"Yes," Larry added, peering over Philpot's shoulder. "You wouldn't even need a full-sized water bottle for that incubus. You could probably get away with using an empty travel-sized shampoo container or something."

"If it was that easy," Serena snapped, "I would have done it already. Now, can we just leave? If everyone's finished having a good gawp at my head, that is?"

Mike pulled her in for a brief hug. "You have to admit," he said, "it is a little bit funny."

Serena smoothed down her bob mutinously. "I really don't see that there's anything amusing about it at all," she muttered as they went out into the corridor. "You try having a spirit wake you up in the night and going all moony over you. It's revolting."

Kester smiled sympathetically. "Ah, it's not really that bad, is it? I mean, it's sad, really. The poor little incubus is probably lonely and love-sick."

"Don't you start." Her withering expression could have wilted fresh flowers in a heartbeat.

They returned to the polished reception hall, then stepped reluctantly out into the cold, noisy street. A double-decker bus ploughed past them, sending a shower of dirty puddle-water in their direction.

"Gosh, I hate London," Pamela said cheerfully, scuttling ahead.

Kester hung back with Serena, who was still patting her head nervously. "So," he began, hoping she'd calmed down a little. "What were your suspicions, then? When you visited my house that night with the chocolates? You never did get around to telling me."

Serena frowned. They deftly dodged past a group of tourists, excitedly snapping photos of a red post-box, then continued down the road towards the station. "It's probably best if we leave it," she said finally, nibbling her fingernail. "I acted rashly that night when I came to your house. I shouldn't have said anything at all, really."

Kester poked her arm. "No way. You're not leaving it like that.

Tell me. What have you got your suspicions about?"

She tugged up her jacket collar, concealing her mouth from view. From behind the beige cashmere, he thought he detected the word "Anya," and something about trust.

"Say that again?"

"I said, I'm concerned that Anya might not be trustworthy."

He pulled up short and stared at her with amazement, ignoring the throngs of people scuttling around them. "What the hell is that supposed to mean?"

Serena winced, then grabbed him by the arm, hauling him across the road. "See? I knew you wouldn't like it. I don't know why I even bothered to say anything."

Kester removed her hand from his elbow, oblivious to the taxi beside them that was currently honking angrily at them to move out of the way. "Why on earth would you think she's not trustworthy? You've got no evidence whatsoever to back that up, and—"

"—Isn't it a bit weird, though? I mean, the Thelemites kidnapped her, then just let her go. It doesn't add up."

Kester took a deep breath and fought back the urge to say something extremely rude. "Look," he replied finally, "I know you're only trying to be protective, but you can trust Anya one hundred percent. Honestly."

Serena rolled her eyes. "Just because she's sleeping with you doesn't mean she can be trusted, Kester."

He thought back to the first time he'd met Anya in the library— her wide smile, her natural friendliness. Anger flared in the pit of his stomach. *How dare she say stuff like this?*

"Serena," he replied in a low voice. "I'm going to let your comments go this time, because I know you're only looking out for me. But—"

"—Actually, I'm not looking out for you at all, I'm looking out for the safety of the agency. And the world, in fact."

Kester gritted his teeth and pushed his train ticket into the barrier. "Whatever your reason is," he called over his shoulder, "I won't let you say that a second time. End of discussion."

Serena glided through the barrier and raced to catch up with him. "Don't be ridiculous, Kester. Look, I didn't mean to upset you . . ."

"Hello, hello, hello; what's going on here, then?" Mike sidled up to join them as they descended the escalators to the underground platform. "You two have been behaving oddly with each other recently. Something I should know?"

"Oh, bugger off, Mike," Serena snapped. "It has absolutely nothing to do with you; you're just being nosy."

"Well, if you two are having some sort of lover's tiff, perhaps you should make sure the rest of us know the situation."

"Mike, we are not having a lover's tiff!" Kester shouted. "Serena was being a cow and insulting my girlfriend. Who, incidentally, is the woman I'm in love with. Get it?"

Mike stepped off the escalator and gave them both a look. "Why are you insulting Anya, Serena? When I met her, I thought she was lovely."

"Oh, did you now?" Serena growled. "How great. I'm so pleased she met up to your discerning standards."

"Gosh, you lot are having a right old row, aren't you?" Pamela appeared behind them, bustling them onto the platform like a goose flapping at its goslings. "I hope this isn't an awkward love-triangle situation. It's never a good idea in the work-place, you know."

"It isn't!" the other three chorused.

Miss Wellbeloved caught up with them just as the train screeched towards the platform. "Will you please show some decorum?" she snapped, looking nervously around them. "Larry Higgins is still within earshot, and I'd rather he didn't see us squabbling amongst ourselves."

Ribero winked, resting briefly on his crutches. "Ah. Young and hot-blooded. I remember it well."

"I doubt that very much, you're far too old," Miss Wellbeloved reprimanded, as they boarded the train. "Now come on, let's hurry up and get home."

They remained in silence as the train wailed into the darkness of the tunnel. Kester fumed inwardly, glaring at Serena, who was doing a good job of pretending not to notice. *How dare she say that?* he thought, feeling even angrier the more he dwelt on it. *What has she got against Anya, anyway? The poor woman got kidnapped by the Thelemites, went through a horrible ordeal, and now she's got this cow-bag judging her unfairly!*

His mood didn't improve for the rest of the journey back. Pamela attempted to cheer him up by offering him a succession of sugary snacks, but even the promised delivery of a chocolate bar failed to raise a smile. Instead, he glared out of the window, watching the tower-blocks and skyscrapers of the capital gradually give way to fields and farmland. It was a long, sullen journey.

"Look, mate," Mike said finally as they arrived at Exeter station. "I don't think Serena meant to upset you."

Kester raised an eyebrow as he stepped off the train. "Since when have you ever stuck up for her? Anyway, Mike, you know what she's like. She's always trying to make me cross. Well, now she's succeeded."

Mike pulled his cap down over his eyes to shelter them from the winter wind, which drove along the station platform like a wave of ice. "Nah, I don't think it's like that," he said. "She was explaining it to me on the way home. She just thinks it's odd that the Thelemites let Anya go so easily. I mean, why kidnap her in the first place if they were just going to release her straight after? You've got to admit, Serena's got a point."

"They only released her because Miss Wellbeloved asked them very nicely."

Mike held his hands up in surrender. "Sure. Whatever. You know her better than we do. But on this occasion, don't hold a grudge against Serena. I don't think she meant it nastily."

Kester eyed Serena, currently lagging back with his father, who was stumbling along as best as possible on his crutches. He shrugged. "Yeah, you're probably right. It just didn't seem fair to attack Anya when she wasn't there to defend herself."

Mike grinned. "So, you've definitely been getting some, haven't you?"

Kester blushed. Mike's grin stretched even wider.

"Get in there, my son! You're a smooth operator, you are!"

"Yeah, alright," Kester muttered, feeling half mortified and half pleased with himself. "Keep it down." They walked out of the station and into the growing darkness of the late afternoon. Christmas lights twinkled in the nearby shops, and well-wrapped people surged past them, weighted down with shopping bags. He would have enjoyed the festive atmosphere more had he not felt so tired and grumpy.

Mike winked. "Say no more. Gentlemen never kiss and tell. Do you want a lift back home?"

Kester looked up at the weighty clouds, looming overhead. "Yes, please. That would be amazing."

"Does that go for me too?" Serena piped up with an anxious look in Kester's direction. He gave her a tight smile in response.

"Ooh, and me, love. My car's in the garage for a service at the moment," Pamela added as she hurried over.

Mike looked incredulous. "Anyone else for the free taxi service then? Funny, you normally all moan about the poor old van, until you actually need it."

Ribero shook his head. "No, I will be travelling back with Jennifer. I do not wish to go in the death-mobile, thank you very much."

"You're the one that bought the bloody van," Mike spluttered. "If it's such a death-trap, why not buy another one for the agency?"

"Because you are so fond of this one, yes?" Without waiting for an answer, Ribero hobbled off, closely followed by Miss Wellbe-loved, who hastily yanked a knitted bobble hat over her head and delivered them a look of silent apology as she went.

One irate, traffic-filled drive later, the van arrived at Kester's house. He was pleased to see the back of Anya's head in the lounge window, watching a television programme about competing catwalk models, if the screen was anything to go by. Less welcome was the sight of Pineapple and Daisy's heads, sitting either side of her. *I do hope Thor has made himself comfortable on top of Pineapple's leg,* he thought uncharitably as he rummaged for his door keys.

"You're early!" Daisy chimed as he stepped into the lounge and eased himself out of his jacket.

Kester looked at his watch. "Only a little," he acknowledged. "There was no point going into the office by the time we got back."

"How did the meeting go?" Anya asked with a welcoming smile. Her eyes glowed brightly in the amber lamplight, making her look almost feline, not to mention irresistibly attractive. He felt his insides stir at the sight of her, turning to nervous, excited liquid.

"Much as we expected." He perched against the armrest of the sofa. "Things aren't going too well so far." He gave a deliberate nod in Daisy and Pineapple's direction, then winked at Anya, who understood immediately not to say anything more in front of them. "So," he continued, changing the subject, "how was your day?"

She shrugged. "I took the day off. The thought of standing in the library all day long, being bored, was too much to bear."

"Really?" Kester absent-mindedly reached down and patted Thor's head. "I thought you loved your job?"

Anya shrugged. "Yeah, you know. There's more to life than working a boring nine-to-five job. Sometimes, it's fun to do something different. So, I went shopping instead."

"We met her in town!" Daisy said enthusiastically. "She helped me choose some new make-up for this party I'm going to at the weekend. I had no idea your girlfriend was so good at understanding colours and everything."

"Yeah, man, she picked some new eyeliner for me, and it was totally a radical departure from my usual gig, you get me?" Pineapple added, stretching his thin legs even further across the carpet.

Kester smiled. "You're a lady of many talents, Anya. Just don't pick any make-up for me. I definitely don't need any."

Anya giggled. "Not even a little bit of blusher to colour your cheeks?"

"Absolutely not." *Especially considering how much I blush already,* he added silently.

"We're watching some super-tight fashion on the TV right now," Pineapple confirmed as he edged along to let Kester sit down. "This well-tasty duchess here is being proper made-over, like smooth, right?"

Kester slumped into the seat. "If you say so. Who enjoys this rubbish, anyway?"

"We do," Anya, Daisy, and Pineapple chorused as one.

Thor wound a tight circle around Kester's ankles, before scampering nimbly up Pineapple's leg and onto his lap. Pineapple seemed not to mind and started stroking his long, limber body.

"You two seem to have hit it off," Kester remarked.

Pineapple gave a soppy grin. "Yeah, this little Thor is a diamond geezer. He's sharing my bed at night, you feel me?"

"Well, I'm glad someone's finally sharing your bed with you." Kester grinned at Anya, who was too engrossed in the programme to notice. "Aren't you and Daisy out tonight, Pineapple? You normally are."

"Nah, we're not in the mood to—"

"I thought you said you were?" Anya interrupted, springing back to alertness. "You said you were going down the pub, didn't you?"

Pineapple looked puzzled, then his brow lightened. "Yeah, we did. You are so right, little lady."

"A trip to the pub would be mega-cool," Daisy added, checking her pink watch. "We should head down now, shouldn't we?"

Kester laughed. "It's only just gone five. Will it even be open yet?"

Pineapple and Daisy winked at one another. "That pub's always open," Daisy confirmed. "And I could do with a drink. Are you ready?"

"Lady, I was born in readiness, like proper rock-steady ready. Right?"

Kester rolled his eyes and took up Pineapple's departed spot on the sofa, pressing his leg gratefully against Anya's own. "Hello," he whispered in her ear. "I missed you today."

"You're sweet." Anya waited until Daisy and Pineapple had left the room before leaning closer. "So, how did it *really* go today? Tell me everything."

Kester groaned and rested his arm over her shoulder. The usual thrill of excitement that she'd allowed him to do it, without recoiling in disgust, passed through him. *I wonder when I'll stop being surprised that she actually likes me,* he thought with a wry grin.

"It was a long, tiring day," he said eventually. "Serena got on my nerves. Well, even more than usual, I mean."

Anya sat up, accidentally dislodging his arm. "Why, what did she do?"

"She was just being overly suspicious," he started, then paused. *Perhaps it's not such a good idea to tell Anya about it,* he thought with a frown. *Why would I even think that, though? Of course I can tell her. She might get cross at Serena, I suppose, but that doesn't really matter.*

Anya scrutinised his expression. "Go on," she said slowly. "What did she say? It was about me, wasn't it?"

"How did you guess?"

Her eyes narrowed. "I *knew* she didn't like me. Tell me what she said."

Kester swallowed. Suddenly, it didn't feel like a very good idea to be talking about it at all. He wished he'd just kept his mouth shut. "It wasn't much," he said lamely, twiddling with the tassels on the nearest cushion. "She was just talking about your involvement in the Thelemites."

"What's that supposed to mean?"

"Oh, I don't know. Who knows with Serena, I mean—"

"—Was she trying to suggest that I couldn't be trusted?"

Ouch, thought Kester. *Right on the mark.* He winced. "Um, yes. Well, not exactly. But kind of."

Anya stood up, flicked the television off, then turned squarely to face him. "And what do you think?"

He gulped. "I stuck up for you, of course. I told her she was being ridiculous."

"Really?"

Kester clutched the cushion against his belly. "Yes, of course. Do you even need to ask?"

Anya's expression clouded over. "I don't know. Do I?"

"No!"

Silence fell. Kester felt like a bug under a microscope, impaled by the sharpness of his girlfriend's stare. *Why did I say anything?* he cursed inwardly. *If I'd have left it alone, we'd be sitting here, cuddled up on the sofa, having a pleasant evening. Now, she's looking at me as if she doesn't know me anymore.*

Finally, Anya broke the silence. "You know, I don't like Serena much. I think she's got a big problem with me."

Kester sighed. "She's got a big problem with everyone. Not just you."

Anya folded her arms and edged slightly away. It was only a subtle movement, but it disturbed him more than he would have expected. He considered reaching out to her, kissing her, or doing something to make it all better, but the rigidity of her posture advised against it.

Slowly, she switched the television back on, and they sat in silence.

CHAPTER 13: THE POSTHUMOUS SONG

A reedy buzz shattered Kester's dream; which wasn't really a problem, given he'd been having a nightmare about being chased by a supersized Thor. He blinked blearily, then realised it was his phone, rattling his bedside table.

"Yes?" He fumbled for his glasses, nearly dislodging his glass of water as he did so.

"Kester, you've got to get into the office, now. Massive news, mate. Massive news."

Kester sat up, rubbing his eyes. "Mike?" A glance at his wristwatch told him it wasn't even seven o'clock. *Mike loves his bed as much as I do,* he thought, blinking in confusion. *Why on earth is he even up yet?*

"Course it's me! Who else would it be, waking you from your beauty sleep? Now, get yourself over here, pronto."

"Over where?" He patted the mattress beside him, then realised it was empty. A single blonde hair lay on the pillow; the only sign that Anya had slept there at all.

"Over to the office! Blimey, you are sleepy." Mike cleared his throat, which reverberated down the line like a gravelly battering ram. "Been burning the midnight oil again? I'll have words with that bird of yours if she's keeping you up—"

"No, I haven't been up all night," Kester replied firmly. "It's very early in the morning, that's all." He sipped his water thoughtfully, then eased himself into a sitting position. "What do you want, anyway? Why do I have to come into the office?"

"He's released another song."

"Who has?"

"Billy Dagger, mate! Keep up!"

Kester sighed. It was a bit too early for all this type of cryptic nonsense. "But Billy Dagger's dead," he said slowly as he massaged his forehead.

"It's one of those pustymouse release things, isn't it?"

"I think you mean posthumous, don't you?"

Mike sniffed. "Yeah, whatever you call it when it's released after their death. Anyway, he's not dead, but alive and kicking and leading the Thelemites, as we all know."

This is all getting rather confusing, Kester thought, and edged down to the bottom of the bed, peering out to the landing. The bathroom door was wide open. *I wonder where Anya is, then, if she's not in bed?* he thought and glanced back at the pillows as though expecting her to suddenly materialise.

"Are you listening, Kester?"

"Sorry, what did you say?"

"I said, you need to come and help me figure out the lyrics of the new song."

Kester rolled off the bed and stretched. "What, now?"

"Yeah, now! Come on, it's exciting. Get down here." Mike paused. "Pamela's coming down too, and she's bringing cake."

"Hmm. Alright then." He hung up, then groped around in the semi-darkness for his clothes. For some reason, his shirt had managed to get caught on his curtain cord, but other than the occasional expletive he muttered while trying to untangle it, the house was silent.

"Anya?" he called downstairs as he went to brush his teeth. "Are you making breakfast or something?"

Silence. Kester sighed, then turned the tap on. *I hope she's not still moody with me after last night,* he thought, surveying his reflection with a frown. His hair was sticking up in all sorts of strange tufts, but he didn't have the energy or inclination to bother sorting it out.

After, he headed into the kitchen, only to find it unnervingly empty. As he pulled his jacket from the peg in the hallway, he noticed Anya's coat was gone.

His heart sank. The empty space on the wall didn't look right at all. Likewise, the telephone table, where Thor's lead had been lying the night before, was also bare.

Either she's taken Thor for an early morning walk, he thought, swallowing hard, *or she's left me.* He had a horrible, sinking suspicion about which scenario was more likely.

Should I call her? he wondered as he locked up quietly behind him. The street was deserted, the first few, feeble fingers of sun just emerging over the rooftops. Every window he passed was protected with a drawn curtain, isolating him from the world around him. He shoved his hands in his pockets and marched on, breath puffing from his lips like a boiling kettle.

How can she have got so upset over something so minor? he wondered, feeling quite nettled. After all, he hadn't done anything wrong, only told her what Serena had said. He did*n't see why she would have flown off the handle so badly.*

But perhaps she hasn't, he rationalised, with a calm inner voice that he'd started to equate with his mother. It was the sort of thing she would have said, anyway. *Maybe she just went to work early. You won't know what's going on until you speak to her.*

Still, it didn't feel great, not knowing what was going on. He stalked into the office, feeling generally irate with the world, only to find Mike and Pamela, wearing matching smiles and suspending a large cake in front of them.

"Chocolate and vanilla," Pamela said, without preamble. "I baked it last night for some friends of mine, but I thought you boys could use it instead."

"I'm supposed to be on a diet," Kester said uncertainly as he threw his coat over his chair. He fondled his belly, then nodded defiantly. "Actually, yes, I would like a slice. A big one, in fact." *That'll teach Anya to storm out without telling me where she's going,* he thought churlishly. *I'll get back at her by eating cake.*

Pamela scuttled off to the stockroom to find a knife whilst Mike gestured to his desk.

"You've got to hear this," he said seriously as he fiddled with his laptop. "This is one of the best songs I've ever heard in my life."

Kester scratched his ear. "Hang on a minute. This is a Billy Dagger song that's literally just been released, right?"

Mike nodded gleefully. "The internet's been buzzing with it for a few days now, and it was finally released at midnight last night."

"Did you stay up to hear it?"

"Damn right, I did!" Mike looked indignant at the mere suggestion that he might not have done. "A true Dagger fan wouldn't dream of nodding off when something this big happens."

"Except he wasn't really Billy Dagger, was he?" Kester reminded him gently as he pulled up a chair.

Mike grumbled under his breath and clicked his mouse. "Right. Listen to this, see what you make of it. It's called 'Ode to Set-Shirker'."

At once, the room was filled with sinister organ music, rendered slightly tinny through Mike's laptop speakers. Pamela poked her head around the stockroom door.

"Not that dreary old thing again, how many more times do we have to listen to it?"

"Have you cut that cake yet?" Mike retorted over the melodious twang of the electric guitars. "Don't keep a man starving, there's a love." He nodded, then added, "And it's not dreary, it's genius."

Pamela sighed theatrically, then disappeared again.

Kester watched the video with fascination. "What the hell is it meant to mean?" he mumbled as he observed the hypnotic swaying of the dancers, not to mention the strange, hallucinogenic backdrop.

"Dunno," Mike said vaguely, "but it obviously means something, doesn't it?"

Kester watched until the end, entranced. After the song had finished, he shook himself, feeling suddenly cold despite the warmth of the office. *That song was eerie,* he thought, the situation with Anya momentarily forgotten. *Though I'm not sure why.*

Pamela emerged bearing cake and tea, which they both tucked into eagerly. She sat on the edge of the desk and watched them eat, tapping her feet restlessly against the carpet.

"So, what do you make of it?" she asked finally. "Miss Wellbeloved and Serena should be in soon, do you think you'll need their help to decipher it?"

"I haven't even had a chance to read the lyrics yet," Kester said as he sipped his tea. "And it's a bit early in the morning for this level of brain activity."

Pamela looked at her watch. "It's past eight o' clock! Dearie me, you youngsters. Always in bed."

"With his girlfriend," Mike added with a particularly lavish wink.

"No, not with his girlfriend actually," Kester said curtly.

Mike wisely chose not to comment and instead started searching for the song lyrics. "Here you are," he said finally. "Dunno how accurate they'll be, given they've only been uploaded this morning, but it gives you an idea."

Together, they scanned the web page.

Left the stage, in a pool of black,
Razor-blade behind my back,
Secret sermons left untold
Shirked my last, left you cold.

I reeked this roost,
Though all was well,
The set-shirker sang,
And opened hell.

The dorkiest heteros heard me call,
That is all, I said, that is all,
I left the stage, to a cave of black,
Sharpened dagger behind my back.

I reeked this roost,
Though all was well,
The set-shirker sang,
And opened hell.

Blackness tightens like a choker,
False religion, theorised stoker,
The stage is dark, under attack,
A justice-sword behind my back.

I reeked this roost,
Though nothing was well,
The set-shirker sang,
And opened hell.

Histories so putrid or . . .
Histories so putrid or . . .
Or nothingness. Blackness. Underground.

"Wow," Pamela breathed, placing her mug down on the desk. "Even more incomprehensible than his last lot of lyrics, if you ask me."

Kester puffed out his cheeks and leant back in his chair. "I think that's his most sinister one yet," he said finally. He wasn't sure if it was his early wake-up call or Anya's absence, but he was thoroughly rattled. He surveyed the windows, laced with a delicate frost, and shuddered.

"Come on, then," Mike said expectantly, polishing off the last mouthful of cake. "What does it all mean?"

"I haven't got the foggiest," Kester replied and massaged his face. "One thing is obvious, though."

"What?"

"This is the most audacious reference to his death on stage that could be imagined."

Mike chuckled. "Yeah. It's pretty blatant."

Pamela bustled in closer, the steam from her tea rising in tantalising little plumes before her eyes. "Well, it makes sense that he'd write about his death, doesn't it?"

"How many singers do you know who manage to write about their own death like this?" Mike chuckled. "Remember, this is supposed to have been written *before* he died."

She squinted at the screen. "He's playing with his fans, then. Making them wonder if he staged his own death."

"Staged his own death on stage, no less," Kester reminded her. Once again, he was struck by the formidable intelligence of the daemon. *Look at the way he's teasing us all,* he thought as he examined the lyrics once again. *He's masterminded all of this, from start to finish. How can we hope to compete?*

He yawned just as the office door flew open. Serena nodded curtly at them all, characteristic red pout in place, then stomped to her desk. Miss Wellbeloved scurried closely behind, quickly closing the door to keep the heat in.

"I got accosted by a group of carol singers," Serena announced with a scowl that suggested it was the most insulting thing that could have possibly happened to her. "I mean, seriously. Who sings carols this early in the morning?"

"I thought they were quite pleasant," Miss Wellbeloved said as she pulled off her mittens. "I was feeling quite festive afterwards."

"I bloody wasn't." Serena grimaced, patting down her hair. "I could do without being deafened by 'Hark! The Herald Angels Sing' before I've had my morning coffee."

"Incubus keep you awake again last night, did he?" Mike asked, with ill-disguised glee.

"Sod off, Mike." She flounced over to the desk and glared at the screen. "How far have you got with the lyrics, then?"

"Give us time," Kester said weakly. "I thought you were meant to be working on something else, anyway? Getting in contact with Whilshin & Sons or something?"

"Done it already," Serena said smugly as she perched on the neighbouring desk. "They're sending me the full report today. You know me, I like to get on with the task."

Miss Wellbeloved gave Kester a wink over Serena's shoulder. "Perhaps we should leave you to it?" she suggested. "Your father will be in a bit later. He wasn't feeling great this morning."

Kester raised an eyebrow. "Is everything okay?"

"Yes, he'll be fine." Miss Wellbeloved didn't look entirely convinced. Suddenly, she clicked her fingers. "Oh, I've just remembered. I spoke on the phone to Dr Barqa-Abu last night. She'd like to talk to you about the case. You'll need to get in touch with her at some point today."

Kester's heart sank. The mere thought of the djinn made him feel rather shivery. "Why does she want to talk to me?"

Miss Wellbeloved shrugged. "No idea, but you'd better not forget. Dr Barqa-Abu isn't someone who likes to be forgotten about. Anyway, shall we all crack on?"

Kester returned to his own desk, already panicking about the prospect of the phone call later. Deliberately putting it from his mind, he flipped open his laptop, waited for the internet to go through its usual, slow machinations, then located the lyrics of 'Ode to Set-Shirker' again.

"Histories so putrid or . . ." he mused as he pressed his glasses further up his nose. *That's got to be another anagram. It's too strange a line to be anything but. Not to mention the song's title, which is one of the weirdest I've ever heard.*

He typed "histories so putrid or" into a few online anagram solvers, but none of them came up with anything. The morning ticked slowly by as the winter sun started to filter through the windows, casting a bleak glow across his makeshift camping table. Finally, he resorted to the good, old-fashioned method of writing the letters down on a piece of paper.

"There are definitely the words 'spirit door' in it," he mumbled to himself, sighing heavily. "Beyond that, I haven't got a clue."

Miss Wellbeloved glanced up. "What was that? Have you figured out any of the lyrics?"

He read out the final line of the song to her, then revealed what he'd discovered so far.

"What are the leftover letters?"

As he told her, she deftly scribbled them down, and started to rearrange them.

"So," she mused aloud, "we're left with an O, an I, an S . . ." Waggling her pen in the air, she wrote down some possible combinations. Kester did the same.

"It's quite fun in a way, isn't it?" she whispered with a surprisingly youthful grin.

Kester laughed. "I'm not sure that's the word I'd use." He changed the order of the letters again, repeating the shuffle until he felt his brain would burst with the pressure of it all. *This is silly,* he thought, staring at his paper, which was starting to look like the deranged scribblings of a certified lunatic. Without much hope, he jotted them down in a different order, then squinted at the results.

His eyes widened.

Without meaning to, he leapt out of his seat, knees crashing into the underside of the table, which promptly collapsed beneath him. Heedless of the crumpled mess of desk, laptop, and various notes and pens, he waved his paper in Miss Wellbeloved's direction.

"Got it!" he announced triumphantly.

The others waited expectantly. Kester beamed. "The last line, 'histories so putrid or . . .'," he began, "is an anagram of 'the spirit door is ours'."

"And what's that supposed to mean?" Serena said indignantly. "They haven't got the spirit door yet—it sounds a bit presumptuous to me."

Miss Wellbeloved looked worried. "I don't like it. It's almost triumphant, isn't it?"

"Gloating, more like," Pamela said briskly, crossing her hands behind her head.

"But it's not like they've succeeded," Serena pointed out. "So, why say that in the song?"

Kester pondered, eyes fixed on the high ceiling. *There's much more to this song than we think,* he realised, running through the lyrics in his head. *It's just a matter of accessing it.*

"I think it's a warning," he said finally.

"A warning about what, exactly?" Serena paced across the floor, heels drumming into the carpet. "This is a song about his death on stage, isn't it?"

Kester scanned the screen again. "Yes," he said slowly. "But that's just the surface meaning. The meaning that's designed to please all the Billy Dagger fans. I think there's a far deeper message in there, hidden from view."

"Like what?"

"Well, like the line 'a justice-sword behind my back', for starters." He rapped the screen. "That tells us that he believes what he's doing is the morally right thing to do."

"It's a bit Old Testament, isn't it?" Pamela said. "Judgement Day and all that."

Kester nodded. "Agreed. And the line 'sharpened dagger behind my back' is a clear reference to his veiled identity as Billy Dagger."

Serena sighed. "What about the reference to a razor blade, then?"

"Perhaps it's meant to be about his faked death?" Miss Wellbeloved suggested. "After all, razor blades are often used in suicides, aren't they?"

Kester shrugged. "I still think we're missing much more. There are probably more anagrams in there. Some of these lyrics are just plain mental."

The room fell silent. Kester knew how important it was to decipher the song and felt the weight of the responsibility pressing down on him. He attempted a weak smile.

"I'd best crack on with it, hadn't I?"

Miss Wellbeloved gave him a sympathetic look. "If anyone can do it," she said gently, "it's you. We'll let you get on."

"By the way, everyone," Serena added as she returned to her desk, "Whilshin & Sons sent through the report."

"And?" Miss Wellbeloved sat straighter in her desk.

Serena frowned. "At first glance, there doesn't seem to be much about Fylgja that we don't already know. There were a few interesting comments though—just let me find them."

They waited patiently as Serena fiddled around with her computer.

"Right." She looked at them all to check she had their full attention. "This is a report from Mr Gilbert Whilshin."

"Benedict Whilshin's father," Miss Wellbeloved muttered faintly.

"Quite." Serena's eyes narrowed at the interruption. "Anyway, he wrote this in 1922. It's quite waffly, but he makes a comment about having to keep an eye on Flygja as she had acted 'with uncharacteristic aggression' on a few occasions. It also says how her behaviour had 'become erratic', and that she had disappeared without trace on a few occasions but had always returned to attend the obligatory spirit registrations."

"Perhaps her connections with Hrschni go back further than we realise?" Miss Wellbeloved said, biting her lip.

"Or perhaps she was just a loose cannon, waiting to blow?" Mike suggested. "Gilbert Whilshin also notes an incident where Fylgja and her human got into a fight," Serena added.

"What, you mean the human she was inhabiting at the time?" Kester asked. "I thought humans were always happy to have daemons living inside them, because it made them successful and beautiful?"

"Most of the time, yes," Miss Wellbeloved said. "But sometimes, the relationship can become fraught. When this happens, the daemon normally does the decent thing and departs—though on very rare occasions, people like myself have had to intervene."

"You mean, spirit conversants?"

"Absolutely." Miss Wellbeloved nodded. "Remember, I act as intermediary between the human and spirit realm. That's what we do."

"Did someone have to intervene with Fylgja and her human, then?" Mike asked, leaning across his desk.

"Looks like it." Serena frowned at the screen. "But it says it was resolved amicably."

"Still," Mike said as he relaxed back beneath the pile of contraptions on his desk, "it tells us something about her character, doesn't it?"

They all nodded in unison. *Great,* thought Kester as he returned to his laptop, *first a power-crazed daemon, and now a vain daemon with a bit of a temper. Could it be any worse?* He sighed, then returned to the song lyrics.

The afternoon passed without incident, apart from Dr Ribero hobbling through the door at about half-past two, glaring at them all, then promptly retreating to his office after announcing that he didn't want to be disturbed until after his three o'clock siesta.

Why does he even bother coming in? Kester wondered. Then he felt guilty. After all, his father was unwell, and he got the impression that he'd taken a much more active role in the past. Kester returned to work. The sky darkened, making the office lights look unnaturally bright by contrast. Finally, Miss Wellbeloved looked up.

"It's probably time to go home now," she suggested quietly before glancing at Kester. "How did you get on?"

He slumped against his camping table. "Nothing to report, I'm afraid. There's definitely more anagrams hidden in there, but I can't work out what they are. I've tried every possible combination I can think of."

Ribero's office door burst open, and the man himself stood at the doorway, smouldering cigarette in hand, crutch hoisted under one armpit. "What is this?" he barked. "No progress? That is not good. The Higgins will laugh if he hears we cannot solve even simple song lyrics, right?"

Kester rolled his eyes. "Dad, I've been working on it all day. I can only do my best, you know."

"Hmm." Ribero stomped into the room, bandaged ankle protruding in front of him. "But I don't want to lose face in front of the Higgins, do I?"

"Oh, really!" Miss Wellbeloved snapped as she shut down her computer. "This is about much more than your silly fight with Larry, you know!"

Ribero drew himself up to his full height and glowered at her down the length of his nose. "I do know that, thank you for reminding me, Jennifer. But still. I do not want the Higgins to have a reason to laugh at us, yes?"

Kester pulled on his coat and seized his bag. "Whatever. I'm off now. It's been a long day."

"Fancy a pint?" Mike chorused. "A nice ale or two to warm you up?"

"Not really," Kester said as he pulled out his phone. Anya still hadn't replied to his text messages. *Perhaps I should try to call her,* he thought as he headed to the door, then he suddenly stopped in his tracks.

"I don't believe it," he whispered. Horror blossomed in the pit of his belly.

"What's the matter?" Miss Wellbeloved asked, wrapping her scarf around her neck.

"I forgot to call Dr Barqa-Abu." Kester groaned. *Could things get any worse?* he wondered.

Mike whistled. "You'll catch it tomorrow, then. She won't be happy."

Serena's eyes glittered. "Yes. You *never* keep a djinn waiting. It's the height of bad manners."

"Should I call her now?" Kester gulped. He knew only too well how terrifying Dr Barqa-Abu was, and now he'd given her reason to be even more frightening towards him.

"Oh, *really,* Kester." Miss Wellbeloved rolled her eyes. "You'll have to just leave it now. I'll let her know you've had a difficult day. But for goodness' sake, phone her first thing tomorrow, okay?"

He nodded glumly, then stepped out into the dark landing, making his way down the stairs and out into the car-park. A loud, rhythmic clanking told him that his father was hobbling close behind him.

"Hey, wait up!" Ribero wheezed, shaking a crutch in Kester's direction. "You go marching off without waiting for me, that's not good! I am an old man, you know!"

"Sorry," Kester muttered, as he braced himself against the cold. "I just wanted to get home, that's all."

"Okay. But why don't you walk with me to the bus stop? I want to have a talk with you."

Kester scratched his head. "I've got to try to call Anya, and I really just want to get back—"

"—Ah, your girlfriend. She can wait, right?" Ribero nodded as though the matter was already settled. "Come. Help me along here, these crutches are killing me."

Together, they paced down the alleyway past tired shoppers

burdened with Christmas wrapping paper and presents. Garish accordion music accompanied them, echoing off the old, narrow walls. Kester flicked a coin into the hat in front of the busker, who gave him a watery smile and a thumbs-up. His father chuckled.

"That is the sort of thing your mother would have done," he muttered as they emerged onto the high street.

"I know," Kester said as he escorted his father over the road. "She always used to say it was important to be kind to people who weren't as lucky as we were."

"That is very true," his father said with a glance to the night sky. "Gretchen was always far wiser than me." He winced, struggling to rearrange the crutches under his arms.

"How long do you have to keep using them?"

Ribero coughed. "A few more days, maybe. But it is my own silly fault, yes? For falling down the stairs like a feeble old man." He sighed and looked down at his hands. "I don't know. Maybe that is what I am becoming, right?"

Kester smiled awkwardly. "Age is only a number, Dad."

"Easy to say when you're twenty-two." He patted his chest mournfully with a look that was suddenly alarmingly vulnerable.

Kester nudged him. "So," he asked as they nimbly avoided a crowd of giggling teenagers coming the other way, "do you stay at Miss Wellbeloved's house often then?"

His father gave him a wry glance. "That is a personal question."

Kester shrugged. "You're my father. Can't I ask whether or not you're romantically involved with someone?"

Ribero grimaced and settled himself on the plastic seat by the bus stop. "It is not like that. When you are old, it is not about the fire and the passion, you understand?"

"Sort of . . ." Kester replied uncertainly.

"Sometimes," his father continued with a pensive stroke of his moustache, "it is just about being less lonely. And me and Jennifer, we go back a long way. We have a lot of the history, yes?"

Kester nodded. "I understand. And of course, it's nothing to do with me anyway. As long as you're happy."

Ribero smiled, his face lighting like a child's. "That is a kind thing to say, Kester. Thank you."

A rush of wheels through the nearby puddle announced the arrival of the bus. Kester helped his father to his feet, where he wobbled unsteadily before straightening himself.

Gazing down the high street, Ribero suddenly clapped a hand on Kester's shoulder. "What are you doing for Christmas?"

Kester smiled. "I've absolutely no idea. Why?"

His father gestured at all the shop windows with their twinkling displays. "You cannot spend it alone. And you must not spend it with that Pineapple person. He is a monstrosity, and I forbid it. Come to my house. It will be nice, right? I will cook a traditional asado."

"What's an asado, again?"

His father snorted with canine irritation. "You are half-Argentinian, boy! You should know these things! It is the finest Argentinian meal, full of cooked meats."

"Oi, mate!" The bus driver waggled a finger in their direction. "You getting on or not?"

Ribero gave the driver his most imperious stare, then began to hobble up the steps. "Is that a yes, then?" he called over his shoulder.

Kester laughed. "I think so. Yes. That would be nice."

"Good! That is the right choice. I will start planning a big meal, yes?"

The doors slid shut, leaving Kester faced with his own chilly-looking reflection. He waved, then ambled back onto the pavement, feeling a little more contented with the world. A child, clutching his mother's hand and licking a lollipop, skipped past. Kester was reminded violently of his own childhood: walking through Cambridge at Christmas time and pointing at all the toys in the window as his mother smiled indulgently over him.

He gulped, embarrassed to feel the prickle of tears in the corners of his eyes. *I still miss you, Mum,* he thought and looked up at the darkening sky. *Wherever you are now. It's pretty lonely sometimes, without you.*

Tugging his phone out of his pocket, he scoured the screen for messages, but there weren't any. He dialled Anya's number and waited.

A flat tone answered him before promptly cutting the call off. *That's a bit odd,* he thought, staring at the screen in the dumb hope that it might miraculously provide him with some answers. He tried again and received the same monotone ring before being cut off.

What the hell? he thought as he gave the phone a frustrated shake. *Perhaps she's somewhere with poor signal, though it's unusual for the phone to just go dead.* He found Anya's landline number and tried that instead.

"Hello?"

It was Wendy, Anya's housemate. He quickly cleared his throat. "Hi, Wendy, it's me, Kester. Is Anya there?"

Wendy paused. "No, I thought she'd moved into yours. Hasn't she?" He could hear the sound of her fingernails tapping against the receiver.

"Well, she was meant to be staying with me for a while," Kester replied uncertainly. "Not moving in, though. Why do you say that?"

Wendy laughed nervously. "When she came in this morning, she packed all her belongings; I presumed she was moving in with you. She's been a bit odd recently, to be honest."

Kester's heart sank. *She's gone,* he realised, and his chest tightened with panic and horror. *I've blown it, big time.*

"What do you mean, odd?" he asked, not sure if he wanted to know the answer.

"Don't know, really. Just not herself. But she hasn't been herself for a while now; not since she disappeared to wherever it was she went to."

You mean, not since she was kidnapped by the Thelemites, Kester corrected silently. He waited for her to continue.

"She was muttering about her clothes and how she hated all of them, which was quite weird. And she left Thor here too, without even asking me. I wasn't too worried, because I presumed she was only at your house. I'm a bit concerned now, though."

Kester swallowed hard. The shop windows had taken on a rather garish quality around him, glaring with fluorescent gaudiness and hulking over him from all sides. He swerved to avoid a man on his bike, who swore at him as he passed. "She didn't give any indication where she was going, then?" he asked, already worried about what the answer might be.

"No. What should we do? Do you think she's safe?"

Kester looked around him at the stalls selling Day-Glo Santa hats and the herds of people making the most of the late-night shopping. He felt overwhelmed, lost amongst it all, and he longed to be back home. "I have no idea if she's safe or not," he said finally, his voice cracking. "But I'll do my best to find out."

Slipping his phone away quietly, he clenched his eyes shut. Fear, sharp and weighty as a lump of lead, settled in his chest, making it hard to breathe. He debated calling his father or Miss Wellbeloved, or even Serena, for that matter—given that he was now concerned she might have been right.

No-one just runs away after a minor argument like that, he realised as he pulled his jacket up tightly around his neck. *And no-one gets that upset. But someone might just flee, if they felt they were under suspicion and had something to hide.*

He winced as the full realisation hit him like a battering ram. *I suspect I know exactly where she's run away to,* he thought, oblivious to the swathes of people mingling around him. *She's returned to the Thelemites. Because she never really left them in the first place.*

Chapter 14: Back to London

Kester spent the following week in a depressed haze. Each evening, he returned home, hoping to find Anya sitting in the lounge waiting for him. However, each evening, the only welcome he received was a chilly, desolate room—or occasionally a chilly, desolate room with Pineapple or Daisy in it, which was even worse.

His conversation with Dr Barqa-Abu hadn't exactly helped lift his spirits either. He received a sharp telling-off, combined with an ominous warning to "look out for trouble," as she was "picking up on some intention towards him." He had no idea what on earth she was talking about and thought it best not to dwell on it for the time being. After all, he had enough to worry about.

To take his mind off of things, he buried himself in his work, trying feverishly to work out the meaning behind the Billy Dagger songs. Frustrated with his lack of success in deciphering the latest track, he focused on the older songs instead and found hidden clues in several of them.

"Open Your Eyes," an old song from the 70s, featured plenty

of anagrams, which he shared gleefully with the others. Mike had been shocked to find that "I spit Maria" was an anagram of "I am a spirit," and that "I, male hematite" was an anagram of "I am a Thelemite."

"It's like he's been playing with us all along," he commented, wide-eyed, as they sat in the Fat Pig on Tuesday night.

Kester fiddled morosely with his beer glass and wondered if he should get a bag of dry roasted peanuts. He no longer cared about his diet, but ironically, since Anya had disappeared, his appetite had completely vanished. In fact, in the short space of a week, his trousers were almost falling off him.

"Still with us?" Serena, who was sitting next to him, waved a hand in front of his eyes. "Wakey-wakey, Kester."

He shook himself and looked blearily at them both. "Sorry, I was miles away. What were you saying?"

"I was just saying about those lyrics in 'Open Your Eyes'," Mike said, polishing his pint off with a slurp. "I can't believe he was leaving clues in his songs, even forty years ago. How come no-one realised?"

"Because they weren't looking for them then, of course." Serena examined her sharp nails, then drummed them irritably against the table. "It's worrying, though. It's all getting rather worrying, in fact." She turned to face Kester. "Have you heard anything from her yet?"

He didn't need to ask who she was talking about. "No," he replied as he cast his eyes to the floor. "I said already, I have no idea where Anya is. And it's probably not worth me being too concerned about it either, since she was probably lying to me right from the start."

Serena's expression softened. "I'm not sure that's true." Sidling along the bench, she wrapped an arm around him in an unchar-acteristic show of affection. "We won't know what happened until we find her."

Kester shrugged her off irritably. "We won't find her though, will we? She's a member of one of the world's most secretive cults. Of course we're not going to find her."

"Yeah, but they might have kidnapped her again, mate," Mike said consolingly.

"Her housemate saw her packing her bags. She wasn't forced."

"Well," Serena placated, "we don't know the facts. She may have been coerced."

Kester thought back to all the times Anya had been so curious about the case, all the questions she'd asked, and how insistent she'd been about getting information. *I should have known,* he thought glumly. *There was me, thinking a girl actually liked me for once, and she was just pumping me for information.* He felt hollow, as though someone had sucked his emotions out with a vacuum cleaner. *How stupid I've been,* he realised, downing the rest of his ale. *I should have known that someone as pretty as her would never be attracted to someone as irrelevant as me.*

"You've gone quiet again, Kester," Mike said, breaking the silence. "Let me get you another drink. Booze always numbs the pain of woman-troubles."

"Since when do you ever have woman-troubles?" Serena snapped. "You don't even have a woman."

"Charming as ever, love." With a parting glare, he stalked off to the bar.

Serena tutted, then leant back against the bench. "You know, I'm not convinced she wasn't forced by the Thelemites to spy on you," she said as she rubbed off an imaginary speck of dirt from her trouser-leg.

"Can we just drop the subject?" He glanced at his watch. It was already getting on seven o'clock; not that there was anything particularly exciting waiting at home for him, apart from a half-eaten bacon baguette in the fridge.

"Why not come with us tomorrow, to the London stake-out?" Serena pressed. The determined expression in her eyes indicated she wasn't going to take no for an answer.

"I don't know," Kester said uncertainly. "What if Anya comes back?"

"Kester, you can't just wait around on the off-chance that she returns with her tail between her legs." Serena eyed Mike at the bar, who was currently sampling a local ale and nodding enthusiastically. "Besides, Miss Wellbeloved has already ordered a twin room for you and Mike."

"Has she?" Kester felt nettled. "I told her I didn't feel up to going."

"Let's all go," Serena said loudly, drawing attention from the group of young men at the neighbouring table. "Come on. It's just what you need, something to take your mind off things. Otherwise, you'll be in the office all by yourself, which will be no fun at all."

"I don't know," Kester grumbled. "I could always start making Christmas decorations to hang around the desks."

Mike returned with a tray of drinks. He placed them down carefully, then grinned. "Thought I'd get us some tequila shots," he said as he removed the tiny glasses and positioned them in a line at the centre of the table. "It They might lighten the mood a bit."

"Oh, for goodness' sake, Mike!" Serena glared at him. "We've got a busy day tomorrow; we can't all turn up with hangovers."

"It's just a sneaky one. Come on, don't be such a party-pooper."

"No." Serena folded her arms and stared mutinously at the glasses. "It's a silly idea."

Mike rolled his eyes, grabbed a tequila, and downed it in one gulp. Then he reached for the next one and did the same again. Kester laughed in spite of himself and quickly rescued the third, before Mike could devour that one too.

"Honestly, you're the most immature man I've ever had the misfortune to meet," Serena snapped. "When are you going to grow up?"

"Hopefully never," Mike concluded with a belch as he started to tuck into his fresh pint. "Lighten up, this is meant to be an evening out, okay?"

"Children, please," Kester murmured. He was starting to get a headache, and their bickering wasn't helping.

"So, Kester," Serena continued, relentless as a terrier. "Are you joining us in London?"

"Yeah, come on, mate," Mike added. "They're putting us up in a fancy hotel. It'll be great. And remember, London pubs are amazing."

"You're not there to do a sodding pub crawl!"

"Stop lecturing me, you old witch." Mike wiped his mouth on the back of his sleeve, then belched again. "So, what do you say?"

Kester rolled his eyes. "Fine. Count me in. You're right, I'll only brood if I stay here."

The other two drummed their hands on the table with delight. "I *knew* I could convince you," Serena said smugly, nudging his shoulder. Despite his moroseness, Kester grinned and raised his glass to her.

That night, he slept badly, as he had done for the last seven nights in a row. He kept rolling over and expecting to see Anya there, breathing quietly in the darkness. Instead, his bed felt vast and empty, making his bedroom desperately lonely. *Where are you?* he wondered, trying to imagine where she might be hiding. Was she with the Thelemites, laughing at his stupidity, making fun of him? Or was Serena right? Had they forced Anya to leave against her will?

Or am I completely wrong, he thought, *and she's actually run away somewhere completely different?* Who knew? Endless questions raced around his head until the early hours of the morning, when he finally collapsed into sleep. It seemed like only minutes later that his alarm buzzed him back into wakefulness, leaving him feeling more exhausted than ever.

The train journey was uneventful, aside from Ribero berating a young man for not giving up his seat for him, then grumbling for the best part of an hour about having to stand in the aisle. Finally, after four hours of travelling, they arrived at Covent Garden tube station and emerged onto the busy street.

"Chaos, as ever!" Pamela announced breezily, navigating a path through the throngs of people. "You've got to love London!" A double-decker bus raced past, creating a sharp breeze that tugged their coats and skirts into the air.

"I take it you're being sarcastic, yes?" Ribero used his crutches to forcibly part the crowd, oblivious to the glares he received in response. "Kester, hurry up with my bag there, and don't pull it through the puddles, I don't want it dirty, right?"

Kester wiped his brow and promptly dropped all the bags on the pavement. "How did I get lumbered with carrying everything?"

"You are young and fit, you should carry things!" his father declared. "When I was your age, I was carrying much more, without even breaking a sweat!"

"Julio, stop nagging the boy," Miss Wellbeloved muttered as she placed her own suitcase down and fumbled in her pockets for a map. "Right, it says the hotel is just up here on the left. Or is it the right?"

Serena groaned. "Hurry up, we're getting in everyone's way here." Sure enough, they were attracting plenty of angry comments from passers-by, mainly due to the fact that they were blocking most of the pavement with their luggage.

Pamela loomed over Miss Wellbeloved's shoulder, then pointed. "We need to turn right. Look. You've got the map the wrong way up."

"Then let us get going!" Ribero declared, hobbling forwards at a determined pace. The others followed him like herded sheep, fighting to keep their suitcases from being battered by the crowds. The smell of roasting chestnuts wafted tantalizingly from a nearby stall, though it was marred slightly by the pungent odour of the traffic, not to mention the general dampness coming from the evaporating puddles.

Finally, they arrived at the steps of what appeared to be a very imposing, regal-looking hotel—complete with pillars, a bronze plaque, and a rather snooty-looking doorman.

"Well, look at this place!" Mike whistled and chucked his battered backpack on the ground. "I don't think I've ever stayed in somewhere as fancy as this."

"This is what you get when you take on a top-level government job," Miss Wellbeloved replied with a trace of self-satisfaction. She handed her bag to the doorman, then winked at the others. "Just don't get too used to it, okay?"

"No, it'll be back to bargain-basement establishments soon enough," Serena muttered, though despite her sarcasm, it was obvious she was impressed.

After checking in at an impossibly-huge, marble reception desk, they were shown to their rooms. Kester's eyes widened as the bellboy opened the door. He hadn't stayed in many hotels in his lifetime, mainly because he'd never been away much when he'd lived at home with his mother. This one was particularly grandiose with high sash windows, billowing velvet curtains, and enormously comfortable-looking twin beds.

Mike looked similarly amazed. Ignoring the bellboy's obvious hints for a tip, he closed the door firmly, then leapt on the bed, sinking into the duvet like a stick into melting marshmallow. "This is the life," he said as he deposited each shoe on the floor with a deft flick of his toes. "Talk about luxurious. I bet those Infinite Enterprise boys get this sort of quality wherever they stay."

Kester chuckled. "Why not work for Infinite Enterprises, then? You always go on about how much they wanted to hire you, back in the day."

Mike propped himself against the pillows. "Well, don't mention that to anyone. It was a long time ago now." Leaping up, he strode over to the bathroom and pointed at the door. "Have you ever seen anything like this? Look, the toilet's got a glass door with pictures all over it!"

Kester nodded. "It's pretty posh, isn't it?"

"We should check out the bar, see what they've got on the menu. Miss W said the government is picking up the tab."

"Yes, but only up to a certain amount," Kester reminded him as he started to unpack his shirts. "Don't go crazy, Mike."

"Ah, come on, mate." Mike bounced up and down on the bed like an excited child. "We've got to make the most of it. Anyway, it'll take your mind off things, won't it?"

Kester sighed and folded his clothes neatly into the chest of drawers. "I doubt it. We'll be talking non-stop about the Thelemites for the next few days, which will only remind me of her."

"Still not heard anything?"

Kester shook his head. He'd been trying to ring Anya constantly. He'd even tried calling her parents in Denmark, even though they didn't speak much English. *Unless she's decided to go on holiday to Antigua without telling anyone,* he realised, *she's obviously sneaked off back to the Thelemites, and I just have to accept it.*

Mike scooped up his backpack and poured the contents all over the bed. In addition to clothes, books, and random pieces of machinery, Kester noticed that several pebbles also fell out, not to mention a large amount of sand, which spread across the pristine duvet in a matter of moments. However, Mike seemed not to notice, and he proceeded to stuff his belongings in an untidy heap in the drawers nearest his bed.

The shrill tone of a mobile phone cut through the quiet. Kester dived hastily into his trouser pocket, studied the screen, then looked away, disappointed.

"It's Miss Wellbeloved," he said in a flat voice.

"Well, go on, answer it!"

He pressed the screen and pushed the phone to his ear. "Hello?"

"Ah, Kester—how is your room?"

"Very nice, thank you. How's yours?"

"Your father seems to have taken up most of the room with all of his suits, but other than that, it's very pleasant." She laughed, then continued, "I've just let Cardigan and Ian know that we're here, so they're on their way to meet us. They've already reserved a conference room."

"Is Larry Higgins here yet?" Kester asked.

"Yes, Larry checked in earlier, with his team."

In the background, Kester could hear his father muttering something that sounded suspiciously like it had the words "*the Higgins*" in it. "Is Dad kicking off again?" he asked.

Miss Wellbeloved sighed. "When isn't he kicking off, Kester? Anyway, we're meeting downstairs in the lobby in half an hour. We'll see you down there."

"Hang on," Mike said urgently, flapping his hands in Kester's direction. "When are we having lunch? It's past two o'clock and I'm absolutely starving."

Kester shrugged. "Did you hear that?" he asked Miss Wellbeloved. "Mike's hungry."

"I'm sure there'll be some food somewhere that he can eat. Tell him to stop thinking so much about his stomach."

Kester looked in Mike's direction to see if he'd heard. His indignant expression suggested that he had.

"I'll have you know that I think of plenty of other things apart from—"

"—We'll see you downstairs later," Kester concluded swiftly, then he grinned at Mike, who was looking rather put out. "Come on, you know she's right. You do eat a lot."

Mike patted his stomach affably. "I have to feed all this rippling muscle, don't I?" He stretched out with a yawn, then pointed to the door. "Come on. Let's go down early and get some bar snacks."

"Fine, but no alcohol."

"Spoilsport." Mike grinned, then bounded to the door. "Last one to the bar is a loser."

Sounds about right, Kester thought glumly as he passed the mirror on the way out. *I don't think many people could be more of a loser than me.*

The bar was no less impressive than the rest of the hotel, and Kester made himself comfortable on an enormous leather sofa whilst Mike ordered in platefuls of chips, which arrived complete with ketchup, mayonnaise, and virtually every other kind of exotic dressing imaginable. Kester forced a few chips down, but only out of politeness. The prospect of sitting through a lengthy meeting with the others wasn't very appealing either.

Finally sated, Mike eased one buttock-cheek up, passed wind audibly, then beamed round the room, oblivious to the horrified expressions of a pair of elderly women on the table opposite.

"Right," he concluded as he slapped Kester's thigh. "Let's get to work."

Sure enough, Serena was already waving crossly at them through the glass door and stabbing a finger violently at her wristwatch. They groaned, then made their way to meet her.

"Seriously, don't tell me you've started drinking already," she chastised the moment they stepped out into the lobby.

"No, actually!" Mike protested. He rubbed his stomach reflectively. "We were just getting a spot of lunch."

"Oh, was it nice?" Pamela asked, peering over Serena's shoulder. "That's made me hungry now, I wonder if there's time for me to order something?"

"No, there absolutely bloody isn't!" Larry Higgins's strident, nasal bark boomed across the polished floor. He marched over to them, then folded his arms over his stomach. "Infinite Enterprises will be here any moment, and the last thing we need is a hold-up whilst you stuff your face."

"Alright, alright," Pamela said affably, giving Dimitri and Luke a wave, who were currently hiding behind Higgins and looking rather embarrassed. "Maybe they'll have biscuits in the meeting, eh?"

"Ah, what is the Higgins moaning about now?" Ribero snarled, sidling over to join them and waving his crutch threateningly in Larry's general direction. "Always with the whining."

Higgins's expression darkened. "You're a fine one to talk, over-dramatic moron. Honestly, everything's always a bloody catastrophe according to you, waving your hands around all over the place and—"

"—Gentlemen!" Miss Wellbeloved hissed as she positioned herself directly between them both. "Cardigan and Ian have just walked through the door, so perhaps some decorum is needed?"

Is he wearing a cape? Kester thought as he watched Ian Kingdom-Green swoosh across the lobby to meet them. Sure enough, as soon as he reached them, he untied the bow at his neck and flung the garment off like a bat spreading its wings. Kester wasn't sure whether to feel awed or amused.

Cardigan, clearly used to Ian's attention-grabbing entrances, merely smiled and extended a hand to them all. "Welcome everyone," he said. "Thank you for coming up at such short notice. As you know, there have been some significant developments. Our surveillance expert, Lili, will also be joining us, but she's been held up in traffic."

Lili Asadi, Kester realised, remembering the pert, slightly intimidating woman from his brief trip to Whitby. He'd got the impression that she'd thought he was a bit of an idiot, but he hoped he was just being paranoid. Quietly, he followed the others through another set of glass doors and down a long, silent corridor. Cardigan flung open the set of double-doors at the end and gestured inside.

"Please," he said politely. "Make yourselves at home. I suspect some of you might not have eaten, so I've taken the liberty of pre-ordering some sandwiches, which should be arriving soon."

Pamela punched the air with delight. So did Mike, despite the sheer volume of chips he'd put away only minutes before. Higgins muttered furiously under his breath, then stalked over to the meeting table.

After they'd settled, Cardigan took his place in one of the large, leather chairs and folded his fingers under his chin.

"Before I get started," he announced, surveying them all calmly, "has anyone got anything else to tell us? Serena, thanks for checking that we received the Whilshin & Sons report, they sent it through to us when they sent it to you. Anyone else?"

"We've been keeping a close eye on the Exeter Thelemite lodge," Miss Wellbeloved said, picking at her nails nervously. "But it's been quiet. Suspiciously quiet, if you want my opinion."

"Have you seen anyone going in or out?"

She shook her head. "Only the cleaner."

Cardigan glanced at Ian, who stroked his beard thoughtfully.

"That seems somewhat irregular," he murmured. "After all, one would think they'd at least have their weekly meeting, if nothing else."

"Quite," Cardigan agreed. He looked at Kester. "How about you? We know you managed to decipher some more song lyrics—did you get anywhere with the latest song? What was it called again?"

"'Ode to Set-Shirker'," Mike and Kester chimed in unison.

"That's right. Surely that must be an anagram, mustn't it?" Cardigan suggested as he leaned closer.

"You'd think so, wouldn't you?" Kester agreed. "But if it is, it's not one I've managed to crack yet. I wonder if he's just playing with us again—throwing it in there as a red herring."

Cardigan browsed through his notes. "Do you think so?" he asked seriously. "Given what we know about this daemon already?"

Kester shrugged. "I'm starting to think that none of us really know him at all, to be honest."

The door lurched open, and Lili Asadi stormed through with a sigh.

"Remind me never to drive in Central London again."

"You say that every time, my dear," Ian reminded her as he graciously pulled a chair out for her. "And every time we remind you, you still insist on driving."

"Yeah, you're right," Lili plonked herself on the chair. "Where are we up to, then?"

Cardigan gestured at the others. "We were just being updated about the song lyrics, but so far, Kester hasn't discovered anything new."

Lili gave him a curt nod. "That's a shame. We were relying on the most recent Billy Dagger song to reveal something important."

"I'm doing my best!" Kester squeaked defensively. Lili shrugged, then gave him a tight smile.

"So," Cardigan continued with a sympathetic glance in Kester's direction. "Lili, could you share your findings with the rest of us?"

She nodded, resting her elbows on the table. "It was Tinker's findings, really; he was the one on observations yesterday."

"Tinker is Lili's assistant," Cardigan explained, seeing the confused expressions around the table.

Ian laughed and flicked his hair off his shoulders. "He's notoriously bashful, so it's unlikely you'll ever meet him. Dear little chap, he is. Looks a little bit like a mole."

"Yes, thanks, Ian, that's quite enough of a description," Cardigan interrupted. "Go on, Lili—tell us what you've found out."

"Well," Lili began dramatically, pausing to ensure she had their full attention. "The Whitby Thelemite lodge has been suspiciously empty all week."

"So has the Exeter one!" Miss Wellbeloved exclaimed.

"And we were watching the Cambridge one," Dimitri added, eyes glittering, "and that has shown no activity all week either. I wonder what is going on?"

Luke rattled his fingers across the table. "That's damned strange, ain't it?"

"It certainly is," Lili agreed. She leaned back on her chair. "To be honest, I don't know what to make of it all. However, something happened yesterday that was of interest."

"Please share it with everyone." Cardigan put his notes down and folded his hands across his broad stomach.

She nodded. "Barty Melville returned in his car, at around midday yesterday. It was odd, because he was in civilian clothes."

"You mean he wasn't wearing his usual circus tent?" Miss Wellbeloved chuckled.

"Exactly. He was just dressed in jeans and a jumper, and he

looked like he was trying to blend in, if you know what I mean."

"So, what the bloody hell did he do, then?" Higgins asked. "Something fishy, I suspect, judging by your expression."

"He went into the lodge, but for some reason, he sneaked in through the back door," Lili continued. "We followed him using the thermal imaging system and saw that he spent a lot of time on the phone. I wish we'd managed to get the government to let us bug the place."

"There's no point," Miss Wellbeloved said primly. "Hrschni would be able to pick up on it in a heartbeat."

"I suppose so," Lili replied. "Anyway, the next thing he did was start packing away loads of files into boxes, then moving them into his car. It was like he was removing all the paperwork in there."

"Now, that is suspicious," Serena piped up. "Why would he do that?"

"Moving to another location, perhaps?" Mike suggested.

Lili sighed. "We have no idea. We trailed him for a bit, but once he'd hit the motorway, there was no way our surveillance van could keep up."

"Perhaps he is in London, eh?" Ribero said.

"Maybe he's gone back to Exeter," Kester added. "After all, that is where he lives."

"Or the Thelemites have got another lodge that we don't know about," Lili said darkly.

They all looked at one another. The frustration in the room was palpable as a fog. *We've got all these clues in front of us,* Kester thought as he knotted his fingers restlessly in his lap, *but nothing solid to go on. The Thelemites are always several steps ahead of us.*

"So," Higgins said, breaking the silence. "The question is, what do we do now?"

"We're going to focus our attentions on the London Thelemite lodge for now," Cardigan said as he adjusted his shirt. "Something tells me that the key Thelemites are gathering somewhere, and it would make sense for them to meet here." He nodded to Ribero.

"We want your team to work in the archives for the next few days, see if you can find anything we've missed. I've already asked the team to pull out all the relevant documents for you."

Kester brightened. He liked research, even under pressurised circumstances. *It's much better than being dragged around somewhere sinister looking for spirits,* he thought. Miss Wellbeloved caught his eye and smiled faintly, reading his thoughts.

"It's strange though, isn't it," Kester said suddenly. He blushed as everyone looked at him. "I mean, nothing really *adds up,* does it?"

"Go on?" Cardigan urged him gently.

"Well," Kester continued. "For starters, breaking into Infinite Enterprises. We all presumed they were trying to get to the spirit door you've got there. But there was no evidence to suggest that was the case. Instead, all you found was some disturbed files in the basement."

"That's because security is so darned tight around the spirit door," Larry retorted, his chins wobbling almost entirely of their own accord. "Presumably, Hrschni had a bloody good attempt to break in and found he couldn't do it."

"Really?" Kester said incredulously. "Then why go down to the archives and mess around with the papers?"

"Maybe he wanted to let us know he'd been there?" Serena suggested.

Kester shook his head. "I don't buy it. I think there's more to it than that. He was looking for something."

"The whole thing about leaving clues in the song lyrics is most odd too," Ian added. "Especially as Hrschni seems to have been doing it since the 1970s."

"Well, that's no time at all to a daemon, is it?" Higgins snorted. "The damned creatures are virtually immortal."

"Yes, but still," Kester interrupted, sitting up in his chair. "Why would he bother? And who are the clues for?"

They all leaned back in their chairs, thoroughly stumped. Kester pushed his fringe out of his eyes and frowned. *I know we're missing something here,* he thought earnestly. *It's all in front of us like a jigsaw. The songs. The break-in. Anya's kidnapping. Barty Melville's behaviour in Whitby. We just need to start piecing it all together.*

"What were you thinking, Kester?" Pamela asked quietly as she touched his arm.

He shrugged. "I don't know. I just think the answer might be glaring us in the face—we just haven't been able to see it yet."

"Well," Cardigan said loudly as he gave them all a significant nod. "Let's hope we start seeing it very soon. For all our sakes."

CHAPTER 15: EXPLORING THE ARCHIVES

Dazzling winter sunshine poured through the windows of the Infinite Enterprises reception as Ribero's team went through the necessary security checks to permit them access to the expansive vaults below.

Kester felt excited in spite of himself. He'd heard a few snippets of information about the archive department at Infinite Enterprises: a vast cave of information, containing every file on every spirit creature, not to mention all the agencies in operation, in the country. *Sounds like my sort of place,* he thought as the lift doors slid shut, blocking out the last of the sunlight. *Just the kind of place I can bury myself in research.*

The artificial glow of the fluorescent lamps made the lift feel otherworldly. Pamela yawned loudly just as the lift doors slid open again.

"I must say," she muttered as they stepped out into the vast, subterranean space, "I couldn't be less in the mood to rifle through old paperwork if I tried. That breakfast is repeating on me a bit."

"Lovely," Mike said, prodding her side. "Are we going to have to endure your stomach gurgling all morning? Mind you," he added with a gentle pat to his own stomach, "I think four sausages at breakfast was a bit much, even for me."

Kester gazed around with amazement. *It's like an endless warehouse down here!* he thought as he took in the long desks with people hunched over laptops, the eerie blue glow of the lights, and the rows of shelves disappearing into the distance. *How far does it go on? It must stretch right under the whole street!*

Ribero leant his crutches against the nearest table. "So," he said, casually slipping his hands into his pockets. "Where are we supposed to start? I presumed someone would be down here to help us, no?"

A rattling noise caught their attention, and they all looked over to see a thin, pale young man with huge bottle-top glasses scurrying in their direction. He was clutching a file to his chest like a drowning man clasping a life-ring.

"Hello, everyone," he said, left eye twitching uncontrollably. "I've been asked to show you around this morning, though quite why they picked me, I have no idea, it's really not something I'm very good at and—"

"—Ah, so you are one of the boffins who works down here, right?" Ribero guessed, eyes twinkling with amusement. "Can you can tell us where all the files are?"

The young man shook his head. "Actually, I don't work in the archives," he mumbled and shifted his collar uncomfortably. "I'm normally on surveillance, and I'm due to head out in a moment— but Cardigan and Lili asked me if I would be able to show you the—"

"—You're Tinker, aren't you?" Kester interrupted. He remembered Ian Kingdom-Green making some comment about moles, and with Tinker now in front of him, he fully understood why. Tinker's round, thick glasses and twitchy, panicky demeanour was very much like a little animal more used to living underground than interacting with others.

Tinker pushed his glasses up his nose and peered earnestly in Kester's direction. "Yes, that's correct," he murmured. "And you're Kester, Dr Ribero's son. I saw you the other week, in Whitby, when we were—"

"Did you?" Kester said. "I didn't see you."

The other man blushed so violently that his hollow cheeks seemed to glow. "Ah, yes. Well, I was in one of the neighbouring buildings, undertaking a surveillance of the Whitby Thelemite lodge, and I watched you walking down the street towards our van, so I—"

Mike slapped Tinker on the back so hard that his glasses jolted to one side, leaving him looking mildly dazed. "That's a bit creepy, if you don't mind me saying," he said jovially. "You shouldn't be spying on people, you know."

"Oh, I must assure you, I wasn't—"

"—It's alright, as long as you're not using your surveillance equipment to peer in on ladies when they're taking a shower," Mike guffawed. The noise echoed loudly before petering off into silence. Tinker squirmed.

"Anyway," Miss Wellbeloved said with a stern glance in Mike's direction. "If you could show us where we need to be, Tinker, that would be most kind."

He smiled, then blushed even more deeply. "Of course, if would be my absolute honour, not to mention privilege, to—"

"—Yes, yes, just show us, eh?" Ribero interrupted. He caught Kester's eye, then smiled apologetically. "Well, we have to get on with things, don't we?"

"Just ignore my dad," Kester said comfortingly as he spotted Tinker's crestfallen face. "He's a grumpy old man—he can't help it."

They followed the young man past shelf after shelf of towering files and folders. There were plenty of other workers down there, either reaching for books on shelves or tapping away at their keyboards. For the most part, they completely ignored the team's presence.

Kester stared, open-mouthed, at their surroundings. He felt more enthusiastic than he had in a long while. *I could spend years reading through all this material,* he thought, itching to get started. *I wonder if they've got any jobs going down here?*

Finally, Tinker halted in front of a large table, an impressive piece of furniture constructed of concrete and polished metal. A huge pile of folders lay in the middle, and there were three spare laptops positioned neatly beside it, fully charged and humming gently.

"Um, so this is pretty much everything you should need today," Tinker began with another nervous cough. "These are all the main files we have on the Thelemites, and of course, anything else you need, you can look up its whereabouts on the system. If you need to ask any questions, just ask any of the people down here, I'm sure they'll help you."

Ribero grunted. "They all look like big nerds to me."

"Shut up," Kester hissed. He looked up and nodded. "Thank you very much, Tinker—you've been really helpful. Are you off to assist with the surveillance now?"

Tinker nodded. "Yes, I just need to collect my camera from the equipment department." He pointed in the other direction. "It's all the way down there, so I'll have to persuade one of the maintenance guys to give me a lift on their buggy and—"

"—Woah," Mike interrupted as he peered in the direction of Tinker's finger. "You mean, it's so big down here that you need a vehicle to get from one end to the other?"

"I'm sure he doesn't mean that, Mike," Serena corrected.

"Well, that's pretty much what I do mean, actually," Tinker said, then looked panicked when Serena narrowed her eyes at him. "Otherwise it takes a very long time to walk, you see. I once timed it, and it took exactly twenty-four minutes and thirty-three seconds to walk at a fast pace from—"

"—Thank you ever so much for your help," Miss Wellbeloved

said with a hint of a smile at the others. She gestured over her shoulder. "I presume that's one of the buggies over there, isn't it?"

Tinker peered over, then beamed. "So it is! What a good bit of luck that is, otherwise I would have had to set aside twenty-four minutes and—"

"—Better hurry up, he's heading off," Mike said with a jerk of his head. Tinker gasped, grabbed his bag, then leapt off in the direction of the buggy.

"I thought he would never be silent," Ribero muttered as he waved his hand towards the ceiling. "He was an even worse talker than you, Pamela."

"Thank you very much!" Pamela squawked, then clutched her stomach. "Oh dear. I do hope it's not twenty-four minutes and thirty-three seconds to the toilet, I'm feeling quite urgent . . ."

Miss Wellbeloved rolled her eyes. "Why didn't you go before we came here?"

"I didn't need to go then, did I?"

"Hurry up and go then," Ribero spluttered, eyes wide with righteous indignation. "Women and their toilet habits. I will never understand them."

Pamela gratefully bustled off, clutching her stomach. They watched her go, then they turned to the mountain of files in front of them with a mixture of dismay, depression, and, in Kester's case, unbridled excitement.

"I suppose we'd better make a start then," Serena said moodily as she reached for the uppermost folder. The rest followed suit.

Kester selected a particularly ancient-looking book, which was nearly as wide as he was. Thumping it down in front of him, it released a pleasingly musty cloud of dust, which then proceeded to settle cross the surface of the desk. He opened it and began to read.

"*The Thelemites: A Hidden History*," he said aloud, then peered at the others over his glasses. "That sounds interesting, doesn't it?"

"If you say so," Mike grumbled. He already looked bored.

"Written by Aloysius Peverall. What a wonderful name!" Kester exclaimed. "First edition, printed 1875. A Victorian writer, how marvellous. Victorian writers are always so creative with their words."

"Kester, will you shut up?" Serena snapped. "I can't concentrate with you wittering on in my earhole."

He pursed his lips together and carried on reading. In typical nineteenth century fashion, the book was filled with lengthy sentences, not to mention considerable waffle, but it didn't matter to Kester—he was in his element. He ploughed through the pages, jotting down occasional notes; he wasn't convinced that he'd found anything useful, though.

After half an hour, Pamela finally returned, wearing an expression that was both sheepish and disgruntled.

"Where have you been?" Miss Wellbeloved asked as she glanced up from her folder. "You've been gone a very long time!"

"I couldn't find a toilet," Pamela whispered as she slid into the nearest available seat. "Oh, it was ever so embarrassing."

"Dear Lord, don't tell me you've soiled yourself," Serena said, wrinkling her nose.

"No, I have not! The cheek of it!"

"Why was it embarrassing, then?" Mike asked, then leant back in his chair, clearly glad of the break.

Pamela reddened. "I managed to find the gents' toilets, but not the ladies'."

"Why's that such a big deal? I've had to sneak into the ladies' toilets plenty of times," Mike replied with a lurid wink in Serena's direction.

"Because Curtis Philpot was in there too!"

Ribero whistled. Miss Wellbeloved shook her head in disbelief. Mike roared with laughter.

"Don't tell me—he was waiting to use the toilet too and heard everything?"

Pamela's face turned the same shade as an overripe tomato. "Yes. You should have seen the look on his face when I came out.

It was awful."

"What did you say?" Serena asked.

Pamela held her head in her hands as though reluctant to relive the event. "I didn't know what to say, did I? I mean, there was me, in the men's toilets, with a very upset stomach . . ."

Mike laughed even harder. "Go on."

"I just told him that he might want to leave it a few minutes before using it."

The entire team burst into giggles.

"That's such a blokeish thing to say," Serena said as she wiped her eyes. "Oh, Pamela. That's dreadful. But hilarious."

"Yes, alright, well, let's forget about it now," Pamela replied stiffly, rearranging her blouse. "I shall never be able to look him in the eye again."

Kester chuckled, gave Pamela a comforting pat on the arm, then returned to the book. It was proving to be a fascinating read. Aloysius Peverall, whoever he might have been, had clearly researched the Thelemites thoroughly. Kester relaxed back into the pages, allowing the words to wash around him, soothing his spirits and calming his emotions. *Who needs a therapist when you've got an author to help you instead?* he thought dreamily as he turned to the next chapter.

An hour slipped away. They continued to read, silent apart from the occasional scratch of pen against paper as they took notes. Kester finished the page he was on, then raised a finger.

"I've just read something quite interesting," he announced, more loudly than he'd intended. The others looked up at him immediately, each fighting to snap themselves back into reality again.

Kester waited until they were ready, then prodded the page with great deliberation. "This whole chapter," he began, "is very curious. Apparently, the Thelemites we attempting to open an illegal spirit door in a secret location. Or that's what they were accused of, anyway."

"Really?" Serena said, with a raised eyebrow. "How come we've not heard of it before, then?"

Kester inhaled deeply. "Well, I suppose because it was never proven. Shall I fill you in on what it says?"

"If you think it is important, then yes, you must!" Ribero exclaimed as he shut his own book with a loud bang.

"It says," Kester began, clearing his throat and flicking back to find the relevant page, "that in the eighteenth century, certain members of the Honourable Infinite Spirit Organisation—"

"—Also known as Infinite Enterprises, before they had to change their name," Miss Wellbeloved added.

"—had grown suspicious about the Thelemites' activities." He scratched his head, then flicked forward to the next page. "Hang on, let me find it. Yes, here it is. 'The gentlemen in question declared that they had unveiled evidence, which pointed most assuredly to—'"

"Just translate it for me, mate," Mike begged. "I don't speak gobbledy-gook."

"That's debateable," Serena muttered.

"Okay." Kester squinted down at the book. "Basically, it says that a group of people from Infinite Enterprises accused the Thelemites of trying to open a door to the spirit world. However, when pressed, they couldn't provide much evidence, and said their lives would be in danger if they revealed what they knew."

"Well, that's not much use, is it?" Pamela huffed.

Kester went on. "All they would say was that the Thelemites had a secret lodge . . . somewhere dark, somewhere cold, somewhere where no-one would think of looking. And *that's* where they were planning to create an illegal spirit door." He looked up. "Typical. It had to be somewhere *dark,* didn't it? Just to make it scarier."

"What happened next?" Serena asked. "Did anyone take them seriously?"

Kester scanned the page. "It says here that their accusations were widely disregarded. The Thelemites protested their innocence and the Honourable Infinite Spirit Organisation—"

"—Infinite Enterprises, let's not give them an even more pompous name that they've got already," Mike growled, then peered hastily over his shoulder to check none of the archives workers had heard him.

"Alright, you've made me lose my place now," Kester said. "Here we are. The accusers had to apologise to the Thelemites, though one person refused, remaining convinced that his suspicions were correct. His name was Ethelred Bunting."

"Now that's a name," Pamela said approvingly.

"What happened to this Ethelred, then?" Ribero asked, leaning across his book like a languishing leopard. "He got into trouble, right?"

"Even worse," Kester replied with a click of his fingers. "He disappeared."

The others sat up straighter at the news. "That's a bit mysterious," Miss Wellbeloved said. "What else does the author say about it?"

"He comes up with a few theories about where Ethelred went to. The most popular idea was that he'd fled abroad." Kester slouched backwards and rapped his chin thoughtfully. "I wonder," he began, "if I look him up on the system, whether anything would come up?"

"It certainly would, if he once worked for Infinite Enterprises," Miss Wellbeloved said, shoving a laptop in his direction. "Go on, log on and see what you can find out."

Kester started tapping hastily, and at once, the screen was filled with book references and a file, all relating directly to the mysterious Ethelred. *Gosh,* he thought. *It's so nice using a computer that doesn't take half an hour to upload for once.*

"Here's his file," he said and rotated the screen so they could all see. "Look at his portrait! What a goatee!" They all stared at the small portrait, which showed a rather portly man with a splendid slicked-back hairstyle, not to mention a very intense expression.

"It says he was thirty-two when he vanished," Kester continued, "and prior to that, he worked in the Department of Spirit Deportation." He looked up. "What does that mean?"

"Spirit deportation is just another word for extinguishing spirits," Serena said. "Like what I do."

"Not quite," Miss Wellbeloved corrected, peering at the screen. "If my memory serves me correctly, the Department of Spirit Deportation focused on sending spirits back to their own realm, usually via a door. It closed down several years ago, due to dwindling numbers of spirit-door openers. I bet you'll find that's what our friend Ethelred's skill was." She pointed further down on the screen, smiling triumphantly. "See? It's confirmed here. A spirit-door opener. Just like you, Kester."

"Gosh, I bet they missed him when he disappeared," Mike said. "Spirit-door openers are hard to come by."

"What else does it say?" Pamela asked.

"This bit doesn't sound too good," Kester said as he read the general notes. "It says here that Mr Ethelred Bunting protested 'loudly and most inappropriately' about the Thelemites and refused to issue an apology when asked. As a result, he was dismissed from his position, then he went missing almost straight after."

"Wow, sacking a spirit-door opener? He must have done something bad," Ribero said.

Kester rubbed his chin. "I'm not sure that any of this is much use to us, though. I mean, this all happened over a hundred years ago."

"Carry on reading," Miss Wellbeloved suggested. "See what else you can uncover."

However, by the end of the day, he'd found nothing else of use, apart from a few minor disagreements between the Thelemites and Infinite Enterprises, which all seemed to be fairly isolated incidents. Likewise, the others had found little of interest, aside from some reference to daemons in an ancient Thelemite text, which none of them could properly decipher.

Exhausted, they caught the train back to Covent Garden station with all the rest of the city commuters, then they staggered gratefully through the polished doors of their hotel. Serena promptly announced that she was going to take a long bath. The others returned to their room to freshen up before dinner-time, leaving Kester and Mike alone in the bar.

"Are you going to let me order a drink, or are you going to say it's too early?"

Kester laughed and rubbed his eyes. It had been a long, draining day. "I personally think a drink is *exactly* what we need right now."

Mike beamed. "Nice one. Let's enjoy the benefits of charging it to the room, eh?" Without waiting for an answer, he sauntered off to the bar.

A couple of hours and seven pints later, Mike was slurring badly and slumping so far into the sofa that it looked as though it was sucking him into a black hole. Kester was still nursing his second pint and laughing openly at Mike's attempt to narrate an anecdote whilst completely forgetting the punchline.

"You'd probably better go a bit easy on the alcohol from here on in," he suggested, patting Mike's leg. "It's not even eight o'clock yet, and you're already fairly hammered."

"This?" Mike droned as he gestured down the entire length of his body. "Thish is not drunk. Not even slightly."

"You said 'thish'."

"That doesn't prove anything." Mike finished his pint with a flourish, hiccupping shortly after. He grinned at Kester, then his face darkened. "Oh no, look who it is. Mr Pompous Prat himself."

Kester turned to see Higgins striding through the door, with Dimitri and Luke trailing wearily behind. At the sight of Kester and Mike, his eyebrows lowered menacingly.

"Good lord, you two!" he exclaimed as he gestured at the empty glasses on the table. "How many have you had?"

"Enough to make me happy," Mike replied, then hiccupped again. "I am a happy little boy."

Luke stifled a laugh behind his hand. Even Dimitri's usually tight lips twitched a little.

Higgins's eyes narrowed to cynical slits. "You'd better not have charged the bill to Infinite Enterprises."

"Why not?" Mike said, rather loudly. "We're allowed to."

"You're allowed to have a couple of drinks. Not take the—"

"We've pretty much finished now," Kester said hastily as he observed Higgins's face slowly turning a deeper shade of purple. "Mike, shall we go and get something to eat? You could probably do with lining your stomach."

"Yeah, come and join us!" Luke said enthusiastically, oblivious to Higgins's ferocious glare. "We can chat about our day."

"Not that we've got mush to be chatting about," Mike slurred.

"You just said 'mush'," Kester whispered. "You really are quite tipsy, Mike."

Higgins folded his arms mutinously, then looked at Dimitri and Luke. "Okay, fine," he barked eventually. "You can join us for dinner. But for goodness' sake, don't embarrass me. No more slurring or hiccupping, is that understood?"

Mike rose unsteadily to his feet and saluted. "Right you are, sir. Lead the way."

As they descended the spiral staircase to the restaurant, Kester's pocket vibrated. He swiftly pulled out his phone, expecting it to be Miss Wellbeloved asking him what he was doing for dinner. However, when he saw who the message was from, he froze.

Dimitri glanced back up at him. "Are you okay, Kester? You look like you have seen a spirit." He chuckled humourlessly at his own joke.

Kester shook his head. "I don't believe it."

"What don't you believe?" Luke asked, pausing at the foot of the stairs. "What's going on?"

"My goodness," he breathed. "It's *her*." Kester grasped the railing, his legs feeling suddenly rather wobbly. "She's finally got in touch." His head felt as though it had been stuffed with cotton wool, and the room began to swim before his eyes.

"Who the bloody hell are you talking about?" Higgins thrust his hands on his ample hips. "I want to have something to eat, hurry up!"

"Anya," Kester whispered. Without being aware he was doing it, he started to walk back up the stairs. *She's finally got in contact,* he thought, blinking furiously. *I can't believe it.*

"Where are you going?" Larry's voice trailed behind him, echoing around the glass stairwell. "Kester, tell us what the heck is going on!"

Kester ignored him and marched through the bar, oblivious to the attention he was generating. *I've got to go to her,* he thought blindly, scarcely able to think properly. He looked down at the message again.

Kester. Need your help. Meet me at Chislehurst Station as soon as possible. Please come alone. Love, Anya xxx

Chislehurst Station? He wondered what on earth she was doing there. What had happened? Was she in danger?

He quickly texted back. *What's happened? Can you tell me anything? I'm on my way, don't go anywhere. K xxx*

Stepping out, he paused briefly in the cool lobby, chewing his lip. *I've got to go,* he thought. *I can't not go to her, not now I know where she is. But what if it's dangerous?*

He dialled Miss Wellbeloved's number. Then, quite without realising what he was doing, he started to make his way out of the building. Before he knew it, he was stalking down the dark street, head buzzing with excitement and anxiety.

"Hello, Kester," Miss Wellbeloved said. She sounded flustered. "We are on our way to dinner, honestly; it's just your father has lost his—"

"—She texted me," Kester interrupted, too excited to remember politeness. "Anya texted me."

Silence followed. He continued to pace steadily along the pavement, now wishing he'd stopped to grab his coat. *I completely forgot it was winter,* he thought as he watched his breath plume out in front of him. *I'm going to freeze.*

"Wow," Miss Wellbeloved muttered finally. "What did she say?"

"Not much. She said she needed help, and that I had to go to Chislehurst Station. Alone."

"What? Why Chislehurst? I don't understand."

Kester shook his head and turned the corner. "I don't either. But I have to go. I think she's in trouble."

"Kester, you absolutely must not go on your own." Miss Wellbeloved sounded alarmed. "It's far too dangerous. Where are you now?"

"I'm nearly at Covent Garden station," he replied, fumbling in his trouser pocket for his wallet. "Don't worry, I'll be fine. Nothing can happen if I'm at a busy train station, can it?"

There was a mumbling down the other end of the line. Kester presumed Miss Wellbeloved was telling Ribero what had happened. Sure enough, a few seconds later, his father's voice rang down the line.

"Come back to the hotel this instant, silly boy! I forbid you to go!"

"Dad, I'm twenty-two," Kester reminded him. "I'm afraid you don't get to forbid me to do anything."

His father made an explosive noise, then coughed, presumably trying to keep his temper in check. "Kester," he tried again in a suspiciously smooth voice. "It is not safe. What if this is a trick?"

"Why would it be a trick? The Thelemites aren't interested in me!" Kester retorted. *At least, I hope that's right,* he added silently. "Look, I've got to go, I'm at the station. I'll call you when I arrive at Chislehurst, okay?"

"No, not okay! You wait there, I am going to—"

Kester hung up and switched his phone off quickly, worried that they'd convince him to wait. *I'll be absolutely fine,* he reassured himself, his heart pounding urgently in his chest. *What's the worst that could happen? She might ask me to join the Thelemites, I suppose;*

but it's not like I'm an idiot who can't think for himself.

He purchased a ticket from the machine, then made his way through the barrier and down into the still, airless tunnels of the London underground. It was still relatively busy, and he felt comforted by the numbers of people around him, laughing and talking without a care in the world. A train arrived almost immediately, and he leapt on, studying the map intently.

Firstly to King's Cross, he told himself, *then across to London Bridge. Then, I should be able to get another train over to Chislehurst station.* In the corner, a hunched lady, laden down with tattered bags, held out her hand towards him. Unthinkingly, he dived in his pocket for some change.

"You are kind, my friend," she whispered and patted him on the arm.

He smiled awkwardly, too distracted to think of a reply.

"Though you should take care. It's getting late, laddie. Don't let the bad things of the night get you."

He felt suddenly cold all over as though he'd been doused in ice. "I'll try not to," he replied quietly.

The woman nodded, then hobbled away.

Well, that was odd, he thought as he switched his phone on again. Sure enough, there were three voicemail messages, presumably from his father and Miss Wellbeloved. *I'll listen to them later,* he thought as he swiftly opened Anya's message again. *I've got more pressing things to worry about right now.*

He remembered that she'd used the word "love" in her text, and hope flared pitifully within his chest. *Maybe she does still have feelings for me after all,* he wondered, hardly daring to hope. *Maybe she was kidnapped by the Thelemites again and managed to escape.*

As the train wailed through endless, dark tunnels, he gripped the rail tightly and stared grimly at his own reflection. Now that the initial excitement had passed, he was questioning his decision. It was unlike him to act impulsively. *I guess that's what caring about someone does to you,* he realised, chewing his lip. *It makes you worry more about their safety than your own.*

Finally, after a couple of changes, he was on the train to Chislehurst station. A friendly woman in a suit had informed him that it usually took around half an hour, so he settled himself into the nearest chair and fidgeted with his phone.

Anya had texted a response—but it was only two words. *Thank goodness.*

What is that supposed to mean? he fretted. *Is she in danger? Has she been hurt?* His mind filled with terrible possibilities, and he struggled to keep his panic under control. Something about the situation didn't feel right, and he was half regretting not waiting for the others to join him. *But she asked me to come alone,* he reminded himself. *What else could I do? She might run away again if she saw me with other people.*

His phone vibrated again. Miss Wellbeloved's number flashed on the screen. This time, he answered.

"Kester, where are you?"

"I'm on the train to Chislehurst," he replied, massaging his forehead. "Don't worry, everything is fine."

"Of course we're worried!" Miss Wellbeloved exploded. "Kester, we think it might be a—"

The line crackled. Kester glanced at the screen—the reception was down to one bar.

"Miss Wellbeloved, can you hear me?" he asked without much hope. "Hello?"

He heard a few muffled words but couldn't make out anything legible. Eventually, he hung up and stuffed his phone back in his pocket. He was reluctant to admit it, but a vague fluttering of fear was welling up inside him, making him suddenly nauseous.

Oh well, he rationalised as the train raced through endless swathes of darkness, howling through the night. *I'm nearly there, it's not like I can turn back, is it?* However, he was feeling far less confident about things now. Most of the other commuters had got off at other stations, and apart from one man nodding off down the other end of the carriage, he was completely on his own.

Finally, at just after nine o'clock, the train slowed, then stopped with a jolt. Kester peered out. In the darkness, he could just see a blue sign with "Chislehurst" written on it. With a gulp, he stood and made his way out.

The cold night air hit him as soon as he clambered off. The doors slid closed with a thin hiss, and the train pulled away, leaving him completely alone, spotlighted by a single, grimy light overhead.

He scanned the deserted platform, then saw a figure silhouetted by a bench. It rose, then slowly waved.

"Anya!" he called out and started to run towards her.

Chapter 16: The Trap

Kester squeezed her tightly, relishing the pressure of her head against his chest and her hands around his waist. The stinging winter air suddenly seemed a million miles away, and he believed, just for a moment, that everything would be okay.

Finally, she pulled away, giving him the opportunity to study her better. Despite the feebleness of the light overhead, he could see that her mascara had run, tracing watery black lines down both cheeks.

"I am so glad you came," she whispered, each word cracking with emotion. "I have been so scared."

Kester seized her hand, pressing it into his own. "What did they do to you?"

She shook her head, then peered anxiously over her shoulder. "We can't talk here. Not like this. We need to hide."

"Hide?" Kester glanced up and down the platform. "What do you mean? Honestly, you don't need to be scared now, I've come up with a plan. We'll take the next train back to Covent Garden, then you can stay with me in the hotel, and—"

Anya winced. "No, it would not work. I would be found again. We have to hide, just for tonight. Please, trust me, Kester."

He caught sight of her expression and melted. *She looks terrified,* he realised as he pulled her close again. *God, what have they done to her? How did she manage to escape?* He was desperate to find out more, but judging by her expression, this wasn't the time press her.

"What did you have in mind?" he asked instead.

Anya pointed into the darkness. "I know somewhere where we'll be safe. A friend told me about it. Follow me."

She led him out of the station and on to the main road. Aside from a few streetlights, casting milky puddles on the pavement, it was unnervingly dark, not to mention quiet. The surrounding trees shifted uneasily in the breeze, as though waiting for something to happen.

Something doesn't feel right, Kester thought inexplicably. His hand crept instinctively to his phone.

"It's this way," Anya whispered, jarring him out of his thoughts. She caught his eye, then smiled. "Aren't you freezing? It is December, you know."

Kester looked down at his shirt. "I am a bit chilly, yes. But I was more concerned about getting to you than finding my coat."

"Kester, you are so kind." She swallowed hard, and for a moment, he thought she was going to start crying. "I don't deserve you, you know."

He felt his insides melt in response. Quite without realising it, his fingers uncurled from around the phone, releasing it back into his trouser pocket. "That's what I often think about you," he replied, squeezing her hand. "I'm so glad to see you again. This last week has been horrible."

"It has been horrible for me too," she murmured. "I have missed you badly."

She guided him across a road, then promptly turned right. *I'm glad one of us knows the way,* Kester thought, looking up at the sky.

A cloud rolled across the moon, muffling some of the light. It was an unsettling sight.

"It is just a little way down here," she whispered, sensing his discomfort, then she glanced over her shoulder again.

"Why do you keep turning around?" he asked, following her gaze. "Do you think we're being followed?" However, he couldn't see anything, only an empty road with a few parked cars lining the kerb. *Mind you,* he rationalised, *if Hrschni or Fylgja were trailing us now, it's unlikely I'd spot them. I'm sure daemons have all sorts of clever ways to avoid detection.*

Anya shook her head. "I think we're safe at the moment."

I don't like this, Kester thought. Despite his joy at seeing Anya again, there was something very *wrong* about everything, a sense of grim anticipation to the air as though something terrible was just around the corner. He reached for his phone again. "I'd better call Miss Wellbeloved back," he muttered. "She'll be out of her mind with worry."

"No, you mustn't call anyone!" Anya said with a look of alarm. "It is too risky. Please, just trust me, just for tonight. You can call her in the morning."

"I have to text her at least," Kester said uncertainly. "If I don't tell them where I am, they'll all come up here to find me."

Anya clasped his arm. "Text her in a minute, when we're out of sight. Okay?"

He nodded reluctantly, stuffed his phone back in his trouser pocket, then followed her across the road into what looked like a car-park. "Where the hell is this?" he asked, scanning the area for clues.

She pointed down a dark road. "We can't use the main entrance," she whispered. "There's another way in down here. No-one knows about it."

"I have literally no idea what you're talking about," Kester said with a smile, "but I'm sure you're right. I'll just follow you."

Anya nodded. "Yes. That's a good idea, you don't need to worry about a thing." Although her expression was calm, there was a skittishness to her movement that suggested nervousness. *Hopefully she'll explain everything when we're safe,* he thought, stumbling blindly behind her and bracing himself against the wind.

Finally, Anya stopped. In the dark, Kester could just make out what looked like a solid mass of tangled bushes in front of them, but nothing else. He squinted, wondering if he was missing something.

"What is—?"

"—Shh. You'll see in a minute." Anya reached out and pulled a mass of tangled weeds away. To Kester's surprise, it revealed a rough hole in the concealed rock.

He gulped. "Are we going in there?"

"Yes, but don't worry, it's perfectly safe. I have a torch in my pocket."

Now this definitely doesn't feel right, he thought. A slither of fear crept up within him. "Anya," he began hesitantly. "What's through that hole? I'm not comfortable about going in, not unless I know what we're going to find there."

She turned. He was certain he spotted a flash of irritation in her expression before her eyes softened again. "We're at Chislehurst Caves," she explained and pulled the torch from her pocket. Her eyes gleamed in the piercing beam of light. "This is a secret entrance."

Not more caves, he groaned inwardly, thinking of the hag o' the dribble, not to mention all the other spirits that probably liked to linger in dark places like these. He took a step back. "How did you know about it?" he asked. "I think we need to discuss this before we go in. It doesn't seem like a very good—"

She grabbed his arm, more roughly than he'd expected, and pulled him towards her, pressing her lips against his. The force of the kiss took him by surprise, but eventually, he melted into the moment, the rest of the world fading into insignificance as he wrapped his arms around her.

A sudden, sharp pain made him gasp. Anya pulled away, eyes

twinkling in the torchlight.

"You bit me!" Kester whispered, patting his lip. It hadn't been hard enough to draw blood, but the area throbbed gently.

Anya shifted on the spot. "I don't know what came over me," she muttered, looking uncomfortable.

That wasn't like her at all, he thought, studying her intently.

"Well, there's more where that came from," she said finally, grasping his arm. To his shock, she started to forcibly pull him towards the hole, with a strength that was totally at odds with her slender frame. "Why don't you come inside and find out?"

That's not the sort of thing she would normally say, he thought, wrestling his arm free. He examined her carefully. The moon cast a glow over her hair, forming a strange halo, but her predatory watchfulness was far from angelic.

A horrible thought, clear as a bell, clanged through his mind. *This isn't Anya,* he realised with total certainty. *I'm with a total stranger.*

His instinct was to run, but he forced himself to remain calm, knowing that any wrong moves could cost him dearly. *Of course it's Anya,* he told himself firmly, forcing himself to think rationally. *Who else would it be? Unless she's got a spirit doppelganger or something.* However, he couldn't deny that there was something profoundly different about her, a note of discord in an expression, a misjudged comment or action. The thought unsettled him deeply.

Anya gave an exasperated sigh. "Kester, you need to come in, we're not safe out here. Now get moving."

Kester took a few steps backwards, hands held out protectively. "No," he said slowly and glanced over his shoulder. The road was deserted. There were no houses nearby. *If I ran for it, what would happen?* he wondered crazily. *God, why didn't I just wait for the others, like Miss Wellbeloved told me to? I'm out here in the dark, completely alone, and no-one knows where I am!*

Anya stepped towards him, pointing the torch directly into his eyes. Kester winced, instinctively holding his hands up against the glare.

"Kester," she whispered, a ghost of sound in the darkness. He could hear her footsteps crunching delicately on the loose stones underfoot, advancing steadily towards him. "Don't make this any harder than it needs to be. Don't force them to get nasty with you."

His heart dropped like a stone plummeting into an abyss. *She's betrayed me,* he realised dumbly. *I trusted her, and she's taken me for a fool again. I'm such an idiot.*

"How *could* you?" he whispered, aching with hurt. "How could you let me think that you—"

"It's not like that," she replied before reaching out to touch him.

Kester recoiled instinctively. "Don't touch me."

"Please. I need to explain things to you. But if you don't—"

"—You don't need to explain *anything* to me," he spat and brushed her hand off him. Taking a deep breath, he started to run.

"Kester!" Her shrill cry tore through the silence as he pounded into the darkness, the icy air already freezing his lungs. He fumbled in his pocket, pulled out his mobile phone and dialled Miss Wellbeloved's number, but lost his grip just as he pulled it to his ear. Horrified, he watched it fly into the undergrowth beside him, before forcing himself to race forward again. There was no time to stop and retrieve it, not now that he knew the Thelemites were somewhere close by.

You absolute moron! he chastised himself. A wave of self-loathing tore into him, so strong it left him breathless. *Not just stupid enough to trust Anya again, but dim-witted enough to throw away your only chance of being saved!*

To his relief, he could see the main road up ahead, along with the reassuring glow of the streetlamps. He had no idea whether Anya was chasing after him or not, but he felt confident that he could outrun her, at least for this short distance. *Perhaps it'll be okay after all,* he thought, picking up his pace. *Maybe I'll make it to the train station and—*

Suddenly, his vision went black. Rough material dragged across his face, smothering him, and his arms were grabbed by strong hands. He cried out, but the fabric was pulled tightly across his mouth, muffling his shouts. To his horror, the unseen arms began to yank him backwards, until his heels were dragging uselessly along the road.

What's happening? he thought wildly as he struggled to get free. He knew that it wasn't Anya pulling him, the grip was far too strong; there were at least two people, pulling him on both sides. He shook his head from side to side, trying desperately to free himself from whatever it was that had been tugged over his face, but he couldn't shift it.

The urge to scream was almost unbearable, but Kester knew there was no-one else around. Instead, he forced himself to listen as hard as possible. Aside from the scrape of his shoes, bumping over the rough ground, he couldn't detect anything, other than a hoarse whisper, which might have been male or female.

Finally, the dragging stopped. His captors hauled him upright, then started muttering, too quietly for him to hear. He looked around wildly, but his eyes only found the blackness of the fabric pressing against them.

Think rationally! he ordered himself. *It's obviously the Thelemites, and they've clearly dumped some sort of sack over my head. But why? What don't they want me to see?*

He took a tentative step to the side, only to be yanked back immediately, so forcefully that he nearly lost his balance.

I'm going to die, he realised with abrupt, horrible clarity. *The Thelemites are going to pick us off, one by one. Or maybe they'll murder me as a message to my father, warning him to steer clear of them. And I'm powerless to stop them.*

A memory came to mind of reading the old book about the Thelemites in the Infinite Enterprises archive department. He recalled the tale of Ethelred Bunting, the Victorian spirit-door opener who'd gone missing after a run-in with the Thelemites. *Why didn't I take that as a warning?* he wondered, a hysterical giggle bubbling in his throat. *Bunting dared to go up against them, and he ended up vanishing. The same thing is about to happen to me!*

An arm enveloped him, constricting his breathing, then started to heave him backwards. His heels kicked against smoother terrain underfoot, and there was a dampness to the air that indicated they'd entered the caves. His heart quickened, thudding painfully against his chest.

What a mess I've made of everything, yet again, Kester thought desperately as he fought against the urge to start crying. *Please don't let me die in here, in the dark.*

He was tugged along for several minutes until, finally, the arm around his chest released him, and he was shoved against a wet, stone wall. Straining his ears, he fought to make out noises that would give him a clue as to who was down here with him, but aside from the occasional footstep and hint of breathing, the space was silent.

He waited, senses alert to every movement, bracing himself for the start of the violence.

Without warning, a hand grasped somewhere at the back of his head, pulling the sack away. He blinked, then stared wildly at the roughly-hewn walls that surrounded him, the oil lamps flickering eerily on the floor, and the surrounding figures watching him intently.

The first person he noticed came as no surprise. *Barty Melville.* Kester nodded grimly, fighting to regain composure. "I expected to see you here," he muttered.

Barty Melville smirked. "Kester. A pleasure to see you again. It's a shame you wouldn't come willingly, but it was only to be expected, I suppose."

Beside him was another familiar face; a petite woman with a sharp suit and an even sharper expression. *Parvati Chowdhury,* Kester remembered, eyeing her with dislike. She refused to meet his gaze, instead fixing her eyes to the ceiling as though musing on more important matters. *Arrogant woman,* he thought.

He'd never seen the two men flanking Anya before. The first was almost unnaturally tall, long-faced and haggard. Under any other circumstances, his appearance would have been amusing, given that he looked almost identical to a stereotypical gravedigger in a bad B-movie. However, there was nothing comedic about it at present. The other man was broad-shouldered as a bulldog and completely bald, with bright eyes that seemed to burn in the lamplight. Barty saw the direction of Kester's gaze and nodded.

"Do allow me to introduce these men," he said smoothly, waddling forward. He gestured to the tall man. "This is Felix Taggerty, Master of the Cambridge lodge. And this," he pointed to the bald man, "is Reggie Shadrach. Master of the Oxford lodge."

"Wonderful," Kester replied sarcastically. "Under normal circumstances, I'd say hello, gentlemen; but you must forgive me, I've just been kidnapped."

Barty looked surprised. "Why do you think this is a kidnapping, Kester?"

"Probably something to do with the fact that you put a bag over my head, then dragged me down here?" Kester snapped back. He glared at Anya, who looked down at the floor.

Barty shook his head, then moved slowly closer. "No, no, my dear boy. That is not what is happening at all. We mean you no harm, I promise."

Kester rolled his eyes. "Excuse me for not believing you."

Parvati turned towards him. Her eyes glittered with alarming intensity—so much so that Kester instinctively shrank backwards. "You're feisty, aren't you?" she said conversationally and strolled over to study him better.

He blushed under the ferocity of her scrutiny. Her gaze seemed to burn through him, making him feel horribly like a specimen under a microscope.

"Look at me," she whispered in a voice that seemed unnaturally deep for such a small woman.

Daring to look up, he stared back, hypnotised by her fathomless pupils, which gleamed with energy. A flicker of movement caught his attention, a tiny speck of flame illuminating her glare, and he realised with horror who he was looking at.

"Hrschni," he whispered. "It's you, isn't it?"

"Clever boy," Parvati replied slowly, each word slipping from her lips like velvet. "I knew it wouldn't take you long."

Kester took a deep breath. *Why didn't we think of Parvati when we found out Hrschni was inhabiting the body of a small woman?* Still, it didn't surprise him, not when he thought about it. Although the woman was short, her intimidating personality made it almost impossible to regard her as anything other than formidable.

"What do you want from me?" he asked finally. "If you're using me to get at my dad, there's not much point. He—"

The daemon laughed. "I don't think so, Kester. Come on, you're wiser than that. Guess again."

Kester shook his head. "No. I won't play games with you, Hrschni. I've had enough of all that. I've been dancing to your tune for the last month or so, and it's been exhausting."

"Dancing to my tune," Hrschni repeated with a chuckle. "That's an appropriate expression, given my previous incarnation. You certainly were dancing to my tune when you came to my final gig, weren't you?"

Kester thought back to the Billy Dagger concert. It felt as though it had happened hundreds of years ago to someone else. "It was a fantastic performance," he admitted.

" was a lot of fun," he agreed. "I'll miss him dearly. Though Parvati has been a most pleasant hostess."

"Why don't you come out of Parvati Chowdhury so I can see you face to face?" Kester challenged, hoping to stall for time. He knew it was almost pointless to do so, but he held out the hope that somehow, his father and the others would manage to find him. *After all, I'm not too far from the station,* he thought, though he knew it was over-optimistic to think that they'd come looking for him here.

Inside Parvati's body, the daemon shrugged, mulling over his request. "Sure," he agreed finally. "Why not?"

Kester watched with fascination as the woman raised her arms, fingers stretching to the ceiling. Eyes closed, her whole body started to shudder, building momentum until she was vibrating on the spot. Then, just as her figure became no more than a blur, Parvati seemed to combust in a violent explosion of light.

Kester blinked, momentarily blinded, not to mention stunned into silence. In the dim light, he could just about see Parvati's crumpled body on the floor, swimming slowly into focus as his eyes recovered. Behind her, glowing piercingly like a wildfire, was the daemon himself.

He looks like a series of flames, tangled into one another, Kester thought stupidly, staring wildly at the pulsing, embryonic form in front of him. The daemon coiled, foetal-like, in the air, though his sharp features were anything but babyish. Slitted eyes poured forth scarlet light, and his wide mouth was full of broad, nail-thin teeth. Above all else, it was the sense of *power* that was overwhelming. The daemon exuded strength like a force-field—an irrefutable authority that was humbling and terrifying.

"Well?" Hrschni asked finally. His voice rang crystal-clear around the echoing cavern. "Lost for words, Kester? I take it you've never met a daemon in the flesh before."

Kester gaped as the daemon uncoiled, revealing a thick, misty tail that flickered above the ground like a restless snake. "I haven't, no," he agreed, feeling alarmingly small and pathetic. The other Thelemites smirked.

"How does it feel, to meet one of the oldest daemons to ever walk the earth?" Reggie Shadrach asked, running a hand across his shining scalp. "It's a great honour, you know."

Kester frowned. *I'm not going to let myself be awed into submission,* he thought. *If I'm going to go down here, I'm going to go down fighting.* "I'm sure it is an honour," he said slowly, straightening against the wall. "But I still don't appreciate being kidnapped."

The daemon moved forwards, sliding through the air as though gliding on ice. "Apologies for manhandling you, Kester. But we needed to talk to you and saw no other way of getting you here."

"So you used my girlfriend to trick me?" Kester snapped, pointing in Anya's direction. She was still staring miserably at the floor.

"Anya agreed that it was the right thing to do," Hrschni replied smoothly. "Like the rest of us, she merely wanted what was best for you."

Kester grimaced. "It doesn't matter which way you look at it. Being hauled into a cave late at night, then held against my will, is *not* what's best for me."

Barty Melville crouched beside Parvati, then eased her gently to her feet. He dusted his gown off before taking a deep breath. Kester braced himself. "My dear lad," he began, in a suspiciously syrupy voice. "Why don't you let us explain why you're here?"

"Yes." Now Felix Taggerty moved towards him, his tall, thin frame casting an eerie shadow on the wall. "You're about to be given the opportunity of a lifetime. Reggie and I have travelled down today to mark the occasion, you should feel honoured."

"Yes," Reggie Shadrach agreed, folding his arms. "It's not often you'll get three Thelemite lodge-masters gathered in one place."

"I have no idea what you're talking about," Kester replied heavily. He felt overwhelmed, exhausted, and more than a little terrified. Although the exit to the cave was unguarded, the passageway beyond was pitch-black, and he knew that fleeing was probably futile. *If it's anything like Beer Quarry Caves,* he thought to himself, remembering the visit they'd made only a few weeks ago, *it'll be a crazy labyrinth of caverns that are easy to get lost in. I should probably take my chances with a daemon rather than die in the dark.*

Hrschni smiled, a sinister stretch of the mouth that showcased his needle-thin teeth. "Let me *enlighten* you, Kester." He swam through the air until he was barely inches from Kester's face, the warmth of his breath settling over them like swamp-mist.

"You are very special," he said slowly, relishing each word. "After all, you are a spirit-door opener, are you not?"

"Supposedly so," Kester replied guardedly. "Though it's a bit hit-and-miss, if I'm honest."

"But you can open doors to the spirit realm?" Reggie asked quickly, glancing at Barty.

"That's what it said in his file," Hrschni said smoothly. "And as we all know, the Infinite Enterprises files don't lie."

Kester gasped, hand rising instinctively to his mouth. "When did you see my file? When you broke into Infinite Enterprises archives?"

"Of course," Hrschni replied. He scoured Kester's face, burning eyes glittering in the light of the oil-lamps. "I needed to be certain that you had the relevant skills for the job. Of course," he continued, "I'd heard the rumours. I read about your dealings with the Bloody Mary spirit and the Scottish fetch with great interest. But I needed to have it confirmed before taking action."

"But I don't understand," Kester spluttered. "I thought you'd broken into Infinite Enterprises to gather information about something important! The others thought you were trying to get to their permanent spirit door."

Hrschni sighed, sending a fresh breeze of heat over Kester's face. "Yes, I suspected they'd think that. Alas, their door is impractical, not to mention costly to run. What we needed was someone with more *natural* talents."

"Hang on," Kester said slowly. Realisation hit him like a battering ram, taking his breath away. "You mean you want me to open a spirit door for you? Is that your plan?"

"Partly," Hrschni replied casually, turning back to look at his colleagues. They nodded, their smiles looking horribly wolfish in the soft, amber light. "But of course, there's more to it than that. To be honest, I'm surprised you didn't work out the message in my most recent song."

"I figured out the last line," Kester said defensively. "'Histories so putrid or' is an anagram of 'the spirit door is ours', isn't it?"

"But you didn't work out the rest?" Hrschni looked surprised. "I felt sure you would solve it."

Parvati laughed. "Especially as it's got your name in it."

"What do you mean?" Kester asked. He felt sick. *I've been well and truly duped,* he realised, *and now, I'm in serious trouble.* The only thing he could do was stall for time and keep them talking.

"The song title is an anagram," Hrschni said. "'Ode to Set-Shirker.' So are many other phrases in the lyrics. 'Theorised stroker', 'Dorkiest heteros', 'Reeked this roost'—how could you not notice? I must say, I'm a little disappointed."

Kester bit his lip. "I knew they were anagrams," he admitted. "But I couldn't work out what. I tried numerous combinations." He suddenly paused and stared at Parvati. "What do you mean, it has my name in it?"

Parvati laughed mirthlessly. "They're all anagrams of 'Kester is the door', of course."

Kester's eyes widened. He ran over the phrases in his mind, then winced, rolling his head to the ceiling. *I don't believe I didn't figure it out,* he cursed silently. *It was there, right in front of my face, and somehow, I completely missed it.*

"Don't beat yourself up about it, boy," Barty Melville said breezily. "I struggle horribly with anagrams. The Sunday morning Cryptic Crossword in the paper gets me every time."

"Why don't you just get to the point, and tell me what you want from me?" Kester snapped.

Hrschni moved backwards, weaving from side to side, as though deep in thought. "Very well," he agreed. "However, I'd like to emphasise, this is a mutually beneficial arrangement. We need your skills to create an opening into the spirit realm. As you probably already know, we believe in freedom of movement between the worlds. A life without borders is so much more *rewarding,* don't you think?"

"Rewarding for whom?" Kester retorted cynically. "It doesn't sound like there's much in it for us humans."

Hrschni winced, closing his glowing eyes for a moment. "That's simply not true, Kester," he said. "That's lies and propaganda. The truth is—spirits and humans can co-exist harmoniously. The level of control that humans place on spirits is appalling. We are restricted by legislation, legalities, ridiculous rulings, not to mention unimaginable cruelty . . ."

Barty coughed meaningfully, and Hrschni nodded. "I veer off-topic," he concluded. "Do forgive me. It's a subject I'm passionate about, as you can see."

"Why should spirits have free access, though?" Kester asked. *If I keep him talking,* he thought wildly, *then I may be able to give myself enough time to come up with an escape plan.* "What's wrong with the current system?"

"It's prejudiced!" Hrschni spat, coiling into himself once more and glowing with even fiercer intensity. "Many of my spirit brothers and sisters are forbidden to enter, despite the fact that they have much to offer. Many others no longer bother to come, as they're so tired of the persecution from the governments of the world. It's time to end it. We need to unite again, be together as we once were."

"'As we once were'?" Kester echoed.

Felix Taggerty licked his colourless lips. "Our ancestors lived alongside spirits," he explained. "It didn't do them any harm."

"Why do you think the government hates spirits so much?" Parvati challenged. "Why do you think they fight so hard to keep them out?"

"Because it would be chaotic if they were all allowed to come in at once?" Kester suggested weakly. The conversation was starting to bewilder him.

"No," Reggie Shadrach replied simply. "It's because of modern society. Things like the effect most spirits have on technology. Unless it's carefully controlled, spirit energy interferes with Wi-Fi signals. It scrambles data. In short, it causes problems for organisations that rely on such things—like banks."

"And the presence of spirits would make people lose their trust in science," Barty added. "How would the world's leaders control the people if the very nature of their modern existence was called into question?"

"It always boils down to economics and control," Hrschni agreed sadly. "It never used to be like that."

Kester massaged his brows, trying to get his head around it all. He knew that in the past, Mike had complained about spirits causing problems with the internet, but he'd never really stopped to think about it much. It certainly sounded plausible.

"That aside," he said slowly, "isn't it fair to say that the sudden arrival of loads of spirits would create chaos? Not to mention frighten everyone?"

Hrschni laughed. Embers flew from his mouth like fireworks before fizzling into darkness. "Is that what you think we're planning? The creation of an opening that allows spirits to flood through in masses?"

Kester shrugged. "If not, what did you have in mind?"

"A fair, organised system with a staggered arrival. We would introduce spirits gently to the human world, to allow for more successful integration."

"Successful integration?" Kester giggled, aware that his laughter had more than a touch of fear to it. "How on earth do you think that will happen? I can only speak for myself, but the first time I saw a spirit, I passed out on the floor! I was terrified! Imagine billions of people, trying to adjust to the idea of sharing their world with spirits? It's a crazy idea!"

"It's not crazy," Parvati snarled. "It requires a significant change of mindset, that's all."

"All revolutions start with a seemingly crazy idea," Barty added, patting his stomach reflectively. "Humans will soon come around. You'll see."

"Anyway," Hrschni added quietly. "Plenty of spirits live in harmony with humans already. Take the famous Dr Barqa-Abu, for example. She's been sharing her extensive knowledge with humans for centuries."

"But she's different," Kester corrected. "She only reveals herself to the students she teaches, who are already aware of the spirit world."

"But look at the difference she's made! How I respect her, in spite of everything," Hrschni continued. "And look at myself. Every human I inhabit enjoys wealth, power, and prestige. They wouldn't have it any other way, mark my words. Fylgja is the same."

"I can't comment on Fylgja," Kester muttered, "given I've never met her."

"Ah, but you have," Hrschni replied slyly. The others laughed, gathering more tightly around him.

There's obviously some big joke going on here which I'm excluded from, Kester realised as he looked from face to face. Only Anya remained silent, eyes still fixed mournfully on the floor. *Is she ridden with guilt?* he wondered. *Sad about how things had turned out? Or does she simply not care?* It was impossible to tell.

He sighed. "Go on then, tell me. When did I meet Fylgja?" Mentally, he whizzed through all the people he'd encountered over the last few weeks. *Could it be Lili Asadi?* he wondered. *Or Tinker? Or even Ian Kingdom-Green? Maybe that's how they've been getting all their information—they've got someone working on the inside.* However, none of those people seemed particularly daemonic. If they were sheltering a spirit, they'd certainly hidden it well.

Anya lifted her head up and met his gaze. Her eyes were full of silent apology. Kester searched her expression for the truth, then all of a sudden, found it. He exhaled, then sank to the floor, his knees buckling uselessly underneath him.

"Anya," he whispered. It was the final betrayal. After her deception earlier, he hadn't imagined that she could hurt him any further, but now he realised he'd been wrong. "How long have you had a daemon hiding within you?"

She bit her lip. "I had no choice."

"That's not true," Hrschni interrupted, circling close to her, winding around her body like an undulating ribbon. "We explained the situation to you, and you agreed. Don't lie."

Anya tucked her hair behind her ear. "Fylgja," she said loudly, "can you leave me now? There's no point in you living within me anymore, I've done what you asked me." She clutched her brow, grimacing. Kester got the impression that she was engaged in some sort of internal dialogue, though he couldn't imagine what words were raging to and from her and the daemon inside her.

Hrschni paused his weaving, peering intently at the back of Anya's head. "Fylgja," he said warningly. The cave went silent. "Come out. Anya is right. There's no advantage to you remaining hidden."

Anya winced again, then let out a small shriek.

"What's going on?" Kester asked with growing alarm. He didn't like the expression on Anya's face at all. It was the expression of someone in turmoil, someone about to crack and break.

"Fylgja," Hrschni repeated, and although his voice was calm, there was a level of menace simmering just under the surface. "Don't forget yourself. Come out now."

Anya shuddered, a full-body convulsion that rippled through her like water, then sank to the floor. There was another flash of vibrant light. As Kester's eyes recovered, he saw the second daemon, hunched in the air, curled in a question-mark of hostility. *Two for the price of one!* he thought, fighting the urge to laugh. The situation was so monstrously awful, it was almost amusing.

The difference between the two daemons was immediately apparent. Hrschni glowed with a crimson light, not dissimilar to a lava flow. Fylgja, by contrast, glittered with emerald brightness; vivid and lustrous as a fresh leaf after rainfall. She fixed her forest-green eyes on Kester, then glided over to him, rustling through the air like the wind.

"Ah, Kester," she breathed and ran a skeletal finger across his cheek, making him shiver. "You beautiful, innocent thing. How I enjoyed getting to know you."

Kester felt a hot tear roll down his cheek. "Whereas I feel like I don't know you, or *her,*" he pointed at Anya, accusation breaking his voice, "at all."

"You were surprisingly hard to get information from," Fylgja continued as she ruffled his hair with unsettling familiarity. "I think deep down, you were suspicious right from the start. You just couldn't bear to admit to yourself that your girlfriend might not actually be in love with you after all."

"Fylgja, that's enough," Hrschni snapped.

Anya wiped her eyes. "Kester, I never meant to deceive you. They forced me to let Fylgja inhabit me. They said they wouldn't release me unless I did."

"So you're saying this daemon was with you right from the start, when we came to collect you from the Exeter Thelemite lodge?" Kester asked, struggling to get his head around it all. "That was weeks ago! The whole time, I thought you really cared about me, and all you wanted was to use me for information."

"It wasn't like that," Anya protested weakly. "Honestly, Kester, you must believe me! I really do care about you. They told me it was the right thing to do for everyone involved."

"Yeah, right," Kester muttered bitterly. *How can I believe you?* he thought as he watched her brown eyes filling with tears. *How can I ever trust you again?*

"Kester, your talents are wasted with your father's agency," Fylgja continued, curving around him, continually touching his body as though fascinated by how he felt through her daemon fingers. "You could achieve much more with the Thelemites."

"Perhaps, in time, your father and his team could join us?" Barty said hopefully. "I was always so fond of Jennifer, I'd welcome her back with open arms."

"Miss Wellbeloved doesn't *believe* in what you're doing," Kester hissed, fingers scraping at the loose gravel around him. "She'd never agree to this ridiculous plan."

Hrschni's eyes narrowed, and he flew back towards Kester, hand outstretched as though to seize him by the neck. Kester flinched, waiting for the pain to start, but to his surprise, the daemon retreated, shaking his head mournfully.

"You do not understand yet," he said as he sank gently, almost to the floor. "But you will. You'll soon have plenty of time to understand, anyway."

"What's that supposed to mean?" Kester asked guardedly. Felix and Reggie glanced at one another and smiled.

"You're not leaving here," Hrschni continued casually, uncoiling himself and stretching his glowing arms behind his back as though easing out a cramp. "You will be staying with us until you *understand*. There will be no going back, I'm afraid."

Kester swallowed hard. "And how are you going to stop me from leaving?"

Hrschni smiled slowly, a stretching of his lipless mouth that seemed impossibly wide.

"By any means necessary," he concluded simply.

CHAPTER 17: EXPLORING THE CAVES

"Do you think we need to tie him up?" Reggie Shadrach cracked his knuckles, much like a stereotypical gangster in a movie.

As far as Kester was concerned, there was one thing worse than being trapped in a cave, and that was being tied up *and* trapped in a cave. He debated trying to make a run for it, but Felix and Barty had moved closer to the exit and were currently eying him warily. *Not a chance in hell,* he realised with a sinking heart.

Hrschni floated down to Kester. The force of his gaze made it impossible to look him in the eye. "I'd rather not have to restrain you," he said softly. "Perhaps if you agree to come with us quietly to the chambers in this cave, I won't have to."

"What chambers?" Kester asked, squinting through the rough doorway—not that he could see anything in the darkness. "Just how much of this cave do the Thelemites own?"

"We've been using this as our secret lodge for centuries," Barty replied, waving boastfully around the shadowy space. "Approximately one quarter of Chislehurst Caves are open to the general public, and the rest is owned by us."

Kester sighed. He remembered what he'd read in the archives earlier, about the Thelemites having a secret place that was somewhere dark. *I wish I'd made the connection earlier,* he thought grimly. "How big are the caves?" he asked, biding for time.

"Are you trying to pump us for information?" Fylgja's eyes widened until they sparkled like emeralds in the dim light. "That's my job, remember?" She winked at Parvati, who chuckled.

"Put it like this," Felix Taggerty said, placing his long, twig-like hands firmly on his hips. "They're big enough to get lost in."

"You'd never find your way out again," Reggie added, a ghoulish grin lighting up his wide, hairless face. "As many people have discovered over the years."

"However," Hrschni said quickly, frowning at the men, "you will find our chambers most comfortable. We've already prepared for your stay, in fact. I know how passionate you are about reading, so I've taken the liberty of providing you with a small, personal library."

"That's kind of you," Kester replied cautiously. "But I'd rather visit a real library, *and* have my freedom too."

"The bed is also very comfortable," Hrschni said, ignoring his comment. "I know humans are partial to soft mattresses, thick duvets, and smooth cotton sheets, so we made sure you'll have them all. We've also provided a personal music player and a computer, should you want to write or entertain yourself."

"I presume it hasn't got Wi-Fi connection," Kester grumbled.

"It's not a hotel!" Parvati snapped. "Of course it hasn't!"

"How long do you plan to keep me down here, then?"

Hrschni sighed, his glow faltering briefly before returning to its former lustre. "I hope not for long. You see, Kester, I want us to get along. It's important to me that you understand the Thelemites and grow to respect our cause."

Kester sighed. "This isn't the way to go about it."

"There is no other way, so just accept it!" Fylgja exclaimed. "Any other human would be honoured to join forces with two daemons!"

"It's not as though you're giving me a choice, though, is it?" Kester said, his voice rising. *I know they're powerful,* he thought, biting his lip. *But they can't just lock me up until I do what they want!*

Hrschni glanced at the others. "Reggie, Felix," he began, smoothly as rippling silk. "Could you escort Kester to his chambers? Make sure he's blindfolded, so he cannot find his way back. Fylgja, let's leave them for now. We'll return in the morning after Kester has had a chance to sleep."

"Grand Master, are you certain you don't want to make him create a spirit door this—"

"Barty, there's absolutely no point. You cannot force a spirit-door opener. The desire has to come from within. Besides, I want him to help us of his own free will."

Barty sighed, then nodded to Felix and Reggie, who, judging by the simmering glares they were giving Kester, were looking forward to dragging him off into the darkness.

Kester looked from face to face, fighting to stifle his rising panic. He knew that resisting them would be pointless, they were far stronger than him, not to mention endowed with spirit powers that could potentially wipe him out in a second. *I need to think cleverly,* he thought, searching the cave for something he could use, *anything* that might give him an advantage, no matter how small.

Hrschni curled restlessly in the air, inching closer to where he sat. There was a knowing glimmer to his expression, something that made Kester suspect the daemon could guess his thoughts.

"We will provide you with an evening meal," he said elegantly. "And anything else you desire, let us know. Felix and Reggie will remain with you tonight, so you won't be alone."

You mean, so I won't try to escape, Kester thought but said nothing.

"Anya, did you want to say good night to your lover?" Fylgja asked with a mocking wave in Kester's direction. Anya met his eyes again, then quickly looked away.

"I'll come back tomorrow." She paused, and for a moment, she seemed about to say something else. However, a moment later, her lips tightened. Eyes still fixed to the floor, she hurried out after the two daemons.

Kester felt a part of himself grow cold and hard. *Good,* he thought, forcing himself to think rationally. *The last thing I need is to be emotional right now. I need to think practically and cleverly instead.*

Barty bent, patted Kester on the shoulder, then gestured to Parvati. "Come, my dear," he said. "We've achieved a lot tonight." He smiled and pressed his hands together. "I look forward to what the morning may bring."

Parvati threw one last, nasty smile in Kester's direction before stalking after Barty. Kester shifted awkwardly on the floor, watching them disappear into the darkness beyond. Reggie and Felix waited patiently until the footsteps of the others had died away into the distance.

There's no way I can overpower them, Kester realised. Even at a glance, he could see the thick muscles lining Reggie's neck and shoulders, and he sensed that Felix was probably stronger than he looked. *What the hell am I going to do?*

"Right." Felix stroked his long chin, as though pondering a philosophical question. "Time to make a move, it's late."

Reggie sighed. "How did we get lumbered with babysitting tonight, eh?" He eyed Kester with open irritation. "If you could just cooperate, you'd make things a lot more pleasant for all of us."

"Calm down, Reggie," Felix interrupted. "The boy has had a lot to take in. You can't expect him to join forces with us just like that. He's been indoctrinated by propaganda and lies."

"That depends on your viewpoint," Kester muttered. They both ignored him.

"We'll need to put this sack back over your head," Felix continued. "To make sure you can't see anything. Will you stay still while we do so?"

Reggie chuckled. "Or will we have to knock you out instead?

Either option works for me."

Something tells me you'd enjoy doing that, Kester thought miserably as he patted the loose pebbles and stones under his fingers. "You don't need to knock me out," he muttered. "I don't want to add a headache to the list of my problems."

"There's a good lad," Reggie replied and extended a hand to help him up. "Perhaps you have got some sense in that thick head of yours after all."

"Reggie," Felix said warningly. "No need for that. Remember, we've heard that this boy is something of a prodigy. Which is why Hrschni's so keen to work with him."

Reggie sneered. "There must be other spirit-door openers out there who can do the job better than this one. I mean, look at him."

"That's a fair comment," Kester admitted. "I have no control over it whatsoever."

Felix Taggerty coughed. "Well, that's what the Grand Master will be helping you with. Now come on, it's very late, and I need my beauty sleep."

"And if we've got to bring you some supper too, we need to get moving," Reggie added.

Kester took a few deep breaths. Now was his chance. If he couldn't come up with an idea to escape now, then that would be it, he'd be imprisoned without a hope of ever being rescued by the others. *Think!* he ordered himself sternly. *Come on! There has to be a way out of this mess!*

"Taking your time there, aren't you?" Reggie's tone had become dangerously amiable. "Time to get up now, please."

"My leg's cramped up," Kester lied and pretended to massage his calf. "Give me a moment."

Felix glanced at his wristwatch, then at the other lodge master. "I believe this young gentleman is stalling for time."

"I'm not!" Kester protested. "I suffer from cramps a lot, it'll pass in a moment." He looked around the space, for something, *anything,* he could use as a rudimentary weapon. However, aside from the oil lamps, which were out of reach, there was nothing.

He leant his head back against the wall, reminded of Beer Quarry, which had been so similar in appearance to these caves. *The situation was a bit different though,* he thought ruefully. *I'd almost welcome a hag o' the dribble now, compared to this pair. At least all she did was throw stones at us.*

"Hag o' the dribble," he murmured thoughtfully and looked down at the ground.

"What did you say?" Reggie growled suspiciously.

That's it, Kester thought with a sudden glimmer of hope. *That's what I'll do.* It wasn't much of a plan, but it was all he could come up with. *I'll copy the hag o' the dribble and see if it buys me enough time to get away. If not, I dread to think what these two will do to me.*

Pretending to wince again, he surreptitiously scooped up as much of the loose gravel that as he could manage. *Here goes,* he thought as he rose slowly to his feet.

"Finally. You took your time about it, didn't you, you—"

Kester seized his opportunity and threw open his palms as forcefully as he could. Dust, grit, and stones flew into the air, and the two men immediately closed their eyes, shouting loudly. Without waiting to see what happened next, Kester turned and fled out of the rough entrance into the darkness beyond.

Why didn't I grab an oil lamp on the way out? he thought desperately as he tore down the narrow passage, hands outstretched to stop himself from running into the walls. Patting the walls desperately, he felt a left turn, just as the two men hurtled out into the passage behind him.

"Come back, you daft idiot!" Reggie's voice echoed flatly off the walls. "These caves are like a maze, you'll never find your way out!"

"Which way did he go?"

"I've no idea. Grab a lamp; you go one way, I'll go the other."

Fighting to control his panting, Kester felt his way along the wall behind him. Soon enough, his fingers detected another passageway, which he instantly fled down as quickly and silently as possible.

I'm still too close to them, he thought desperately, eyes straining in the darkness. *All it would take is one shine of the lamplight and they'll find me. But I don't want to get lost!*

He carefully edged backwards down the passage, trying to mentally plot the route he'd taken so far. Finally, he stepped out into a larger space. Judging by the uniformity of the walls, he guessed it had been roughly carved out by hand, but it was difficult to tell just by edging around the perimeter.

Count your footsteps! he ordered himself, struggling to remain calm. He knew that if he started to panic, he'd never find a way out, and dying of starvation in the darkness wasn't a prospect he relished. Slowly, he counted his steps around the edge of the room until his fingers curled around the edge of another passageway.

"Kester, where are you?"

The voice sounded far away but not distant enough for his liking. Biting his lip, Kester retreated still further into the ink-blackness. It was getting increasingly hard to keep tabs on where he was going, but he knew his life depended on it.

Why did I run away? he berated himself, cursing his stupidity. *At least if I'd have stayed with them, I would have had a chance to escape another time. Now, if I get lost, I'm dead.*

His heart pounded against his ribs so hard that he was worried it would give away his location. He waited for another shout from one of the men or footsteps echoing along the stone floor, but to his relief, he heard nothing.

Somehow, miraculously, I've managed to get away, he thought. He wasn't sure whether to be pleased or not. *Should I call out to them and get them to come and find me?* he wondered, taking a deep breath. *Or is there a chance I can find my way out of here?*

"Calm down," Kester told himself quietly. "Come on. You can do this. After all, when they dragged you in here, they didn't drag you that far, so the entrance has to be somewhere close by."

He froze, suddenly convinced that he'd heard a noise. Straining to hear, he pressed against the cold, damp rock. Aside from the steady drip of water from some unseen place, it was completely silent. Eerily so.

Thank goodness, he thought. He was sweating, in spite of the chill in the air.

The noise came again, unmistakeable this time. *Footsteps!* Kester realised with panic and started to creep backwards.

"Kester?" The voice lingered in the cool air before fading into silence.

He waited, back pressed against the wall.

"Come on," the voice continued. "I know you're here some-where. I can hear your breathing."

To his horror, the floor in front of him was suddenly bathed in an orange pool of light, which swung gently to and fro. *It's Reggie Shadrach,* he realised. *And in a few seconds, the light from his oil lamp is going to hit me.*

Without thinking, he stumbled blindly back into the darkness and broke into a panicked jog, still tracing the passageway wall with his fingers.

Right, right again, left! he repeated to himself. *If I don't remember the order of the turns, I'm done for!* After a few minutes, he stopped, daring to turn back round again. To his relief, he was once again surrounded by thick, oppressive blackness. The noise of his breath was deafening, sharp and ragged, more like a wild animal than a human.

Tentatively, he massaged his stomach. A tight cramp spasmed in his right side, though his physical pain was nothing compared to the tangled mess of his thoughts. *I'm doomed,* he realised and bit back a laugh. *I had the chance to tell Reggie where I was, but instead, I fled like a rabbit onto a motorway. For someone who prides them-selves on being able to solve problems rationally, that was a pathetic display of panic.*

He had no idea what to do for the best outcome. Instead, he retreated to the memory of Anya's face: the thing that made him happiest, up until recently. A succession of painful images passed through his mind: the morning after they'd first spent the night together; her hair spread across the pillow; her lashes flickering restlessly in her sleep. All those times she'd laughed at his jokes with her gap-toothed grin. And most agonisingly of all, the raw regret on her face down here in the caves.

He slumped down to the floor and groaned, clutching his head in his hands. *Why did I ever believe you liked me, Anya?* he thought desperately, and a single, hoarse sob escaped from his lips. *You let me believe that I was something better. That I was worth more. You made me think, for just a little while, that I wasn't a complete no-hoper after all.*

Perhaps I'm better off staying down here in the dark. After all, what have I got to live for? I have to endure horrible spirits on a daily basis, my mother's dead, and my girlfriend never really liked me.

Finally, wiping his nose on his sleeve, he admitted to himself that he was just being fatalistic. The faces of his father, Miss Wellbeloved, Mike, and Pamela came to mind, which brought a hint of a smile to his face. *I'd probably even miss Serena a bit,* he conceded. In the months that he'd known them, they'd become his family. An odd, inept, and slightly embarrassing family—but a family nonetheless. He knew they'd be devastated if anything happened to him.

I just wish I hadn't been so stupid as to drop my phone in the bushes earlier, he thought. *I know I wouldn't have picked up a signal down here, but at least I could have used it as a torch.*

Standing slowly, he listened once again to ensure there were no footsteps following him. It was completely silent. *Right,* he realised, rolling up his sleeves. *Now I need to figure a way out of here.*

Quietly, Kester edged back in the direction he'd come from, trailing his fingers along the walls to navigate the way. *I need to turn right at some point,* he thought. *Then two lefts, and that should bring me out into that larger space . . .*

He staggered onwards, focused entirely on the task at hand, trying not to think about unseen people lurking in the dark and waiting to jump out at him. The passageway seemed longer than he remembered as he travelled along it. *But that could be because I'm taking it more carefully,* he reasoned. There was no point fretting now, he needed to focus on the directions instead, if he was going to make it out alive.

Time passed. Too much time for comfort. After several minutes, he still hadn't found the larger cavern. Instead, his fingers collided with solid wall. *A dead-end.* He gulped and patted the sweat off his brow.

"That's not good," he mumbled, more to console himself with the sound of his own voice than anything else. Quickly, he retraced his steps. *Where did I go wrong? I must have missed a turn somehow.* Feeling along the wall, he turned back down the right-hand passageway, then probed the wall, trying to locate the turning that he'd missed.

After five minutes or so, he stopped. His chest was painfully tight, a sure sign that a full-blown panic attack wasn't far behind. *Why isn't there another passage to the right?* he thought, forcing himself to think things through carefully. *Where did I go wrong here?*

Stumbling further along, he eventually hit another dead-end. Kester gasped. "I don't believe it." His voice sounded dull and muffled in the narrow space.

What now? he thought miserably. *How the hell am I going to find my way out?*

With vivid clarity, he suddenly remembered the time his mother had taken him to a maze made of corn, out on a farm near their old house in Cambridge. *I must have only been about six or seven,* he realised. He recollected the height of the corn plants, the rough husks jutting across the path, the stodgy mud beneath his feet. And his mother's voice, guiding him through the labyrinth. The only reliable constant in a maze of slippery ground and shifting paths.

I'd run away from her, he remembered with a rueful nod. *She must have been terrified, poor Mum. But she never lost her nerve. She kept calling my name, I kept following her voice. And I got out in the end.*

And that's what's going to happen now. It was a more practical inner voice now, the one he always associated with his mother. *You will get out of this, Kester. It may take some time, but you'll manage. You just need to create a map in your head, work out where you've been, and keep exploring until you find the exit.*

"As long as there is no Minotaur in this maze," he muttered aloud. Given how many other frightening creatures there were in the world, nothing would surprise him anymore, not even a mythological bull-headed beast.

Slowly, he crept along the passageways, comforting himself with the knowledge that the walls were straight, dug out rather than naturally formed. *These caves were clearly used by humans in the past,* he told himself, *much like Beer Quarry. And if humans made these passages, then they must lead somewhere.*

Minutes passed. Hours, perhaps; it was impossible to tell. Kester groped and stumbled his way along the network of passages, carefully mapping out the route in his head, bumping into dead-ends and low ceilings, and fighting to ignore the constant prickle of doubt and despair at his back. After a while, he almost forgot he was in darkness. His hands started to become adept at detecting shapes and distances, enabling him to picture his location more clearly.

A low, trickling noise stopped him in his tracks, and he paused, motionless, like a dog scenting a fox. *Is that water?* he thought, wondering if his ears were playing tricks on him. He squinted through the darkness, and to his amazement, he saw a low glow up ahead.

"That's light!" he mumbled. His voice sounded hoarse and tinny. "I don't believe it!"

Instinctively, Kester hurtled towards it, noting with pleasure that it grew wider the closer he got to it. The trickling noise also increased in volume, and soon, he realised what he was looking at. However, even though he knew what it was, it didn't make much sense to him.

Before him was what looked like a pool of water. How deep it was, he couldn't tell. The glowing light was coming from underneath the pool, which he presumed meant there was an illuminated space on the other side of the rock face.

But who's lit the cave beyond? he wondered. *Will I just find Felix Taggerty and Reggie Shadrach on the other side, ready to throw a sack over my head?*

"Or maybe it leads outside," he told himself, smoothing his hair down nervously. "Maybe that's a street light casting that glow."

Kester knew there was only one way to find out, but he didn't relish the prospect at all. *I hate swimming at the best of times,* he thought, nibbling his fingernail anxiously. *Let alone swimming in a cave.* To make matters worse, it was impossible to tell how long he'd have to swim underwater. The light looked close, suggesting that the neighbouring cavern was only a short distance away, but he knew that water did strange things to the light, distorting and lengthening it.

Tentatively, he bent down and touched the pool. Ripples eased lazily across the surface, dancing outwards into the dark. As he'd expected, the water was freezing. Wildly, Kester ran through other possibilities in his mind. *Should I try to find another route?* he wondered. *Should I just start shouting and hope someone hears me?* He smiled joylessly, suspecting that if he started bellowing, he wouldn't be able to stop. *And that way leads to madness.*

Sighing deeply, he took off his glasses and shoved them into his trouser pocket. *This might possibly be the worst thing I've ever experienced,* he thought, running through all the other times he'd recently thought that. A catalogue of horrible events paraded through his mind, but none could quite equal the unspeakable horror of having to swim in a dark cave pool, at night, in the bitter cold. *Without even knowing what's on the other side,* he thought with a shudder.

Kester stepped into the water before he could change his mind. The cold hit him with brutal force; his feet threatened to cramp at any moment. Taking a deep breath, he waded in further, until he was suddenly out of his depth and gasping for breath.

Stay calm! he urged himself as he sized up the pool in front of him. *Just keep breathing and get it over with!* It didn't help that the water was freezing. He was no scientist, but he knew the human body could only withstand such extreme temperatures for a short period of time.

What if I run out of air halfway through? he wondered, then wished he hadn't. With that frightening thought in mind, he swam as close to the wall as he could, took a huge breath, and dived below the surface.

Cold pierced his face and scalp, abusive, raw, and unrelenting. Kester pulled and kicked earnestly, propelling himself forwards, aware that his chest was already burning, desperate for air. Rising nearer the surface, he extended a tentative hand upwards, but felt only hard, wet rock.

Keep going! He swam with greater urgency, the urge to breathe growing stronger with every stroke. Glancing upwards gave him no clues; the water made everything seem dreamlike, an endless tunnel of strange, shifting rock. The light seemed to be growing stronger, but it was difficult to get his bearings.

With frantic energy, he pressed forwards, his body naturally bobbing upwards, lungs burning like embers. *I don't want to die!* he screamed internally as he hauled himself through the water, reaching out with desperate fingers. He knew he couldn't hold on much longer. The pain in his chest was excruciating, a ball of needles rolling around inside, ripping him to shreds. Releasing his breath in a torrent of bubbles, he pushed forward with a final burst of energy. This time, rather than rock, his fingers wiggled in glorious, empty air.

Kester erupted through the surface of the water, spluttering and choking. *Another second and I would have been breathing water instead,* he thought, splashing weakly towards the side. *A few more seconds, and I would have drowned.*

Clasping the ragged sides, Kester clambered out of the water, though his muscles protested every movement. The icy air of the cavern only made him feel colder, especially with his wet clothes clinging to his body. It was futile trying to prise the fabric away from himself. In fact, it only seemed to make it worse.

But I did it. He allowed himself a moment to recover. *I was terrified, I thought I was going to die, but I made it through. And that's something to be proud of.*

A series of coughs tore through him, and he collapsed, every inch of his body aching, cold, and miserable. Finally, he raised his head and looked around.

"Where the hell am I?" he whispered. It wasn't what he'd been expecting. The space was smaller, more cramped than he'd imagined, and instead of the light-source being right here with him, he now realised that it was emanating from a further cavern with a low entrance framed by stalactites.

Still, Kester thought as he tried to console himself. *At least if the Thelemites are all waiting in that other room, they might not notice me. I can sneak through the entrance and see if it's safe first.*

He shivered, a full-bodied quiver that made him realise how weak and exhausted he was. It was tempting to just give up, to find a corner somewhere in the dark, shut his eyes, and forget about everything.

"No," he whispered quietly. "I've come this far. I've got to keep going."

The cavern beyond was completely silent. Kester wasn't sure if that was a good thing or not. *Either it's deserted,* he thought as he started to creep beneath the low-hanging rock, *or someone's waiting to pounce.*

Finally, he dared to look up and peer inside. The first thing he noticed, to his great surprise, were chairs. Rows and rows of wooden chairs, laid out to face what looked like a rough altar. Then, to his horror, he noticed something far worse. People. Three of them sitting down, the final person standing, motionless.

Kester screamed. He simply couldn't help it. The noise reverberated along the rock surface, then died, just as he realised his mistake.

They're not people at all. With a hysterical giggle, he clamped his hand over his mouth. *They're mannequins! That's why they're completely still! I've managed to find the tourist section of the caves!*

He leant against the wall, almost out of his mind with relief. *I'll be able to get home now,* he thought crazily. *I can find my way out of here now. I don't believe it.*

"I'm alive," he whispered aloud and started to chuckle.

One of the mannequins turned around, eyes sparkling darkly in the dim light.

"So you are," it announced cheerfully.

Kester screamed again, and this time, he didn't stop.

CHAPTER 18: WINNING THE BATTLE, NOT THE WAR

"Hey, hey! Calm yourself, silly boy!" The mannequin rose awkwardly to its feet, moustache bristling ostentatiously under its nose. It was only then that Kester realised he was looking at his father.

Kester collapsed onto the nearest wooden chair. "Oh, thank god," he spluttered and clutched his chest. "I don't think I've ever been so glad to see you. Though you nearly gave me a heart attack in the process." *It's like the corn maze all over again,* he thought, almost delirious with relief. *Except this time, the person waiting for me on the outside was my father, not my mother.*

Ribero scooped up his crutches and limped over. Without warning, he pulled Kester into a ferocious bear hug, then released him just as quickly. "Come on," he said, glancing over his shoulder. "We need to get you out of here quickly. It is not safe." Leaning back, he surveyed Kester sceptically. "Why are you wet? Have you been swimming?"

"I'll explain as we go along," said Kester as he followed his father out of the cavern. Walking past the mannequins, he could now see that it was a recreation of an underground church, presumably during the war, if their outfits were anything to go by. "You're right, though," he added, "it's not safe. It's the Thelemites, Dad. They kidnapped me, and they're probably still looking for me now."

They hobbled as quickly as possible through the network of caves until they found the others, who were gathered in one of the larger caverns, bickering about where to continue looking. At the sight of him, Miss Wellbeloved let out a cry of relief, immediately whipping off her cardigan and enveloping him in its musty softness.

"Julio, why didn't you offer Kester your jacket?" she snapped. "Look at him, he'll get hypothermia if we're not careful!" She hugged him tightly, rubbing at his back with the energy of a groom preparing a horse for a show.

"Ah, I am an old man, right? I did not want to get cold." Ribero ran a hand across his well-oiled hair, looking mildly abashed.

Kester grinned, then wriggled free of Miss Wellbeloved's embrace. "How did you find me?"

"Tinker," Mike interrupted before tugging Kester into a bear-like hug. "The man's a genius. He managed to trace your mobile phone, so we knew exactly where you'd ended up."

"Wow," Kester breathed, rubbing his face with amazement. "So, me dropping my phone wasn't as disastrous as I thought."

"No, it was lucky you were trying to call me at the time," Miss Wellbeloved said. "That allowed us to carry out a proper trace."

"Tinker did it in the back of the surveillance van," Serena added. "Which was no mean feat, given how fast Lili Asadi was driving. Thank god they were at the hotel; we never would have found you otherwise."

"Lili's here too?" Kester said, shivering like a drowned puppy. "How many of you came?"

"As many as we could gather at short notice," Miss Wellbeloved retorted. "Thankfully, when we arrived, the security guard was still on the premises. After a phone call from Curtis Philpot, he let us in willingly enough."

"But we were starting to despair, yes?" Ribero added. "We looked all over the caves and couldn't find you. The Thelemites, they took you to another part of them, right?"

"Yes," Kester confirmed as he wrapped his arms tightly around himself. "There's a secret entrance around the side. Anya tricked me. Just like you suspected."

The team glanced at one another. Pamela wrapped a comforting arm around his shoulders. "Look at you," she said with maternal ease. "You've had a rough night of it, haven't you? We should get you out of here before anything else happens."

"Do you think they're looking for you?" Miss Wellbeloved asked, peering anxiously into the shadowy corners of the cavern.

Kester nodded. "I'm almost certain they are." Through chattering teeth, he quickly filled them in on what had happened, right up to the moment his father had scared him half to death.

"Yes, he screamed like a little baby!" Ribero confirmed gleefully. He hastily straightened his expression when he caught sight of Miss Wellbeloved.

"I'm not surprised!" she spluttered as they made their way towards the exit. "After what he's been through tonight, I'm amazed he's even still standing. I'd like to see you try to stay calm whilst being chased through pitch-black caves, Julio."

Ribero muttered something in Spanish under his breath, then gestured ahead with his crutches. "Here we are. Let's get back to the van, I need to get back to bed."

"Yes, don't go running off like that again," Serena chastised once she'd stepped out into the open. "It's been a total nightmare trying to find you."

"Yes, but I've managed to find out exactly what the Thelemites are planning," Kester replied, blinking in the moonlight, which felt oddly unreal after his time in the darkness. "Surely that's worth something."

"Well, yes," she admitted reluctantly. "But not at the cost of your safety, I suppose."

Mike grinned and slapped her on the back. "Hang on a minute, was that you being *concerned* about someone for once? I didn't know you had it in you."

"Oh, shut up Mike. I'm perfectly capable of being—"

She faltered, eyes widening. Mike opened his mouth for another witty comeback, followed the line of her gaze, then promptly closed it again.

"Oh dear," Miss Wellbeloved said quietly as she instinctively moved in front of Kester. "It seems that we have company."

Reggie Shadrach and Felix Taggerty emerged from the shadows of the car-park. Their silhouettes would have been comical under any other circumstances; one almost unnaturally tall and thin, the other broader than he was high. However, given the expressions on their faces, this was clearly no time for laughter.

"I don't know how you pulled that off, Kester," Reggie growled, expression full of menace. "But I'm impressed. You hadn't struck me as the enterprising type."

Kester shivered. "I'm not going with you, so just leave us alone."

"Yeah, go away," Mike growled.

"Kester, please." Felix stepped forward, fingers weaving restlessly in front of his stomach like a nest of adders. "You've badly misunderstood us. We don't want to hurt you. We don't want to hurt any of you. By the way, may I say how charming it is to see you again, Miss Wellbeloved? It has been a long time."

"Hello, Felix," Miss Wellbeloved said in a tight, strange sort of voice. "I heard about you becoming Master of the Cambridge branch. Quite an achievement. However," she added, linking arms with Kester, "regardless of how powerful you may be now, you're in no position to order Kester around."

"And you should not be kidnapping people either." Ribero shook a finger in their direction. "How dare you treat my son like that? No respect! No respect at all!"

"It wasn't a kidnapping," Felix replied smoothly. "We merely needed to discuss things with Kester, important things. Miss Wellbeloved, you should understand this. After all, you were once one of us."

Kester felt Miss Wellbeloved stiffen against him. "I no longer support what you believe in," she said quietly. "You've gone too far, and you know it. I agree with Julio, you had no right to treat Kester like that. Look at him!"

"Yes, we really do need to get him out of those wet clothes and into a warm bath," Pamela added, looking worried. "He's shivering like mad."

"I am here, you know," Kester said with a small smile. "And I can speak for myself. Mr Taggerty, Mr Shadrach—I'm not interested in what the Thelemites have to say. I'm working with my dad, for the agency, and that's how it's going to stay. I'll be reporting you to the government too, so don't think you'll get away with what you did tonight."

Reggie laughed, a rough, guttural sound that clanged discordantly in the still, quiet night. "If you think the government will be able to do anything, you're sadly mistaken." He stepped forward, rubbing his hands together.

Serena paced in front of Kester, shielding him completely. "Don't even think about it."

Reggie laughed. "Oh, dearie me. Get out of the way, little woman. I don't want to have to hurt anyone."

"Hurt anyone?" Serena sneered. "I'd like to see you try. And don't you dare call me a 'little woman' ever again, you patronising moron."

"Serena, be careful," Pamela hissed. "What are you doing?"

"I could snap you like firewood," Reggie retorted. "Get moving. Now." He reached out and seized her by the arm. Serena shrieked as he shoved her out of the way.

"You shouldn't have done that!" Mike stampeded forward,

and in an instant, his fist had connected with Reggie's shoulder. However, the other man hardly seemed to notice. Instead, he drew back his own arm and punched Mike directly in the face. Serena screamed again, covering her mouth in horror.

"Mike!" Miss Wellbeloved shouted, anxiously gripping Kester's arm. "He's stronger than you, trust me, I know! He was a professional boxer before he joined the Thelemites."

Kester stared, open-mouthed, as Mike threw another desperate punch, which glanced painlessly off the side of Reggie's face. With reflexes that were almost too quick to follow, Reggie returned the blow with a fist that smashed into Mike's chest, pushing him to the ground.

"You bastard!" Serena wailed, immediately swooping down to join him.

Kester watched in horror, then noticed something odd moving in the air above Serena's head. *What is that?* he wondered, blinking, overwhelmed by the chaos in front of him. *That little, brown, squidgy thing, that's growing bigger every second?*

He watched, stupefied, as the thing swelled to several times its original size before lurching at Reggie with abrupt ferocity. Although it was difficult to see in the dark, Kester could just about make out the flailing of spectral arms beating wildly at Reggie's face until he retreated, bellowing in confusion.

Pamela pointed, then started to laugh. "It's the incubus! Look! He's defending Serena!"

Rising like a vengeful goddess, Serena tossed her hair back, glaring at Reggie with open fury. Her eyes glittered, patent-leather stilettoes shining in the distant lamplight. "That's what happens if you mess with us," she shouted, placing her hands firmly on her hips.

Mike groaned on the ground, hands wrapped protectively over his chest. "Why did no-one tell me he was an ex-boxer?"

"I still box, I'll have you know!" Reggie spluttered, wrestling with the incubus. "Now, will you get this horrible thing off me?"

"I thought you loved all spirits?" Kester retorted with a glimmer of amusement. "After all, you're the one who wants to let them all come into this world, willy-nilly."

"Spirit!" Felix called out, ignoring Kester's comment. "Desist this nonsense. You're fighting the wrong people!" He proceeded to try to prise the incubus from Reggie's face, without much success.

"Uh-oh," Pamela suddenly hissed in Kester's ear and pointed towards the nearest tree. "Do you see what I see?"

Kester peered through the darkness, then flinched, heart sinking. "Oh no," he whispered. "I know exactly what that is."

A low, amber glow hovered above the ground, meandering towards them with casual ease. It grew in size, forming limbs and a head, burning with greater intensity with every passing second. The others gasped. Even the incubus ceased its mad scrabbling and paused, momentarily stunned into stillness.

"I take it this is Hrschni?" Miss Wellbeloved's mouth hung open with obvious awe. "Gosh. It's been a long time since I've seen a daemon in the flesh."

Hrschni's face came into sharper focus. The narrow, scarlet eyes scanned them all for what seemed like an eternity. Kester held his breath, fear blossoming in his chest like a deadly flower. *If he's angry with me,* he realised, *then I'm probably already dead. I suspect he could finish me off in a second.*

The daemon opened his mouth, and Kester instinctively cowered, waiting for the pain to start. However, instead of focusing his attention on Kester, Hrschni turned to the incubus and held a hand out towards him.

"Fellow spirit," he hissed softly. "You trouble yourself for nothing. Now, return to where you feel happiest."

The incubus hovered silently in mid-air, his round, black eyes locked onto the larger spirit who glowed with such authority that he eclipsed everything surrounding him. The incubus floated uncertainly towards the daemon, before drifting back to Serena. Finally, he vanished with an audible plip, leaving the air shimmering slightly in his wake.

Hrschni bowed his head, then glided through the air towards Kester. "I take it you were not that enthusiastic about my offer?" There was a note of wry amusement in the question, combined with obvious disappointment.

"Being trapped in a cave wasn't the most tempting proposal I've ever had," Kester replied bravely. "Nor was being forced to open spirit doors against my will."

Hrschni sighed as though the response pained him. "I never would have forced you."

"Then why drag him into the caves in the dead of night?" Ribero challenged, eyebrows bobbing violently up and down. "Why put a bag over his head, eh? Why frighten him to death with your two bully-boys here?" He gestured angrily at Reggie and Felix, who looked rather put out at the description.

"And why get his girlfriend involved?" Miss Wellbeloved added. "You've caused him nothing but pain. Can't you see that?"

Hrschni hovered more closely to the ground with a thoughtful expression. "That was not my intention," he said finally. "One day, I would like you all to understand our cause. Who knows? Together, we could change the world."

"This isn't a revolution," Miss Wellbeloved replied angrily. "This is terrorism. There's a big difference."

"You have no idea what you're talking about!" Reggie growled. "Find out the facts before you pass judgement, you silly old woman."

"Reggie, that is enough!" Hrschni wheeled around, blasting the bald man with the force of his simmering aura. For a moment, the daemon looked ready to attack, but then he reared back, still glaring. "You forget yourself!"

"Apologies," Reggie muttered, still looking darkly in their direction.

"We are going home," Ribero declared finally, spine straight, gaze fixed defiantly in Hrschni's direction. "We are getting my boy back to safety, and we will not take no for an answer. That is clear, right?"

Hrschni closed his eyes briefly. "Very well," he said finally. "But you know you cannot stop us, don't you?"

"We can if we've got the spirit-door opener and you haven't," Mike wheezed from the ground, still clutching his chest.

"This is not the end," Hrschni replied gracefully. "But only the beginning. Kester, we will meet again. I am confident of it."

The last words chilled Kester to the core. *He means it,* he realised, studying the daemon and seeing the steely resolve. *This isn't over.*

"And after all," Hrschni continued as he coiled around himself like an undulating ribbon, "the main purpose has been achieved. You now know me. And I *know you.*"

"You don't know me at all," Kester muttered, keeping his eyes to the ground.

"I know you better than you might imagine," Hrschni replied. He extended a thin, spectral hand and briefly touched the side of Kester's face. It tingled across his skin, like a rush of anaesthetic. "And in time, I suspect you may understand me better."

Retreating abruptly, he gestured to Reggie and Felix, who were watching with open confusion. "Let's leave," he said softly. "Our work is done . . . for tonight, at least."

"But Grand Master, this seems a little—"

"—There is nothing more to say, Felix. Sometimes, we must be gracious in defeat in order to win the battle another day. And there *will* be another day. Very soon."

The daemon bowed low to Ribero and his team and, casting one final, significant nod in Kester's direction, disappeared into the night. Felix and Reggie, who both looked decidedly confused, grumbled under their breath before pacing slowly out of the car-park. Once they'd gone, the team released a collective sigh of relief.

"I thought we were in trouble there," Pamela said as she pulled her coat more tightly about herself. "Goodness me, a real daemon, right there in front of us. I've never seen anything like it before. And the way he was looking at Kester, not to mention you, Julio; well, it was downright peculiar."

"Like he knew me from somewhere before," Ribero said, scratching his head. "It was most strange."

"You were very brave, Mike," Miss Wellbeloved said as she scooped him to his feet. "A bit stupid, perhaps, but very brave, nonetheless."

"You could have warned me that he had a left-hook like Tyson," Mike moaned as he clutched his face. "Seriously, I think he's dislocated my jaw. Not to mention snapped a few ribs."

"You made yourself look like a bit of an idiot, didn't you?" said Serena smugly as she sauntered down the driveway. "Luckily, I was there to protect you."

"You mean your lovesick spirit was," Mike corrected as he limped after her. "I didn't see you throwing any punches."

"Didn't need to."

"Couldn't, even if you tried. Your arms are like pipe-cleaners."

"Well, yours aren't as muscly as you think, if your feeble punches are anything to go by."

Miss Wellbeloved sighed and took Kester by the arm. "Normal service resumes," she whispered with a chuckle. "For once, I think I'm glad to hear them bickering again."

Kester nodded. "I know what you mean."

They arrived at the van, which was parked crazily over three spaces. The skid-marks on the gravel revealed just how fast they'd been driving to get here, and Kester gulped, feeling suddenly overwhelmed with gratitude. *Thank goodness for friends like these,* he realised, thinking back to everything he'd endured in the last few hours. *Where would I be without them?*

Inside, Lili and Tinker were waiting anxiously, surrounded by a sea of technological contraptions. Lili waved a large, metal, funnel thing in their direction, then gestured to her headphones.

"I recorded it all," she announced with a stern smile. "We

picked up the entire conversation from here."

"And I used the thermal tracking device to see where they went," Tinker continued, looking rather flushed. "As far as I could tell, they made their way approximately fifty-five metres down the road before climbing into a car, which of course, I've got the registration number of—not that it'll be much help, as I wager they'll have hired a rental vehicle for the purposes of—"

"—Anyone got a drink?" Mike interrupted as he squeezed himself into the van.

Tinker pressed his lips together. "I have some water, if that's any good at all. Well, I've haven't got a lot left, but—"

"—I meant something alcoholic," Mike retorted as he sat on the unit, disturbing numerous pieces of important-looking paper as he did so. The others clambered in behind him until the van was stuffed to the brim with bodies.

Ribero snorted. "Goodness me, you are thinking of the alcohol at a time like this, Mike?" He tutted loudly, then waited until Miss Wellbeloved had looked away before pulling a hip-flask from his pocket. Mike's eyes lit up as he sidled a hand across to grab it.

Kester rolled his eyes, then leaned back against the side of the van as Lili started the engine. He'd never felt more exhausted in his life. Visions of the evening flashed before him like movie stills: the horrible blackness of the caves, the oily tang of the sack over his head, the bitter cold of the water, and most of all, Anya's face. *I hate her,* he thought with sudden passion. *I hate her, because she made me love her. And that was just cruel.*

The journey back to the hotel was mostly silent, apart from the occasional muted slurp as Ribero and Mike took it in turns to sip at whatever it was inside the hip-flask. Judging by Mike's increasingly beatific, not to mention glazed, eyes, it was something fairly strong. Pamela and Miss Wellbeloved seemed to have nodded off on each other's shoulders, though how they managed to remain upright with the van swerving along the quiet roads, Kester had no idea.

Finally, they arrived outside the hotel. A tired-looking doorman was still standing determinedly by the entrance even though he looked as though he might fall asleep at any moment. He nodded sleepily as they headed in, watching with bleary interest as they swept silently through the marble-floored reception area.

Just get me to bed, Kester thought as they waited for the lift to arrive. *Get me out of these soggy clothes and under a warm duvet. That's all I ask.* He just wanted to sleep, to pretend, just for a while, that he'd never been lost in a cave. That he'd never nearly drowned in the dark. That he'd never seen Hrschni's glowing, haunting face.

The lift finally arrived, and they clattered in. At their floor, Kester quickly hugged the others. "Thank you," he said quietly. "I know I haven't said that yet, because I've been too wet and confused by all of this, but thank you, all of you. I know it would have been a very different story if you hadn't come to rescue me."

"Ah, do not mention it," Ribero mumbled, but Kester could hear the affection in his voice. They hugged briefly. "Go on, you get yourself warmed up. We don't want you sick now, do we?"

"Yes, and please take care," Miss Wellbeloved added, looking concerned. "I'm glad Mike's in the same room. I wouldn't be happy with you being alone."

"And don't go running off again," added Serena with a yawn. "Once, I'll forgive you for. Twice, and I'll kick you up the backside so hard, you won't—"

"—Yep, good night, Serena," Mike said firmly. "Save your moaning for tomorrow, eh?" With one last, wicked smile, he pressed the button to close the doors of the lift, then ducked out quickly, before she could think of a witty retort.

"That girl, she never shuts up," he concluded, then patted Kester on the shoulder. "Come on. You need to strip off, I need to get some ice on my poor face. Do you think reception will send some up?"

"Probably."

"Am I getting a big bruise? I don't want to ruin my youthful good looks, you know."

Kester ran the keycard down the sensor, and the door clicked open. "No, Mike. Your youthful good looks are preserved, don't worry."

He made his way into the bathroom and closed the door firmly, oblivious to Mike's chatter behind him. It was blissful to finally peel the soaking shirt from his back and slide out of his trousers. In the mirror, he could see that his skin had an alarmingly blue tinge and that his lips were so pale, they seemed to blend with the rest of his face.

I'd better have a shower to warm up, he realised, alarmed by his own reflection. *I had no idea how ill I looked.*

A knock at the door startled him out of his thoughts. "You alright in there?" Mike bellowed above the running water. "Not passed out or anything?"

"I'm fine," Kester called back, allowing the heat of the water to cascade down his body. He felt fragile as a lamb and almost numb with relief at being back in the safety of the hotel. It all felt strangely surreal, like a theatre-set with the real world hiding just behind.

Finally, he clambered out and dried himself off, savouring the softness of the fluffy towel against his skin.

"Mike?" he called, "could you pass me my pyjamas? I forgot to bring them in with me."

He waited. Silence greeted him in response.

"Mike?" Kester opened the door and peered out. "Mike, is everything alright?" A knife of panic cut through him, and he hastily dived out into the room, fist held up in readiness, even though he was horribly aware that he wouldn't be able to beat a fluffy kitten in a fight at present.

Mike, to his great relief, was lying on the bed, mouth open, hand still clutching the remote control. The gentle rise and fall of his chest made Kester want to weep. *I'm a complete bundle of nerves,* he thought as he retrieved his pyjamas from the drawer. *I'll start jumping at my own shadow next.*

With a wry chuckle, he made his way back to the bathroom.

Mike let out a grunt and rolled onto his side.

It was only when he pulled on his pyjama trousers that Kester noticed something strange lying on the floor by the door. It was an envelope, sealed with what looked like a blob of red sealing wax. Kester froze, staring at the letter with growing dread.

Where did that come from? he thought, rubbing his eyes, hoping that it was just his imagination. Sadly, it wasn't. *How the hell did it get in the room? It's too bulky to have been pushed under the door.*

Trembling, he scooped it up, holding it at arm's length. The envelope was heavy, and he could feel something inside, though he hadn't a clue what it was.

I don't want to open this, Kester thought fervently. *I can't take anymore. I really can't.* However, despite the voice in his head advising him strongly against it, his fingers started to prise the envelope open of their own accord.

To his surprise, a key fell out. Slipping through his hands, it fell to the carpet with a soft thud and lay there, shining dully in the light. He peered inside the envelope, heart beating fast, and tugged out the note inside. The paper was of a high quality, almost parchment-like in colour, and the words upon it had been written in red ink.

When you're ready to see the other side, he read silently, *the key will guide the way.*

And that was it. No signature, no further words to give any clues about the sender or their intentions. However, Kester knew well enough who it was from, as the motif stamped on the wax seal revealed it clearly enough. The pentagram symbol of the Thelemites was immediately, sickeningly recognisable.

Still clutching the note, Kester picked up his phone and called his father.

About the Author

Lucy has enjoyed inhabiting worlds of her own creation from a young age. While her initial creations were somewhat dubious, thankfully, her writing grew as she did. She takes particular delight in creating worlds that closely overlap reality . . . with strange, supernatural differences.

Lucy lives in Devon with her husband and two children. She immerses herself in the wild, rural landscapes and loves seeking out hidden locations. More of a book-python than a bookworm, she devours at least one novel a week, and loves the written word so much that even her day job involves writing and editing.

Kester Lanner had never liked doors. As a small boy, wide-eyed and duvet-wrapped, he refused sleep until his mother opened his bedroom door with a sigh. The thunder of the school toilet cubicle doors forced his skittish heart into arrhythmia, and the mere sight of his mother's closed bedroom door threw him into an immediate state of loneliness. Fortunately, as he swelled into rotund young adulthood, fear deflated to scanty wariness, as he realised that doors were disappointingly mundane.

However, he'd never come across a door like this before. It was truly remarkable, and for all the wrong reasons.

More relic than modern business entrance, its surface was coal-smudged and splintered, with a tinge of odious decay. Its grubby demeanour, combined with a whiff of mildew, rendered it vaguely organic—as though sprouted from seedling instead of hinged by human hands. The surrounding alleyway was stagnant, simmering in the still afternoon air, and the silence steeped it in secrecy.

Kester surveyed it nervously, trying not to look too closely at the details. If he squinted, it looked just about acceptable. Quaint even, if he took off his spectacles and let astigmatism do its work. But, on close inspection, the spidery cracks, pock-marks, and gritty, crumbly bits were a bit too much to take in. He especially protested at the sight of the moss blossoming from the unspeakably greasy crannies. Bright against the gloomy wood, they were like tiny, mouldy limes, luridly acidic and indecently bold. All in all, it was not a door that he liked at all.

This can't be right, he thought, tugging the letter out of his satchel. The gold-embossed letterhead glinted in the dusty light. *Dr Ribero's Agency, 99 Mirabel Street.* And this was certainly that street. The mottled Victorian road sign on the red-brick wall confirmed it.

The letter had implied something grander, something with a bit more style. He'd imagined a stained glass affair, complete with polished brass letterbox and neoclassical pillars. Instead, a tumble-down building confronted him, without even a mounted plaque to announce the name of the business. It was unceremoniously wedged between a barber shop and a boutique selling voluminous hippy skirts, and had a shifty look about it, as though trying to squeeze surreptitiously between the two.

"Well, this is strange," he muttered, looking around him. "Very strange indeed."

He'd never even heard of Dr Ribero until two weeks ago. The name had been one of the last words his mother had said, as the disease pulled the final moments of life from her body. He remembered the night well. It was unlikely he'd ever forget it. It had been ten to midnight, and the moon, unnaturally bright, had sent a trail of milk-whiteness across the bedspread to his mother's upturned head.

"You must find Dr Ribero," she had said, eyes urgent-bright, clutching his hand in hers. "I ask nothing else of you, my boy. Only that you find him. Find him and tell him who you are."

Who this mysterious man was, or why his mother had insisted that he be found, remained an enigma. She had died only a few moments later, her wheezes subsiding to hollow silence. All was quiet, and the room the more dreadful for it. Kester had not wept; only remained at her side, still holding on to her hand, which gradually turned icy as the next day rose behind him.

In the solitude following her death, he forgot her final words, submerged in the grief of losing his only parent. However, a few days after, when he had a chance to compose himself, he found himself recollecting that strange, foreign-sounding name. In his practical way, he had immediately set about searching for her leather-bound address book.

He located Ribero's name straight away—the only "R" in the book. There was no phone number beside it, only a tightly folded, official-looking letter tucked into the page. It was a strange note, indicating a level of intimacy between sender and recipient, but beyond that he couldn't discern much, only the name and address of the mysterious agency. A search on the internet revealed nothing. Likewise, a visit to the library and a flick through the business directories drew another dead end. *Who is this strange man?* he wondered. *And how had Mother known him?* In spite of his grief, which was still raw, his interest was piqued.

And so it was that he found himself here, a fortnight later, armed with nothing more than his toothbrush, a change of clothes, and a book, standing outside the curious door.

It doesn't look like much of a business, he thought. He peered through the window of the shop next door, hoping to see a member of staff to whom he could ask a few questions. However, he couldn't see a soul through the tie-dyed blouses and velvet waistcoats, only his own owlish reflection staring back at him.

Kester was only twenty-two, but his image suggested older; wispy hair already starting to thin, watery eyes floating behind thick spectacles, not to mention the paunch tucked uncomfortably into his ironed slacks. He was the very epitome of middle-aged academic, squeezed inexpertly into a younger man's body. He turned away, refusing to dwell on his appearance, and focusing instead on the problem at hand. He'd travelled a long way. Should he simply retreat, board the train, and go home again? Exeter was nicer than he'd expected, with its squat cathedral and swarming streets. Its people bobbed along pavements like contented honey bees, and, in spite of his melancholic mood, he was reluctant to leave it so quickly. The city's blend of traditionalism and modernity soothed his spirit in a manner that he hadn't enjoyed for many months, making him feel a bit more like his former self.

However, this forgotten alleyway reeked of an earlier era. The twenty-first century hadn't touched its cobbled streets. The atmosphere of the Dickensian era still roamed unabated, uninterrupted by modern glass frontages or neon signs. It hung from the wrought-iron lamp posts and the dark beams overhead. It pressed against him in the very weight of those red-bricked walls.

Edging forwards, he studied the door more intently and pondered what to do. There was no intercom, no bell, no buzzer to alert the people inside of his presence. It went against every ingrained rule of etiquette to rap upon such an uninviting entrance. But rap he must, if he was going to solve the mystery of the strange Dr Ribero. Delicately, he knocked. The door felt oddly spongy underneath his fist, like brine-soaked wood that had dried out in the sun. Kester decided unreservedly that this was the most unpleasant door he had ever encountered in his twenty-two years of life.

There was no answer. The alleyway lingered with the echo of his fist. Somewhere nearby, a bird cawed, taking off in a clatter of feathers. He shivered, in spite of the afternoon's warmth.

So, what am I supposed to do now? he wondered. *I've spent fifty quid on a train ticket, forty pounds for a room for the night, and it doesn't even look like the building's occupied.* It was frustrating, but also a relief. The whole experience thus far had been far too surreal for his liking, and now he felt that he had licence to depart with a clear conscience.

I tried my best, Mother, Kester thought. He smoothed his sweaty fringe and gave the door a final once-over. *Obviously it just wasn't meant to be.* He turned to leave.

A strange feature in the centre of the door caught his attention, and he narrowed his eyes, surprised. A perfectly circular knot sat roughly at eye level, darker than the surrounding wood, indeed, almost ebony in appearance. He could have sworn it hadn't been there before, though now, he doubted his own senses. After all, it had been a long journey from Cambridge, and he was exhausted, both mentally and physically. Perhaps it had been there all along, and he had simply missed it? It was unlike him not to notice a prominent detail like that, he took pride in his observational skills. *My little Kestrel,* his mother used to call him. *Always scanning the surroundings like a bird of prey.*

Instinctively, he brushed it with his index finger, noting its peculiar glassy smoothness. It felt warm and glowed a little, as though lit from within by a lightbulb. Feeling a little foolish, he pulled his finger away furtively, like a child caught with his hand in a biscuit barrel. To his amazement, the door swung open, revealing nothing but darkness beyond.

Blimey, Kester thought, peering in. *Now what do I do?*

The meagre light of the alleyway revealed the beginnings of a narrow corridor, and not a lot else. A threadbare Persian rug formed a burgundy road into the blackness; a blood-red path into a rather eerie hallway.

"Hello?"

His voice wavered in the silence. It was tempting to turn away. After all, he had tried. He had travelled for hours to find this blessed business, and now, no one was in; if indeed anyone had ever been here. The place looked as though it had lain empty for years, decades perhaps. It had the cobwebby look of something long since forgotten, neglected and left to crumble away in the sombre hands of time.

The emptiness of the narrow corridor unsettled him, even spooked him a little. It was all rather strange, and as a general rule, Kester didn't like strangeness. He preferred the predictable, the reliable, and the well-established. Anything that stepped outside those parameters he tried to ignore as best as possible. It was as his mother had always advised, when he'd awoken from nightmares as a child, "Turn your mind from it, Kester my love. Then, you'll find that it's simply not there anymore." It was very tempting to follow that wise advice now, and return to the train station, go home, and forget all about it.

The smell of age wafted from the enclosed space with the musty scent of air that had spent too long sealed up in darkness. He glanced over his shoulder. The alleyway was still empty. Even the neighbouring shops appeared deserted. It was worryingly silent, as though someone had pressed a pause button, sealing everything into stasis.

"Oh, this is ridiculous," he muttered. Shunting his black-rimmed spectacles up the bridge of his nose, and trying not to dwell on the darkness too much, he stepped over the threshold.

It was noticeably stuffier inside, and sweat prickled at the back of his neck. Beside him, remnants of parchment-dry wallpaper peeled and curled like dead ferns. The ceiling was low, so low that if he were to extend his arm, he would be able to place his palm easily on its surface. It was an unpleasant space, hot, dusty, and stale—and it reminded him of a tomb.

The dead end at the back of the passageway loomed in the shadows, confusing him. Instead of the expected door leading to offices, there was the vague outline of a spiral staircase, coiling snake-like in the corner. *It looks like something waiting to pounce,* he thought, tugging at his collar. *I don't like this one little bit.* He felt as though he'd stepped into the underworld itself.

He crept along the Persian rug, tiptoeing deliberately over the places where footsteps had already worn holes through to the floorboards.

"Hello?" he called out again, louder this time.

There was still no answer. He scarcely knew what to do. Nerves and a sense of impropriety stopped him in his tracks, and he looked uncertainly at the staircase, unsure how to proceed. *What in god's name am I meant to do?* he wondered, fiddling anxiously with the straps of his satchel. *I don't want to burst in on this Dr Ribero uninvited. If indeed he's actually here, which I seriously doubt.*

And, in truth, he was feeling more than a little uncomfortable. The narrow corridor was oppressive, the walls seemed ready to squash him like a bluebottle, and his heart was beating faster. It was an unfamiliar sensation. Normally, Kester had his late mother's calm demeanour, combined with a quite remarkable lack of imagination. Fear of the unknown was not an emotion that generally troubled him, as he seldom ever thought about it. Superstition and the supernatural were only fanciful concepts for him, nothing more, nothing less. However, the events of the last fortnight had shaken his sensible foundations, leaving him more sensitive than usual. His normally sturdy brain had been shaken, rocked like a ship lost at sea.

Right, he thought firmly, straightening his spine and staring at the stairs. *I've come this far, I'm inside the building now, so I may as well carry on. After all, what would Mother think if she could see me now?* As a matter of fact, he knew perfectly well what she would say. He could almost hear her soft voice now, gently urging him to continue, to find that bravery deep within him. She had always had such faith in him, even when he had none in himself.

Kester gulped, suddenly lost in the memory of her. She had always been his most devoted supporter: giving him a standing ovation when he wheezed in last in every school sports day race, and whooping with delight when he was given his degree certificate at Cambridge, in spite of the sombre silence. A strong sense of her presence came to him now, lingering behind him and shooing him tenderly into the darkness. It made his heart heavy with her loss once again.

Do it for her, if not yourself, he thought. *After all, it was her last wish. She said to find Dr Ribero. And now you're here, you'd best go and find him, whoever he may be. Judging by the state of this place, you're not likely to find him unless he's a skeleton, propped up in the rooms upstairs.*

With that unpleasant thought in mind, he began to climb. The first step of the spiral staircase clanged under his polished shoe, echoing into the blackness above. Unnervingly, the stairs simply disappeared into utter blackness. He had no idea what might be lurking up there, if indeed there was anything up there at all. Still, he knew that the only way of finding out was to venture upwards, despite the fact that every part of him really didn't want to. He ascended, setting off a discordant din of metallic bangs and leaving the last of the light behind him.

Who is this peculiar man, and why on earth does he choose to work in such a hovel? he wondered as he climbed. The building was obviously ancient, at least three or four hundred years old, and, Victorian staircase aside, didn't look as though much had been altered since the time it was built. Many old buildings had charm and personality—this wasn't one of them. So far, all he could detect about this crumbling monstrosity was that it looked ready to be condemned and demolished. Kester wasn't particularly sensitive to atmosphere, but even he could detect something hostile, watchful, and downright eerie about the place. Had he not made a solemn promise to his mother, he'd have walked straight out again.

At last, Kester arrived at the final stair. Panicking, he groped for a wall—anything to provide him with clues about his surroundings. Aside from a dim semi-circle of light coming from the stairwell, he was lost in blackness; he couldn't even begin to work out where he was, or for that matter, who was up here in the dark with him. He shivered at the thought.

"Is anyone there?" he called. "I'm looking for Dr Ribero, am I in the right place?"

Once again, silence was the resounding response. *It's rather like one of those horror films,* he fretted, not that he had much taste for the genre. *I suppose this is the point where the unseen monster leaps out of the shadows and starts doing dreadful things to my person. Well, that's a nice thought, isn't it?*

Fighting to remain calm, he squinted around him. Somewhere in the dense darkness, he could make out the tiniest line of light running along the floor. *Aha, a door,* he thought, with a sense of triumph. *So someone is here after all. I wonder why on earth they didn't come out to greet me when I called out?*

He marched towards the glimmer of light, and pushed at the hard surface that met his outstretched fingers. To his surprise, it immediately gave way under his touch, swinging open into the room beyond.

Kester blinked in the sudden light and gawped. He wasn't sure what he had been expecting, but this certainly wasn't it.

"Hello?" he stammered, eyes widening. His greeting was met with only silence.

Kester looked from face to face, scanning the room with disbelief.

Four pairs of eyes returned his scrutiny, staring at him in bafflement, curiosity, and vague annoyance. They peered from behind their desktop computers as though a creature from another world had just stumbled into their lair.

The room itself was airy and fresh, and clearly a professional office space. It was as shockingly different from the hallway below as could be imagined, and it astounded him into slack-mouthed silence.

There was an indeterminable pause, as Kester surveyed his surroundings, and was surveyed in return. There was something about the collective glares that made him feel like a field mouse under the glare of a flock of falcons, and he didn't much like it. He was unsure how to proceed, how to protect himself against such an appalling lack of social finesse. It certainly wasn't what he was used to at Cambridge.

Finally, for want of anything better to do, Kester coughed. The silence and staring continued. He coughed again and smoothed down his shirt for good measure, waiting for at least one person to smile. Then he waited for a few seconds more. His cheeks, normally ruddy at the best of times, reddened to a deep shade of puce.

The eldest person, a severe-looking woman perched behind the largest of the leather-topped desks, raised a steel-grey eyebrow.

"Can we help you?" she said eventually, ice dripping from every syllable.

Her fingers pressed against one another, forming a sharp triangle of disapproval. She looked as though she was surveying something a passing dog might have deposited onto the carpet, and her quivering nostrils suggested that she disapproved of every inch of his person.

He read the brass plaque standing at the front of her desk. *Miss J. Wellbeloved, BA, MA, MPhil.* Kester looked up again. Then down. Then up once more, just to double-check. If it had been a different situation, a different place and time, he would have laughed out loud. He'd never seen a surname so ill-suited to its owner. The name suggested warmth and gentleness. Cuddliness, even. In stark contrast, this woman had all the natural warmth and gentleness of an over-sharpened pencil.

"I . . . I did actually call out several times," he stuttered. "I knocked too, but no one answered."

"I see," Miss Wellbeloved said. Her lips tautened to a thin line, and she leant back, glowering over half-rimmed spectacles.

He cleared his throat. The room was so much at odds with the rest of the building that it had completely thrown him off guard, leaving him as confused as a hook-caught fish hauled from the water. Why they chose to leave the downstairs corridor in such a horrendous state when their actual office was pleasant was completely beyond him. It was as though they didn't want visitors, and were using the horrible entrance to discourage entry. *But what sort of a business would operate like that?* he wondered, feeling more perplexed by the second. *How on earth do they get any customers?*

Unlike the ancient hallway downstairs, the office was clean and spacious, with fresh paint, high ceilings, and elegant panelled walls, lending it a sense of gravitas. The faintest hint of a summer breeze drifted in from an open window, and four computers hummed quietly, each with a person behind them. Their modernity was a stark contrast to the rest of the setting, which was austere, timeless. At the end of the room, there were two simple wooden doors, leading to goodness knows where. *Ugh, more doors,* he thought, feeling his stomach lurch. Kester felt thoroughly displaced, an astronaut exploring alien territory. The sensation was an unsettling one.

"Oh Christ, I don't bloody believe it," one of the other occupants growled, a series of burly consonants slicing through the quiet.

Kester looked over to the source of the sound, just in time to spot a flurry of sparks erupting from one of the desks like a miniature volcano. He grimaced, surprised to see what looked like two large car batteries perching squarely in front of a bearded, baseball-capped man. The man glared at Kester, all hair, bristles, and sheer bulk. Kester shrivelled, wishing that he could somehow creep back out of the office without any of them noticing him.

"Mike, you shouldn't be doing that at the desk, you'll start a fire one of these days," Miss Wellbeloved tutted with a disapproving shake of the head.

"That's why I treated my desk with fire-retardant paint," Mike retorted. His desk was a wild sea of electrical contraptions and wires. Jabbing a screwdriver in Kester's direction, he continued, "Anyway, it was his fault for distracting me."

A younger woman with a sharp black bob, and an even sharper chin, rolled her eyes from the neighbouring desk. "According to you, everything's a distraction," she scowled. "A sneeze is a distraction. Me itching my neck is a distraction. Someone breathing too heavily is a distraction. We should get you some earplugs."

"Well, your neck scratching is a bloody distraction, it's like an ape searching for fleas," Mike barked back, folding his arms across his sizeable check-shirted chest.

Kester coughed again, feeling uncomfortably as though his presence had already been completely forgotten. "Erm," he started, then stopped. At once, all eyes were on him again.

"Yes?" Miss Wellbeloved said. Her eyes narrowed to granite slits.

"Look, I'm terribly sorry to disturb you," Kester continued, fumbling for his letter. "But I'm looking for someone, someone who I don't think is here actually, judging by . . . well, judging by all of you. But perhaps you know where he might be? I presume he once worked here?"

A plump woman sitting in the furthest corner peeped over the top of her computer monitor. She had been so well concealed by her enormous computer that he hadn't really noticed her before. Now he had the chance to study her more closely. Her face was doughy and mottled, giving her the general appearance of an overcooked dumpling. However, she looked slightly less annoyed by his presence than the others, which was a certainly a start.

"Well," she said, in a voice that was almost kind, "why don't you tell us his name? Then we might be able to solve the mystery for you."

Kester smiled gratefully, tugging the letter open. He wafted it in her direction, a pointless gesture given that she couldn't possibly read it from that distance.

"My mother," he began, then stopped. "Well, you see, my mother, when she died, she told me to come and find this man. Only she didn't give me any other information. So I did some research, and I drew a complete blank, but I did find this address. It took me a while to decide to come here, I really wasn't sure what the point was initially—"

"How about *getting* to the point?" the black-bobbed woman snapped, rapping a biro in a staccato of ill-concealed irritation. "Just a suggestion?" She frowned, plucked eyebrows forming a sharp V above her weasel-sharp eyes.

Kester shrank under the weight of her contempt. He felt as though one glare of those bright green eyes might be enough to deflate him, puncturing his flaccid body with a single needle-sharp stare. It was something he was used to. Most girls found him rather an unappealing prospect. Attractive women, like this one, even more so. And they generally weren't afraid to let him know how they felt, in no uncertain terms.

"Serena, be kind," the plump woman said with a frown. Turning back to him, she nodded, encouraging him to continue. Kester pulled at his collar, trying to ignore the audible tutting from across the other side of the room.

"Of course, I appreciate I'm wasting your time here," he said stiffly. "I don't even know why I came up really. I should have realised from the start that you weren't the type of business to welcome visitors. And it's now obvious to me that there's no one called Dr Ribero here. Please excuse me for interrupting you."

He turned, the blush still firing his cheeks. *What a pompous group of people,* he raged silently. *And I've wasted all that money coming down here for nothing.* He felt like a fool. He hadn't managed to get a job since graduating and money was tight, too tight to waste on pointless trips to the West Country, regardless of how pretty the landscape might be.

"Wait!" an imperious voice commanded. Kester paused. He peered reluctantly over his shoulder.

Miss Wellbeloved had risen from her seat, erect as an obelisk. "Dr Ribero, you say?"

Kester nodded. She clicked her fingers impatiently at his letter, which he obediently handed over. Like a schoolboy in front of a headmistress, he waited, twiddling his thumbs together as she scanned the paper.

"Where did you get this?" she asked eventually.

"I just found it in my mother's address book."

Miss Wellbeloved reached over, shaking the letter in the plump woman's direction. "Read this, Pamela," she said, ignoring Kester. Silence descended as the larger woman scanned the contents of the paper.

"Goodness me, how on earth did you come by this?" she said finally, handing the letter back to her colleague.

Kester shrugged with confusion. "Well, I suppose it was sent to my mother. It is addressed to her. I don't understand it though; it made no sense at all."

"Your mother was Gretchen Lanner?" Miss Wellbeloved asked.

Kester nodded. The woman gasped, iron composure shaken. She slumped forward, pressing her palms against the desk, and breathed heavily.

"My goodness, does that mean Gretchen is dead?" Pamela said. She covered her mouth, eyes widening.

"She died two weeks ago," Kester said quietly. He still hated saying it aloud. He wondered if he would ever get used to saying it. Right now, faced with these strange people, he realised with an even greater pang of pain that she had been his only real friend in the world.

"My goodness," Miss Wellbeloved murmured, closing her eyes. Her face had gone remarkably pale.

"Hang on a minute," Serena said, striding the room and seizing the paper. "Are we talking the about famous Gretchen Lanner here?" She looked at Kester, pursing her lips in disbelief. "And you're her son? Are you serious?"

"Serena, there's no need to be unkind," Pamela said, squeezing out of her chair. She padded over to Miss Wellbeloved, giving Kester a sympathetic look. "I'm so sorry for your loss. We knew your mother a long time ago." She paused, and a look passed between her and Miss Wellbeloved that Kester couldn't decipher. "She was a wonderful woman," she concluded, nodding.

"You knew her?" Kester said incredulously. His mother, like himself, hadn't been one for socialising. To the best of his knowledge, she had only had two friends. Only one, if you didn't include Mildew the cat. The other was their elderly next door neighbour, Mrs Winterbottom, who popped round for the occasional chat about the garden. Aside from that, he and his mother had simply enjoyed one another's company, and had never really needed anyone else in their lives. She had never mentioned these people. He was sure he would have remembered her talking about such a strange cluster of individuals.

"Your mother was . . . a friend of mine," Miss Wellbeloved muttered, looking out the window. "Though we have not spoken in many years. Decades, in fact. And now it seems, we never shall again. Or at least, not in the conventional manner."

Kester raised an eyebrow, but was distracted by Pamela placing a bundle of kindly, sausagey fingers on his arm. "I didn't know your mother so well," she explained to him. "I had only been here about a year or so when she left. But she always seemed very friendly." She glanced at Miss Wellbeloved, who nodded. "She was very kind to me when I arrived; she really helped me to settle in. You must miss her terribly."

"I do," Kester said, clearing his throat. He felt strange discussing his mother with these people. Who were they exactly? And why had his mother never talked about them? It was all most mysterious, given how open she had been about every other aspect of her life.

The young woman with the black bob sighed. "Look, I didn't mean to be nasty," she said. Leaning over, she extended a hand with cat-like grace, albeit with a lingering air of hostility. "I'm Serena. I didn't know your mother at all, but heard some impressive things about her. She was great at her job, from what these ladies used to tell me. It's rough luck, you losing her. Sorry about that."

Kester duly accepted the slender hand. He looked up, observing her pointy chin, wide cheekbones, and bright green eyes, which gave her the look of a cunning, but very pretty, pixie.

"My mother never talked about any of this," he replied. "I feel a little confused, to be honest."

Miss Wellbeloved and Pamela shared another meaningful look.

"Why don't you sit down?" Pamela suggested, gesturing to a worn leather sofa tucked snugly against the wall behind him. "I'll make you a cup of coffee."

"I don't drink coffee, but thank you anyway."

"Tea? Everybody drinks tea."

"I'll have a cup of tea if you're brewing, Pam," Mike shouted from behind his desk.

Pamela sighed, giving Kester a conspiratorial look, as if to say, *see what I have to put up with?* He felt himself brighten at the show of comradery, in spite of the circumstances. "Milk and sugar?" she asked, with a flash of a dimple.

"Yes, three sugars please."

"Three sugars? Blimey," Mike commented. "Fast track to a heart attack, that is."

"Oh Mike, do put a sock in it, will you?" Serena chided. Lowering herself onto Miss Wellbeloved's desk, she added, "Though it is bad for you. You should consider cutting back. Sugar does terrible things to your body." She nodded at his generous waistline. Kester folded his arms over his stomach, trying to breathe in as much as possible.

"Goodness, leave the poor boy alone!" Pamela exclaimed, scuttling through one of the doors at the back. Her voice echoed back through the office. "Last thing he needs is a lecture."

"Might we ask what your name is?" Miss Wellbeloved asked, after allowing him a minute or so to get settled on the sofa.

"It's Kester, Kester Lanner," he replied. "I take it yours is Miss Wellbeloved?"

"Wellbelov-ed," she corrected, emphasising the final syllable. "That is indeed correct. Serena Flynn has already introduced herself, I believe, and Pamela Tompkin is the final member of the team."

"Oh, don't I exist then?" Mike boomed indignantly from his cluttered corner, like a disgruntled thunderstorm.

"Mike's just the IT guy," Serena explained.

"There's no 'just' about what I do," Mike retorted. "It's an integral part of this company, as you well know." He scraped his chair back along the floorboards, ambling good-naturedly over to join them. "Sorry I snapped at you earlier," he said, shaking Kester's hand with a bear-like grip.

Kester noted the contrast to his own pale hands, complete with his unsightly patches of psoriasis. Up close, he could now see that Mike's baseball hat was from Legoland, a strange choice of style given that he looked almost exactly like a muscular lumberjack who had never stepped foot outside the Canadian Rockies.

"That bloody machine has been driving me mad all morning," Mike continued to explain. "I just can't make it capture the right frequency. It needs to be so sensitive to capture spirit noises, and—"

"Spirit noises?" Kester said with alarm.

Miss Wellbeloved tutted, glaring at her colleague. "Mike likes to come up with all sorts of preposterous inventions," she explained quickly, entwining her spindly fingers across her hollow stomach. "Don't listen to him."

"None of the rest of us do," Serena added.

"Preposterous?" Mike squawked. "Honestly, you ladies have no appreciation of what I do. I'm the one who makes all of this possible, and you know it. I'm what keeps this company modern and cutting edge."

"I do not believe there is anything 'cutting edge' about this place," Miss Wellbeloved snipped. "But let's not get off the subject. Kester, will you please tell us more about why your mother sent you here?"

Kester shifted uncomfortably, crossing one leg over the other. "There's nothing much else I can tell you, really. On the night that she died, she told me to find Dr Ribero. Until that night, I'd never heard the name before." He gratefully accepted the mug of tea that Pamela gave him, though he now felt guilty about the three sugars. His mother had often told him to cut back, but he liked the taste too much. He swore it helped him to think better.

"I fully understand why she didn't mention it," Miss Wellbeloved muttered. Her expression darkened, and she turned away. Kester studied her intently, unable to interpret her reaction. *Did she have a problem with my mother?* he wondered. There was something going on here, but he wasn't sure quite what.

"What do you mean?" he asked, sitting straighter.

"Well," Pamela said, sipping from a chipped porcelain cup. "It's not really the sort of thing you can easily explain to people, dear." She winked at him, then looked at Miss Wellbeloved with concern.

Kester frowned. There was something strange going on, a mystery that united these four people, from which he was firmly excluded. He couldn't even begin to imagine what it was, and by now he was feeling too exhausted to ponder on it much. It had been an odd day—perhaps one of the oddest in his life—and now that he had sat down, he felt his mind unravelling at the seams with tiredness.

"So," he said suddenly, struggling to stir himself. "Is there a Dr Ribero here or not? I presume that there once was, given your reaction when I mentioned his name. Did he work here too, at the same time as my mum?"

Pamela and Serena looked at one another and laughed.

"It's his company," Pamela explained, pointing to one of the doors at the back of the room.

"Does he not work here then?" Kester asked.

"He certainly does," Miss Wellbeloved answered. "Just through that door is his office."

Kester frowned, confused. "Well, can I talk to him?"

All four colleagues looked upwards at the clock mounted above the window.

"No, not quite yet," Miss Wellbeloved said finally.

"Why not?"

"He's always asleep until three o'clock," Serena replied with a grin. "And there's one rule in this office. Never, ever disturb Dr Ribero when he's having his siesta."

Kester looked at the clock. "It's practically three o'clock now," he said.

"Yeah, practically. But not actually. And that's a big difference," Mike replied, slamming his mug on to the desk and spilling tea over the leather.

Kester paused. "So," he said, mulling it over, "does that mean he'll be awake soon?"

"In two minutes and thirty-two seconds precisely," Miss Wellbeloved confirmed.

What sort of a man is this? Kester thought with bewilderment. *Who has a daily siesta that runs until exactly 3:00 pm, and not a second less?* And, more importantly, why had his mother decided that it was so important for her son to meet him? None of the facts were adding up, and it was making his head ache to think about it. He drank the rest of his tea, watching the slow progression of the clock.

As the long hand clicked into place at the twelve, he heard a low buzzer from somewhere behind Dr Ribero's mysterious office door.

"That'll mean it's safe to knock on his door now," Pamela explained kindly, tapping her watch for good measure.

"Shouldn't I give him some time to come to, if he's just woken up?"

"Oh no," Pamela replied, "he's always up like a bullet as soon as his alarm goes off. Let's go and get you two better acquainted."

Miss Wellbeloved took his empty mug, giving him a strange look. "I hope you're prepared for this," she muttered, pursing her lips together.

"What should I be prepared for?" Kester asked. He looked over at the door with growing anxiety, expecting it to fly open on its hinges at any moment. There was an air of pregnant expectancy in the room, and it was making him instinctively wary. This wasn't helped by the secretive glances the others were giving one another.

The two older women exchanged another meaningful look,

just to further ignite his anxiety. Pamela raised an eyebrow, and Miss Wellbeloved shrugged. She smiled tightly, gesturing to the door. "I'll knock for you," she said. "Get back to work, everyone. Tea break is over."

Kester shuffled reluctantly towards the door, following the older woman like a large ship being pulled into harbour by a fast-paced tug-boat. She paused, bony fist hovering in the air, then knocked smartly in a series of authoritative raps.

"Come in," a low voice rumbled from within.

"Dr Ribero," Miss Wellbeloved said, as she pushed open the door. "This is Gretchen Lanner's boy, here to see you. Kester, I'd like to introduce you to Dr Ribero. Your father."

To continue reading about Kester's fateful discovery
of the supernatural, look for
The Case of the Green-Dressed Ghost.